Every Version of You

Contents

Book Cover by Vera Osipchik & Sloan Spencer

Illustrations by Vera Osipchik

First edition 2024

Content Warnings

What you're about to read is a fluffy romantic comedy, but based on these content warnings, it will seem like a dark romance. It is not.

Pregnancy, consensual nonconsent, primal play, stalking, gunplay, light BDSM, breeding, degradation, pegging, somnophilia, dubious consent, choking, hypothetical cheating in a daydream, Domination/submission.

Playlist

Spotify

1. **We're Going to be Friends** by The White Stripes
2. **Despacito Remix** by Luis Fonsi, Daddy Yankee, Justin Bieber
3. **Shape of You – Stormzy Remix** by Ed Sheeran and Stormzy
4. **Let's Go** by Trick Daddy, Twista & Lil Jon
5. **Stubborn Love** by The Lumineers
6. **Vivir Mi Vida** by Marc Anthony
7. **My Love Mine All Mine** by Mitski
8. **Bad Girls** by Donna Summer
9. **Get UR Freak On** by Missy Elliot
10. **Alone at the Ranch** by BRELAND
11. **I WANNA BE YOUR SLAVE** by Måneskin
12. **Super Freak** by Rick James
13. **Grace Kelly** by Mika
14. **Roses** by Outkast
15. **No One** by Alicia Keys
16. **Ghost Ride It** by Mistah FAB
17. **Fancy** by Iggy Azalea, Charlie XCX
18. **Shaky Hands** by VACAY
19. **Wrecking Ball** by Miley Cyrus
20. **Mr. Brightside** by The Killers
21. **Run Away With Me** by Carly Rae Jepsen
22. **I Think I Like You** by The Band CAMINO
23. **Angel** by Shaggy and Rayvon
24. **Micaela** by Sonora Carruseles
25. **Rainbow** by Kacey Musgraves
26. **Teenage Dream** by Katie Perry
27. **No One** by Alicia Keys
28. **Say You Won't Let Go** by James Arthur
29. **A Pedir Su Mano** by Juan Luis Guerra

To those who never knew where they fit in.

American Rugby Terminology

- **Boot** — Cleat.

- **"Boot up"** — Get ready to warm up.

- **Fifteens** — A full eighty-minute rugby game with fifteen players against fifteen players. Typically played in the fall and spring.

- **Kit** — Usually a duffle bag full of boots, uniform, and a change of clothes.

- **Line out** — A means of restarting play after the ball has gone out of bounds (into touch). Typically two players will lift another player into the air to catch the ball as it is being thrown back into play. The opposing team will do the same to try and gain possession of the ball.

- **Pitch** — Field.

- **Scrum** — A formation of players, used to restart play, in which the forwards interlock arms and heads, and push forward against a similar group from the opposing side. The ball is rolled into the scrum and the players try to gain possession of it by kicking it backward toward their own side.

- **Sevens** — A shortened version of the game, typically

played in the summer tournament style. Seven players against seven players, played for seven-minute halves.

- **"Shoot the boot"** — Chugging alcohol out of someone's shoe.

- **Sir** — The referee, regardless of gender.

- **Social** — A little party right after the game with both teams. There's food, beer, and sometimes drinking songs. Everyone is dirty and tired. General comradery.

The positions:
Forwards (very strong, tackles the most, members of the scrum) :
   #1 & #3 — Prop (Loosehead & Tighthead)
   #2 — Hooker
   #4 & #5 — Second Row (Number 4 Lock & Number 5 Lock)
   #6 & #7 — Flanker (Blindside & Openside)
   #8 — Eight man (Number 8)

Backs (fast and agile runners, score most of the game points) :
   #9 — Scrum Half
   #10 — Fly Half
   #11 — Left Wing
   #12 — Inside Center
   #13 — Outside Center
   #14 — Right Wing
   #15 — Fullback

Rugby is played at all different levels and age brackets throughout the world, and in most countries where the sport is popular, there are professional teams. The US has one international men's team and one women's team. There is also Major League Rugby, which is fairly new, and Divisional rugby.

Colleges and universities have rugby clubs and some have school-sanctioned teams known with division titles as well. *Every Version of You* follows a Division I club team.

Outside of college, cities across the country have club teams ranging from Division I to IV that play below the MLR and International team. Some larger club teams have more than one division to allow all their players the ability to compete, like I have written about for the Philadelphia Men's Rugby Team.

For the purposes of this book and series, I have changed the names of these organizations.

Prologue
Rafael

"You're going to have the best first day of [1] school, *mijo*," my mamá says, her sweet, muffled voice barely perceptible as she squishes me and my younger sister tight in her arms. When she releases us, she finger-combs my thick black hair and her eyes pop over my head. "Okay, the bus is coming," she continues in Spanish. "I know you're a little scared to start a new school, but this is going to be your favorite year yet."

I highly doubt that. How can living across the country from my papá result in my best year yet? I guess Mamá does seem happier now that she's not living with him. We moved in with her girlfriend, Christina, here in Radnor, Pennsylvania two months ago. It's nothing like my home in Texas. And I guess it's nice not listening to my parents fight anymore. But being the new kid? It's like I'm being handed one uncomfortable situation after another.

"Mamá," I whine. "Why couldn't you drive us today?"

Screeching to a slow stop, the school bus throws open its doors as the few other kids at the bus stop start to file up the steps.

"Because this is a public school, not a private school like your last one. The bus is fun! Now go on. You're going to make lots of friends today, I just know it. Go on. Take

---

1. *We're Going to be Friends* by The White Stripes

Gabriela's hand. I love you, *mijo*. Love you, *mija*." She smiles, then places a kiss on each of our heads.

Grabbing my backpack straps, my sister and I trail the student in front of us and I turn back to reluctantly wave at Mamá. When I reach the top level, the bus driver, a white man with a whiter beard and a sucker in his mouth, smiles at me. "Good morning and welcome to bus 302! I'm Mr. Murphy. We're going to the trash dump, right?"

Uncomfortably laughing, I say, "No."

"We're not?"

The younger kids in the front row of seats giggle and shout as we make our way past them to find a spot. "No! We're going to school!"

"School? Well, I guess that sounds better than the dump, huh?"

When I find an open seat in the middle of the bus for us and sit down, the bus jerks and starts to move away. Waving back to Mamá, I watch as she blows a dramatic kiss, and I imagine myself catching it to keep me safe. I'm almost ten years old after all, and only little kids catch kisses. But as the bus bounces along down the paved road, I lean my head against the shaky window and watch the morning mist-covered ditches and driveways pass by.

Other kids are talking and singing all around me. As badly as I want someone to be my friend already, I can't bring myself to turn away from the window. My body is frozen solid and my heartbeat is getting louder and louder and...

And then everything in my body quiets when the brightest spot of color emerges from the gray mist. Standing at the end of a driveway with two other small boys, a girl wearing all yellow—my favorite color—waves joyously at the school bus. When Mr. Murphy opens the doors for them, I'm too far back to hear what he says to her, but every tooth in her smile shines as she hugs the man.

After helping the younger of the boys she boarded with find their seat, she floats her way down the aisle closer to me, her head bobbing from side to side like she's singing a tune in her head. Her brown hair is up in two crooked ponytails, and she's even wearing a yellow headband. When she spots someone she knows, she quickly arranges herself next to them and asks in English, "Did you really go to SeaWorld? Jenny said you did."

For the next five stops, I'm engrossed in her conversation, but I keep my eyes trained outside. I like her voice. I like how goofy she is.

The bus pulls up to my new school and everyone herds off like sheep. Yellow Girl walks in front of me and I'm not sure where I'm going. I came here last week with my mamá, so I have a vague sense of my surroundings, but following her seems to be my only focus. Shuffling into the school, a teacher spots my sister and moves her with the other first graders, and Yellow Girl and I merge with the crowd, making our way to the same classroom. Even though the school is new to me, it still smells like my last school. The familiar scent of construction paper, wooden pencils, and cafeteria french toast sticks soothes me.

Waving her hands in the air, a tall Black woman I remember as Miss Carter calls us over. "Welcome fourth graders," she trills. "Find your lockers, drop off your lunches, and then come on in to find a desk!"

Ducking my head between other students, I finally locate the large name label *Rafael Jimenez* and open it. The locker to the left says *Tyler Gordon*, and to the right of mine says *Angel Johanssen*. When my locker opens, Yellow Girl skips right next to me and whips open the locker. "Hi!" she beams. "Are you new?"

"Yes," I mutter, keeping my face tight as it burns from embarrassment.

"That's cool!" She looks up at my name. "Ra-Raf..."

"Rafael," I supply. "But you can call me Raf."

"Okay. I'm Angie."

"Hi. It's not..." I point to her name label. "Angel?"

"What? Oh! *Ugh*. No, it's technically Angela," she groans as she takes off her yellow sweater, revealing more of her short-sleeve sunflower dress. "But please don't call me Angela. I don't like it."

I realize then I mixed up the letters and read them incorrectly. "I'm sorry."

When we're done at our lockers, with notebooks and pencil cases tucked under an arm, Angie surprises me by grabbing my hand and pulling me toward our classroom. Part of me settles down and relaxes when she does. "Miss Carter? Can Raf sit next to me? He's new and he doesn't know anybody!" Her face is as sincere as she is determined.

"Hello, Angie, it's nice to see you again. Go ahead. I think I sat you two next to each other anyway. You'll see your names on your desks."

"Thank you, Miss Carter."

"Thank you." I smile at our teacher. The fierce grip Angie has on my hand as she leads me around is a little alarming, but by doing so, she's erasing all my new-kid jitters, and for that, I could not be more thankful.

Pulling out our chairs and setting down our notebooks, Angie's bright blue eyes watch me carefully. "Alright, I'm warning you right now, Raf: if you cross this line," she indicates an imaginary line with her forearm down the middle of our shared table. "I will leave snack crumbs all over your desk for all of eternity."

I squint. "You wouldn't..."

"Try me."

Chapter 1

March 23rd

Angie

T onight feels like an end and a beginning. That might be the tequila turning me sentimental during Rafael's housewarming party, but I don't think it is. Because once again, Rafael Juan Dominico Jimenez is living in the same city as me.

The way it should be.

For the last eight years Raf has lived one hundred and fifty miles away in Washington DC, working as a financial controller most recently. That was until our other best friend, Cora, hired him at her architecture firm as her new Chief Financial Officer. If you would have told me twelve years ago, when we were raving in college, that my two best friends would be running a whole-ass company together, I would have told you to pass me whatever you were smoking. But people can change a lot in a decade.

Some things don't though. Like how fine Raf looks in that white Henley, showing off his rich terracotta skin and bright, a-ton-of-money-went-into-this-mouth smile. Oh, and let's not forget about those devilish dimples punctuating either side.

It's like, *we get it*, you're hot. Can you cover it up sometimes? It's incredibly distracting as someone who is only supposed to be a best friend. Unfortunately for me, I *made* him become my friend at an innocently young age when we were simply two pudgy kids with less-than-ideal family dynamics. Well, that part was mostly me.

And sure, throughout our twenty-two year friendship, there have been heated moments where I
thought...maybe. *Maybe* he felt the same unspoken spark
that I have tried relentlessly to deny. But time and time
again Raf has proved me wrong. He has stuck to his guns,
continued the patterns, and perpetuated his no-roman-
tic-commitment approach to dating.

Simply put: Rafael Jimenez is a slut.

Don't get mad at me for using that term; he self-iden-
tifies as such. It works out for him. I know he's upfront
with his sexual partners, man or woman.

But for two best friends who, in a way raised each
other, we could not be more different. While he's sowing
his wild oats, I've been looking for the real deal. This
doesn't mean I'm some virgin by any stretch of the imagination, but I'm thirty-one years old and I want a fucking
husband. I'm not ashamed to admit that either. Not just
any husband—I'm not that desperate.

What I want is someone to be obsessed with me the
way I am about them. I want an all-consuming love
bracketed by commitment. I want to laugh with someone about the dumbest, most cringe-worthy moments
until we could pee ourselves, and then we'd laugh even
harder from the sheer disgust. I want to go to the
grocery store together, and he'd know that I like the
expensive dill pickles you buy in the refrigerated section, not the green-dyed shelf-stable ones. And that
he prefers the store-brand sandwich cookies over Oreos—you know, like a psycho. And I'd know he likes it
when I write dirty things on sticky notes and leave them
around the house to find.

Or...something like that.

That's what I want and that's not what Rafael has in
him. Not that he is even remotely aware of my unrequited, soul-crushing love for him. Oops. I mean, super tiny,

insignificant, barely a whisper of— now that I really think about it...is it even really...

"That's our [1] song, Angel!" my best friend booms his nick-name for me over the salsa music. "Drink this and dance with me!" He hands me another shot of tequila as I swell with excitement. Holding limes in one hand, he already has salt stuck to the top between his index finger and thumb.

"Wait, I want salt too!" I giggle and try to step out of his way to head into the kitchen. But he stops me in my tracks and holds his hand to my mouth.

"Do it," he dares, the salt taunting me.

Hell, I'm well past buzzed at this point, so without any hesitation, we cheers the way his family taught me all those years ago. "Pa'riba, pa'bajo, pa'centro, pa'dentro." Our tequila shots travel from above our heads, down low, to the center of our chests, but before we throw them back, I do it.

I lick his strong hand.

Telling myself not to linger, I quickly remove my wet tongue from his warm skin, but his eyes don't remove from mine. Furrowing his brows almost imperceptibly, he then lets out the smallest huff of laughter—like he can't believe I actually did it. In the grand scheme of our friendship, we have performed far more sexually-inciting acts, both on purpose and by accident—all in the name of comedy, of course.

He licks over the remaining salt on his hand and my insides go tight.

But this—with his eyes boring into me—there's a charged energy. More than what his housewarming party alone is providing.

---

1. *Despacito – Remix* by Luis Fonsi, Daddy Yankee, Justin Bieber

I shake myself out of it and knock back the tequila as he does the same. Quickly handing me the lime, we both suck until the bitterness calms the surge. He promptly discards the shot glasses and rinds before making his way back to grab my hand and spin me out. He must have miscalculated my trajectory because he flings me right into our friends Cora and Jay, who are attempting to salsa dance as well.

"Sorry," I giggle as Raf pulls me back into his orbit.

Jay laughs over the music. "Do you think more alcohol will make this dance easier?"

"Come on, babe, you got this," Cora says to her boyfriend. Well, one of her boyfriends. She's in the most beautiful polyamorous relationship with two men. I'm not talking *beautiful* in the sense that all three of them are gorgeous—which they are. I'm talking *beautiful* in the sense that their relationship and the love and support they have for each other is *goals*.

"You're one of us now, Jay," Rafael says as our feet find their practiced placement in combination with our swaying hips. "You can expect dancing at any Jimenez hang-out. It's practically the law."

"Is that how you know how to dance so well?" Jay asks Cora, moving his hands from their place at her lower back to her ass and grabbing tight.

"She learned from the best," Raf says. And it's true. Raf and I met Cora our freshman year of college. Within that first week of meeting her, he was teaching her the same way he taught me as kids.

I was over at the Jimenez-Webber house so often as a girl that I not only had a key, but his moms had a permanent spot at the dinner table for me. I required no invitation. For a girl with no mother figure, Ana and Christina fucking showed up to be exactly that.

Rafael pushes me away and pulls me back in as the muscle-memory takes over. "This one is my favorite."

"This song?" I ask. "You say that about every one of our songs. There's like four hundred of them at this point, Raf."

That's also true. We spent a large part of our childhood immersed in all kinds of music. Really, our entire relationship now that I think about it.

As a girl, I wanted nothing more than to find where I fit in. I bounced from group to group, club to club, tried on all kinds of potential friends and clothing styles to match; but nothing and no one ever stuck in those days—no one except Raf of course. He was always along for the ride. And any interest he had, I gladly wanted to explore too. *Maybe this is my thing*, I'd always think to myself when trying something new. The thirst young me had was real.

To this day, I still don't think I ever found my *thing*. There's nothing that's *mine*.

What I have collected over the decades, however, is a smorgasbord of interests and the most eclectic (aka random-as-fuck) musical arsenal. A huge part of this passion of music should be credited to Raf's bonus mom, Christina. She works for a music event production company that plans everything from small, intimate venues for independent musicians to huge arena-selling bands. As a perk, she got free tickets often. Free tickets that she used to take us to see live music of all kinds. Rock bands, orchestras, EDM shows, folk singers, pop stars—we saw them all.

And we had the fucking outfits to match the vibes too. Oh my god, the outfits—*the pictures*.

Pulling me back into his chest and the external conversation I should be participating in, Raf smiles down at me. "Four hundred? Is that it? I thought there were more. But no, that's not what I meant. I meant this dress you're wearing. It's my favorite one."

"Oh," I smile as my stomach drops. "Old faithful here?" I tease. It's a simple sleeveless yellow chiffon dress with a high halter neckline. The hem stops just above my knees, and the skirt flows and swishes so beautifully, it makes me feel like a little girl. It's a great dress for dancing, but it's honestly out of style at this point. I don't make much money as a children's counselor, so I rewear my clothes until they're threadbare, not out-of-fashion. Let's also add to the mix that I teeter between a plus-size eighteen and a twenty on any given day; so finding clothes that are both beautiful, fit, and make me feel good is the trifecta. This is a gold-standard dress in my opinion, even if it is nearly ten years old and Raf has seen me wear it dozens of times [2] now.

"I like old faithful. It's always looked good on you," he says seriously.

"I think you're drunk."

"I'm not as drunk as your brothers...yet," he says nodding over to my three younger brothers who look like they're trying to convince Marco, Cora's other boyfriend, to join their club rugby team.

Oh god...they're trying to lift Jonah in the air like a line out. But the ceiling isn't that high in the kitchen, and as Isaiah and Dane lift him from the knees, Jonah makes impact with the ceiling fan and—Thwack! Thwack! Thwack!—the blades smack him in the head and arms.

"Ah shit! Put me down!" he bellows with laughter as my other two idiot brothers drop him.

All three of them, plus Marco, are dying in a fit of giggles.

"How fucking embarrassing for you, bro," Dane musters through the tears pooling in his eyes, like he wasn't the one who lifted him.

"This is what I can expect if I join?" Marco asks, falling back against the wall and clutching his chest to catch his breath.

"More or less," Raf yells over. "You won't hit the ceiling, but you will make impact often."

Raf and my brothers have been playing rugby together since high school. Well, since Raf and Isaiah were in high school. Raf and I are two years older than Isaiah, followed by Dane, four years younger, and Jonah, seven years younger. My sister Ivy is nine years younger than me, but she's living in Guatemala right now training to be a midwife.

The Johanssen and the Jimenez-Webber families have been interwoven forever it seems. Even when Raf was in DC, he still played for their DI club team and played against my brothers all the time. They're all relatively smart and capable men on their own, but when they're all together like tonight, I swear they have one collective brain cell they share. Don't even get me started on the ridiculous tattoos and nicknames they all have.

Right before the song ends and rolls into the next one, Raf ends it with a flourish and dips me, something we've practiced and perfected over the years. Except, I think he was lying about his level of drunkenness, because he loses his grip and we tumble to the hardwood floor in a mess of chiffon and limbs.

"You big klutzy animal," I cry through my belly laughter as he goes limp on top of me, adding his full weight like a lead blanket. I groan, "You're doing this on purpose. I can't breathe!"

His head pops up and he stares down at me with a huge grin and glassy eyes. "You can't? She needs resuscitation," he jokingly slurs to everyone. But when his eyes land back on mine and then lower to my lips, I stop breathing entirely.

Am I dying? Can I actually breathe? Because why else would my best friend have his mouth so close to mine? Why would he be looking so intensely at it?

All I can hear is my own heartbeat thumping wildly in my chest as both of our bodies lay motionless against one another. And as soon as he wets his lips, I tilt my chin up the tiniest amount.

"Guys..." Cora says cautiously. "Whatcha doin'?"

If at all humanly possible, both of us go even more still. I'm too stunned to fully register what just happened—what *almost* happened. But when Dane comes stumbling over, he lifts Rafael's shoulders and promptly pummels him to the ground, knocking him into the couch playfully.

"I'm gonna pretend you didn't just try to kiss my sister!"

And I'm going to pretend I didn't feel Raf's bulge.

Oh my god.

What the fuck just happened? Why did he have a bulge? I'm not his type. I *know* I'm not his type.

"Party foul man," Jonah says. "Shoot the boot!"

"Yes!" Dane agrees as Isaiah is already taking his shoe off to fill with a bit of everyone's drink.

Oh god, I've seen this happen countless times before and it never gets any less amusing or disgusting. As soon as Dane hauls Rafael up, the shoe filled with beer, tequila, and sangria is pushed into his chest as the chanting starts. Rafael chugs the horrendous concoction like he's a twenty-one-year-old college rugby player, not a thirty-one-year-old CFO.

"Down in one, down in one, down in ooooone," everyone sings. But before I can watch Raf finish, Cora takes me to the bathroom, bottle of tequila in hand, and locks the door behind us.

"What. Was. That," she says—not a question.

"I have no idea!" I squeak.

"Has something been brewing behind the scenes you didn't tell me about?"

"Cora, you're my bestie—"

She cuts me off. "So is he!"

"He's my bestie with testes. You're my bestie with...breasties," I wince, hoping that the rhyme lands and I didn't just slur the whole thing.

Cora starts to untuck her shirt. "Swear on it?"

Like a reflex, I lift my shirt up and press my tiny breasts against Cora's enormous ones. Except I realize I'm wearing a dress and the whole thing lifts.

Oops. Oh well.

It's like our secret little BFF handshake, except a lot of people have seen us do it.

She tucks her top back into her skirt. "How do you feel? What was it like?"

Trying to work through the drunk fog that's getting thicker by the minute, I ponder that. "I don't know what to think." In theory, I should be doing backflips, but in reality, "I'm confused. I think I need to drink more to forget this happened."

Cora opens the half full bottle of 1800. "I'm right there with you. It's jarring watching your friends almost kiss, not gonna lie."

We pass the bottle back and forth, and the next thing I know, sunlight is blinding me as I wake up in Rafael's bed.

Chapter 2

March 24th

Angie

There's a good chance I'm a raisin at this very moment. God, my mouth is like a desert. My head has its own pulse and...I'm in Rafael's bed.

Fuck me. I never drink like that. At least not since college. Why did I get white girl-wasted?

Opening both eyes, I confirm that he, too, is here with me. This certainly isn't the first time we've fallen asleep in the same bed together, but with so many missing pieces as to why we're in here now...yeah, that's new.

Dragging my line of sight from his disheveled raven hair down his aquiline nose, slightly parted full lips, and Adam's apple, I get to his bare chest and inspect the letter J tattoo over his heart—the one we share. And then I stop myself.

Wait, what am I wearing?

Popping the covers, I take a peek below and see I'm only wearing my nude titty cutlets and high-waisted panties. Sexy.

"Why are you in my bed?" Raf's raw and gravelly morning voice scrapes out.

I quickly close the covers back over my chest and stare at him. "I don't know. I wasn't planning on staying the night. You don't know why I'm in your bed either?"

He shakes his head slowly and we simply lay there, silently trying to put the scraps of memories together.

I narrow my eyes. "We didn't...?"

"No," he says quickly. "There's no way we'd... No," he huffs, then sits up in a flash and turns to open his nightstand drawer. He lets out a huge sigh of relief when he shows me a cellophane-sealed fresh box of condoms. "I've never had sex without one before. There's no way I would ignore that step. It's ingrained." But then he drops the box and studies me. "Do *you* think we did?"

I shift my body weight around feeling for any soreness, anything out of the ordinary, and...nothing. "Other than my pounding hangover, I'm okay. Plus, I'm on the pill, so even if we did..."

"Which we didn't."

"Definitely not, because—"

"Because we're best friends—"

"And that would be so—"

"Stupid."

"Completely wrong." There's a long pause between us. "We should call Cora."

Five seconds later, her sleepy voice answers. "Hello?"

There's no point in sugar-coating the truth when I know I'm going to tell her about this sooner or later and Raf knows everything anyway. "Girl, why am I in Raf's bed?"

"What?" she drawls. I hear a low snicker come from her side of the phone.

Marco clears his throat and speaks next. "I tried getting you a driver last night, but you refused and told me you were staying there. Raf said you could sleep in the guest room."

"What are you wearing, Ang?" Jay asks, and I can *hear* the smirk through the phone.

"Um...that's not important."

"Oh, I think it is," Cora replies.

"Thanks for your help! Please go back to your little love nest and we shall all forget about this as soon as I hang—" I ramble, then press the end call button.

Raf lets out a huge exhale. "Alright. Are you okay, Ang? Tell me the truth."

"I think we're chalking this up to be more than it is. We simply fell asleep drunk," I say, but remember then that he almost kissed me. I have to get to the bottom of this. "What was the last thing you remember?"

"Did we take shots?"

"Yeah. You had me lick the salt off your hand."

His thick eyebrows dart up. "I did?"

"Yeah."

"Okay," he sighs. "I must have blacked out somewhere around then." But then his expression turns interrogative. "Did you try to kiss me?"

"Me?" I blurt. "You're the one who tried to kiss me!"

"Was not. You tried to jump me."

"You're delusional," I scoff. "You were literally laying on top of me after dropping me during a dip."

All of a sudden his eyes round with another memory. "Fuck. I shot the boot, didn't I?"

"You did."

"Whose shoe was it?"

"Isaiah's."

Raf makes a gagging sound. "I'm going brush my teeth. And shower. You can take mine since all the good stuff is in there. I'll take the guest bathroom and meet you downstairs. You wanna go to White Dog Cafe? You can buy me brunch as an apology for trying to kiss me."

"I did not! But yeah, let's go. You're paying. We'll need to stop by my place first so I can change."

"Sure," he says, like we didn't just talk about how we almost broke our twenty-two year no-kissing streak. He gets out of bed, showing off the way his broad muscled shoulders taper down to his tight backside covered by his black boxer briefs. His upper right arm is covered in wave tattoos, and Prison Mike stares at me from his bicep.

Locating my dress pooled on the floor, he gently turns it right side out and inspects it before draping it over the edge of the bed neatly. "Looks to be in order and still clean. Good," he says smiling at me. "I would hate for something to happen to that dress."

God, why is he simultaneously the sweetest and most confusing human? I want to grab him by his big, stupid, handsome face, shake him and say: *Stop being so nice, it turns me on.*

I cover up my chest a little tighter with his soft, dark green duvet. "It would have been fine. That dress was like forty bucks. She doesn't owe me anything."

"Stop," he says, shaking his head and moving toward the bedroom door. "That dress is special and I know you feel great when you wear it." His dimples dig in even deeper before he pops out of the room.

·····•·••···

Escaping to Raf's bathroom is exactly what I need right now. It's beautiful and modern, but I don't pay much attention. I can't focus on how well I'm cleaning my body with the whirlwind of thoughts placating my brain. Washing off my stupidity and replacing it with a fresh version of myself is rejuvenating. But then my traitorous brain reminds me... *Raf almost kissed me.*

Obviously we were both drunk because I know better than to give into those stupid urges. Not that I have any. But if I did...

No. Shut it down.

Leaning my forehead against the porcelain tile wall, I slough off the dangerously theoretical situation like my head and my heart are teflon. The shower takes longer than normal, but I needed a little more time to think. Even though all the aftermath makes sense, the blacking out part is still frustrating.

I'm worried I said something I'd regret to Raf. Like maybe I said something foolish that friends don't say to friends. Things that shall not be labeled or given a name even within the confines of my brain. My only saving grace is knowing that he blacked out too. So if I did say something stupid, he doesn't remember either.

Stepping out of the shower, I take my time inspecting everything he has stocked. He has a large collection of cologne, but I spot his go-to and take a whiff. He's also an after-shave kind of guy apparently. That's new. He never used to be.

Mmm, that smells good too. His cologne is a strong bergamot and lemon, but this aftershave balm is light like chamomile.

Listen, I'm as turned-on by a rugged mountain man as the next person, but there's *something* about a man with a whole skincare set up, a beautiful grooming kit, and cologne collection that gets. Me. Going.

When I'm satisfied with my pampering, I reapply my sticky bra and throw on my dress from last night and head out.

We make a quick pit stop at my place where my chunky orange cat Razzel Dazzle yells at me for disturbing his peace. This dude is twenty years old and just *won't die.* Not that I want him to. I've had him since I was a preteen and he's been through too much with me. I think all my childhood trauma is keeping him alive honestly.

Snickering, Raf plucks one of my dark romance novels from the bookcase, fingering through the pages to the well-worn sections as I change into a cute spring sweater, jeans, and sneaks.

I'm grateful he's distracted and not paying attention to my little rented one bedroom that I know he hates. He's been here countless times over the last few years. It's in a house with a family I know through my old job, but it is in a rougher neighborhood. A neighborhood Raf grunts his indignation at every spare moment he's here. Like if he grunts enough I'll finally find a safe neighborhood with cheap rent.

Pete and Sarah Boyer were kind enough to let me live with them for a reasonable rate. I wasn't stretching the truth before: I make very little money even with a bachelor's degree in psychology and a master's degree in counseling. I work in the non-profit mental health field at a few different public elementary schools—you know, where teachers and staff alike are notoriously paid well from the endless pot of gold the government gives them.

By the time we make it to White Dog Cafe, one of our favorite spots, the lingering unease from this morning fades away with that first clink of our mimosa flutes. "I'm so happy you're back, Raf. Cheers to the way it should be."

He gives me a feline smile. "*Are* things the way they should be if you're going to keep kissing me?"

Chapter 3

March 25th

Rafael

When Monday morning finally rolls around, the hangover courtesy of my housewarming party Saturday night has finally subsided. I made a promise to myself Sunday morning that I would never drink like that again. What got into me? Angie and I are almost never like that. College us? Yes. All day. But I know for a fact we're both more like two or three drinks a week kind of people.

I still can't believe I almost kissed her. Will I ever admit that I leaned in first? No. But I will forever tease her that she tried to kiss me. The vulnerability is easier to ignore that way. Plus, I love teasing her.

Right as I park my car in the lot, a notification pops up that Angie has just posted a new song to one of our many shared playlists with the caption *Have a great first day!* Popping in an ear bud, I listen to *Let's Go* by Trick Daddy, Lil Jon, and Twista.

How does she always know the right song for the moment? She's a witch. A musical witch.

I glance around at the other cars in the lot and don't see anyone, so I let myself succumb to the banger and pretend I'm performing on stage—and by doing so, I hype myself up. Blood rushes through my body as my SUV rocks in tandem with my driver's-seat dancing.

I'm fucking ready.

"Good morning," Cora smiles, greeting me as I walk into the lobby of Define Architectural Group. I was here once before for a formal interview with Cora (the CEO and senior architect), Jay (Director of Human Resources and her boyfriend), as well as Dayo (Director of Interior Design). In all the years I've known Cora, never once have I been in a room with her in such a professional manner. It feels like we are still the wild and reckless freshman masquerading as adults with important jobs; when in reality, that's exactly what we are. All three of us—including Angie—have been dedicated to succeeding in our respective fields. But just like when I get together with my rugby teammates, I naturally default to being goofy with those two.

"Good morning," I say, extending my hand to her like a moron.

"Oh. So formal," she smiles, and shakes my hand.

"That was weird."

"Yeah," she winces. "Let's never do that again. Alright, follow me and I'll show you to your office where IT will get you all set up."

She hands me my badge and we scan it against the receiver on the wall to enter into the office area. Walking past the cubicles, some folks are settling in for the day while others are in the kitchen area pouring coffee. Noticing their more casual office attire, I feel a little overdressed. Cora's wearing jeans and a light blue oxford shirt.

Clearing my throat I ask, "What's the dress code here?"

"Oh, whatever you like. It's mostly office casual but some people wear business formal. I have to visit a construction site this afternoon, or else I would be a little dressier. Jay is usually wearing a suit too, so don't worry."

We approach an office with floor to ceiling glass walls. It's a good size with a large wooden corner desk and a seating area with fancy red armchairs. I take a mental note to start learning about furniture and design because those are probably special. Now that I look around more, the entire office space is special. Everything from the carpeting to light fixtures to the exposed brick walls around the perimeter all lend to a high-end vibe. It certainly represents an architectural firm taking notice of its historical Philadelphia roots and marrying that with a modern-day style.

"Oh good, he's here," Jay says, walking into the office with me and Cora, while another man trails in behind him. She wasn't kidding. Jay's wearing a dark green three-piece suit. So I'm not the dressiest person in the office afterall. Might need to step my game up if this is what he wears on a regular basis.

The other man is scruffy-looking and wearing all black and Jay introduces him. "Rafael, this is Stuart, our IT specialist. He's gonna get you set up, and then I'll be back in an hour to take you to the morning meeting where we'll introduce you to the whole Director-level team. Then my colleague Courtney and I will go over all the benefits information with you. Sound good?"

I set my bag down on the desk and smile. "Sounds good."

After Stuart helps me set up my laptop and mobile phone, I attend the morning meeting and am introduced to several department heads. Define has over two hundred employees, so this isn't some small mom-n-pop shop, even though Cora's late father did start this company.

By the time Courtney and Jay go through their whole spiel and I've enrolled in my health and financial benefits, it's nearly noon.

"Okay, one last thing, Rafael," Courtney says. "Did you want to list your address as the one you're living at now or the other property?"

I told her about the huge fixer-upper on Chester Ave in Philly that my brother Joaquín and I are renovating. Well, that I'm financing and he's leading. With the apartment building we sold in DC, we've decided to renovate historic homes here. Some will stay single-family, like the one we're fixing up now, and some will turn into multi-family estates. I plan to split my time between two places, so it's a valid question from her.

"The townhouse I'm in now on Pierce Street will be fine. I'll let you know when I move into the other property."

"That works," she says, closing her laptop and flipping her long blonde hair behind her shoulder. "Welcome to the team, Rafael!"

"Ready for lunch?" Cora asks, rapping lightly on the door-frame as Courtney leaves. "It's kind of a first day tradition for me to take out new hires."

"Yeah sure," I say, standing up and buttoning my navy blue suit jacket.

"I'm coming too," Jay stands, throwing his jacket back on. Jeez, he's tall. I'm six foot-four and he's close to my height. He'd make a great second row—him and Marco both. Wonder if I could convince them to join our DIII club team?

We step outside to a bright spring afternoon, when I ask him, "Jay, have you ever played rugby?"

"No," he says curtly. "Now, tell me exactly what happened with you and Angie."

Choking on nothing, I then turn to him and lean over to peer down at Cora on the other side of Jay. "Excuse me?"

"You heard him," Cora says. "We want to know."

"Didn't she already tell you?"

Jay scoffs. "That wasn't nearly enough intel. We need the play-by-play."

When did this fifty-three-degree spring day start to feel like Florida in July? But I plaster a smile on regardless. "Guys, we literally called you from the scene of the—" I cut my own words off as they both stare wide-eyed at me. "From my bed. We got too drunk, blacked out, and woke up there. It's not the first time something like that has happened."

"Mhmm," Cora hums with a furrowed brow.

Jay opens the storefront door to a Middle Eastern restaurant. "You both skirted my question before when I asked what you were wearing."

"I...was wearing what I always wear to bed: boxers."

"Wait," Jay stops me in front of the hostess stand. "Boxers or boxer-briefs?"

"That doesn't matter."

"It certainly does!"

"Boxer briefs, okay?"

Jay gasps. "You slut."

"You know you're my HR Director, right?"

"No, I'm your friend right now," he says, shaking his head. "Now tell me, what color were the boxer-briefs?"

The hostess gives us a weird look but takes three menus and leads us to a small table where we sit.

"Does color honestly matter? Guys, I'm telling you, nothing happened." They both stare silently across from me, making me uncomfortable with their gaze. When I can't stand it anymore, I open my menu and pretend to read it before clearing my throat and whispering, "Black."

It's Cora's turn to gasp. "You like her."

"What?" I hiss. "How did you—I usually wear black. Where the fuck is this coming from? I'd also like to know what color boxer-briefs would indicate that I'm not a slut and not interested in my best friend?"

"Orange," Jay says flatly.

"Novelty patterns," Cora adds.

I stare at the menu again and shake my head slowly. "Alright, looks like I'm picking up some new underwear today to convince you two freaks that I'm not into her."

Why are they pressing me about this? Cora has been around me and Angie since before we could legally drink—so why is she suddenly suspicious of our platonic relationship?

"You know what sounds good?" I ask, ignoring their in-terrogation. "Chicken shawarma."

Jay leans his forearms on the table and clasps his hands. "There was tension at your housewarming party, dude."

"No, there wasn't," I say defensively.

"You almost kissed," he says, raising his eyebrows.

"We were inebriated and in close proximity."

Cora clicks her tongue and looks lovingly at Jay, grabbing his hand, "Remember the first time we were inebriated and in close proximity?"

Jay smiles sugar-sweetly at her. "The back seat of my car still smells like us."

"Okay," I groan, pinching the bridge of my nose. "That's more than I need to know about you two. Let's settle this once and for all: Nothing happened between Angie and me. Nothing will ever happen, because we're friends. Always have been. Always will be."

Jay turns his smirk to me. "Did I ever tell you about the time I fell in love with my best friend Marco?"

"You mean your other partner?"

He pauses briefly and huffs a little laugh. "Yeah."

Chapter 4

March 30th

Rafael

"I'm kind of embarrassed that I haven't visited your moms much since you've been away," Angie says, looking outside the window as we roll up to my moms' house in Radnor—a mere half-mile away from her childhood home. They've been here since Mamá, Joaquín, and I moved here from Texas when I was nine. Back when Joaquín was Gabriela. Fuck, it's weird to think about him before he transitioned.

"It's okay," I say. "We were here at Christmas time with them."

"Yeah, but I feel like I should have been here on my own when you were living in DC. They're as much my moms as they are yours at this point."

Something irksome kicks up inside me when she says that. "Don't worry about it," I say, stepping out of my Range and coming around to open her door, like I always do. "You usually come with me when I'm back in town anyway."

She steps out of the SUV looking so...Angie. Which is to say cute and sophisticated. Tonight she's wearing a casual, long, olive-green wrap dress with sleeves. It's a far cry from the ensembles we wore in high school, but Angela Johanssen's style has certainly found its mark in the last five years or so. She shows herself off now. Gone is the insecure chubby girl hiding behind her once-long brunette hair and massive costume jewelry. Now, she's a woman who knows her body—knows it looks good. Knows how to expertly style herself, even if it is with out-of-fashion clothing. She can make any garment look like it was just invented.

But that's always been my Angel. She's always reinventing herself. Exploring. Trying something new.

When we reach the front steps to the house, the door swings wide open before we're even in range of the doorknob. "¡Bienvenido a casa!" Christina, my bonus mom cheers, opening her arms wide to grab the both of us for a tight hug. She's a good foot shorter than me, with short-cropped auburn hair that's whiter these days, pale-as-snow skin, and her signature cargo pants and basic cotton long-sleeve. Her 'home uniform' as Angie and I lovingly refer to it as.

"Hi," Angie says, switching to Spanish. "Do I smell tamales?"

Mom lets go of us. "Of course."

"The spicy ones?" I ask, charging inside to make my way to the kitchen.

"We made them extra spicy for you two."

"Yes," Angie bellows. "Thank you!"

Being second generation Mexican in this country, I grew up speaking Spanish in the house and English outside it. Mamá was determined her children would speak it since most second-generation kids lose it. Since Angie was in our home constantly as a child, she picked it up quickly, and subsequently, her brothers and sister did too.

I set the bottle of wine down on the counter before hugging Mamá at the sink. As always, her black hair is perfectly curled and flowing down her back. She's wearing simple leggings and a long sweater, and of course, her makeup is flawless. The only time you see Ana Webber without makeup is when she's about to go to bed and before breakfast is ready. Even working as a nurse practitioner, Mamá always looks like she's ready for the cameras. Like she's expecting paparazzi to show up and take notice of her normal, suburban American life. Like the tabloids will finally see the rags-to-riches story she made for herself—where she dragged herself out of a fractured hetero-presenting marriage, and finally became herself when she found her true partner.

The partner who supported her and wanted her to achieve her dreams. The partner who stuck by her and held her hand when our ultra-religious family back in Mexico tried to shun her for being outwardly queer. She forced her way back into the family and made them accept Christina and herself. Then did it again when I came out as bisexual. Then did it again, with way more ferocity, when Joaquín transitioned.

I'll never forget the way she yelled at my *tios* and *abuelos*, told them right to their faces, "If you ever want to see us again, you will call him by his name and love him as you love everyone else!"

Hearing her say that to them was earth-shattering. In our family, children never speak to their parents or elders like that. Never. There's a huge respect barrier between the generations, and even if you know you're right, you don't talk back. You don't yell. You don't sass. To us, family is everything; so to hear her say she would cut ties with them if they didn't accept him—us—was a huge risk to our familial connection.

Except for the occasional slip up every now and again, they've been pretty good about it. Do they secretly refer to us as the gay side of the family and pray for our souls? Sure. But I don't know anyone with a perfectly accepting extended family.

I've been a little luckier with the family's acceptance than Mamá and Joaquín though. Seeing as I've never brought any love interest around them, there's been no human proof of my bisexuality—and I think to them, that's been easier to digest and ignore.

Whatever. It's not my job to show off my queerness to them.

Do they still sometimes refer to Christina as Mamá's friend and not her wife? Yeah. I'm not thrilled to say it took me a while to come around to Christina too. It wasn't that she was a woman; it was that she wasn't my papá. Regardless of the borderline hostile way he treated my mamá, their relationship and their presence was what I knew; it's what I was comfortable with. As a kid, I didn't realize that comfort was just my conditioning and lack of knowledge on how a healthy parental relationship should work. That's all I knew. It wasn't until I was in the sixth grade that I finally saw Christina as a parent rather than Not My Dad.

Secretly, there's still a part of me that wishes my bio parents were still together. I know that's fucked up to say given the way he treated her, but a childish part of me still thinks I could have done something to prevent them from separating. Don't get me wrong: I wouldn't trade mom for anything in the world—she's the best and she's exactly what Mamá needs. But there's still a feeling of *you can fix this* that I harbor for my mamá and papá.

If I just did better at school.

If I just worked more efficiently.

If I just made more money.

If I just listened to his advice.

Maybe *then* I could make my dad proud. Proud enough to earn an elusive *te amo*. My father's love is hard-won, but possible.

"Mijo," Mamá sighs, wiping her hands on a tea towel and turning to face me. "Have you grown since I saw you?"

"Since my housewarming party?" I raise an eyebrow. "That was last weekend."

"I know. But I swear you're taller every time I see you."

I know my moms were there at the beginning, but I have no idea when they left. Better to leave that stone unturned. I don't want them to know as much as our friends already do. If my mamá even gets a whiff of scandal, she's like a hound dog—relentlessly chasing the scent until she finds the evidence.

Releasing from her hold, I turn to see Angie helping Mom set the table, so I grab the silverware and head over.

Once we're all situated, Mamá says grace, immediately followed by our wine glasses clinking. Like always, the conversation never dies or has a lull. Mom tells us about the last concert she coordinated at the Wells Fargo Center, and mamá tells us about how she's thinking of retiring in the next year or so—to which I twitch with excitement. I've been my parents' financial advisor for the last ten years and I know she's been hesitant to pull the trigger, so this is huge.

Sitting next to me, Angie sniffles, causing me to look in her direction. "I'm sorry," she says, dabbing her cloth napkin to her tear-streaked face. "That's incredible news, Ana. But these tamales," she shakes her head and lets out a little whistle.

"Oh no, *mija*. Are they too spicy?"

"No, no!" Angie replies quickly. "They're perfect. *Pica rico.* You know it's good when it's so spicy it makes you cry."

Mamá smiles with a worried look, because she knows how freakish Angie can be about her spicy food, but it also encourages Mamá to pile more on our plates. Way more food than a normal person should eat in one sitting.

"That reminds me," Mamá says, sitting back and placing her hand on Mom's shoulder next to her. "We're going back home for Fernanda's college graduation in May. Do you two want to come with us?"

By home, she means Guanajuato, Mexico, where most of my family lives. Both sides. I love visiting them and the city is stunning. Between the rolling cliffsides overlooking a vibrant city to the culture, architecture, and energy this place exudes, it's no wonder we try to go back at least twice a year. Angie included.

Always included.

I've never taken anyone else. Certainly not someone I was casually seeing, which is anyone I've ever "dated." I don't know what you'd call how I date other people. Interludes? It's something between a one-night stand and a fling. Nothing lasts more than a month and that's by design.

"I'd love to go," Angie says. "Fernanda is wild. I wanna see who is willingly giving her a bachelor's degree."

My excitement dies down when I remember. "I can't," I sigh. "Rugby playoffs are at the beginning of May, and if we win it all, it'll seep into the end of May."

"Oh, you're right," Angie drawls. "Well, I don't want to miss any of those games either. Who's going to bring orange slices for the players?"

I huff a laugh. "Why do you keep doing that?"

"The guys love it!"

"They love adding the slice to their beers after the game."

"They've come to expect it from me," she says seriously. "I cannot disappoint them."

She's so funny. "So that's a no?" Mamá asks.

"Yeah, sorry," I say. "We'll plan another trip soon, I promise."

Once we're about done cleaning up, I cover the last of the leftover rice, beans, and tamales in Tupperware containers that Mamá will be sending home with us and place them in the fridge. But I stop when I see a few new pictures they've added near the ice dispenser. These pictures of me, Joaquín, and Angie have adorned this surface forever. Mostly from the concerts we attended. But these new ones make me curious.

"Where did you find this one?" I ask no one in particular as I stare at eighteen-year-old Angie and Rafael wearing black and white full-face makeup, ready for the Insane Clown Posse concert.

"Oh my god," Angie groans, coming up next to me as I wrap my arm around her and pull her in close. "Was that when we tried to be Juggalos?"

"Yes," Mom laughs uncontrollably. "I think that was the first concert you guys went to where you had no prior knowledge of the band."

Mom's laughter trickles to Angie. "That's one hundred percent what happened. We looked up how we were supposed to dress and nothing else."

All four of us are peeling with laughter now. "That was not our vibe," I muster out. "Wait, wait, what's this one?" I ask, pointing to the picture next to it.

Mom steps in closer to look at an image of a sunburnt Angie sleeping on a towel next to a tent—not in the tent—next to, and I'm crouched beside her with a huge grin and two thumbs up, wearing my swim trunks and a cut-off tank. "Oh, I found that one in the basement the other day. That was the summer after your sophomore year in college when we went river tubing and camping down in West Virginia. It was right before you went back to school."

"I loved those camping trips," Angie says fondly, squeezing me a little tighter around my torso.

"Me too," I sigh, letting her hold me a little longer as we look back on our memories.

The pair of us have always been affectionate like this. Until Cora came into our lives, Angie was the only girl outside of my family I was comfortable being my true unfiltered self with. I guess to this day I'm still not nearly as affectionate with Cora as I am with Angie. That could largely be because Angie has been around since before I had my own opinions. Before I formed my hardened exterior to outsiders. That's not to say I'm not still friendly and goofy with people I meet and other friends—I just don't let those people inside the way I do with Angie.

My eyes travel to the one picture of my papá on the fridge. I've always been surprised my moms have kept it, but I've never said anything about it in fear that they'll take it down—as if they've never noticed it, and by me mentioning its presence, they'll correct their mistake. It's a photo of him, me, and Joaquín before he transitioned. I'm about fourteen, which would make Joaquín about eleven. My dad stands between us on his front porch in Redbird, a well-to-do suburb of Dallas. I remember my mamá took the picture right before she dropped us off for a month that summer. She and Mom were heading to Mexico to visit family afterwards.

It was one of the last summer trips to Papá's house where my moms traveled with us. I remember being beyond excited to be there. We only got to see him in the summer and the occasional Christmas spent together in Guanajuato. We'd still see my father's side of the family in Mexico whether he was there or not, which, often, he wasn't.

To say I look up to my dad is an understatement. Whenever I had one of those class assignments that asked who my hero was, my dad was always the answer. He was cool and fun and strong—he was everything I wanted to be.

And I wanted to show him that. I wanted to prove to him I was worthy of his love beyond reasonable doubt. I still do.

To this day, I still get excited when I get to see him. Though, it's been almost five years since I have—the longest stretch of time we've ever gone. It's not on purpose; we've been busy. He never had a chance to make it to DC when I lived there, but that's okay. I know he has a demanding job working in the oil and gas industry down there. Plus, his hobbies keep him occupied. I get it.

I should visit more. That's on me. I'll plan to visit him soon. He'll be so happy if I do. Maybe that will convince him to come visit me too. Shoot, the last time José Juan Jimenez was on the east coast was... huh. Was it when I graduated from grad school? Wow, it's been forever. Not that he visited much anyway, but that's okay. Other than us, he didn't have any family here or reason to visit.

"Oh my gosh," Angie sweetly sighs, pulling me back to the other memories in front of us. She points to another photo. "I can't believe you let me bleach your hair back then."

I chuckle. "You said you knew how! I believed you!"

"What sixteen-year-old knows how to properly bleach hair, Raf?"

"You were very confident," I shrug. "You've always tricked me into doing things with your unwarranted confidence."

Chapter 5
April 30th

Angie

Having Rafael back in my life full time is even better than I thought it would be. It's also kind of worse, but in a way that's easily ignorable. Over the last month, we've been hanging out after work at least a couple nights each week, usually in the evenings when he doesn't have rugby practice. Sometimes by ourselves and sometimes with friends. Being with him—in any capacity—is like breathing. It's natural.

Sometimes we'll simply hangout, watching trash TV and eating ice cream as I self-medicate my period cramps. Which was a minor relief when I did get my period a couple weeks ago. I know we said nothing happened, but it's still a relief to get that confirmation each month.

Our playlists seem to be getting out of control in the best way. We started curating them once we both graduated with our master's degrees, and he moved to DC. It was a way we still connected to each other outside of the near daily text messages, at least weekly video calls, and monthly trips to visit one another. Playlists for trips we took to Mexico together, for holidays, for camping trips, and everything in between. Our master playlist holds the largest assortment of music—all four hundred plus songs that we deem our favorites or at least have some memory associated with it.

But now, instead of songs being added once a week or so, we're sharing multiple times a day. I want to share everything with him—every thought and feeling put to a melody.

We haven't spent every free night together though. We're not that codependent. There have been a few nights where each of us went out on dates. Raf saw some guy named Charles for a few nights and it ended exactly the way it always does for him. I went out with a couple guys I met on a dating app—both of which ended on-brand for me. One guy took one look at me, eyes round, turned, and left the bar without saying a word. You know, I go to great lengths to make sure my profile photos capture my fatness. I clearly indicate that I'm five-foot eight and thick. What is so surprising to these fuckwads?

The other guy, who asked me out and made the plans at a trendy expensive restaurant, showed up, ordered a ton of food and four drinks for himself, then conveniently forgot his wallet. This is not the first time this sort of thing has happened to me. So when he asked me if I could spot him, I said, "Sure. Let me just head to the ladies' room and I'll be right back." I got up, found our server, paid her for my portion and tip, then left without looking back. I blocked that mooch before I even got in my rink-a-dink car.

That was over a week ago and I've been pinching pennies since then to make up for the unexpectedly high price of that dinner.

The whole dating situation makes me sick. Or maybe that's just my physical body; I haven't been feeling my best lately. Maybe I need more sleep and fewer fucks to give about men.

"I think we added too much Old Bay to this batch," Raf says, digging through our shared popcorn bucket. I gasp, but he chuckles. "I know. I never thought I'd say those words either."

We're sitting on my tiny sofa watching Love Island. My rented room is barely big enough for my queen size bed, a loveseat, circular coffee table, TV, and bookcase. I do have a large closet, which I'm eternally grateful for. My room is cozy and decorated just the way I like it—which is to say whimsical and weird and a little bohemian. Lavender is the most prominent color choice, but there's fluffy white bedding, mushroom decals adorn the white baseboards, and fairy lights twinkle along the ceiling's edge. The trickling sound of a tiny plug-in water feature sits atop a floating shelf in the corner; and below on another shelf are essential oils and crystals.

Alright, so I'm a little crunchy. It's not like I tell my students amethyst and patchouli will solve their problems. It's not that deep; I'm simply here for the vibes. Meditation on the other hand—that's one I'll share with the kids who need it.

As a kid, I never had much choice in my décor. I was too busy taking care of my four siblings and sharing a room with Ivy to have any time to discover what my style was. So now I'm a thirty-one-year-old woman with a funky, ultra-feminine bedroom and I savor it.

There are dried flowers hanging everywhere, as well as fake sunflowers in a vase on my nightstand. It's a plastic vase, but that's only because Razzle keeps knocking it over. He has one eye and the other barely works, but somehow, he knows where the flowers are and must disrupt the peace.

Fucking orange cats, man.

Thankfully he's distracted by Rafael's generous rubs as he lounges in his lap, so the sunflowers live to see another day. But when a light knock sounds on my door, he abruptly launches himself into the closet to hide.

I live in a family's home with Sarah, Pete, and their two young children, so whoever is knocking can only be from that very short list of people.

"Come in," I call.

When the door slowly opens, Sarah's head pops in. "Hey," she smiles. "Can I talk to you for a minute?"

Sarah and I used to be colleagues when we were foster care case workers. But when I moved on to being a children's mental health outpatient therapist, we kept in touch. When she found out I needed a new place to live a few years ago, she offered her place to me.

"Yeah, come on in." There's no more room to sit down, but Rafael gets up and offers his spot while he goes to sit on my bed.

When Sarah sits, I just know she's about to unload something on me.

"There's no easy way to say this," she sighs. "So, I'm just going to get it over with. Pete and I have decided to sell the house. We're moving back to Harrisburg."

I stare at her with a slack-jaw. She simply stares back at me with a wan smile, like she knows it's going to take me a few seconds to register everything.

"So," I drawl. "You need me to move out."

She winces. "Unless you want to buy our house."

Ha. Like I could afford this place. "You and I both know I couldn't." I let out a long exhale and look up to the ceiling—the twinkling lights mocking me. With resignation, I ask, "When do you need me out by?"

"June first?"

"That soon?" Raf interjects.

"I'm afraid so," she says. "I know this is hard. I'm sorry." Sarah stands up and makes her way to the open door. "I don't want to take up any more of your time," she says, gesturing to the pair of us sitting there dumbfounded. "I'll let you get back to your night. I'm sorry again, Ang."

"It happens," I sigh. "Thanks for letting me live here though. It's been nice."

"It has," she says with a smile and then leaves, closing the door gently. My room is quiet for a long moment while I continue to process what happened.

Rafael seems lost in thought too until he jumps up from my bed and lands next to me on the sofa. "Move in with me."

My head jerks in his direction. "What?"

"Yeah," he nods. "Why not? We've lived together in college. What's so different now?"

I study him. "The difference is we were both broke in college," I say. "And now you're a friggin' chief financial officer and I'm—" I wave to my small room. "I should be living within my means."

"How is this any different than what your current situation is?" he asks seriously. "You're living with people who make more money than you and offered you a place to live."

"Um," I try to think it through.

"Exactly," he says flatly, and then takes my hands in his. "Come on. You can live with me for free."

"Absolutely not, dude!"

"Okay! Okay. Just pay me what you are currently paying here. Fair?"

"Raf," I say, trying to reason with him. "Your townhouse is way nicer than this place."

"You don't know how much they pay for this house. But that's not the point," he says, squeezing my hands a little tighter. "The point is, we spend all our time with each other anyway, we've lived together before and fucking excelled at it, and I'm in a position to be able to offer this to you."

Chewing on my lip, I ponder the possibility.

He continues. "Do you think you don't deserve to live somewhere nice just because you don't make much money?" I roll my eyes at the accurate statement. "Angel, you could be making more money than me working at a private practice. Instead, you've chosen to work with kids who need you. With families that don't always appreciate you.

You've chosen to work for those who could never afford to pay you out of their own pockets. Stop making yourself believe you're only as worthy as your salary."

My eyebrows lower as I pout at how right he is. "Okay," I sigh. "That was really nice of you to say."

"So you'll move in?"

Should I? Based on previous experience, I know I can. But that tendril of unrequited...emotion...I keep locked away... what about that? I've been able to keep it at bay—the feeling that shall not be named. At this point, it's like your favorite pair of shoes suddenly have a little squeak to them, and you think, *Well, that's annoying. But I'm never going to throw away these shoes. They're the best.*

I can live with a little squeak—I've been doing it for years. I can keep it up.

Letting out a sigh, I look at him in his deep brown eyes and I give in. "Yeah. I'll move in."

"Fuck yes!" he cheers, grabbing my arms and shaking me like I'm a magic eight ball. But Razzle thinks he's attacking me, so he jumps to my rescue and starts biting his arms. Again, how can he see? "Ow ow! Okay, I let her go! Stop!" he screams, jumping up and running away to the safety of my bed. "You know, you're moving in too, big man. I wouldn't be so aggressive to the person sheltering you."

Razz curls up in my lap and starts loudly meowing at him—like he's setting the ground rules.

Good boy.

Chapter 6

June 1st

Angie

L ast night I woke up in a panic. It wasn't from a dream or anything like that. I literally woke up dizzy. I didn't know you *could* wake up from that. But lo and behold, with my room spinning and an aching emptiness inside my gut, I held onto my bed for dear life. It was unlike any spinning hangover I've ever experienced—far worse. Somehow, I made it out of bed and downstairs to the kitchen where I took a sip of juice and felt mildly better. I tried to drink water but gagged in my efforts. There's something about water that's not sitting right with me lately—like I need to add *something* to it to make it more palatable.

When I finally got back to bed, I managed to fall asleep again and I woke up with my alarm. Glad the dizziness was mostly gone, I started packing the remaining last-minute essentials before everyone arrived to help me move.

Is it overkill to have all three of my brothers, Marco, Jay, and Cora here to help? Maybe. But also, Cora isn't lifting a finger. She just found out she was pregnant, and Marco and Jay are being hyper-vigilant. They just got back from a long vacation where they decided to get married without anyone else present!

Married without me.

I'm not salty at all.

Fuckers.

But also, I've been crying with happiness for them non-stop since they told me.

Dane and Jonah pull up in the small U-Haul right as Raf comes out of the house with a heavy box. I wave to them as Isaiah pulls away from the curb, opening a spot for the truck.

Man, even lifting my arm to wave is difficult and I'm tired suddenly. I let my hand flop down but shake it off. Bending to lift a box of clothes, I have a rush of lightheadedness as my heart rate picks up dramatically, and with no thought, I fall to the sidewalk.

I think I'm conscious, but my senses are lowered somehow. I can hear, but everything is quieter. I can see, but everything looks white-washed. I can feel, but only the dizziness buzzing in my head.

"Angie! Angie!" I hear a powerful voice push through the fog, and then hands are on the back of my neck holding me upright as I sit limply. Rafael stares at me with wide eyes. "Are you okay?"

Vaguely sensing everyone else gather around, I manage to whisper, "I'm...so dizzy." My eyes shut of their own accord, but Raf shakes me.

"I'll go get her some water," I hear Cora say.

Ugh. No, please anything but that, I think to myself, but can't utter the words.

"Stay awake, Angel. Talk to me."

I barely get out a simple, "Okay." Fuck, what's going on with me? Gone are my senses.

"Did you eat today?"

"No. I...got up and...finished packing," I whisper.

"Isaiah—"

"On it, Raf. I'll be right back."

"Keep talking, Angel. Have you been feeling well?"

God, I want to close my eyes so badly. But I try to speak. "Last night...was...weird."

"Here," Cora says, shoving a plastic cup of water in my face and forcing me to drink. But as soon as I try to swallow, I gag so hard I start coughing.

"What the fuck is going on with you?" Raf asks, his eyes bugging out as he continues to hold me on the sidewalk.

"I don't know," I cry—literally. Where the fuck did all these tears come from? All of sudden I'm now a blubbering mess.

"I found this breakfast bar," Isaiah says, hunching down to push the unwrapped rectangle toward my face.

When I try to lift my arm, again it's exhausting. Barely gripping it, I take a quick bite and my hand drops to the ground with it. I feel pathetic. I'm chewing and crying at the same time, exhausted beyond belief, and I just want everything to quit being so spinny for one goddamn minute.

"Guys," Raf says. "Can you guys wrap up here? I'm taking her to the hospital."

"Of course," they all say in some manner.

"Door code is 0220," he says, standing up and then lifting me like I don't weigh over two hundred pounds. Walking away, I rest my head against his shoulder as he calls back to everyone, "Thank you! Don't worry about unpacking anything."

I hear the passenger door open and Cora's there, helping Raf guide me into the front seat. "Keep me updated, Raf," she says.

"I will."

He enters the driver's side and shuts the door. Cora squeezes my hand. "Keep trying to eat that granola bar, Ang."

"Okay," I sob.

"You're going to be fine, hun. Raf has you. Okay?"

"Okay," I repeat, then attempt to take another bite.

She releases my hand and says, "I love you. Drive safe, Raf."

"Will do. I'll call you."

As soon as the door shuts, he pulls away from the curb fast as lightning. If I thought the world was spinning before, it's nothing compared to being in this vehicle now. I shut my eyes in an attempt to quell my new nausea.

"Keep your eyes open, Angel."

"I can't," I cry. "Too sick."

"Okay. Okay just...keep talking to me."

I try to form another sentence, but my queasiness builds. Shaking my head, I hope he can see and understand that I can't.

"Are you gonna throw up?" I shrug. "Okay. Hold my hand then," he demands. "Every time I squeeze, I want you to squeeze back. Okay?" I nod and squeeze his large hand as it settles in my lap.

We make it to what I assume is the closest Emergency Room, and I have no idea what Raf has done with his SUV, because all I know is I'm being carried into the lobby and placed in a wheelchair immediately.

"Sir, there's going to be about an hour wait before she's seen."

"Like hell there is!" I hear him roar. "She's almost unconscious! She can't stand up, she can't talk without being sick, she can barely lift her arms!"

"I'm sorry, sir, but she's going to have to wait like everyone else."

"We'll see about that," he seethes, pushing me away at a snail's pace. A few seconds later I hear him speaking in Spanish. "Hey, Mamá. Angie's at the ER on Convention Ave. I'm with her. Who do you know here? She needs to be seen immediately. Thank you. I understand. Yes. Thank you so much."

His hand squeezes mine and I return the touch, still unable to open my eyes or speak. Within a few minutes, I hear a voice call out, "Angela Johanssen?"

"Right here!" Raf calls back and starts wheeling me.

After taking my vitals, Raf gives the nurse the situation, and I do my best to open my eyes and acknowledge what he's saying.

"Her blood pressure is dangerously low," the nurse says. "I'm going to run some tests and start her on some intravenous fluids. She's incredibly dehydrated as well."

That part checks out—between gagging from water recently and sobbing from Cora's happy news—yeah, that seems about right.

Shit. I need to take better care of myself.

The nurse, Aleigha, I think she said her name was, sticks me with a needle and within minutes I'm feeling marginally better. When she leaves, I turn to Raf as I lay back on the crunchy plastic hospital bed. "Thank you for being here."

Sitting in the chair next to me, still holding my hand like it's a life preserver, he smiles up at me. "Of course. I wouldn't be anywhere else, Angel."

Angel. That silly little nickname he's been calling me since we were kids holds a punch. I don't think he's aware of it. And if he is, then he knows exactly what he's doing when he says it to me. He says it often, but especially when he's trying to convince me to do something because he knows I'll fold like a lawn chair.

By the time the doctor comes in twenty minutes later, I'm more alert thanks to the IV and able to coherently speak without crying. She's a short Black woman with natural hair that's been straightened and curled to perfection. She's incredibly beautiful. "Hi, Angela," she smiles, rubbing her hands together after pumping some antibacterial foam on them when she walks in the room. "I'm Dr. Asare." She takes the chart out from under her arm and flips it open. "Looks like you're in here for dehydration, low blood pressure, and fatigue, is that right?"

"Yes, that's right."

She looks at Rafael and comes back to me. "Would you like to be alone for the rest of our visit, or would you like for him to stay?"

"Oh, he can stay. He should be my emergency contact anyway."

"Alright," she says calmly, then looks back at the chart. "Did you know you're pregnant?"

A long pause stretches between us, freezing me. "Did...you...know that's the wrong chart you're looking at?" I ask.

She simply shakes her head and says, "No, it's not."

I choke on my own words but finally push out, "That's not possible. I'm on birth control and I haven't missed any periods. I *just* had a period."

"Some people never stop their periods while they're pregnant. It's more common than you think." She says simply, like it's common-fucking-knowledge. The doctor continues, oblivious to my turmoil. "Says here, you're about twelve weeks pregnant. Which really means you're ten weeks pregnant. I've never understood why we always add two more weeks from before conception, but here we are. You're almost in your second trimester."

My vision defaults to a dolly zoom on Dr. Asare.

She can't be serious.

I can't be pregnant.

How the fuck did this happen? I haven't had sex with anyone in nearly a year.

"I'm going to give you some privacy to adjust to that news, and Nurse Aleigha will be in here shortly with some juice and snacks to help with your blood sugar levels. I'll come back a little later with more information and some obstetric doctor recommendations in case you don't already have one. Okay?" she says cheerily, as if she hasn't handed me a live grenade.

On reflex I nod, unable to blink as she walks out of my line of vision.

"Ang," Rafael whispers.

Slowly, I turn my face to him, and all thoughts are completely wiped from my brain. "Yeah?"

"Who did you sleep with?"

"What do you mean?" I ask, blinking like a deer caught in headlights. "I didn't sleep with anybody."

"Well...that's just...not how things work. What did she say? You're twelve weeks, but really ten weeks?" he asks, pulling out his phone and sitting on the edge of the bed. "That would be..." he drawls, but then his eyes go wide. "No. That—that can't be right." He rapidly counts aloud from one to ten, his index finger hovering over the screen. "That would mean...the week I moved back..."

"No," I bellow. "But we didn't do anything!" I blurt.

"I know!"

"How could—"

"Are you sure you didn't sleep with—"

"I would know, Rafael!" I shout.

He paces the small room. "Okay. Okay. Okay. This is... Okay. We're just... We're gonna... Holy fucking shit." He presses the palms of his hands against the wall and kicks his butt out, hanging his head below his shoulders. He takes a few deep breaths, then suddenly spins around and launches himself at me, straddling my thighs and holding my cheeks. "You're pregnant," he states, clearly trying to work through the same puzzle as me. "What's going through your head right now?"

"Buffering," I reply quietly but it comes out a little mumbled since Raf's hands are squishing my cheeks together.

He smiles. "Yeah. Same." But then his smile fades and he moves his hands from my face to my upper arms. "What do you want to do?"

His meaning catches up to me. "Oh. Yeah," I say, pinching my brows together. "I have options, don't I?"

Raf nods solemnly, unblinking. "Yes. This isn't my choice, Ang. But... I promise I'll support you with whatever you decide."

·· · • · · • · · ·

Rafael

Five hours after arriving at the hospital, Angie is released with instructions to stop taking her birth control, stay hydrated and eat often, as well as a folder full of pregnancy information. I texted Cora, her brothers, and my mamá to let them all know she was going to be fine and that she was just dehydrated. That's what we agreed I would send them. Not the full truth that my best friend is pregnant because of me.

I'm still trying to fully process this and allow her to do the same, but as I open the car door for her and help her up, I can't stop thinking about everything we'll need. When I get to my side and shut the door, I look into the rearview mirror at the backseat.

I'm going to need a car seat, I think to myself.

And a stroller.

And a crib.

And tiny pajamas.

What's going to happen to my social life? I don't give a fuck, *because I need to start investing my money differently and—*

"Raf?" Angie asks with concern.

"Huh?"

"Are you going to drive?"

"Oh," I smile weakly. "Yeah. Sorry," I tell her, pulling away from the hospital. "Just thinking is all."

"Yeah," she whispers, looking out the window. "Do you mind if we just...not talk until we get home?"

"I get it. We both need to... Yeah. I'll shut up now."

It's late afternoon so the trip back to our place takes nearly an hour in traffic. And in that time my brain whirled between degrading insults about myself to planning my future child's college tuition. It's been a fucking rollercoaster in my head, but I know it's ten times worse in hers.

When I pull into my tight one-car garage, I shut the car off and we sit motionless in the even-quieter silence.

"Angie, I'm sorry," I blurt out, the sound of my voice like a jackhammer on a Sunday morning. "This is all my fault. I did lean in that night," I admit, but continue to blabber uncontrollably. "But I swear to god I don't remember anything after that. I can't believe I could do something like this—both of us were so drunk. I'm a piece of shit and I understand if you hate me for it because I totally deserve it—"

"Raf," she tries to interject.

"You must feel so violated, Angie. That's the last thing I would ever want you to feel, and if you want to cut me out of your life because of it, I understand, but—"

"Hey, hey, hey," she says, placing her hand on my arm. "I'm not mad."

"You're not?"

"No," she whispers. "What happened was a mistake. But the more I think about it," she says, placing her other hand on her belly. "I don't think *this* was a mistake."

That shoots my eyebrows up. "Really?"

"Yeah. I mean, this could have happened with anyone. And if that's the case, there's no one in my life I'd rather have a baby with than you," she says softly, then adds, "Well, except for Cora. But she can't get me pregnant; the science just isn't there yet."

An unexpected laugh bursts out from my lips as my heart pounds so loudly in my chest that I'm positive she can hear it.

How can she make jokes at a time like this? I fucking love her for it.

"Does that mean you've made your decision? Because you can take more time if you need it—not that I'm pressuring you to go one way or the other."

"You know," she nods. "I thought I would need more time too, but, halfway through the drive I started telling myself I was going to have a baby, and I let that thought settle in. I don't know, I guess that thought stretched out and got comfortable. But hey, where are you with this? I know you said this was my decision, but what are you feeling?"

"To say I'm shocked is an understatement. I'm scared."

Angie grabs my hand. "Me too."

"I have no idea how to raise a child," I huff, and a small smile makes its way through. "But we've always made a good team, haven't we?"

"You're my first pick," she smiles.

It's my turn to squeeze her hand back. "Okay," I say, my voice only a little shaky. "Let's have a baby."

Chapter 7

June 8th

Rafael

I t took me four solid days to process the fact that I'm going to be a father. I went to work and rugby practice this week, but the whole time I was thinking about Angie and what she needed. Every spare moment was consumed with pregnancy education and crippling fear of telling my parents the news.

During our work days, we'd send each other articles and apps that we found informative or helpful. In the evenings when we got home, we'd eat together and talk endlessly about what we learned each day and what she's experiencing.

Like her gums bleeding. She said it only happens when she brushes her teeth, but it's freaky. She's also experiencing a constant need to pee, which we both find strange since the baby is the size of a peach right now. Thankfully her morning sickness isn't too bad. She said she only feels mildly nauseous for most of the day, but nothing that requires upheaval.

I still feel awful though. It may have taken me four days to come to terms with being a father, but I still can't believe I did this to her.

There is a very selfish part of me though—fuck, it's even hard to give this brain space—that feels cheated from not remembering the act. Because having sex with your very attractive best friend—a woman so wildly confident and beautiful—is something I would have liked to remember.

It's almost not fair that I can let all those nights of meaningless sex with people I didn't truly care about live in my head for the rest of my life, but I'm not allowed to remember the way it felt to be inside her. Or the way she sounds in the heat of the moment. Or the way her soft body would feel against mine.

I've been robbed.

"Start bootin' up, boys," Coach Batsakis hollers. "Warm up in five."

It's already seventy degrees at 9:30 am, which means today's sevens game is going to be a hot one. Thankfully we only play fourteen-minute games instead of eighty minutes like in a standard fifteens match.

Rugby in the summer is always for fun. The games don't matter and they don't count for anything. You can whore out for any team you want, but I usually stick with a smaller version of my DI club team. In the summer, The Philadelphia Men's Rugby Team turns into The Philly Fathers when we show up at sevens tournaments. We claim the name has meaning rooted in the country's founding fathers—but really it was for the sexual innuendos.

The Daddy jokes are endless.

Make a great tackle? Cheer for your teammate by whimpering, "Yes, Daddy!"

Get lifted in a line-out by only one teammate? "You're so strong, Daddy!"

Make a perfect spiral pass to your backline? "I love your hands, Daddy!"

Is it weird to hear Angie's brothers say that to each other? Yes. But we're all perverted and it makes everyone laugh. Rugby players by and large are deeply unserious people.

"Okay, I gotta get ready," I say to Angie as I help her lay a quilt on the grass.

"Wait, there's Cora and the guys." She points just ahead as they make their way towards us. "We have to tell them now, Raf. I can't hold it in any longer."

I chuckle, "Okay. We can tell them." We abandon the quilt and meet up with the trio a little bit further away from any unnecessary audience.

Immediately Cora and Angie go in for a hug and I give the guys a quick embrace and thank them for coming to watch.

"How are you feeling?" Cora asks, concern written all over her face. "You scared the shit out of us last weekend."

"Yeah, um," she nervously giggles and then to my surprise, she wraps her arm around my waist and before I can even set my hand on her shoulder, she spills it. "Apparently, I'm pregnant and Rafael is the father."

The three of them stare at us like we're aliens.

Cora looks from Ang to me, then back again as I give my biggest smiling wince, waiting for her to say something.

Finally, she throws her hands into her hair and screams, "What?"

"I'm going to faint," Jay exhales, dramatically grabbing his chest and Marco's at the same time.

"I knew something was up," Marco smirks.

"You did not," Angie accuses.

"Let's go, guys," Coach Batsakis yells from down the field. "Take a lap and get movin'!"

Feeling guilty, I give Angie a quick hug and start jogging back to the rest of my team. "I'm sorry, guys, I gotta go. I'll see you between games."

"You can't just throw that out there and then ditch us!" Jay calls.

Twisting around, I shout back, "I'm ditching you guys, not her!"

Alright, so not the ideal way to tell our friends we're having a baby, but if that's what Ang needed, I'll give it to her.

It's time to focus though. I've been distracted all week, but now that we've told our secret to someone, I'm a little lighter and more confident. That is until Jared Holloway—aka Hollow—comes into view, pulling one of our jerseys over his long dirty blonde hair.

Wasn't expecting him. I thought he played for Trenton, New Jersey? I'm playing prop today, so I bend down and grab the number one jersey when Hollow spots me.

"Jimmy!" he exclaims with that ever-present smile I've always wanted to smack off. "Hey man. How'ya been?"

My nickname progression goes as follows: Jimenez—Jimmy (keeping the Spanish J). It's a short progression.

"I've been alright." We start on our lap around the field and Hollow stays next to me. *Ugh.*

"You just moved back from DC right?"

"Yeah."

"That's awesome. I just moved back from Jersey. This is my last season though. I gotta get knee surgery at the end of July and I'm throwing in the towel after that. Gonna retire."

Good, I think to myself.

"Hey, is that Angie and Cora over there?" He nods over to where they're sitting on the blanket with Marco and Jay. Cora's clearly still processing the news. His question irks me though. It better not be going where I think it's going.

"Yeah," I say as we round the half-way mark on our lap.

"Oh, cool. I didn't realize you two were still friends. You're still...just friends, right?"

Fuck. Not this again. Jared and Angie used to hook up in college pretty regularly. He's a total fuckboy, and at the time that's exactly what Angie wanted. So this itchy internal ache that I have when he's around? It's my own fault, really.

As much as I'd like to, I can't forget that November night freshman year.

Angie was flirting with Jared at a rugby house party; it was fucking clear as day. He had his forearm pressed against the wall above her head as she leaned against the wall. His other hand was snaking up the side of her waist, lifting her sparkly pink top just enough that he could touch her skin.

Something in me snapped. I ate up the distance between us and grabbed her by the elbow and pulled her away. She protested as we wove through other students and players, but I ignored her until I got her into an empty bedroom and shut the door.

"What's wrong with you?" she asked, setting down her solo cup.

"What's wrong with me? What's wrong with you? Jared? Hollow, really?"

"So what?" she shrugged. "He's literally so nice and funny and...yeah, he's fucking hot, so what if I wanna go home with him?"

"You're a virgin."

"I'm aware, Raf," she said through clenched teeth. "And I'm trying to do something about it."

"But with him?"

"Do you have a better suggestion?"

"Yeah," I said, clearing my throat. "Someone...you trust. Someone who really knows you."

"You lost your virginity to Kimberly Washington last year, so don't try and tell me my choice is any different than yours when you didn't give a shit about her." God, I hate when she's right. Her eyes narrowed on me as she thought. "Someone I trust? Someone who really knows me? And who would that be, Raf?" My words dried up instantly. "Are you offering?"

"I...I think you've had too much to drink." I deflected, then reached for her hand. "Let's just... Let's go back to the dorms, Angel."

"No," she said sternly, pulling her hand away from mine. "If you're not offering, then I'm going home with Jared tonight."

Did she not hear me call her Angel? That...that always works.

Oh my god, is she serious? Does she want me to offer? I mean, no one deserves her, that's for damn sure, but...could I?

My papá's voice then echoed in my head. "Women will only ruin your life, mijo. Never get close."

Angie has always been the exception. But to cross this line, even though I've thought about it too many times to keep track, would be too risky. She's the one perfect exception I've made to the rule; and if I cross this line with her...everything will fall apart. I know it.

Angie stood there, waiting for me to say something—anything—but I was frozen because I realized I can't stop her. She'd made up her mind, and regrettably, so had I.

"That's what I thought," she choked out, then grabbed her solo cup off the dresser and left me there to melt.

"Raf?" Jared asks, nudging me in the shoulder to bring me back to our conversation. "You alright? You spaced out there for a minute."

"Yeah, I'm fine."

"So... Is Angie still just your friend?"

The secret is barely out there now, but I can't exactly tell him she's pregnant with my child. And I can't tell him we're... Fuck, I don't know. Sighing, I simply grunt my confirmation.

"Cool," he smiles. "Glad to know you two are still hanging out. I love seeing old friendships like that. You guys were always so fun to party with."

Hollow must be oblivious to my disdain for him because ever since that night Angie lost her virginity, I've been nothing but surly toward him. They continued hooking up on and off for the rest of undergrad, and while I'm not happy about it, I will acknowledge he was as respectful as a fuckboy can be. Angie never had problems with him, and she always seemed content with their casual hookups.

I'm just the poor bastard who had to keep playing rugby with him and act like I was cool with it.

By half time of the first game, my mind is finally back to where it should be: on the pitch with my team. Normally, I play the position of eight man, but when we're playing sevens, that position doesn't exist any longer, so I usually play prop. There's something in the rhythm of play, the cadence, the closeness I feel inside the pack, even if it is only two props and a hooker, that makes me relax into the play. That's not to say rugby is relaxing—far from it. But I've been doing this so long that it's second nature.

Sevens rugby is played differently than fifteens. With seven players against seven players on the same size pitch, there's more space than usual. Therefore, less tackling, more running, more tries.

We came here with only ten players, and on the field right now are myself and Dane/Pony as props, Tom/Tum Tum as hooker, Tyler/Small Fry as scrum-half, Jonah/JoJo as fly-half, Jared/Hollow as center, and Colin/Wheels as winger.

Why all the nicknames? Rugby culture. It's as synonymous as having a beer at the social after every game. Even if you know your teammates outside of the sport, were friends with them before you ever played, you still call them by their nicknames when you're in a rugby crowd.

By the end of our first of three games, I'm out of breath but feeling good. Wheels and JoJo scored a combined three tries and Hollow kicked for points, leaving us with the W over Pittsburg.

Between games, we have a little time to recoup and refuel. I take that time to talk with Angie and our friends, which is mostly them peppering us with questions. I do my best to deflect, and when I see a tent set up across the field for a massage therapist offering ten-minute sessions—a fairly common vendor you'd see at a rugby event such as this—I tell Marco he should consider doing that since that's his job. Thankfully, that topic seems to take root and Angie and I are saved once again.

The next two games play out and the Philly Fathers take first place in the tournament. Dragging myself off the pitch, I collapse while pulling my jersey off my sweaty body. I hear Angie's giggle coming closer and when I look up, she's blocking the scorching sun from my eyes, and holding a large plastic bag of orange slices.

"You wouldn't want one, would you?" She smiles knowingly.

I groan and chomp at the air. "Please," I beg.

Her soft chuckle is all the confirmation I need to know that she's satisfied. "Here you go," she says, dropping a handful into my palm. I'm too tired to get up, so I lazily chew on the sweet citrus. "Cora and the guys had to leave a little bit ago. They said they're definitely coming back to watch more games."

"Angie has orange slices!" Pony hollers.

"I'll be right back. I'm gonna go pass these around. You good, Raf?"

I take a deep breath, "I will be."

Sauntering off to where the rest of the team is, she offers it to everyone. Her brothers give her a huge sweaty hug, making her cringe, and I chuckle at the sight. She says she likes to bring the orange slices because everyone loves them, but I think it's residual mother-henning she can't shake.

In the years after her mom died in that car accident when she was ten, she became a mother to her whole family by default. Should she have been? No. But her dad, Neal, just didn't step up. I understand he went through immeasurable grief, but he was a shell of a man—a shell of a parent. So Angie took charge and took care of everyone.

When all the guys grab their orange slices, I watch as a shirtless Hollow slowly walks up to her. With his stupid fucking chest and his stupid defined hamstrings on display, he goes in for a hug. I'm about twenty feet away, but I can just barely make out what they're saying.

"Oh my gosh," she smiles as he hugs her. "It's been so long, Jared, how are you?" Her white tank top rides up the slightest bit when she does.

"I'm good," he says, then releases her as she fixes her top. "Wow. You look great, Ang." She fluffs her wind-blown shoulder-length hair. Her cheeks are pink and I swear to god that better be the fucking sun's fault and not blush.

"Thanks. What are you doing here? Do you play for Philly now?"

"Not for long. I just moved back from Jersey and this'll be my last season before I retire."

"Oh, okay. Well, you played great today. You've certainly gotten better over the years. You didn't miss a single kick."

"You noticed?" He grins, then crosses his arms in front of his chest, flexing his goddamn vanity biceps.

"Are you...flexing in front of me?" Angie accuses playfully.

Good. Call him out on his bullshit, girl.

"Maybe," he smirks again. "Is it working?"

She arches an eyebrow. "Are you serious?"

"Are you single?" he asks darkly. She chews on her lip with a smile but doesn't answer him right away. "Hmm, I'll take that as a yes," he drawls, then slowly sucks on an orange slice as he stares her down.

You're about three seconds from taking my foot up your ass, Hollow.

"You still have the same number, Angie?"

"Yeah."

"Good. I'll call you later." *The fuck he will.* "Thanks for the treat," he says, gesturing with another slice, and then slowly walks backwards to the rest of the team packing up their bags.

Before she can even get to me, I'm up and marching over to my own bag, throwing my boots in and slipping on my slides. I toss my jersey in with the others and head back towards Angie, who's folding up the quilt. It's too damn hot to bother with a shirt right now. That's what I tell myself at least as I approach her, letting her eye me.

·· • • •· • • • ··

Angie

When Raf doesn't stop where I'm standing, I move to keep up with him. "Why are we walking so fast? No one else is leaving for the social yet."

"We're not going to the social," he huffs.

"Why not? I love socials. Drinking beer with the players after a game is the best part."

"You can't even drink, Angie," he says harshly.

What the fuck crawled up his ass? They just won.

He turns his face to see my pout. "Is that why we're not going? You know I'm allowed to have a beer every now and again, right?"

A frustrated puff of air whooshes out of him. "Why didn't you tell him?"

"Who? Jared?"

"Yes, Jared."

"What was I supposed to tell him?"

"Oh I don't know," he says sarcastically, unlocking the Range with the fob and letting the hatch open on its own. "Maybe that you're pregnant."

I forcefully throw the quilt in the back, staring at him. "First of all, we've only told our closest friends that information, so it's not something I'm ready to tell everyone else yet. Did we not agree on that?"

"We did," he relents, placing his kit in the back and shutting the hatch.

When we get in the car, I continue. "And second, I *am* single. Do you assume people don't want to fuck me or date me because I'm pregnant?"

He rolls down the windows to let the hot air dissipate. "You were leading him on, Angie."

"Who says I'm leading him on? And *what* is there to lead on? You know full-well him and I were always—"

"You're with me now!" he shouts, shaking his hands in front of him.

My head rears back instantly. "What? When the fuck did this happen?"

"I...I have to take care of you," he says in a softer tone.

We sit in silence for a moment as I let that sink in. "Raf, I'm truly grateful that you're doing this with me. You're going to be an excellent birthing partner, and co-parent, I'm sure of it. But..." *Shit.* How do I say this next part without hurting him? "I'm not *with* you. You don't do commitment. I do."

He finally looks at me. "I'm committed to our child."

"I know you are," I smile. "But that doesn't mean you have to force a commitment to me. It's not in you, Raf."

Gently leaning his forehead on the steering wheel, he lets out a sigh. "Yeah."

"So you're not going to stop me when I wanna get my rocks off," I say. "Just like I've never stopped you."

"You're right, Ang. I'm sorry. I don't know what came over me."

"Maybe your protective Papa Bear mode kicked in or something." That makes him smile. "You just played a blood-thirsty sport all day; your hindbrain has clearly taken over and you've now resorted to baser urges."

"Is that your professional diagnosis?" He grins.

"It is. Now can we please go to the social? I heard there's a barbecue and you need to feed your pregnant friend."

"I thought you said meat was making you sick lately?"

"It is," I confirm, as a little wave of nausea rolls in at the mere thought. "But where there's barbecue, there's fixin's—and I plan on scarfing down some potato salad."

Finally, he shows me his pearly whites. "Let's get you some fixin's then."

Chapter 8

June 25th

Angie

C ora texted me around lunch time asking if I wanted to have happy hour with her after work today. I know we've both been getting creative with mocktails recently, so I texted back immediately confirming the plans.

Even though it's Tuesday, Raf didn't have practice tonight, so he's heading over to his historic fixer-upper to tear up stuff. Floors, maybe? Walls? I forget. That's another ridiculous symptom I've been experiencing: memory loss. Sure, it was minor at first, like forgetting to put mascara on after a full face of makeup and only realizing when I looked in the mirror at work. But then it got worse. Like forgetting where I'm driving. Which is why I'm thirty minutes late to Cora's place in Rittenhouse. Her gorgeous, historic home that should honestly be featured in magazines.

I love coming here.

"Sorry I'm late," I sing as I barge through her front door. The Lumineers[1] are playing softly from the speaker perched on one of her built-in bookcases. "Pregnancy brain had me take a different route."

"You do that too?" Cora asks, standing up from the white couch in her front sitting room and giving me a hug.

---

1. *Stubborn Love* by The Lumineers

"Yes. Don't tell Raf, though. He already hates my car, and if he finds out I'm sure he'll make me get rid of her and make me get something with a nav system."

Cora gives a dignified snort. "Your car is barely holding on, so I'm with him."

"Shh," I tell her, looking over my shoulder. "She might hear you."

She heads to the kitchen before saying, "I'm making lime seltzer with a splash of pomegranate juice. Want one?"

I follow her. "You're so good to me, queen."

"How's work going?" she asks, pulling the ingredients out from the fridge.

I lean against her white marble countertop. "Oh, you mean besides being the hardest thing ever because it's impossible to stay awake?"

"Oh god, you too?" she asks, dispensing some ice into the glasses. "I don't know how we're expected to function in any capacity at work whilst growing a human. Jay's been secretly letting me sleep in his office every day."

"All I want to do is sleep," I whine. "But I did have an interesting session today with an eleven-year-old."

"Oh?"

"Their mom has been incarcerated for almost a year now and they miss her terribly. They said listening to *Fancy* by Iggy Azalea makes them happy because it reminds them of her."

Cora pours the pomegranate juice over the lime seltzer and ice. "That song seems a little mature for someone their age."

"That's what I said," I smile. "But they said their mom would blast it and they'd dance and sing along."

Cora smiles and hands me my drink as we clink our glasses. "That's what I want."

"To be incarcerated?"

Cora chuckles. "No. The dancing."

"Me too."

I think I resonated with that student because that's something I remember from when my mom was still around. Music filled our home when she was still alive. She played piano and sang boisterously. She was a burst of summer sunshine personified. With golden hair she brought from her Polish family—which she passed down to only Jonah and Ivy for some reason—and an infectious laugh, she could light up any room. And she did.

When she died though, that light extinguished in our family, so I did my best to take over—to fill our home with joy and love again. To be there for everyone else. I didn't realize my dad used me like a crutch until I was in grad school where I learned what a parentified child was and immediately recognized I fit that bill.

It was crushing discovering my childhood was robbed from me because I took over as the mother my siblings needed. As the parent my dad could not be.

Thankfully, I had Ana and Christina Webber fighting for me. Showing up. Inviting me to be a child as they loved on me. As they arranged to watch my siblings while Raf and I would spend an afternoon building a fort. Or taking the whole Jimenez/Johanssen/Webber clan to the shore for the day.

They saw me and gave me the childhood that could have so easily evaporated.

Am I still dealing with siblings that treat me like their mother? Yes. But I'm working on it and setting boundaries with them.

Cora knows all about this, so all it takes is *one look* for her to know what I'm thinking. Isaiah's calling because he needs to know how to make bolognese? Dane is texting me about how Jonah isn't listening to him when he's trying to be a good team captain? All it takes is one eye roll from my bestie (with breasties) and I know she knows what I'm going through.

God, I'm grateful for her. More than anything, I'm grateful for her humor.

A notification buzzes from my phone in my butt pocket, and I peek to see it's a new playlist Rafael has created for us called *The Pregnancy Era*.

"What are you smiling about?" Cora asks as she sips her mocktail.

"It's nothing," I hum, but pick up the phone and show her the screen.

Cora shakes her head slowly. "You two and your playlists."

"It's our friendship language," I explain.

"Yeah," Cora says, giving me a side eye. "It's a totally normal thing to do with someone you *definitely* don't have feelings for."

"Cora," I warn. "If you bring up that one tiny lapse in judgment freshman year—"

She cuts me off. "Of course I'm bringing it up!"

"I regret telling you about that night."

"No, you don't," she smirks and gestures for us to move to the front sitting room.

She's got me there. As one of my closest friends, she deserves to know everything—almost everything. She doesn't need to know about that tendril of emotion I have for Raf—the one that shall not be named. If I can't bring myself to name it, then I won't share it.

What kind of counselor am I? Hiding from my own feelings like this? Why is it that everything else I can talk about, explore, dig into—but this?

This is nothing, don't worry about it, I tell myself.

"Alright, I'll leave it alone for now," Cora sighs, as we cozy-up on her couch like it's a sleepover and we're going to gossip late into the night. "You know what I really want?"

"Hmm?"

"Dick twenty-four seven."

I nearly spit my drink back into my glass. "You already have two dicks. By the way, where *are* your husbands?"

"They're on a date," she smiles. "But seriously, I'm so fucking horny, Ang. I need it every day. Preferably twice. Sometimes Marco and Jay have to take shifts."

Throwing my head back, I cackle until I can't breathe. "I fucking love you, you diva."

"Aren't you going through that too?" she asks.

I roll my eyes. "It's nothing that my vibrator can't handle at this point."

"Did I tell you I bought a strap-on?" she says excitedly, pulling her phone out and tapping the screen. "This one."

I gasp. "No! Do you love it? More importantly, do *they* love it?"

"I'm a new woman, Ang. Here, I'll send you one."

"I have no idea when I'll get to use that, but you're a real one, Cora-babe."

"If you're not buying your best friends sex toys, are you even best friends?"

"No!"

Chapter 9
June 26th
Rafael

"**G**ood morning, baby brother," I huff out after tapping my ear bud to connect the call.

"Sounds like you're out running, too?" Joaquín says through labored breath. It's not even 7:00 am yet, but the sun is already up, peeking through the trees and reflecting off playground slides as I run through another neighborhood park.

"It's gonna be ninety degrees before noon today," I say. "Gotta get my workout in before it's too hot."

"Same," he says.

A knowing smile crosses my face before I ask, "Does that mean you're wearing a shirt?"

He chuckles. "Absolutely not."

Joaquín had his top surgery six years ago, and if he doesn't have to wear a shirt, he's not. He's fucking happy with his body finally so he should feel proud and be able to show it off.

"So what's going on?" I ask, coming to a traffic crossing. "What's on the agenda today?"

"I have a meeting this morning with our broker about cleaning up that sale on Garfield in Arlington," he says. Joaquín's been living in DC and commuting between there and here for various real estate projects. He's been an invaluable partner to have since we launched Jimenez Brothers Properties almost a decade ago when we bought our first fixer-upper. I got a nice little chunk of change from my *abuelo* for graduating from undergrad, so I put it towards real estate. Between the two of us, we've amassed three smaller apartment buildings, all in DC, as well as two storefronts in Philly, the historic house we're currently renovating down the street from me, and after the sale of the Garfield complex, we'll acquire four large, abandoned historic Philly homes that we plan on turning into multi-family residences. They're all within the same city block, so it'll be convenient for the construction crews, too.

We both want to see the city we love look its best and serve the families that live here. I'm looking at every fucking penny to make sure we do right, not only by restoring these homes to their former glory, but also provide affordable housing.

It's my job to make the money work—and do some light work like demolition occasionally. Joaquín's my property manager. We have a few other employees like our Project Manager in DC and one in Philly.

"Good. That place was a headache." We've had that apartment building for only five years, but it's been a nightmare property.

"So with those profits coming in, we should be ready to pull the trigger on that block in Philly."

"Perfect," I exhale, as I make my way through another city park, passing a mother pushing a stroller. An urge to peek and look at her baby forms inside me, but I don't want to be a creep, so I keep my eyes trained ahead of me.

"How are you doing with all this, Raf?" he asks. "There's a lot on your plate." I don't miss his worried tone. Is working as CFO for Define and Jimenez Brothers a lot? Yes. Throw on top of that rugby and becoming a father? Yeah, it might be too much; but I've always thrived under pressure. You can't have a father like José Juan Jimenez and not tirelessly work yourself to earn his admiration.

Yes, it has irrevocably shaped me for better or worse. But honestly, I'm alive with energy when I'm busy like this.

We told Joaquín he was going to be a tío last week and he started crying. It was adorable to watch. He was beyond thrilled for us. Surprised, of course—but thrilled.

"I'm doing fine right now. You know I can't sit still."

He laughs incredulously. "Understatement. When was the last time you actually relaxed?" he asks, his breathing rougher. "When was the last time you went camping? That's always brought you peace."

That's true. "It's been a few years," I admit. Has it really been that long?

"Why don't you take a little weekend trip soon? Go breathe in the forest and exhale all the stress you're pretending you don't have."

"That's," I consider, "not a bad idea actually."

"Ha! So you admit you're stressed."

"No," I grouse. "I'm agreeing that it's a good idea to get out of the city and hug a fucking tree."

Angie would love it too. My mind replays a memory of the first time the two of us went camping without my moms. We had just finished our senior year of high school, but graduation wasn't for another week.

We went with a small group of friends we had collected over the last few years—people I haven't talked to since come to think of it. But that's fine; because I still have Angie and that's all that matters.

We spent most of the afternoon drinking screwdrivers and laughing our asses off while we made fun of our teachers. Angie's imitation of Mr. Forton was always spot-on. From his unexplainable and widely-known dislike for cats, to his much younger wife, the man had a lot of material for us to work with.

But when the sun set low and the temperatures stayed high, the strands of our friendship began to fray with each sip of vodka. And when someone admitted in a game of Never Have I Ever that they had never played Spin the Bottle, a gust of wind blew over the tightrope of our friendship.

To this day, we've never talked about what happened that night. We can talk about everything else, but never that. We can dance around every other facet of that camping trip, but neither of us bring up that moment.

It's probably for the best. Especially now.

Because now that she's pregnant, there's something inside of me gnawing at my heart. It's fucking uncomfortable—that percolating desire I've kept buried since we were teenagers has been growing hotter. I've always seen her as beautiful because it's a fact; but now...it's like her aura has changed and she's drawing me into her orbit. Is she Aphrodite?

Angie might be mildly sick and tired these days, but she's so vibrant now, which only serves to remind me of our friendship. Never in my life have I had to remind myself how seriously platonic we are as often as I have recently.

Never get close to women, mijo. They'll only ruin your life.

I know, Papá! Get out of my head.

You're not enough, my mind tosses back.

"Raf!" Joaquín's voice twinges in my ear. "Are you listening to me?"

Shit, I zoned out.

Taking this opportunity, I slow my pace to cool down. "Sorry. I got distracted," I huff out. "Hey, when was the last time you talked to Papá?"

He groans. "When he called us at Christmas."

"Has it been that long?"

"Considering I haven't seen him since before I transitioned, that's on-brand for him."

"Does he still not know?"

"No," Joaquín grumbles. "I'm not hiding it from him. But the day he actually asks how I am or about my life or makes an effort to see me again, I'll gladly tell him."

"You'd think he would hear the difference in your voice by now."

"Yeah," he sighs. "Doesn't make me feel self-conscious at all that he can't tell the difference."

"And you don't want me to say anything?"

"No," he says. "It's not your responsibility to do that. But hey, when are you going to tell the rest of our family that you're having a kid with Angie? Do the Johanssen's know yet?"

"Not yet," I wince as I look both ways before crossing the street back to my townhouse. "We're telling everyone this weekend."

"Please video call me when you do. I have to see their reactions in real-time. Mamá is gonna kill you."

Chapter 10

June 28th

Angie

"I don't feel good, Raf," I announce as we pull into the long driveway of my childhood home.

"No?" he asks, bringing the vehicle to a stop behind several other familiar cars. "Is it your stomach? I have your ginger chews and Tums," he says, putting the Range in park and digging through the center console.

"It's not that," I whine. "I'm nervous."

"It's not like your dad has any room to judge. He got your mom pregnant out of wedlock."

"I know," I sigh. "I can't pin-point why I'm nervous. It's just... It's a big deal what we're about to do."

"I get it. Like by telling them, it's officially real."

I let out an unladylike sigh. "Yes."

His body turns towards me as he rests his head against the seat and smiles. "Yeah. But it's been fun pretending so far with you," he says, playfully leaning into my worry. Firmly grabbing my hand, he brings it up to his lips and kisses the back of it. "Let's go make it real, Angel."

When my stomach flips for an entirely different reason, I take the opportunity to open the door, but Raf gently chastises me. "Absolutely not. I'll get your door," he says, jumping out of the SUV and running to my side.

He's been doing this a lot more lately—the extra layer of chivalry. There's always been a certain low level he's maintained throughout our friendship, but it's reminding me of all our trips to Mexico. As soon as we land, he always kicks it up a few notches. I've played it up to the culture there. Men, no matter if they're a stranger, a friend, or an *abuelo*, always treat women with reverence. At least that's been my experience. Doors are always opened for me. I'm expected to serve myself first (or be served first). Chairs are made available to me as soon as I walk into a room. I expect it when we go to Mexico—I don't expect the same level back home. Apparently Rafael's chivalry is alive and well here in the US now that I'm pregnant.

Can't say that I hate it.

He's wearing another white Henley, pushed up to expose his strong forearms, and a pair of navy blue chino short-shorts that some people might find indecent from the way his massive, hair-dusted quads bulge.

Me.

I'm some people.

Damn rugby thighs.

Offering his hand for me to grab as I step down, Rafael eyes me appreciatively, but his gaze takes a longer drag over my chest. "Is that a new dress?"

It's a sleeveless, red maxi dress with a low v-neckline. I love it because it's stretchy, flowy, and has pockets.

He's seen it before.

What's tripping him up that he's not putting words to are my growing tits. While I'm ecstatic at their size, I'm not so thrilled about how sensitive and achy my new C cups are.

"I've had it for years actually," I smile, stepping onto the concrete driveway as he hums something that sounds an awful lot like appreciation.

As we approach, [1] salsa music is playing from the outdoor speakers, which means Ana has taken over the music already. We've disguised tonight's announcement in the

---

1. *Vivir Mi Vida* by Marc Anthony

form of an early Independence Day cookout, but it's no less nerve-wracking as we round the side of the house to the back yard, where Christina is cooking on the grill and Dad is pointing to the foul-smelling meats while holding a beer bottle—most likely questioning Christina's grilling abilities, which are far superior to his.

The backyard is nearly a half-acre, which is much larger than most of the other houses in the neighborhood, but our house is the smallest by far. We didn't have much money growing up, and after Mom died, it got even tighter. Dad still works as an engineer, but since all his kids have moved out, he's been able to cut back on the side projects he did to make ends meet. Small engine repair was what kept us afloat mostly. Everything from push lawn mowers to motorboats my dad could fix. So while he was out financially supporting our family, I was emotionally supporting them at home. He would maintain the house, and I would maintain the family.

Again—parentified child. I might have been upset when I found out what I had become, but it never made me love him any less. It's complicated between us, yet lately, I can't help but feel like something's changing with him.

When Dad spots us, he abandons Christina and makes his way towards us with his arms wide open. "Hey, bunny," he calls to me, using the first nickname I was ever given thanks to a stuffed animal I was attached to as a baby. His hug is tight and comforting.

"Hey, Dad. I missed you."

"Missed you too."

He gives Raf the same level of hug and then offers us each a beer. We take one but I give a stage sip to keep up appearances.

It's a small gathering tonight. Just me, Raf, Dad, his moms, and my brothers. Joaquín is back in DC still and Ivy is in

Guatemala. They're both aware they'll be getting a video call soon. Only Joaquín knows why.

Speaking of brothers...

"I thought we were going to be the last ones to show up," Raf says. "Where's Jonah?"

"Late as always," Dad smirks. His features haven't changed much over the years. Still a wide smile—once so rare that you'd forget his deep laugh lines around the corners of his mouth existed. Still dark brown hair now with a smattering of white around his temples and fading into the sides.

He looks...a lot better than I've seen him...ever. There's a liveliness to him making him seem more youthful. His clothes look new and fit properly. He's only fifty-six, but when he smiles like he is now, he looks so much younger.

When Jonah makes an appearance an hour later, his shaggy blonde hair is still slightly damp from the obvious shower he took recently. The sun is already lowering, casting this old, forested suburban neighborhood in a beautiful pinkish glow. The yard lights I strung up last year adding to the ambiance.

Ana has been forcing Isaiah to learn to dance with her, which has been comical to say the least. Between their height difference, Ana's bouncy personality and his grumpy one, it's been a special night already.

But when Ivy video calls me at our pre-scheduled time, my heart starts to pound in my ears. When Raf sees my phone, he bites his lower lip. "It's showtime, Angel," he whispers.

Nodding, I slide open the call and see Ivy's beautiful face light up the screen. "Ah!" she screams. "How are you? How's everyone? Let me see everything!"

Chuckling, I say, "We're good. Here, I'm going to set you down so you can see everyone."

With Joaquín on Raf's screen too, he sets down his phone and my entire body temperature drops as stage fright takes over. A big warm hand finds the space between my neck and shoulder, and I look up at my friend standing next to me with a steady smile.

Like he always does.

"Can you?" I plead in a whisper. "I don't think I can do it."

"Of course. I've got you," he whispers back, then turns down the music on the speaker next to where we're standing.

"What's going on?" Dane shouts, then notices the phones on the table pointing toward us. "Who's on the—" He perches around, leaning over Jonah like he doesn't exist. "Joaquín?"

"Oh," Joaquín says, his voice cracking. "Hey, Dane."

"How are you? What's going on?" he asks in an uncharacteristically joyful way.

"Okay! Everyone please take a seat," Rafael announces. "We'll let everyone catch up on the phones in a minute. But first, we have some news we want to share."

Ana rolls her eyes. "We already know you two moved in, *mijo.*"

"It's not that. We, um..." His shaky hand moves from the crook of my neck and slides down my side to my stomach. "We're having a baby together."

Silence.

Silence for all of three seconds before chaos erupts.

Screaming loud enough to puncture eardrums, Ana stands, then squats, repeating the process over and over again as Christina clutches her chest, then clutches Jonah by the arms while still staring at us.

Then the questions start shooting in like machine gun fire.

"Are you fucking serious?"

"What the fuck?"

"How did this happen?"

"Can I be your doula?"

"Are you two together?"

"How far along are you?"

Ana runs up to her son and repeatedly smacks him across the face and chest, cussing him out and praying to God in Spanish. He tries to duck away, but he knows this is something he must take.

But then she catches my eye and stops assaulting her son to cry and pull me into the tightest hug.

"*Mija*," she sobs.

I sniffle. "*Lo siento.*"

"No," she says sternly. "Do not be. This is good news. This is a blessing." She releases me and gives Raf a death glare. "You are lucky this happened with her."

Dane and Jonah jump in a circle and force a shocked Isaiah to join in. "We're gonna be uncles!" Jonah bellows.

"Oh my god, this was better than I imagined," Joaquín says from his little perch on the patio table.

Ana whips around to clutch the phone. "You knew about this?" she seethes.

But all that chaos fades away the second I focus on my dad. On my dad who's crying, which is making me cry because I've only seen him tear up at funerals.

Fuck, I didn't expect this.

Before I can think it through, I'm running into his arms and bawling, "I'm sorry, Dad. It was an accident, I swear."

I don't know what has come over me because I'm not sorry at all. But some innocent part of me desperately needs his love and approval right now, and maybe if I apologize, it'll be easier for him to give it to me.

"Hey, hey. It's okay, bunny," he soothes as he sniffles and rubs my back gently. "Don't apologize. Are you happy?"

"Yes," I sob, fisting the back of his shirt with shaky hands.

"Then I'm happy too," he says. "It's surprising, but you're going to be the best momma."

I rub my face against his shirt, uncaring that my eye makeup smears everywhere. I pull away enough to look at him. "Thank you, Dad."

Wiping the tears from my eyes with his thumbs, he smiles through his own. "You can do this, Angela." Then his focus shifts over my head. Being the shortest member of my family, everyone's always looking over my head. "And Rafael is the father?" I nod. "By choice or biologically?"

"Both."

He looks back at me. "Did something happen between you two?" he whispers.

My shoulder lifts. "I mean, something obviously happened but...nothing's happening, you know?"

"Okay, bunny," he says, pulling me back into a full embrace and kissing the top of my head. "We'll follow your lead."

Chapter 11

July 4th

Angie

When Rafael suggested we go camping for the long holiday weekend, I was all-in. After we told his father the news over a video call, we were both feeling uneasy. His father's reaction was, let's just say, less than enthused. I think Rafael actually preferred Ana's reaction because at least she was excited underneath all the hitting and praying. His father was cagey—he tried changing the subject a few times over the course of the fifteen-minute call, and by the last time, I think Rafael got the hint to end the conversation.

I know my friend's relationship with his father is strenuous. He acts like it's not, but when his father is around or on a call, it's easy to see Rafael become a shallower version of himself. He hides a lot from his dad but shows off when he thinks his dad will be proud. Then Raf will do what he always does after talking with him—he's going to bury himself in work and rugby and numbers until he feels better about himself. Until his father approves.

And that's exactly what he did this last week before our camping trip. He buried himself in work at the office, but he also created an entire spreadsheet for our child's college fund including pie charts of what investments will yield the best returns. He talked with his brother about buying more properties here in Philly, then met with his real estate agent. He adjusted his 401k and updated his will. Then he made me a will.

So yeah, this camping trip came at a good time. He needs to get out of his head and away from his computer. He needs to recenter himself.

What I need right now is a strong, cool breeze. I'm fifteen weeks pregnant, and while I'm still not showing, it's taking a lot more effort to do things. I'm sweating profusely.

Rafael looks like a freakin' pack mule in front of me as he carries most of our belongings. I'm carrying a small backpack with my essentials—snacks, water (infused with electrolyte powder because regular water still makes me gag), and ginger chews. But honestly all this fresh air is putting my nausea at bay. Maybe I should live in the forest and give birth here. I already have a crunchy side to me; I could lean in and rock the Earth Mama look.

Raf's teammate, Wheels, offered his family's sixty acre-property near the Catskills. We have the whole place to ourselves, including the "cabin" near the front of the property. It's a "cabin" in that it has a rustic aesthetic, but it's huge and filled with every modern amenity you'd find at a high-end resort.

We didn't come here for the resort lifestyle though. We came to camp and hike and be one with nature.

I will, however, be taking a long shower before we leave—mark my word.

"It's only a little bit farther," Raf says. "We'll be right along a creek, so we can wash up after setting up camp."

"Yes," I groan. The idea of glorious cold creek water on my body makes my imaginary dick hard.

"It's beautiful here," he muses.

"I can't believe you know someone that owns *this* much property in this location."

"Wheels has that *old* family money."

"Clearly."

"It's right up here. Do you hear the creek?"

I inhale. "I can smell it." There's already a clearing with a small fire pit, big enough for a couple tents between tall evergreens and oak trees.

"According to the DNR's website," he says, sloughing off his heavy bags, "Smokey the Bear says fire danger is low today, so we should be able to have a fire tonight."

"Well, if Smokey says it's okay, let's do it."

"Alright," he sighs, assessing our surroundings. He's wearing dark khaki hiking pants, boots, and a natural green long sleeve shirt with a black baseball hat. "I'll set up the tent. Why don't you take a break by the water and eat something?" he asks, looking at his wristwatch. "It's been about three hours since you ate." He takes a water test strip from a little package he kept in his pocket and bends down to dip it in the creek.

"Are you keeping track of how often I eat?"

"Of course I am," he states matter-of-factly as he leans back up. "The doctor said you need to keep eating even when you don't feel hungry to keep your blood sugar up."

"Raf."

He narrows his eyes on me, setting the test strip down on a nearby rock. "Ang, you're not winning this one. Go put your bare feet in the water and eat, please."

I am hot. And a little hungry. "Fine," I mutter, as if this pains me.

"Thank you," he says in a sing-song tone as he leans over to unhook the tent from his pack.

Sitting down on a stump close to the water's edge, I roll up the bottoms of my slate gray pants to my knees, pull off my hiking boots, and peel off my thick socks. [1] Already feeling twenty percent better, I grab a protein bar from my bag and scoot down from the stump to the creek's

---

1. *My Love Mine All Mine* by Mitski

edge. Dropping my feet in the crystal-clear water, I allow the freezing sensation to shoot through my body like an orgasm.

"You okay over there?" Raf asks.

"What?" I reply in a trance.

"You sound like a ghost was expelled from your body," he laughs.

"Oh," I giggle. "It's nothing. I'm just having an orgasm courtesy of the creek water."

He mutters something unintelligible, but I'm too lost to my own experience to care. Ever since Cora told me she's been uncontrollably horny, it's like my own arousal has increased ten-fold.

It doesn't help that I live with a goddamn rugby player either. With his stupid fucking legs and his stupid fucking team crest tattooed on his upper thigh like a hussy. And his stupid fucking gorgeous pectorals that he can't seem to put away. And his ridiculously broad shoulders with more slutty tattoos flowing down his bicep.

Don't even get me started on that pornographic happy trail. Or his bare feet. Fuck—when did his feet become attractive? He's an athlete for Christ' sake—he shouldn't have such beautiful, tantalizing feet.

Fuck.

I told Cora it was nothing that my vibrator couldn't handle, but that was then. Hormones? More like whore-moans, because that's what I've been reduced to. If I could be attached to my vibrator—preferably two or three of them—all day, then *maybe* that would be enough.

But as much as I love my collection, it's never the *real* thing. It's never as warm as skin. It's never as unpredictable as another partner.

It's never Rafael Jimenez.

It's never Rafael Jimenez when he's doing things he's *great* at.

It's never Rafael Jimenez looking so barbaric while playing rugby.

It's never Rafael Jimenez when he's nerding out on numbers.

It's never Rafael Jimenez when he's dancing.

It's...never him.

By the time I finish my protein bar and drink some not-water, I decide to strip off my shirt and pants, leaving me in a pair of black cotton panties and sports bra. Rafael has seen me in far more revealing clothing, so I don't think twice before I lay down across the narrow riverbed. The water is only six or seven inches at its deepest, so my mouth and nose are still above the burbling stream.

The cold current flows over me and my body clenches in response. My lungs seize for a moment before forcing my body to accept the shocking sensation. With my jaw hanging wide-open, I take in the deepest lungful of fresh air.

I'm a Pisces; I belong in the water. I always have. I've always felt the call, the pull, the need to be close. Water, in any form, has always been my center; and right now, it's serving me. It's finally giving me what I need—so why has my body been rejecting it? Water is a literal building block to life, but my stomach is repulsed by it?

But like a light switch, my repulsion turns into desperation.

Maybe I just needed to reconnect.

With my eyes closed and my chest heaving, I throw my hands above my head and let the current push them down. Allowing my hands to search my body, they crawl up my stomach where I caress and enjoy the feel of my own skin.

"Thank you," I whisper to myself.

To the water.

To any higher power.

With one hand on my baby, the other glides over my sternum, my neck, my jaw. My body cuts through the stream like a boulder.

I am a rock.

I am this child's *rock*.

There's a very real chance I'm having an out-of-body experience at this moment—but I've never felt more clear-headed and saner in my life.

Then all at once, the desperate need to drink water overtakes me—real, fresh water. My mind reels back to earth, back to here, back to now; and I remember Rafael.

He tested the water.

"Raf!" I call, finally opening my eyes in search of him. I have to lift my head ever so slightly to find him, but my ears lift out from my submersive escape to find him standing on the bank, his arms folded over a wide chest. He's watching me with his lips slightly parted—almost expressionless.

"Yeah?" he says thickly.

"Is the water safe to drink?" I ask desperately.

His throat works before answering. "Yeah. It's safe."

Closing my eyes again before submerging, I tilt my head to the right, my mouth ready, and I take my first real drink of water I've had in months.

Cold, fresh, *real* water.

Nothing has ever tasted this good.

Gulping down as much as my body demands, I allow the creek to nourish me. To heal me from everything I didn't realize was broken.

When at last my body and mind are satiated, I take one last inhale from my water bed, open my eyes to the blue sky, and smile.

· · · • · • · • · · ·

The rest of the afternoon passes as we settle into camp. Rafael has been a little aloof, but that's okay. He's giving me peace and quiet to read on my Kindle next to the babbling brook while he... What is it he's doing now?

He's mumbling to himself—again—as he stokes the fire. The sun hasn't quite set, but we'll have to make dinner soon. I'd rather prepare dinner while we still have the light.

Uncrossing my legs that have been covered back up with pants, sans panties, I make my way up the slight incline to where Raf is milling about. "Ready for dinner?" I ask.

"Uhhh, yeah," he says, barely able to make eye contact with me. "I have the stir fry stuff right here."

Grabbing the pan and placing it over the cooking tripod he's set up, I then walk up next to him where he's digging through the food bag. "I'll take the veggies first and throw them in," I say, extending my hand to him. He looks up at me with what appears to be panic with the way he's breathing.

My eyes narrow on him. "Raf, what's going on with you? You seem...untethered."

"Nothing," he says quickly. "You're having a nice time, right? You're...comfortable, right?" His eyes shoot to my chest for the briefest of seconds.

Oh.

I look down at my shirt and back at him. "Raf, do you want me to put my bra back on?"

"No," he says, an octave too deep. "It's wet and that would make you uncomfortable so don't worry about it. Hey, look, a teriyaki packet. This is going to be a great stir fry."

Deciding to hide my real reaction to how weird he's being in fear that he'll become weirder, I wordlessly grab the raw chopped veggies, sauce packet, and ready-made rice pouch. "Okay," I smile. I saunter back to the fire. "You'll let me know if it makes you uncomfortable, right?"

Standing, he wipes his hands on his pants and reverts to mumbling huffs, where I think I catch a *yeah* somewhere in there.

"Hey, Raf?" I ask, pouring the bag of veggies into the pan.

"Yeah?"

"Why don't you take a turn relaxing near the water. I'll make dinner and let you know when it's ready. Okay?"

"Do you need any help?" he asks.

"No," I say lightly. "I got this. Go connect with the water." When I cock my head in his direction, he nods to himself, then make his way to the creek. I plug in my phone to the little speaker we brought, and Donna Summer's *Bad Girls* plays first.

I love this song.

When dinner's ready fifteen minutes later, he's already making his way back. "Smells good," he smiles, and I can already tell he's settled back into himself.

Handing him the collapsible bowl piled with hot veggie stir fry and biodegradable spoon, he takes it. "Thank you."

"You're welcome."

Finding a downed tree near the creek's edge, we both take a seat and dig in.

"Whoa," Raf says after his first bite. "This is better than I expected."

"I think it's that added *fire* flavor that really enhances it," I smile.

"Everything does taste better over an open fire."

Memories pop up like a hot spring. "Oh my god," I groan. "Like when we made kettle corn over the fire on that camping trip before graduation."

"That was so good," he mutters with a mouthful of food while his eyes roll back dramatically.

"Where did Alex even get the ingredients for that?" I ask before taking another bite.

He shrugs. "I have no idea. One minute we were drinking screwdrivers, and the next kettle corn was being passed around."

Uh-oh. We've hit dangerous territory. When the *before-graduation* camping story comes up and screwdrivers have been mentioned, it's time to tread lightly.

But something is making me bolder. Maybe it's the similar scenery. Maybe it's how close we're sitting. Maybe it's the out-of-body experience the god-blessed creek gave me—but I'm curious to finally know.

I want answers.

"Hmm. You know, to this day I still can't drink screwdrivers."

Like a jungle cat lowering its body and dilating its pupils, his body stills next to mine. "No?" he whispers.

"No," I confirm.

"Huh," he says, but it doesn't sound like a realization.

"Yeah, you know, it's strange. I can drink mimosas no problem. But there's *something* about screwdrivers that triggers that...associated memory."

"Yeah?" he asks, before clearing his throat and shoveling three large bites of food in his mouth.

"But you know what's weird? I have the strongest memory of that night, but there's something that I never *quite* figured out."

Okay, Angela, you are playing with fire here!

The corner of Rafael's eye finds me. "What's that?" he asks, like he doesn't know where this is going.

"Why didn't you kiss me?"

Cue atomic bomb.

He huffs a disbelieving laugh. "What are you talking about?"

Oh no. I didn't come this far for him to back out. This is so far past where I promised myself I would ever take this conversation. I've passed the point of no return, and I'm dragging him with me.

I push my stir fry around with my fork. "I'm talking about Spin the Bottle. And how you kissed every person the spin landed on." *Fuck*, I'm doing my best to stay calm and poised right now, but I am sweating bullets on the inside. Regardless, I continue. "You kissed Alex. And Jess. And Pakhuri. And Austin," I drawl. "But when the bottle finally landed on me, you... What? Decided enough was enough?"

For a *very* long time after that night, I thought he wouldn't kiss me because I was fat. You'd never guess I had those insecurities from my confidence level now, but young Angie was deeply insecure.

There were six of us there. Five trim people, and one me. That tendril of insecurity only grew when I watched Rafael time and time again only date—only hook up with—other fit people. By the time I grew out of my body-hatred and started loving it in my mid-twenties, I thought I had wiped my slate clean. It wasn't until the end of our graduate studies that I realized his rejection probably wasn't about my body, and it most likely about him not wanting to ruin our friendship. That made more sense, but it never fully erased my first suspicion.

But to this day, I've only ever seen Rafael's hookups in one form—lean. I still love and appreciate my body, but every time I meet one of his fleeting partners, I can't help thinking, *Of course. That's his type.*

Many times I've had to remind myself, *It's fine that I'm not his type—people's attractions can be varied and narrow and it's all valid.* But a dark part of me wants him to admit it now.

"Angie, we don't need to talk about—"

"No, we do," I cut him off. "I'm tired of pussyfooting around this, Raf. Tell me why you couldn't kiss me."

"I *wanted* to kiss you!" he blurts, with a ferocity I've only seen when he's playing rugby. "Fuck, Angie. Why did you have to bring this up?"

"What?" I ask—*seriously* ask. Because that honestly surprised the shit out of me.

Abruptly, he stands up and takes my almost-empty bowl along with his and sets them to the side. "Why didn't I kiss you?" he asks with eyes wide and his fingers combing through the dark, wavy mess on his head. "Other than the fact that we're *just* friends?"

"We were there with other friends."

"*They*...weren't *you*, Ang! Don't you see that?"

Suddenly, I feel small under his heated gaze. With a voice that's equally as small as I feel, I say, "It was just a game, Raf. There was no need to take it seriously." I want to poke him. I want him to admit the real reason.

"I couldn't kiss you because I was afraid of what it would mean. I've kept my distance for so long, yet it *hasn't* become second nature. I've kept my distance because you and I both know I could never be what you need."

"What? Committed?" I ask. "How could you even know at eighteen years old that you wouldn't want commitment?"

"It wasn't that," he sighs.

"Then what was it?"

Looking down at the ground, Raf waits a beat before saying, "It was a few things, but mostly, I didn't want to ruin what we had. It was perfect." He lifts his gaze up to mine. "It still is. I don't have what we have with anyone else. I don't want it with anyone else."

"And what if things have changed, Raf?"

"What do you mean?"

"I mean I'm insatiably horny *all the time* and it's because of you," I grunt, letting my filter disintegrate. I place my hand on my belly. "You gave me this incredible gift and now you parade around in your goddamn short-shorts with your juicy fucking booty like it doesn't affect me, and I'm going insane in this hormonal tornado you've thrown me in!" *Oops, that may have been too much.* "But noOoo, you can't even touch me because it'll *ruin things*," I say in air quotes. "And I'm not your type."

His face contorts. "What do you mean you're not my type?"

"Come on, Raf." I roll my eyes. "Name *one* partner you've had that looks even remotely like me." His jaw clenches in response. "Exactly." I sigh heavily and push past him for the tent. "This was a mistake. Forget everything I said."

He snatches my hand before I can grab the zipper. "No," he grits.

"I've embarrassed myself enough tonight, Raf. Let's drop it."

"I've never been with someone that looks like you because every time I've tried, they've reminded me of you. And if I was going to be with somebody that looked like you...I'd be fucking pissed that it *wasn't* you."

My entire mind goes blank. Time doesn't exist. I don't know where I am.

"Angel? You okay?"

"No," I reply in a fog. "You just hit the factory reset button in my brain." I stare at the man in front of me for too long, and when his gaze lowers to my lips, I remember what I'm doing.

I'm digging my hormonal heels in.

"What are you thinking about?" I ask.

With his hand clasped around my wrist, his trance only intensifies. "I didn't bring a bottle with us, but I still want to kiss you."

My breath is stuck for a moment as I study him, but a tiny smirk climbs into the corner of my lips. "Wouldn't that ruin things?"

"Fuck it," he huffs and yanks me toward him. Before I can place my hand on his chest, he's kissing me. With one hand on my back, and the other cupping the side of my face, Rafael Juan Dominico Jimenez is finally—*actually*—kissing me.

His mouth on mine is like finding a treasure trove I've been searching for my whole life. But it's so much more than I anticipated. The way his soft lips devour me, like I'm the only meal he needs.

He tastes like lusty energy born from nervousness. Like a summer evening spent swapping details of yourself so private, you realize you've never admitted them before this moment. He tastes like a memory—the funny kind. The romantic kind. The devastating kind.

Any second now, he's going to pull away. Any second now, he's going to abruptly stop and say something like *There. See? It's no big deal.* And if that's the case, then I'm going to milk every second for all it's worth.

When his tongue seeks mine, I eagerly open for him. With my left arm wrapped tightly around his back, I squeeze that side muscle I don't know the name for as my other hand drags down his chest to his chiseled abdomen. As if my hand is a magnet, I slide it under his shirt, feeling his warm skin.

"Angel," he whispers.

Whatever he has to say can wait. "Shhh. Don't ruin it, Raf." I grind against him, where I can feel him growing hard against my stomach.

Fuck yes. I *do* turn him on.

"Tell me what you need," he rasps, feverishly kissing me.

It's almost too hard to form sentences. My brain is caught up in him. In the way he smells and feels and towers over me. But I manage to whisper, "I need to come. I need *you* to make me come."

He breaks the kiss, which I'm about to protest, but he plants his forehead on mine and nuzzles me. "Are you sure?"

"Rafael, all I can think about lately is getting off and needing *you* to do that for me."

"Say no more," he says, lifting me up and wrapping my legs around him. *Yup.* He's got something under those pants for me alright.

He squats down with me in his lap as I hold on and kiss his neck and ear while he unzips the tent. The music still playing from the speaker has switched to *Get Ur Freak On* by Missy Elliot and I inwardly laugh. Of course.

He makes it one step in before throwing me on the double high queen air mattress. Bouncing, I giggle as he kneels to remove my boots, socks, and shuck off my pants with those intense game-day eyes. When he discovers I'm not wearing any underwear, his jaw drops and he freezes.

"Where are your panties, woman?"

"They were wet," I say with fake demure.

Rafael runs his hands up my thighs and grips them tight and the growl shakes me like an earthquake. "It looks like you're still wet."

"It's your fault," I say before biting my lower lip.

He crawls closer to the apex of my thighs and hovers there, his hot breath puffing against my sex, his eyes trained on mine. "It's not my fault, Angel," then he tenderly kisses my mound with a feather-light touch that only makes me ache for him more. "What it is, is my *job*," he rasps, then closes his eyes and licks a long, wet tongue against my seam, sending my back arching. He gently pulls my labia into his wet mouth, alternating between kisses and nips. "If you're wet and needy, then it's *my job* to take care of that, do you understand?"

"Yes," I pant.

"I put this baby inside you," he growls, before shoving his long tongue inside me, lapping at the evidence that brought us here. "I'm responsible. Say it."

"Yes," I whimper. "You did this to me. You need to—*oh god yes, keep doing that*—you need to take care of me."

"That's right," he mumbles through my body. Working his jaw in tandem with his tongue, his rough stubble from his usually clean-shaven face rubs against my sensitive skin. Fuck, it's so good.

Rafael's oral game is on another level—yet another thing he's great at apparently.

When he sucks at my clit, my hands fly to the pillow behind my head, to the sheets, then to my own hair. I can't decide where to put them.

"Grab on to me, Angel. I wanna know what makes you feel good."

They fly down to his thick black hair and I'm grateful for the few inches he leaves on top—just enough to hold on so I can ride his face like the wanton little whore I am.

Still sucking at my clit, he never lets it go; he keeps the suction while undulating his chin into me. His beautiful aquiline nose is buried so deep I don't understand how he's breathing. But I don't have to understand. What I *do* understand is how my orgasm rips through my body like lightning. Without knowing, I clamp my legs shut and squeeze his head between them like I'm a pair of pliers and he's the stubborn nail I'm pulling.

For the first time ever, I let myself scream his name at the top of my lungs instead of under my breath or muted into a pillow.

Take your trophy, Rafael. You fucking earned it.

Apparently he's not settling for just one, because when I release his head from my large, dimple-covered thighs, he lifts his head up with a gasp like he's resurfacing from the water and the biggest smile on his face. "Goddammit,

Ang," he huffs. "That was so fucking hot." He shifts his body so he's kneeling before my splayed-out self, then stuffs a finger inside me. "Take your shirt off. I'm not done with you."

"Again?" I ask, but I listen because this dominant side of him is *doing things* to me.

"Yes," he growls, crooking his finger inside me like he's coaxing the next one out of me. "You're going to come on my hand." He leans down and lays next to me, our bodies automatically turning on their sides to face one another. When I lift my bare leg over his hips, he adds another finger inside of me, then leans in and attaches his mouth to my neck. When it travels down to my breasts, his tongue dances over my hardened nipples, and I stroke the back of his head, the other hand on his shoulder.

Why the fuck is he still wearing clothes?

"These tits," he moans. "You were driving me fucking crazy with them today." His hand pummels into me as he adds a thumb to pull on my clit. My hips buck and thrust into his touch.

"Was I?" I pant.

"When you were laying in the water, your nipples were rock hard. They were begging to be touched," he whispers, then pulls one into his mouth. "Begging to be sucked. And *you*," he drawls. "Laying there. Your body writhing and *desperate*."

"I am," I whimper.

"I know you are, dirty girl." He fucks me with his fingers harder, but there's something I need more than coming again from his touch.

Scrambling to unbuckle him, I say, "Need you. I need to feel you."

His mouth releases from my chest, when he looks down at where our hands play with each other. "You don't have to, Ang."

"I want to," I breathe. "I need to see it. I need to hold it."

When his erection releases from his pants, the tightness I was carrying in my face relaxes as I stare at Rafael's massive cock.

"Jesus Christ, Raf! How the hell do you walk around all day with this between your legs?"

He chuckles. "It's not that big."

"Are you joking? This is a porn dick, dude! How big is it?"

"I don't know," he smiles. "I never measured it."

"Bullshit. Tell me."

He sighs. "Ten inches."

"And you're uncut? You know, you could be a lot cockier in real life because of..." I gesture to the monster, "this."

He rubs my G-spot. "Shut up, Ang. You wanna talk about it or *be* about it?"

"Be," I moan, then start stroking his enormous dick—that I still think he might be downplaying its true size. When he grunts, I take it as a personal victory. His mouth finds mine as our tongues mingle like they've known each other for years.

This should be awkward. This should be strange. But it's not. It has that exciting *new* feeling, with all the safety that comes with knowing someone for decades.

Our hands work each other as ferociously as our mouths claim. I took his cock out so he could put it inside of me, but there's something incredibly necessary about what we're doing right now, that breaking from it would be wrong.

His expert fingers stroke inside me and his palm pushes against my clit with the perfect amount of force. I'm already climbing to my peak, but listening to him lose himself to *my* touch is what sends me over the edge.

"I'm coming, Raf!"

"Yes," he grunts, spilling himself between us as my entire body clenches around his hand. I ride my orgasm out for as long as possible and he peppers me with kisses and *good girls*, making me a whole new level of woozy.

When my body finally relaxes, he removes his hand, closes his eyes, and sucks his fingers clean of my arousal. "Mmm," he groans and finally takes his shirt off, tossing it to the tent floor, before settling himself back between my legs. "I need to clean up."

Oh my god.

Chapter 12

July 5th

Angie

R afael gave me three more orgasms with his mouth and fingers last night. I have no idea how I'm awake already—I should be zonked out, but if anything, all those orgasms have stirred me awake. I need more. It seems what he did to me last night only poked the horny bear.

This can't be good.

Raf is sound asleep behind me as we lay on our sides. I'm reading my Kindle because I've been awake for a little while but didn't want to disturb him. The temperature actually dropped last night and—oh no, would you look at that?—the blanket is still on the floor folded up next to the air mattress. When it got a little too chilly, Raf slowly snuggled into me, rendering the blanket useless.

A low gasp whooshes over my ear. "What are you reading?" His morning voice is like gravel as he peers over my shoulder and pulls me closer, nudging his morning wood into my backside.

I guess he is awake. "A why choose dark romance."

"How many dudes are fucking her right now?"

I smile. "Six."

He leans in a little closer to read, "...Drake held his gun to my head as he fucked my throat and Lazzaro entered my ass once again. You want my knife, hellcat?... Jesus Christ, Ang," he chuckles. "This stuff really gets you going, huh?"

I snort. "Everything gets me going these days."

"Yeah, but you've always had a thing for these books. How many do you read in a year?"

I feign shock. "That's private. A lady never tells."

It's his turn to snort. "I know what color menstrual cup you wear, how many sexual partners you've had, and I watched you writhe in a creek yesterday. But knowing how many dirty books you read in a year? That crosses a line?"

"I'm glad you understand."

Rafael hums his amusement before a lingering pause settles between us. "So," he drawls. "I meant what I said last night, Ang. I want to be able to take care of your needs in this way."

"You're sure?" I ask, setting down my Kindle and turning to my back as he leans on one arm to look down at me.

"Only if you are."

There's no one I trust more than Rafael. He's a loyal friend, and he clearly knows his way around a woman's body, so why wouldn't I take this opportunity?

Oh, yeah.

Because for the better part of two decades he's given me unwanted butterflies. Because he said he wanted to kiss me all those years ago. If I want to protect my heart from his commitment-less lifestyle while getting my primal urges taken care of, then we're going to need boundaries.

"We should set some rules."

"What were you thinking?" he asks, pushing a lock of hair away from my face. I'm sure I look like the picture of a debauched wilderness queen.

"I think we should only do this for the duration of my pregnancy."

His gaze becomes unfocused for a moment before nodding. "Yeah. That sounds fair."

"That should help us keep things casual," I say with the confidence born from a prayer.

"Okay. I have a rule I'd like to submit," he says.

"Shoot."

"No one else. Neither of us sleep with anyone else during this time."

Oh god, I don't know about this one. On the one hand, I love this exclusivity aspect. All his attention? Of course I want that. But on the other hand...

"I don't know about that, Raf," I sigh. "I think if we leave this open, it'll help us make a clean break when it's over, you know?"

Furrowing his dark eyebrows, he smirks. "Don't think I can keep up with you?"

"Please," I roll my eyes. "Cora has two husbands and even they have to take shifts."

"I'll redact my rule, but I will take it as a personal challenge."

"Speaking of personal," I drawl. "When was the last time you were tested?"

"Pretty recently. I'm clear. It was after Charles. There hasn't been anyone since. Why? You want it bare?"

"I'm already pregnant, so yeah, I wanna seize this opportunity."

"Fuck," he smiles then adjusts himself under the sheet. "Just the thought of it..."

A giggle escapes me as desire creeps into my belly. "I was tested when I was at the hospital last. I'm clear too."

I lose track of Rafael's devilish grin when he lowers himself to kiss my neck. "We," I breathe. "We should talk about other things. Like what we want and what we don't."

He kisses up the column of my neck. "I already have a BDSM limits document filled out."

"You do? I didn't know you were into that. I've always...wanted to explore that," I pant.

When he pulls his mouth off and stares at me with round eyes, I want to protest. "Really?"

"Yeah. I've only read about these things or listened to erotic audios," I admit. "But I've never felt comfortable enough with a sexual partner to ask."

"But you have an idea of what you like?"

"Oh buddy, I have more than an idea."

"I am very interested to know. Do you want me to send you a blank version of the limits form I have?"

"Yes please," I smile, as those butterflies start multiplying.

He grabs his phone from the ground and taps away. "There. Sent you a blank and mine." He pushes up and pulls on a pair of old rugby shorts over his boxer briefs. "Why don't you relax and read them over while I make breakfast."

"Okay," I say, snuggling into the bed a little deeper. "So we're doing it, huh? Just two best friends, sharing our kinks with each other?"

"Totally normal stuff," he grins, then ducks to exit the tent.

Opening his filled-out form, I eagerly read every word and his interest level for each activity. We seem to share a lot of interests, but one thing in particular catches my eye.

Switch.

The pounding in my heart catches up to the throbbing ache in my pussy. He's a switch—which means he likes to dominate, and he likes to submit.

Fuck yes.

The thought of Rafael dominating me... Oh my god. I'd be drunk with lust. But the reverse is just as alluring. Him submitting to me? I need that.

Reading further down the document, I start to wonder if he'd let me... Bingo. That's happening.

This is fascinating. It's like knocking down a wall in a home you've lived in all your life and discovering a secret room—or a kinky sex dungeon.

When I get to the end of his list, I realize some things weren't covered. I call out to him from my comfy spot. "Hey, Raf? Would you be into financial domination?"

He chuckles. "I don't know. Why?"

"I once read about a Leprechaun king who was into that. It was hot."

"Your mind is a fascinating and deranged place, you know that Ang?"

"That's not a no," I tease.

"Let's table that."

By the time we're sitting for breakfast, perched back on our downed tree next to the water, I've completed about a third of my own form, but I notice myself holding back with my real answers and interest levels. Debating over how much of my desires I should show Rafael.

When would I ever get the chance to act out my real desires? What if I end up marrying someone who only likes vanilla sex? There's nothing wrong with vanilla sex—I enjoy it immensely too—but I want to explore this part of me that I've only been able to experience in Romancelandia.

"How far did you get with your form?" he asks before taking a bite of his apple.

"Not too far," I drawl.

"Is something the matter?"

I pause. "I want to be truthful with what I share with you, but I don't want you to think I'm weird."

"That ship sailed long ago, Ang. You are weird and I like it."

I chuckle. "Yeah, but there's a difference between *Angie reads monster romance and was part of the underwater robotics club in high school*, and *Angie likes to be stalked and fucked into the dirt*."

Rafael's eyes bug out, but he smiles. "Do you want to be stalked and fucked into the dirt?"

I play with my food. "Maybe."

"I'm totally down for that," he says eagerly.

"Okay," I giggle, giddiness bubbling inside me. "I'll be as truthful as I can, but I was thinking, I don't know when I'll be able to be in a situation like this again, where I can explore my interests like this. So, that's what I'd really like to do. Explore those things I've always wanted—within your limits too, of course."

"I'm glad you trust me enough to do this. Unless I have a hard limit, I promise I'll only be supportive of your desires. There will be no kink-shaming between us."

"Okay," I smile. "So... I couldn't help noticing you had a high interest in primal domination."

Chapter 13

July 5th

Rafael

As the sun starts to set, my senses start to heighten. Or maybe I'm method acting a little too hard with this wolfish persona I've adopted. It's not too much of an act really—I have always wanted to do this—but it's not easy to tell your one-night stand you want to chase them in the woods. Apparently that freaks some people out.

Not my Angel though.

No, she gets off on it—and that gives me a smug confidence boost. Because even though I've never done this before, I know I can give her what she wants. Not only that, but she trusts me to do this for her.

Getting her off with fear is my mission. I want to make this night memorable for her. When she said she wanted to keep this arrangement open, it rubbed me the wrong way, like sandpaper against skin. But I want to give her what she needs, what she desires. So I've taken this as a challenge: I'm going to make myself available for her every time she's needy. I'm going to rock her fucking world so hard that she won't even consider another partner.

We've somehow found ourselves in a temporary friendship loophole, and I, for one, will be taking full advantage of this. It's like the universe has handed me this perfect, thick gift I've secretly pined for but could never have. With a timeframe and expectations in place, it's my one chance to have Angie without hurting her.

Between taking my father's advice and knowing she wants a full commitment—that's what has always stopped me. When we didn't kiss on that high school camping trip, it really was because I didn't want to ruin our friendship. She's my closest friend, and if I kept her only as a friend, then I'm still obeying my father's advice. I'm still in his good graces.

Being her best friend has always been a priority. It's not like she would ever stand to be in a relationship with me—she'd see soon enough how inadequate I am, how far short I'd fall from her expectations and—well, it's better the way it is now. Just friends. And if that means my heart needs to take a hit so she can get what she wants, then I'll always do that for her. I'll always be that for her.

And if she wants me to chase her in the woods, who am I to deny her?

We took the afternoon to fill out the rest of her BDSM interest form, which fascinated me endlessly. She's exactly my brand of kinky. She's open to an array of interests—things I've never considered, but with her interest piqued, so is mine.

Tonight's activities require safewords since the whole point is her running away from me, fighting me, telling me no. So in honor of one of our favorite musical pairings, her safeword is Dolly Parton and mine's Kenny Rogers.

While she was filling out the form, I took a long run through the woods to get the lay of the land, keeping a mental tracker of where all the dangerous spots would be and to avoid them. I want her to be scared, not injured. I also thought about how to prevent her from tripping. My biggest fear of what we're about to do is her falling on her stomach. Thankfully, there is a narrow pathway I told her to stick to since it's fairly clear of tripping hazards. But I've also seen this girl tussle with her brothers and I once watched her compete in a Tough Mudder course. This woman is agile and has reflexes better than a cat—Razzle Dazzle notwithstanding.

He's a million years old and almost blind; he gets a pass.

We ate an early dinner and dusk is about ten minutes away. I've already hidden myself high up in an evergreen as I watch her tighten the laces of her hiking boots. She then takes a bite of a protein bar and a swallow of water.

Good girl.

I can't hear her from where I'm perched, but I watch as she hypes herself up—little jumps side to side as she shakes out her arms and rolls her neck—like she's about to step in a boxing ring instead of a hike through the wilderness.

God, she's perfect.

Tonight, she's wearing black leggings and a tight white tank top. Her hair is a little wavy from the lack of styling products we have available to us, but it's setting me off. I want her hair to be a mess of twigs and leaves when I'm done with her. I want that white top so stained nothing will ever remove the memory. I want to yank those leggings down and find her wet cunt quivering, scared, and ready.

Leaving the safety of our campsite, she makes her way through the thick forest, looking around for signs of life. When a squirrel runs down a tree beside her, she nearly jumps out of her skin, and I chuckle to myself.

This is going to be fun.

Angie makes it about fifty yards before I decide to scale down the tree and follow her from a safe distance. There's enough tree coverage that I can hide easily when necessary. As she moves through the path in the woods, I can see her posture relax a little—like she's growing used to the environment.

Can't have that.

Picking up a few large stones at my feet, I find a decent hiding place behind a fallen tree and chuck the rock in her direction. It lands far away enough it won't hit her, but close enough for her to hear impact. She stops in her tracks and quickly spins around looking for where or what the sound came from. As she continues her walk, I then release a series of crow-like caws, making her head spin again.

Continuing to stalk her, I wait for the sun to finally dip just low enough to create the perfect blanket of fear. Just dark enough to make it hard to see, but light enough that when she finally catches a glimpse of my body—bounding between trees—she panics and starts to run.

I'll catch you, little creature.

She runs faster than I've ever seen her, but with panic surging through her, she falls forward, making my heart lurch, but she extends her hands, catching herself on a tree trunk. She may have saved herself from harm, but with that tiny amount of fear now erupting like a volcano inside me, I'm taking no more chances.

I'm close enough now that when I stop only a few feet away, she's fully aware of my proximity. But before she can turn around to find me standing there, I let out a howl and duck low to grab her ankles.

She screams at the top of her lungs as she kicks her way out of my grasp. "No! No!" she cries, scrambling to run away. Her fear ripples off in waves and I swear it only fuels me. Consensual nonconsent was something she marked as very interested in, but only in certain situations such as this—and I must hand it to her: this is fucking hot. The longer I stalk her, chase her, the more I become wholly a hunter.

The more I need her.

My dick is rock hard and begging to be buried deep inside her. When she manages to slip away and sprint toward the creek, all I can think is, *Catch her.*

There's a decent-sized hill leading down to the creek from where we currently are on the path, but my little creature runs for her life down the hill. I halt myself just before the drop off and watch her look back up at me, eyes wide with fear, as she tries to hastily get to the water. But it's too steep for her to run down.

"Fuck, why did I think this was a good idea?" she whimpers, trying to use a downed tree as leverage.

With a plan in place, I watch her slowly struggle to get down, slipping every few feet and trying her best to escape. I can tell she's being as careful as possible, which I appreciate, but I can also see the fear. When she's almost to the creek though, I jump, landing on my ass and sliding down the slope with my legs extended. Dead leaves cover the forest floor, providing me a fast route as I push away from obstacles. Landing with my feet in the cold creek, I spin around with my hands on the bank in front of me, watching as Angie's eyes bug out.

"Shit!" she hisses, trying to scramble back up the hill, but she's too close to me now. I've got her right where I want her. I quickly clean off my hands in the creek, then climb up the bank and flip her to her back, making sure to gently lay her down. Her scream punctures through the soft rustling of leaves and I shift myself lower to grab both of her ankles and pull hard. "No! No! No!" she sobs.

"Mine," I growl as her feet land in the water next to my own. Wasting no time, I pull off her tank top and shove her sports bra up to expose her exquisite chest.

"What are you doing?" she pants, her face painted with fear.

"Taking what's mine," I bark before latching my mouth to her nipple and sucking hard. I lower my hips against hers and with one hand, I hitch up her leg around me. She begs and pleads with me to let her go, but her leg is staying wrapped around my back all on its own.

And I don't hear her safeword.

With my mouth still firmly planted on her chest, she writhes under me, her warm center grinding against my cock. I shift my body just enough to yank the stretchy fabric down from her waist. Releasing her nipple from my mouth, I stand up and quickly unbuckle and unzip my pants. When she tries to make a run for it, I throw my hand against her neck and pin her down. I love a good choke, but she's pregnant and we agreed not to take any chances. What we're doing is risky enough. So my grip is light on her throat—just enough that she knows it's there, but it never constricts her airway.

"I don't think so, little creature," I whisper. "I hunted you. I pinned you. I own you." I take my other hand and slide two fingers across her pussy, feeling the overwhelming evidence of her arousal. "I can do whatever I want with you."

"No," she chokes out. "Please let me go. I promise to leave you alone."

"I don't want to be left alone," I sneer, leaning into our scene. "It's my job to keep you safe, and here you are running away from me?" I shove those two fingers deep inside her warm pussy.

"I'm sorry," she whimpers as I push my hand against her jaw, still not squeezing, but the threat still lingers.

"You're not sorry. You want this fucking punishment, don't you?"

"No," she cries.

"Then say it. Say the word now and I'll let you go. But if you don't, I will take what belongs to me," I growl. When she says nothing, her throat works beneath my palm. I grab my cock at the base and press the shaft against her slit before saying, "That's what I thought," then I thrust inside her pussy—the pussy I *earned*.

"Fuck!" she bellows.

As badly as I wanted to fill her completely with one hard stroke, I know she's not ready for my full size, so with great restraint I only push in half-way.

Leaning down to cover her body fully, I kiss her neck as she breathes heavily. Our pants are around our thighs, limiting our movements, but that doesn't seem to matter because for the first time—that I can remember—I am inside her.

When my nose brushes against her ear, I whisper, "I know how badly you want this cock." I inch myself forward a little more. "How badly you needed that perfect little pussy fucked by my cock."

"Yes," she whimpers, grabbing on to the outsides of my shoulders and digging her fingers in for every ounce of leverage she can hold.

"You need it all, don't you? You need every last inch buried in this cunt."

"Please," she groans.

"Stretch for me. That's it. Yes," I drawl, sliding into my rightful place.

"Fuck, that's good," she says. Once I'm confident she's ready, I thrust into her hard, and she pulls me closer. "Raf!" she cries.

"That's it, Angel. Tell the whole world who fucks you this good."

"You," she cries again. "Yes, Raf. Right there."

"Right here?" I ask, keeping one hand folded gently on her neck as the other finds her clit buried beneath her soft mound. Her sharp inhale lets me know I'm right before her words do.

"Yes," she chants and howls.

I chuckle as if a demon has possessed me. "How quickly your no's have turned into yes's, little creature. Say you're mine and I'll give you what you really came out here for."

"I'm yours," she shouts, and her pussy squeezes me. The sounds of flesh slapping against flesh cracks through the forest like the sound of trees splitting. Her pussy clenches tighter when I rub her clit with more precision and press it hard, sending her hips bucking into mine. "Please," she begs, before taking my mouth.

Completely lost to her, I force my tongue against hers and growl nonsense into her. Unsure if they're words or sounds, I succumb to the moment. I savor the wet warmth between our bodies. Her lips. The way her soft body allows mine to dig in. It's all too much.

"I'm going to come," she breathes. "Don't stop." I keep my hips thrusting against hers and the pace of my fingers exactly the same as she digs her nails into my shoulders and screams—for me.

"Raf! Fuck yes. Yes, keep going please," she sobs.

Like I could stop. I keep pumping into her, watching her bloom before me. She rides her climax out for several minutes before I can't take it anymore.

"Now you're gonna take my cum, you disobedient little whore. I'm gonna fill you up. I'm gonna mark you so you can never run away from me again."

"Yes," she pants, and I finally take my hand off her neck, pushing myself up and grabbing her lush hips as I stare down at where I'm fucking her.

I thrust even harder. "I didn't ask for your permission. I own you," I grunt. "You're mine to watch. Mine to chase. Mine to fuck and fill and breed."

"Oh god, yes," she whispers.

My balls tighten and the coil of arousal that wraps around my spine finally breaks and my thrusts staccato. "Fuck," I grit. "That's... Fuck."

And then, my mind goes beautifully blank.

Several moments later when I come to, my forearms braced on either side of Angie's head. She's looking up at me like I hung the moon.

"Sir," she smiles. But not like Sir in a Dom way, like sir in a playfully respectful way. "That was incredible."

"Yeah?"

"That was better than my wildest fantasies," she sighs. "You really commit to a scene—holy fuck, dude."

The way Angie can deliver such sincerity in such a funny and lighthearted way makes my entire body soar. Something childlike wrestles free from a bound place inside my chest when she compliments me like that. She always knows how to make me feel good.

Chuckling, I thank her. "I'll take my award for best Primal Dom."

"Oh, your award is the second baby you just put in me," she says furrowing her brow as I stay buried inside her. "Seriously, I think you got me pregnant again."

A full belly laugh rolls out of me as we both lay there, giggling like we always have. See, we can do this. We're fucking nailing this temporary friends with benefits thing.

When we finally break apart, I pull out a clean handkerchief I brought with me and soak it in the creek before wiping her clean and checking on her. With nothing physically or emotionally hurt and minimal scratches on either of us, we make the long walk back to our campsite, recounting every detail of the scene and talking about our favorite parts.

When we make it back, I prepare another hot meal for us and make her drink plenty of that arousing creek water she's so fond of now.

I smile to myself.

What a little freak I have.

Chapter 14

July 20th

Angie

"I don't understand why they don't make full rugby kits for infants," Rafael muses as we sit in the dilapidated sunroom of his historical fixer-upper, scrolling our phones and adding items to our baby registry. I've only been here a few times so far, but each time I visit, it's getting better and better.

"Probably because it's impractical," I hum, setting my feet up on the old milk crate in front of me. The first time I was here, I considered checking my online medical chart for the last time I had a tetanus shot. The kitchen was nothing but cheap cupboards that appeared to be actively disintegrating. Both the paint on the walls and the laminate floors were peeling. Grime and dirt coated everything. The back deck was one strong wind away from collapsing altogether.

Since then, everything has been gutted, save for a claw-foot tub. Before tearing out its guts, the house felt huge. At over thirty-one hundred square feet with six bedrooms and four bathrooms, this place now feels like a mansion. A scary, barebones, possibly mold-ridden mansion. But with a wrap-around porch, a formal parlor and giant custom pocket doors, I can look past the rough exterior and see the charm Rafael and Joaquín saw in this place.

We came here today so he could do some yard work. He grumbled when I told him I would help, so I had to remind him he literally chased me in the woods a few weeks ago and that I could handle a little lawn maintenance. After an hour pulling weeds in the blistering sun though, he sent me inside to rest and hydrate, but not before I could daydream wild scenarios between the two of us.

Like when he used the flat head shovel to pry up some old brick pavers.

[1] *I imagine he was lifting hay to feed the livestock outside our humble barn. Our, meaning my husband's. Because in this fantasy, I'm a married woman, standing on the porch of my Texas ranch in 1970 wearing a dress that screams I don't do manual labor, watching our farm hand work up a sweat. Watching the muscles of his strong back move under his shirt as he lifts another pile of hay. Watching the sweat pour from under his cowboy hat and soak through his button up.*

"It's awfully hot out here today," I'd drawl in my best southern belle accent. After, he'd throw his hay, look over his shoulder and I'd saunter toward the fence line with a single glass of lemonade, the condensation beading like his tanned skin.

"It is, ma'am," he'd say, tipping his hat and turning on his heel to face me as I walked through the gate.

"Would you like a little refreshment?" I'd smile, arching a single eyebrow.

He'd swallow thickly, his eyes going from the glass in my steady hand straight to my lips. "Don't your husband mind you talkin' to me?"

Fuck, he sounds good with a southern accent.

"He's not here right now... he's gone to town all day," I'd say, unbuttoning the neckline of my dress and dragging the cool glass across my chest. "And I've been stuck inside. Lonely."

He'd prop the pitchfork against the barn wall. "Well then, seems it'd only be gentlemanly of me to keep you company, ma'am." Then he'd slowly step forward, closing the distance

---

1. *Alone at the Ranch* by BRELAND

between us as my thighs clench, until he's only a couple inches away, and the shadow of his hat would cast over my face.

"Would you like some lemonade, Rafael?" I'd whisper, biting my lower lip, looking up at him and inhaling his musky working man scent.

"I'd like you to take a drink first, ma'am." When I do, my eyes stay trained on his deep brown gaze. Pulling the rim away from my mouth, I try to lick the drip of tart sweetness away from the corners of my mouth, but he stops me dead in my tracks, his hand caressing the side of my face and his thumb brushing the bottom of my lip, while the other pulls in my waist. "Allow me, ma'am."

And right there in the open, he'd kiss me. He'd taste me—lick every last drop of juice from my tongue as I melted in his strong arms. Then he'd carry me back to the porch, and when he'd kick the door open, he'd murmur against my lips, "I worked hard today, ma'am. I'm gon' need more refreshment than that."

And that's why when real-life Rafael forced me to go inside and take a break, I listened. Being hot from working is one thing, but being literally hot and bothered by him is another.

I need to stop reading cowboy romance. This is getting dangerous.

When he came back in an hour later, looking like he just played a full rugby match—he was even wearing those short rugby shorts that show off all his thick, defined legs. He sat down next to me on the one piece of furniture in this place—an antique couch that should be thrown to the curb. After taking one long swig of my giant thermos of ice water, he saw I was creating a baby registry, and all thoughts of yard work flew out the window.

He's been sitting next to me ever since, oblivious to my hormone-fueled daydream, adding impractical things and researching the hell out of the practical things.

It's been weird in the most normal way possible: after our Catskills camping trip, after finding out that Rafael actually wanted to kiss me all those years ago—that he in fact did not reject me because I'm fat—my brain chemistry changed. I believed a lie that I fabricated, and I'm embarrassed to admit that I took that hurt with me for many years. I let it seep into my self-esteem. It wasn't until much later that I finally forgave him for what he unknowingly did to me. Forgave him in the sense that I never spoke a word about it to him, but I released that negative energy from my being and built my confidence from there.

Whatever possessed me that night next to the creek to demand he tell me what really happened, I'm grateful for. Because now I'm sitting next to my best friend, picking out car seats and onesies, and I know as soon as we get home, he'll be on his knees with his face buried between my legs, relieving the ache that's already formed from watching him do manual labor in tiny shorts.

That's if I ask him. Since we got back from our camping trip, I haven't been totally forthcoming about my needs. We've only been together two times since then because I've been afraid of wearing him out—of letting him see how much and how often I need the relief. It's borderline embarrassing if I'm being honest. It's shocking to see my sexual appetite increase so dramatically. He's been nothing but willing and eager when I approach him at home, but there's something holding me back from showing him the whole truth.

Even with this drastic shift in our friendship, it hasn't seemed drastic at all. That's the best fucking part. Sure, we're experimenting with our kinks and that's thrilling to say the least, but the fact that we added this whole new sexual layer to our relationship is simultaneously mind-blowing and right.

And maybe that's what scares me.

"What's impractical about a tiny rugby jersey, shorts and socks?" he asks, settling his head on my lap as he continues to scroll, one long leg splayed over the sofa's edge and the other planted on the chipped tile floor.

"Considering my due date is December 28th, I don't think we need to worry about a proper rugby kit until the summer."

"Fine," he mumbles. "But I'm adding this USA Valor onesie."

Humming a small laugh, I look down at him. "Maybe Robyn can sign it next time we see her," I say, referring to our friend who plays for the highest level of rugby one can in the United States and our Olympic team.

"I love watching her play on TV. She's a beast," he smiles, then looks up at me from his phone. "You know I brag all the time that I know her?"

"So do I! Have you seen her on social media?" I ask. "She's all about body acceptance and giving the haters a solid middle finger."

"I know. She's a fucking badass."

"Whatever happened with her and Isaiah? They were such good friends once upon a time."

"I was hoping you knew," he frowns.

When my phone starts buzzing with an incoming call from Dane, I say, "Maybe he knows," before swiping to answer. "Hey, little brother."

"Angie-Pangie, what's going on?"

"Sitting here with Raf in his decrepit fixer-upper." When he pokes me in the side, I smile, but slap his hand away. "You?"

"Driving to Dad's house to help him with the sump pump."

"He can't fix it himself?"

"Of course he can," Dane huffs smugly, before his tone turns sober. "I think he's lonely now that everyone is out of the house."

"Yeah," I sigh. "We should probably make sure to invite him to more stuff."

"Yeah," he drawls.

"So why'd you call?"

"Oh yeah," Dane says. "Jonah is being a little brat. He's always ten to fifteen minutes late to sevens practice if he shows up at all. And when he is there, he's half-assing it. I'm the fucking captain of our team now, and he's making me look like I can't lead." My eyes draw to Raf's where his lips thin and he nods in confirmation. "He was never like this when Isaiah was captain."

"I'm sorry, Dane. That sucks. Do you have a plan?" I ask, hoping he doesn't involve me. But alas, a person can only change so much.

"Can you talk to him, Ang?"

Rafael shifts to get a better look at me, watching me silently sigh. He knows how hard I've been trying to set boundaries with my siblings. I've been their default mother for most of their lives, and I've been trying to back off. Trying to let them be more self-sufficient so I can stop being their emotional support—their fixer.

"Dane," I say calmly. "If you think you're capable of being captain, then you're capable of handling this. You don't need your big sister cleaning up for you."

"But he'll listen to you," he whines.

"Figure out a way to make him listen to you. Or else he never will and you're going to be going through this again and again with him."

He groans loud enough to make me turn my speaker volume down. "Fine," he mutters.

When a new call pops up, it's the devil himself. "Hey, Jonah is calling me right now. Hang on, I'll be right back."

When I do, my baby brother's cheery voice fills the room. "Hey, sis! Do you wanna go to the shore tomorrow?"

"Hey," I smile, fighting the urge to fix my brothers' issue immediately. "Yeah, I don't have plans." I look down at my best friend still laying in my lap. "Raf, you coming?"

"Count me in," he smiles.

"Yes!"

"Hey," I say with trepidation. "Have you talked to Dane lately?"

"Ugh. Yeah, he's being a dick. Can you tell him to stop being such a jerk at practice?"

Pinching the bridge of my nose, I sigh. "No. You need to talk to him yourself."

"Fine, whatever," he says as if Dane being mad at him isn't affecting him. "Hey, do you have a spare TV I can have?"

That has me chuckling. "No, Jonah. Who just has a spare TV laying around?"

"I don't know. You just moved, I thought maybe you had enough TVs at Raf's place."

I roll my eyes. "I keep my TV in my room. Nice try. What happened to yours?"

"Um..." he drawls, panic evident in his tone.

"Jonah," I say through a tight smile. "What happened to your TV?"

"My dog knocked it over."

"When did you get a dog?" I exclaim. He's nowhere near responsible enough to own a dog—and this is why!

"Um, last week...when I got two from the shelter."

Rafael jerks upright and spins to face me, his knee bent across the cushion, as if to gain more leverage to understand the situation. "You what? You got two?" I scream.

"They needed me!"

"Jonah, oh my god. You just barely graduated college, are subletting an apartment with three roommates, and whatever happened to the dog you adopted in college?"

"Paris and I broke up! She took the dog, you know that."

Yeah. I do. And I warned him then that he shouldn't get a dog with a girlfriend he's only been with for two months—especially while living at college.

"Jonah," I sigh.

"You can meet them tomorrow! I'll bring them to the beach with us. Hey, I gotta go, see you tomorrow!"

"Jonah, youcantbringdogstotheshore—" I try to scramble out before he hangs up. Raf's laugh shakes the sofa as he leans his shoulder against it. When I see my call with Dane has been disconnected as well, I toss my phone on the cushion, throw my head back and let out some cross between a sigh and a scream.

"I'm sorry," Rafael chuckles. "I don't mean to laugh. But you're doing great, Angel. Really. As difficult as it may be, you're setting those boundaries. And Jonah will get there. He's gonna man up some day. You can only do so much to help that kid."

"He's gonna give me gray hairs before this baby ever will."

"Oh shit, that reminds me," Raf smiles, leaning his tall frame down to show me the top of his head where he's parting his dark hair. "I found these the other day."

"Gasp!" I hiss, clamoring to push his hands out of the way and see for myself. "Oh my gosh, there are so many white hairs! One, two, three, four—"

"Alright, that's enough," he chastises me and sits upright again. "No need to count them all. That stays between you and me."

"Until everyone else can see them," I smirk, inclining my head in search of more.

"Leave me alone!" He slaps my hand away and jumps off the couch, running to the creaky door and letting it slam shut.

With a smile, I pick up my phone to see a text from my sister.

Ivy: why are Jonah and Dane texting me about rugby? i'm kind of busy delivering babies in another country. can u fix this? luv youuuuu

Chapter 15

August 1st

Angie

"Raf, wake up," I squeal, barging into his bedroom as the sun barely illuminates the space. "It's here!"

"Huh?" he says semi-unconsciously.

"My bump is here," I exclaim, shoving my legs against the side of his bed and pushing my stomach out even more so he can get the full effect as I lift my pajama top up. Snatching one of his hands, I place it on my belly. "See! It's definitely bigger. And I haven't eaten anything yet, so it's not a food baby—it's a *real* baby!" I may have woken up stupid-horny, but when I saw my full body reflection in the mirror this morning, I forgot all about the ache.

I'm twenty weeks along and I've been growing frustrated at the lack of evidence. According to all the sites, most pregnant people show starting around sixteen weeks. But not me! I want strangers to see my belly and ask me when I'm due just so I can act shocked and tell them, "I'm not pregnant."

There's a sick satisfaction I would get from it.

Yes, something is wrong with me.

"That's great, Ang," Rafael smiles as he rubs the sleep from his eyes and sits up to get a better hold on me. "Oh yeah. It's definitely here. Just in time for today."

Biting my lower lip and unable to contain my excitement, I shimmy back and forth, widening my stance, then thrust my hips, grunting like an animal. Rafael falls back against his headboard, holding his sides as he laughs that rich baritone that makes everything inside me better. I love his laugh, and I don't care if it's *with* me or *at* me; I just want to hear him be happy and know that I made that happen.

When his alarm goes off, I tap his screen to stop it. "Okay, let's get ready," I cheer. "I'll make breakfast today," I say, already moving back to his bedroom door. "T-minus sixty minutes before we have to leave for the ultrasound!"

As I leave his space, his chuckle lingers inside me as I head to the kitchen with a pep in my step.

··········

Encouraged by my new visible baby bump, I threw on a form-fitting daffodil maternity dress before heading to my new obstetrician's office with Rafael. Apparently my old OB/GYN retired last month, so I'm getting assigned a new doctor today in addition to my twenty-week ultrasound.

Looking dapper in his light grayish-blue slacks and tucked-in crisp white shirt, Raf signs me in at the front desk as I hand over my insurance info to the receptionist. His big wristwatch glints under the fluorescent lights, momentarily mesmerizing me. We're both headed to work after this, but I can't help my wandering mind from thinking about playing hooky and strolling about the city looking as good as we do right now. Even though we have different clothes and different bodies, we somehow feel like a matching set.

Mentally slapping myself, I refrain from any more ridiculous couple imagery.

Stop leaning in.

"Angela?" A woman's voice calls my name as she opens the door that heads back to the patient rooms.

"Right here," I say as Raf stands with me, placing a hand at my back as we walk with her.

"You're here for your twenty-week ultrasound, correct?"

"Yes," I smile as she leads us into a dark room with low lighting and a few monitors on the wall.

"And are you the father?" she asks Raf.

"I am," he grins.

"Perfect. Have a seat and lay back, mom. I'll give you this blanket to cover up your legs if you'd like. Will you please lift your dress so I can access your belly?"

A prick of nervousness zaps through me as I lay down. I'm not sure why. Maybe it's just the excitement of it all culminating as little tingles inside my body.

The ultrasound tech taps away at her computer as Rafael helps me get situated. Taking his own seat, he scooches the chair as close as he can to me and holds my hand with both of his. When I look at him, he brings my hand to his mouth and kisses my fingers with the biggest smile I've ever seen.

It's a genuine but nervous smile and a matching one to mine.

The tech squirts the cool jelly on my beautiful belly and begins telling me how she's going to take a lot of measurements first, then review everything with me in a few minutes.

I don't like this part at all. Because even though I am watching exactly what she's doing on the screen in front of me, I have no idea what she's seeing. But when Rafael squeezes my hand, he centers me back to him.

"I was thinking Lance for a boy," he says quietly, causing me to jerk my attention fully to him.

"Absolutely not," I frown. "Have you forgotten about that terrible date I went on with that douche-canoe? He literally lived on a boat."

"Oh yeah," he smirks. I *think he does remember.* "What about Parsley for a girl? We could spell it P-A-R-S-L-E-I-G-H."

My giggle turns into a low chuckle that turns in a belly laugh that I'm trying to keep quiet. Wiping the tears from the corners of my eyes, I muster out, "Yes, of course. Love it."

"Or maybe for a gender-neutral name, we could go with Zillow," he says, like it's the best idea he's ever had.

Full-on snorting and struggling to breathe, I finally get out, "Like the website? Why not go even further with Apartments.com?"

He takes my hand and wipes his own laughter from his eyes. "They could have...two middle names," he wheezes. "Dot and Com."

"Alright, guys," the ultrasound tech gently interrupts our giggle fit. "Excellent names. You're going to have a hard time choosing amongst them, I can tell. Are you ready?"

"Yes. Please," I say, trying to catch my breath. "But we don't want to know the sex."

"No problem," she smiles, modifying something on her screen at the request. "Have you felt any kicks yet?"

I groan. "No."

"That's okay, and totally normal at this point either way. The good news is they are lively. Can you see the hearts beating? See that movement right there? And there?" My breath catches in my chest watching our baby squirm about. There's a lot of movement all over the image. "Oh my, they are hard to catch," the tech smiles, chasing the baby with the ultrasound wand.

When I peek at Raf, he's tearing up but it's not from residual laughter. Choking back a little sob, he watches me like I'm the most incredible thing he's ever seen. He leans over to plant a lingering kiss to my forehead and murmurs, "Look at what you're doing, Angel. ¡Dios mío! Gracias."

I'm grateful I'm already crying a little because him thanking me for carrying this baby pulls at my heartstrings harder than I've ever experienced. This man is one of the most special people in my life and he's given me this unexpected gift—the most amazing, life-changing gift.

"Everything looks really good, and all their measure-ments are right where they should be," the tech says, tapping her keyboard several more times. "The good news is both heart beats are strong. And your blood pressure is right where it should be too."

Wiped away is every previous thought and emotion I was holding. "Excuse me, what?"

"Yeah," she smiles. "Your blood pressure is one-ten over sixty-eight and the babies each have a heart rate of a hundred and fifty beats per minute."

"Each?!" I screech and Rafael shoots out of his chair.

"Yeah," the ultrasound tech drawls, furrowing her brow. "You're having twins. You didn't know that?"

"No!" I cry.

Her eyes widen. "They didn't catch that at your twelve-week ultrasound?"

"I just found out I was pregnant *at* twelve weeks!" My heart is pounding like a jackhammer and my whole body is paralyzed. I can sense Rafael pacing next to me in the small dimly-lit room.

This can't be right. This is a mistake. What is with all these medical professionals giving me shocking infor-mation recently? Are they conspiring against me? Is this all some elaborate prank? I *still* think they've all mixed up the charts. There's no way. You know, I'm not entirely sure I'm actually pregnant now that I think about it.

The tech looks at a folder on her station. "Looks like you had Dr. Clarkston," she sighs, making me no less at ease. "She just retired. I'm wondering if this slipped through the cracks."

"Ya think?" Raf huffs his indignation.

"Well, we're here now," she soothes, clearly trying to calm us down. "And you are carrying two babies. You're still measuring at twenty weeks along, and everything looks just as it should be." My eyes bug out. "With twins," she adds quickly.

"We're having two babies," Rafael whispers to himself with his hands on his hips, unblinking.

The technician finishes up by showing us each image and measurement, printing out the pictures for us to take, then leaves us in the sterile room to collect ourselves privately. When the door gently closes, I sit up, adjusting the skirt of my dress into place and stare at the man before me.

"I'm dreaming, right?" I ask. "Did what I *think* happened, just happen?"

Rafael must be further along in the acceptance process because he crouches before me and wraps his arms around my middle, pressing his face into my belly. "Yes. We have two babies, Angel. You're carrying twins."

Letting out some version of a sigh or whisper, I try to say the word. "Two," but I'm speechless and still too dazed to move any more than I already have.

Rafael then looks up, and noticing my blank expression, he stands to his full six-four height. He pries my legs apart and stands between them, then takes my hands and has me wrap them around his middle. Holding my head tight to him, his stomach rises and falls in a slow cadence, and I close my eyes, inhaling his cologne.

Bergamot.

Lemon.

Cedarwood.

Between his inviting scent and the warmth of his body, my focus shifts back to reality, and I smile. "We're having twins."

···•••••··

Rafael

Angie and I took the rest of the morning off to collect ourselves before going into work, but not before she called an emergency lunch for us and Cora where all three of us proceeded to scream like banshees. Thankfully we had grabbed some takeout sandwiches and were sitting at a park for this, so we only disturbed a few nearby walkers.

Every second since finding out we are having twins has felt like I'm in an alternate universe. Simply walking between meetings and interacting with colleagues has been like some bizarre, suspended reality. All I want to do is tell everyone. Have them share the hand-trembling excitement and surprise that I'm going through. Have them celebrate with me. Have them talk endlessly about what it's like to be a parent and the earth-shattering life change that I've been bestowed. But the best part of this is—I'm doing it with Angie. I'm doing this with the best fucking person I know.

The sweetest.

The funniest.

The smartest.

If it weren't for her, I have no idea how I would be handling this. Truth be told, I never put much thought into having kids because I planned on being a bachelor my whole life. But now that I'm here, becoming a parent with my best friend, of course we can do this. Just like everything else we've ever accomplished together, everything we've gone through, everything we've struggled with—there's no one I'd like to struggle with more than her. There's no one I'd rather celebrate with more than her.

She's my soft spot and my rock.

And she just texted me.

Angie: I just doubled everything on the registry <woozy face emoji> <upside-down face emoji> <face holding back tears emoji>

Rafael: Aww. Good idea. How many times have you cried since you got to work?

Angie: Only three times. You?

Rafael: I'm a MAN Ang. I don't—two. I've cried twice.

Angie: LMAO

Rafael: I'm leaving work now, so I'll see you at home in a little bit. Are you still on your veggie taco kick?

Angie: Yes! But the hot salsa we like must have been a bad batch or something bc I can't taste the heat at all! I'm gonna buy another one on my way home.

Rafael: Really? I didn't think so. But ok. I'll see you soon.

Rafael: Please remember to use your GPS so you don't forget where you're going again.

Angie: <Salute emoji> <grimacing face emoji>

When I get home, I start sautéing the cauliflower and chickpeas—it's a far cry from the street tacos I've grown up with, but if Angie can't stomach meat, then I won't subject her to being around it. While that's simmering on the stove,

I quickly head to my room to change into comfortable gray lounge pants and a black T-shirt. My rugby kit is already packed for this weekend's tournament in Saranac, New York, so I grab the duffle and head back downstairs to the main floor. Right before I hit the last step, Angie walks through the front door with a paper grocery bag and a smile that quickly fades when she sees me.

"Where are you going?" she asks, closing the door with her shoulder as I set my bag on the floor next to her and take the groceries from her.

"The Can-Am tournament in Saranac is this weekend, remember? I'm leaving bright and early," I say warily, but my gut sinks when she doesn't look like that's the reason she's worried.

"What?" she bellows. "You can't leave me like this. I just found out I'm having two babies at once. All I'm going to do is panic and masturbate all weekend."

The image of Angie getting off in her bed over and over is both arousing and painful to think about. She said she would come to me for relief, and I promised I would take care of her. I have to make this work because if I don't, she might find someone else to ease her ache. We may have promised this was open, but I'm going to try my damnedest to make sure she doesn't need someone else.

"What I told you when we were camping wasn't an empty promise," I say confidently. "I told you I'd take care of your needs, right?" She nods. "Well, pack a bag because you're coming with me."

"Really?" she perks up as I walk to the back of the townhouse and set the grocery bag on the counter.

Pulling my phone from my pocket, I press Dane's contact and hold it to my ear. "Of course, Angel. You're coming with me in more ways than one," I level a seductive stare at her. "Hey, Dane. Your sister is coming in Saranac—I mean to.

She's coming to Saranac. Any chance you could room with someone else so she can stay with me?"

"Ang is going? Sweet," he says on the other line. "Yeah, I'm sure I can share a room with someone else on the team. Don't worry about it." He knows there are no hotel rooms available anywhere near that tiny town six months in advance of this weekend. And I love that her brothers are so used to us platonically being together that they don't even question why we would sleep in the same room. Sure, they know I got her pregnant, but to them and everyone else, it was a one-time thing.

"Thanks. I'll see you tomorrow." When the line cuts, I set the phone on the counter and turn to stir the taco filling as Ang stares at me with a grin. "I take my responsibilities seriously, Angel. Don't forget it."

Chapter 16

August 2nd

Angie

W hen Rafael said he was leaving bright and early, he actually meant dark and late—4:30 am to be exact. This isn't like the short two-hour drive to NYC from Philly. This is damn near six hours to Saranac, located in upstate New York at Lake Placid. He was sweet enough to pack the whole car for us and guide my sleepy ass to the passenger seat with a blanket and pillow.

I also caught him having an adorable man-to-man chat with Razzle before we left, too. "Any intruder is fair game, amigo. I'll bail you out of jail and get you a good lawyer."

Boys.

The Can-Am tournament is one of the only east coast rugby events I've never attended with Rafael nor my brothers, but I've always heard them speak of it like it's Christmas or something. Raf explained in the car that this tournament serves as the unofficial kick-off to the fifteens season—meaning that's when summer sevens rugby ends, and full rugby games take over with fifteen players against fifteen for eighty-minute games. Why anyone would agree to play multiple games in a day is beyond me, let alone all weekend. Thankfully for the teams, they only play twenty-five minute halves for this tournament.

But Christmas it is not. Based on the way Raf and the rest of his team are interacting with the hundreds of players here, I'd say it's more like a family reunion. Endless hugs, bantering and back-slapping pepper every moment between games. The rugby community is tight like that—whether you played against them once or played with them for years, everyone seems to remember each other. Or at the very least, they have a very specific memory tied to every player.

Or a spectator, like me. I know the Philadelphia Men's Rugby Team like a family—mostly because three of them are by blood—but even the guys who have been playing for only a season know me by now. So do their wives, girlfriends, and partners.

Rafael might be taking the field right now, but I'm fielding endless questions thanks to my new baby bump that I can't stop touching.

"Angie," I hear a familiar voice bellow before I'm wrapped up in a hug from my friend Robyn. She's wearing a clean uniform of a team I don't recognize.

"Hey," I sing, hugging my lean friend back and then releasing her. "Is this the new USA Valor kit?" I ask, gesturing to her black and yellow jersey.

"Oh no," she smiles. "The Valor aren't playing here. I'm just whoring for another team today."

"Lucky them," I say, knowing any team that gets Robyn is getting one of the best rugby players in the country. They're getting an Olympian.

Rafael and I met her in college. She's a couple years younger than us, but the men's and women's rugby team at Penn Valley University are a tight bunch, so in her freshman year we got to know her well.

"Is it true?" she asks, pointing to my belly timidly.

I chuckle, "Yeah."

"Oh my gosh. Congratulations! Does that mean you and Raf are together now?" She's not the first person to ask me this today. It's the most common question, but it's also the most painful. It's a simple question that I'm capable of shrugging off with a smile.

"No, just two best friends, co-parenting." It's the truth, but it stings like a lie.

The smile she gives me is genuine, but there's a hint of disappointment underneath. "Well, if anyone can do this, it's you two. You guys make a great team."

"Thanks. That means a lot." My eyes catch on the pitch in front of me for a second and I see Isaiah crouched in the middle of a scrum.

She must see the same thing I do because she asks, "How's his knee?"

"Not fully healed," I mutter, annoyance bubbling up at my stubborn brother. "Same with his neck."

"He's gonna get irreversibly hurt one of these days," she sighs.

"He asks for my opinion on everything, but when it comes to me telling him to get physical therapy, he ignores me."

Robyn folds her arms as we watch the ball fly from our scrum half's hands to the back line. "At least he talks to you," she says with a shake to her head.

"What happened between you guys?" I ask, remembering the brief time when they were friends, when Raf and I introduced them.

"Good question. I wish I knew."

When Robyn leaves to join her team, my focus turns back to Raf. I watch him charge forward with the ball cradled against his forearm after a kickoff, juking the other team's players trying to tackle him and I'm overcome with pride and desire.

He's as close to being mine as he'll ever be, and I know I have to make every second with him count. This arrangement between us will only last until December. At some point, someday far in the future when I can emerge from my new mama cocoon, I'll have to try even harder to find the right man to be my husband. To be my life partner. Someone who will want that same obsessive, loving commitment to me as I have to him. Someone who will be equally committed to my babies.

An ache tightens in my chest at the thought of someone else—someone new—being that for us.

Just enjoy this time you have now, I tell myself. Enjoy him. Enjoy the view.

Enjoy the view I shall.

At the tail end of the scrum, Rafael's long, muscular body attaches to his second row players, his head squeezing between their hips; his hamstrings and calves contracting with every inch they gain as a unit. They're less than five meters from the try line when Raf unlocks his head from the scrum and my heart races. I've been watching him play for over a decade and it never ceases to thrill me when he performs this play. In a flash, Rafael makes for an eight-man pick by snatching the ball from the ground just below his chest and sprinting for the try line with Jonah (his number seven flanker) trailing him as support, and helping push him into the end zone through a wall of opposing players.

Apparently my feet have their own agenda, because I'm being carried by them to get the best view from the sidelines, cheering like the super fan I am, shouting like I'm playing in the game myself, as Raf dives for any available real estate he can touch. Several opposing players try to force their limbs under the ball, but it's no luck when the sir blows his whistle and throws his arm straight in the air.

"Yeeees, Jimmy!" I holler his nickname, jumping up and down and throwing a wild cheering fist into the summer breeze. "That's what I'm talking about! That's my babies' daddy right there!" I didn't mean for that last part to slip out, and even though I'm embarrassed I shouted it, I wouldn't take it back.

When Isaiah extends his hand to pull Rafael from the rubble of men, both my brother and my best friend are laughing at me. Philly takes their place behind the goal posts as they gulp down water and hit Raf on the back for a great try. I can't hear what they're saying, but from the way everyone keeps looking over at me and the way Raf smiles and ducks his head, they must be both praising him and giving him shit.

But then his eyes lock on mine and the world falls quiet. Words so powerful and so real threaten to escape. Terrible, awful, beautiful words—poisonous and perfect—and I can't look away. Can't move. Can't stop my heart from racing.

It's only when his teammates start jogging back to midfield to take their positions, does he break the spell—but it's only the spell that connected us in that moment. Because while he's focusing on winning this barbaric sport, I'm focusing on how beautiful he is when he's great at something. How turned on I can get by his stride, his precision, the way he supports his team. The way he communicates to them with a pointed finger at the end of an outstretched arm. The way he handles an impending tackle, throwing his shoulder into their abdomen and wrapping them up at the waist, dragging them into the dirt, only to get back up a split second later and do it all again.

It's the physical toll he takes willingly that makes me want to ride him—that makes me want to breed with him.

Fuck me, I'd do this all again if I had a choice. I'd do it all again with this man who can think on his feet and protect his people like they're an extension of himself.

Damn hormones.

And damn my pussy for being so connected to my heart. It's like my cunt has feelings.

My logical, educated, therapist brain pipes up reminding me having affectionate feelings for a sexual partner is totally normal and, in most cases, a healthy thing. But here I am, with friendly affection-turned-romantic attraction to my best friend. Alright, so maybe this has been simmering for a long time, but thanks to these babies inside me, that attraction has grown uncontrollable.

Undeniable.

I love him.

Shit.

I've been hiding that very thought in the darkest parts of me for so long—that to finally let myself accept it feels dangerous.

We fundamentally want different relationship structures. For the life of me, I've never understood why Raf wants to be unattached. He can't possibly be taking after his father on purpose, can he?

He's never given me a real answer about it. For someone who tells me everything, who sends me songs that express his mood or that jog a memory, who lays his head in my lap and treats me like a partner more than anyone—he won't tell me why he doesn't want the real thing.

Rafael Jimenez comes from love—mothers who have shown nothing but a strong committed relationship to themselves and to him. A brother who loves and trusts him unconditionally. A best friend who has let him be his true unguarded, goofy self. He's not some alpha-hole wannabe who listens to a podcast of idiots talking about finding some fit, high-value, virgin bride. He's Raf—the silliest, dancing rugby nerd with a heart of gold and a laugh so big and bright the sun is jealous. The man no single trope or characteristic can contain. The man who explores, who finds new interests and keeps polishing the old ones.

Maybe that's it.

Maybe there's too many interesting people out there that he can't settle on only one; and I'm the old friend, the original interest that he keeps close to his chest, polished and special. The one he's so clearly proud of, just not confident enough to commit to.

The only reason I feel a mild satisfaction instead of anguish at that thought is because I know Rafael, and he doesn't let go of the things or people he loves. So I will hold on to that reality, I'll let it steady me, and someday, I'll meet someone else or he'll say something stupid that will turn off the spigot of my unrequited love. It's been more than a decade of waiting for either of those things to happen, but I am nothing if not patient.

By the end of the first half, some players are subbed out for fresh legs as an unexpected storm cloud looms closer, causing the temperature outside to cool slightly—but the fire inside me burns hotter as he tackles player after player, and with each pointed pass. With only fifteen minutes left in the match, the dark clouds above us finally open and dowse everything in sight. But ruggers and fans alike are never fair-weather. We either came prepared with ponchos and umbrellas, or we didn't—either way, no one is taking shelter.

The rain permeates my teal maternity T-shirt and baseball hat which match the team's colors. It's all the coverage I need for spectating. For fan-girling. For yelling at the sir for a bullshit call and not seeing the high tackle the other team's inside center just got away with.

The match has already gone over time, but with the remaining drive to finish the play, Isaiah makes a rare prop move, and scores the final try with Raf's assist and the sir blows that victorious whistle.

Philadelphia—27

Toronto—25

It isn't until I stop jumping and screaming, waiting for the teams to shake hands and walk off the field wearing mud like war paint, that I feel the unmistakable sensation of a little kick coming from inside me—two.

Two little sets of feet cheering for their daddy too. *Ese es tu papi.*

"Are you okay?" Rafael asks through exerted breath, surprising me as he comes to stand in front of me. "What's wrong?" He places his hands on my belly, just as I am.

"Do you feel it? They're kicking!" I squeal. "They're kicking!"

Gasping, his eyes light up when he feels the little knock against his palm. "Yup. We definitely have a couple rugby players in there," he smiles. But when his eyes travel from my belly to my eyes, I'm locked in his spell once again—transfixed by how the rain drips off the ends of his messy hair and his long dark eyelashes hold back the trailing moisture. By his full lips, parted slightly in a sexy grin that could make anyone mad with desire. By the way his disgusting and muddy jersey clings to his chest.

His brows furrow. "Are you sure you're okay?"

"I'm not okay," I swallow, then clench my thighs together. "I need you."

That sexy grin turns into a smile you'd see on an orthodontic advertisement. "Yeah? Did you enjoy the game?"

"Too much."

Releasing my stomach, he jogs over to his team to grab his soaking-wet kit and sprints back to me, grabbing my hand and making me run alongside him. "Let's go, Angel!"

"Don't you have another game?" I giggle.

"Not until tomorrow."

"What about the social?"

"We'll go later. Also, who the fuck cares about the social? You have needs!"

Chapter 17

August 2nd

Angie

I wish I could say we ran through the lobby like a pair of wanton lovers, like nothing could distract us, but unfortunately this entire town is filled with ruggers Raf and I have known for years. Exchanging pleasantries as fast as possible was its own game. Dodging around corners and shouting back to old friends that we'll see them at the bar later—yeah right. This man won't be able to walk, let alone speak, when I'm done with him.

Even the goddamn elevator was crowded—the sexiest place to makeout in all romance books and media, and we're stuck with three other people all headed to the fourth floor with us. And could it be any slower? Fuck. I have no idea what these Boston accent buffoons are saying in front of us, because the only sense I have is feeling the radiating heat from Rafael's chest against my back. He's leaning against the wall of the elevator and I'm only inches away. Thankfully, these other men don't know us, and Raf must pick up on the fact that they're not paying attention. A single soft fingertip runs up the back of my bare thigh and my breath hitches. It's searching under the hem of my rain-soaked maternity shorts and finds the natural crease of my ass. My entire body lights up like a live wire and I'm hyper-alert to every miniscule sensation. His finger teases along the curve, and when he gets closer to my center, he pushes that finger into my panties and gently strokes me.

He's barely grazing my seam, but it's the secret naughtiness that's edging me further into this delicious moment.

If these doors don't open in the next ten seconds, I'm mounting him right here in front of these strangers.

Trying exhibitionism must not be in the cards tonight because the chrome elevator doors part and the Boston ruggers file out. They head in the opposite direction we do, and when we notice no one else occupies our hall, he guides me with his hands tight on my hips. When we're mere feet away from our door, I pull out the key card from my back pocket as he crowds me against the door—his erection noticeable already.

[1] "Hurry," he says on a ragged breath and presses his hips into my backside. The green light signals, and with one push we're inside, quickly shutting the door behind us. In a split second I force myself on him, pressing him into the wall as our mouths crash into each other. Our wet clothes grow warmer against one another as we grind fruitlessly. His hands are in my hair, his tongue down my throat, and his knee between my legs.

Ravenous—we're completely, mindlessly, ravenous for each other.

My fingers dig into the double-layer waistbands of his small black rugby shorts and compression shorts and I don't dare waste any more time. "Get these fucking shorts off, you slut," I demand.

"A slut?" He chuckles, but it's erased when he sees I'm serious and his responding tone switches to obedience. "Yes, ma'am."

He's already taken his socks and cleats off before getting in the car, so when he kicks his sandals off, I squat down

1. I WANNA BE YOUR SLAVE by Måneskin

and peel the wet shorts off him completely. His large, proud cock points directly at my face, but I'm too entranced by his legs—covered in mud, grass, scratches, and bruises. Unable to stop myself, my hands are drawn to slowly skate over them—his coarse hair adding friction to my devotion.

"If you let me shower, I can—"

"No," I interrupt, still fixated on his powerful legs, the defined muscles, the sinew between it all. "I want you like this. Dirty. Ragged."

He huffs a disbelieving breath. "Are you sure?" My domineering stare tells him he needs to finish that question properly. "Are you sure, Ma'am? I smell awful."

When I stand up, taking my time to palm his impressive thighs and ass, I sink my hands under his tight jersey and force him to take it off all the way. "That's kind of the point, Raf," I smile and throw his dark teal jersey on the bathroom floor next to his shorts a few feet away. "I want you like this," I say, then bite my lip, stroking my hands over his abs and chest. It must be the hormones and the way his chest rises and falls that puts me in a trance, because I can't filter my words. I dig my nails into his thick pecs. "You were so hot out there today. I love watching you tackle other men into the ground. You're all so *rough* with each other. It makes me feral."

"Oh yeah?" he drawls, causing me to finally look into his eyes. He moves to lift my shirt, while pushing me toward the two beds. "Tell me more."

Oh, he thinks he's leading this? Fuck that noise.

"Shirt stays on," I bite out, causing him to freeze with only a foot until we're on the bed. My mind replays what his BDSM chart said, and I sift through what I want to use. Reluctantly taking my hands off him, I take the opportunity to tease my aching breasts over my shirt. "If you're a good boy and make me come, I might let you see them."

"What would I have to do to touch them, Ma'am?"

"Don't get greedy. You're mine to use," I smile, not only at my words but the fucking power surge coursing through my body. I didn't know I had this in me. Sure, I've read about femdoms and listened to endless erotic audios that got me off, but I didn't know I could *actually* be this assertive.

"I'm sorry, Ma'am," he pouts. My god, he *pouts*. I've never seen him pout. It's fucking adorable and sexy, and I want to rub my pussy all over that mouth and claim that pout as my own.

Pushing off my denim shorts with a gigantic maternity waistband that stretches clear up to my ribcage, I don't bother feeling embarrassed. He watches me as I kick them to the side along with my panties and sit down on the edge of the bed, the cool white duvet giving way softly under my ass.

"Kneel, slut." Fuck, this submissive name I've given him is sending chills across my body just saying it. He must like it because the excitement in his eyes is undeniable as he sinks to the carpeted floor, and I spread my legs before him. Rafael tries to lean in, but I place two fingers to my seam, dragging my arousal around, playing idly in my short curls, teasing us both. With my other hand planted behind to prop myself up, my head drops back, and I close my eyes, letting my fingers work their magic.

This isn't what I really want, what I really need, but I love making him wait like this. His little whimpers cut through the silence like a knife. "Please, Ma'am? Please, can I touch you? I promise I'll make you feel so good."

"I don't know," I taunt. "I've been thinking about you all day. Maybe the stakes are too high now."

"No, Ma'am. Please—*please* let me take care of you."

Rocking my head back down to look at his pained expression, my teasing loses all merit. "You sound so pretty when you beg. Eat."

"Thank you, Ma'am."

My stomach flips when he dives in with a grunt of satisfaction, his massive hands spreading me wide. "That's it,"
I pant as he licks long, languid stripes through my core,
already causing me to cant my hips into him. "Yes." His
disheveled wet hair begs for me to grab it, and when I do, he
lets out a prideful little grunt. "You like it when I dominate
you?" He nods eagerly, but he doesn't dare take his mouth
from the center of my thighs. "Me too," I smile.

The ache that's been building inside me all day as I
watched his muscular body slam against others begins to
relax; the ache transforms to pleasure at the touch of his
wet tongue against my clit. The drag of his taste buds
against my soft flesh, so tender then so taut. His little
appreciative sounds turn up to moans mixed with a growl
or two that send my stomach tightening—the sensation
traveling north until it's lodged as heat in my chest.

I've never experienced such noisy oral. Noisy in the best
way—in the most arousing way. I've listened to erotic audio,
hoping one day I might be able to have that kind of experience with a partner who can make me feel like eating me
out is a luxury, not a chore, not a necessary step on the way
to penetrative sex. But like they *want* to be here. They *want*
to pleasure me because it brings them pleasure.

And then it hits me all over again: here kneels my best
friend, the man I trust more than any other, giving me
the best, the most eager head I've ever known—and he
looks like he's having the time of his life. He just played
a full eighty minutes of rugby; he should be bone-tired
and needing some aspirin, a beer, and medical attention
honestly. But here he is, eating me like I'm the only thing
that could help him recover from such ferocious exertion.

When Rafael starts incorporating his teeth along with
suction, I'm hurtling toward the finish line sooner than expected. I read somewhere that this heightened sensitivity
has something to do with the increase in blood flow in my

body now that I'm pregnant—it's causing me to be more sensitive down there. But I won't stop him, and I don't warn him. I lean into the free fall from atop my mountain high and allow him to collect his reward.

"Yes, Raf! Yes, that's a good boy. Don't stop," I encourage, already hungry for another release. I desperately want to tell him to use his fingers, but I know they're filthy, and even though I crave him that way, *those* will not be entering my body until they're clean. What he does, however, is place both thumbs on either side of my opening, just outside the pillowy tissue of my sex, and applies pressure while massaging it.

"Oh my god," I whisper, tilting my head down to gaze hungrily at his beautiful naked kneeling form and stroking my fingers through his damp wavy hair. "That feels amazing. Keep doing that. Give me another one. And apologize for turning me on so badly today."

His words are muffled through my tender pussy, but he repeats them again and again as he continues to devour me. I can't see his cock from this angle above him, but I'd wager anything it's hard as a rock right now.

"Use one hand to touch yourself," I command. "Be a good boy and stroke that big, heavy cock for me. But don't you *dare* come." His right hand wastes no time flying down below my line of sight, and when his shoulders relax and his moan reverberates through my cunt, I know he's begun stroking. "That feel good, baby?"

Shit. I didn't mean to say that. *Baby* is too personal a nickname for us. For me. Sure, what we're doing right now is arguably one of the most personal things you can do with someone.

His eyes catch mine with every ounce of thrill showcased like priceless displays in a gallery. "Yes, Ma'am," he smiles, those deep glorious dimples making me forget everything I've ever thought up to now. Nose nuzzling against my clit, he closes his eyes and sighs. "Yes, I can be your baby. Please."

Shit. This vulnerable submission from him is unsteadily potent and heady. Power rockets through my being at his words and touch, his expression.

I want him to be my baby too.

We have rules and a timeframe and boundaries for a reason—but what was that reason again? Right. So that when this is all over, I can step away without hesitation or heartbreak.

But I've always been in love with him, haven't I? It's going to hurt regardless. I'm hoping it won't hurt any more than the constant underlying pain I've put myself through loving him all these years. Ignoring that feeling became a habit. I only hope my heart can handle that reset.

Baby.

Fuck boundaries. Fuck rules.

Chase this feeling, the hormones inside me whisper in a tiny voice. *Him*, they encourage.

"Yes, baby," I cry out with closed eyes, my second orgasm catching me off guard as I lose myself in the imagery of *us*. As Rafael and Angie.

Together at the beach.

Together making dinner.

Together salsa dancing.

Together in bed on a lazy Sunday with kids climbing over us, giggling and bouncing.

"Thank you," Rafael hums, kissing my sex delicately.

My mind and body are floating too high to comprehend reality. Did he just thank *me* for dragging him away from his friends, demanding he make me come, and calling him a slut all while denying him an orgasm?

Yes, he did, the hormones giggle. *Do you think he could call you Mommy next time*, they ask.

Alright, they're fired. Officially out of control.

"What?" I ask, then look down at him, his head leaning against my inner thigh and both hands gliding against my legs until they reach my backside and rest there. "I'm the one who should be thanking you." I move my hand to cup his square jaw and gently push him so he's sitting on the backs of his feet, then lean down and place a slow kiss to his perfect lips. The taste of my cum evident inside and outside his mouth. It coats everything from his expensive smile to the five o'clock shadow that darkens and defines his handsome features.

"The pleasure," he hums against my lips, "was all mine. Can I help relieve you some more?"

"Hmm...tempting. Let me wash you first," I say, keeping the kiss going.

"You wanna shower with me?"

"Not just shower with you, baby. I want to wash you."

He hums again, his smile against my own. "I like when you call me that."

Breaking our affectionate kiss, I slowly stand and hold out my arms for him to do the same. "Is that the subby name you'd prefer I call you?"

When he stands, his erection makes itself known by poking me in the stomach and we make our way to the bathroom. "I..." he hesitates. "Yeah. I love being called your little slut too, though. I like both. I love the mix of degradation and praise."

Opening the expansive door to the walk-in glass shower, I turn the chrome handle and let the water warm up, then promptly take my damp shirt off. Rafael smiles and watches me—like he's been doing it for years instead of a handful of times. I stand next to him in only a white, soft-yet-supportive tank-bra, while he helps me peel out of it, and our bodies immediately gravitate toward each other—our hands slowly searching, learning each other intimately like it's the only thing we'd ever want to be educated in.

"Well then," I murmur, my fingers tracing over his collarbone. "Let me praise you a little more. You were incredible today, baby."

"You're just saying that because you're sex-drunk," he smirks, pushing a lock of hair behind my ear.

The heat of the shower ghosts over my back, so I open the door, guide us both in, and shut the door. "No, I'm serious," I say, nudging him into the hot spray that relaxes his body. "Watching you play rugby is fucking sexy, Raf. You played so well today. You scored that try and an assist. You commanded your teammates. You listened. And your body," I say in awe, pumping body wash into a cloth and gently scrubbing his shoulders, then massaging them. "Your body is like a work of art."

The smile I gave him fades as he relaxes deeper into my touch, and he inhales the steam. He enjoys the moment as I continue to wash him. The soapy bubbles form and fall away in a waterfall down his abused body, marred with both new and old bruises.

When I'm finished washing him, I move on to his hair, asking him to sit down so I can properly scrub and massage his scalp and he grunts in the process. "I couldn't help but envision you as this protective, dominant, rugged man-beast," I say, which in turn makes him chuckle. "I'm sorry if I came on too strong, though."

"No, not at all. Come on stronger if you want. It was refreshing," he says as I start to work the conditioner in. "I've never been dominated by a woman before. It's always been other men if we were playing that dynamic."

A pang of jealousy spikes through my body at his admission. I know better than anyone that he sleeps around, but something extra painful bites at my heart knowing other people have dominated him. In a logical sense—a sense that once mostly controlled my life—I know sleeping with other people is normal and expected outside the confines of a platonic relationship. But my pregnant ass doesn't see it that way. I don't like it one bit.

"Ang, I'm all for the spa treatment, but can you remove your nails from my scalp?" he chuckles, and I leave my mental war. He continues, unaware and happy. "Honestly, I thought you'd be asking me for more action since we started this arrangement."

"Oh," I drawl, not expecting him to say that.

"Don't get me wrong, I've loved what we've done so far but, I don't know. I thought you needed me more."

"Oh," I repeat. The last of his conditioner is rinsed away, so I have him stand and lean him against the white tile wall. I lean into him, my round belly pressing against his flat one. "I actually haven't been very upfront about that."

"What do you mean?"

"I mean, I didn't want to freak you out with just how often I need..." *Say relief. Say orgasms. Say anything but* "You."

"Oh, Angel, none of that now," he says with a sad smile. "I'm serious. Anytime you need me, I'll make myself available." That sad smile transforms into a devilish grin though. "Afterall, it *is* my fault for being so sexy on the field today."

The corners of my mouth curl up at that. "You know, with all that tackling and testosterone flying about, you'd think there'd be more players kissing in a ruck."

His rumbling laugh vibrates through my body. "You'd like that, wouldn't you?" he teases.

"I just watch you guys and I'm like *kiss kiss kiss*. And I could ask you the same thing."

"Oh, I've thought about it before, trust me."

"It's the ultimate rivals to lovers story," I say coyly.

"Speaking of which, what other sexual scenarios do you wanna try courtesy of those spicy books?"

"How do you feel about role playing as a [2] kraken?"

· · · ● ● · ● ● · · ·

Rafael

I stare at her, jaw unhinged and eyes unblinking, but amused, nonetheless. "Never in a million years did I think *those* would be the words that would come out of your mouth."

Biting her lip and looking anything but shy, her hands smooth down my hips and grip my thighs before saying, "Maybe it's the fact that we're in this shower and all wet..." she hisses, the obvious hunger clawing its way back into her body. My cock twitches as she begins to writhe against me—her full breasts sliding against my torso.

"You need me to be your kraken, Angel?"

"Yes please," she breathes heavily.

"What's the scene?"

Without hesitation, she launches into the backstory. "You're a thousand-year-old grumpy kraken who's been exiled from your community and the only way you can come back is if you steal an innocent human—me," she nods, pointing to herself as if that isn't obvious. "And bring her back as a sacrifice. But when you find me, you're so entranced by my beauty and charmed by my sunshiny disposition that you simply cannot sacrifice me, *cannot live* without me," she enunciates in a lower register, really getting lost in her own story. "And so you must choose

---

2. *Super Freak* by Rick James

between your exiled aquatic life or coming to land with me, where I must show you what your life could be like if the sea witch grants you your one wish."

"There's a sea witch?"

Her brow lowers. "Of course there's a sea witch."

"What's the thing I must give in return to the sea witch?"

"I don't know, it's not important."

"Oh, *that's* not important to the story," I tease.

"Shut up."

Removing the smile from my face and widening my stance, I hold her wide hips and study her face. Invested, I ask, "Okay. So we're on land or in the water at this point?"

Her eyes light up again. "We're on land, in my shower because you haven't transformed into a human yet and I have to keep your skin hydrated. Secretly I want you to stay in your kraken form forever," she adds.

"And how many tentacles do I have?"

"Eight."

"Suckers?"

"So many."

I grin. "Okay." True excitement swirls under my skin as I push off the wall and pin her back to the same place I was. I hitch her leg up and her knee interlocks in my elbow as I dive right in. "How could I have sacrificed this perfect little human," I growl, lowering my head into the crook of her neck and licking the water droplets away. She gasps and I challenge myself to bring more of them to her lips. My cock has been begging for relief since we left the field. I grab a firm hold at the base of my shaft, crouching down to line myself up against her pussy, *still slick with the arousal I gave her*, I think smugly, and maybe a little bit possessively.

"Yes," she whines, her small fingers digging into my shoulder muscles and making me want to submit all over again. Which in a sense, I am right now. I may be the dominant one in this scene, but she's given me explicit direction in the form of a wildly imaginative and monstrous setting.

I'm all too happy to indulge her.

My crown teases her warm cunt and it glazes my needy cock—or rather... "You want my tentacle in this sweet little human hole?"

"Yes," she begs, lost to the scene already. Lost in the most beautiful and ethereal way.

My tentacle cock teases her more, just the tip slipping inside her for a second. "You wanna feel my suckers play with your clit, sunshine? You wanna feel them inside you—the suction on that *one* sensitive spot driving you to bliss?"

"Yes, Rafael."

I can't help exit the scene for a quick moment and smile. "Is that my kraken name?"

"Of course it is," she says, still writhing and pushing her hips into mine, trying to get me to go deeper.

"Got it," I say and shift back into my new persona. Taking her earlobe between my teeth, I whisper, "You want this big kraken to please you, little human?"

"Yes!"

I start to push in earnest, luxuriating in every slow inch being welcomed in. Sliding into her is like falling into bed after a long, exhausting day—the comfort of familiar smells and textures, the relief, the safety of *home*.

"Look at you giving yourself to me. Riding my tentacle like a good girl," I groan. "Fuck, you feel so good, baby."

Whoa, that slipped out way too easy. When Angie did earlier, I was so high with lust that I didn't think twice. No one has ever called me that before, and I've never either. I've never been in a relationship where that level of comfort and sweetness existed—a level where loving nicknames like *baby* are said freely and generously. Hearing it come from the lips of my Angel didn't feel strange or wrong though. My body had a visceral reaction to the sound. I wanted to hear it again from her, and clearly, my subconscious wanted to say it back.

God, it sounds good.

It feels good.

She looks down at where I told her to, watching me pump inside her slowly, watching our dark curls kiss with every thrust. With my other hand, I extend my index and middle finger, curling them under and finding her sweet clit waiting for me.

She lets out an adorably sexy whine when I start rubbing it in rhythm with our hips. In fact, it's too damn tempting to ignore that when she makes it again, I have to capture one with my mouth. I have to take every last moan and whimper from her body and keep them like the treasures they are.

Her lips taste so dangerously sweet. What we're doing as friends is far more than I've ever done with sexual partners before. Intimacy like this was never in the cards for me, and now I'm wondering *how* I ever lived my life without it? Does everyone know how great sex can be with someone you actually care about? With someone you want to give more pleasure to than you'd ever want in return? With someone who will make you laugh while you're balls-deep, pretending to be a kraken?

No. I don't think everyone knows, because someone would have told me by now, right? Sex for me has mostly been hot, mutually beneficial, and a little fun. But with Angie it's depraved in the best way; it's hilarious... It's special. It's so fucking different, and I don't know how I'm supposed to go back to what I was doing before.

What was I even doing before?

I certainly wasn't leaving hickies all over people's bodies so they'd have evidence from their kraken lover's suckers later on. But *dios mio*, look at her... covered in large red marks across her chest and shoulders—marks I'm sure will darken in an hour or two. I want to cover her body in them.

I want to strangle her thick thighs with my tentacles like bondage rope and leave even more marks.

I want everyone to know that Angela Zofia Johanssen belongs to *me*. Even if it's temporary.

Shit.

This is temporary, I remind myself, but even I'm not convincing that liar. I want to keep doing this with her. I want to keep playing these games and playing with control. I want to keep this good thing we have—with this perfect person who just so happens to be creating my children and driving me wild with desire at the same time.

"Yes. Harder," she begs, grabbing two handfuls of my ass and squeezing.

A delightful rumble rises from the depths of my chest. "Whatever my little human needs, she gets." Her eyes slam shut as I slam into her with as much force as I can, her head falling forward against my chest. "Do you want to keep me, human?" I ask, not entirely sure if that's me or the kraken speaking. "I may have tried to steal you, but *you* have stolen me...body and soul."

"Oh—*fuck*," she cries out, her pussy clenching at me like a vise. "Yes, I'll keep you!"

I don't have time to unpack that and decipher our words and if they hold more meaning than they should, because all I can see is the try line and getting us both there. It doesn't take much longer for me to follow her. In fact, her climax is still holding on to dear life as liquid sensation coils in the base of my spine and she milks my cock—*tentacle*—for all it has.

"*Unghhh*," I grunt out, my entire body taught. "Good...little...human," I manage to say through otherworldly pleasure.

Letting go of her leg, I allow her foot to return to the shower floor, but then wrap her in my arms and stroke her back. Her head willingly presses into my chest and her soft arms wind around my middle. "That was incredible, Ang. How do you feel?" I murmur into her wet hair as the shower runs over our shoulders.

"Fucking perfect," she says with a squished cheek to my pec.

"Was I a good kraken for you?"

"The best," she sighs.

"Good," I smile. "Maybe next time we can involve our toy collections for a real multi-tentacle experience."

The snort she lets out makes me instantly giggle along with her. "It's a date," she says.

I let her rest against me for a long while, holding her close enough to feel her heart beating and her rhythmic breathing. I wonder if I stay here long enough if I can feel our babies kick against my own stomach.

"Can I wash you too?" I whisper into her brunette crown. With a hum and a nod, she allows me to lather the shampoo and slowly massage it through her shoulder length hair. "So, what have we learned today?" I drawl.

"That your role play game is fire."

"No," I chuckle. "How about: you *will* tell me when you need me. Every time."

She snorts again. "Okay. But I'm warning you, Raf—I wake up horny and borderline angry that there isn't a cock already inside me."

"Well, there's a very simple solution to that, Angel," I smirk, tilting her head to rinse in the spray. "I'll sleep in your bed."

Chapter 18

August 24th

Angie

"What are we getting again?" I ask, taking his hand and stepping out of the Range into the parking lot of Wegmans.

"We're grabbing dessert and salad to bring to moms." He shakes his head. "Did you really forget?"

Shutting the door, he then locks the car and pockets his keys before I roll my eyes. "I didn't forget where we were going. I only forgot what we were getting. That's pretty good for me these days. The pregnancy brain is getting better."

We make our way from the blistering hot pavement inside the heaven that is Wegmans grocery store. It's kind of like Whole Foods. There's a restaurant here with amazing food, a whole beer department where you can sip on a cold one, and then walk through the store to do your shopping.

Like I said, heaven.

And we must be in the clouds because Rafael is looking extra fine tonight. He's wearing a modern, black Hawaiian shirt with a striking pale pink and blue floral pattern. And those fucking short-shorts again. To top that, he's wearing leather deck shoes with no socks like a harlot.

I thought having on-demand sex with Rafael would ease my craving, but no. In fact, I'm having the opposite problem. After he fucks me within an inch of my life nearly every morning, by the end of the workday I'm either rearing to go another several rounds or so exhausted I fall asleep as soon as I walk through our door. And on those pass-the-fuck-out before 5:00 pm nights, I'll wake to a small plate of food on my nightstand. Grapes, a concha Ana made, a dish of trail mix maybe—just something to munch on in case my blood sugar or pressure drops.

And when I wake up, he's always right there—his body warming my bed and my stupid heart. No one is more thrilled than Razzle Dazzle though. Now he gets to choose who he sleeps with each night. He usually starts with laying on my belly until the twins start kicking, then promptly swats at my stomach for disturbing him and transfers locations to cradle in my friend's arms.

But Rafael's not the only one I have my eyes on these days. There's someone else turning me on in a surprising turn of events.

Me.

When I look at myself in the mirror, my bump now prominent, I become the most conceited person ever. I had healthy self-esteem before I was pregnant, but now? Fuck me, I'm gorgeous! My hair, skin, attitude, body, everything is the epitome of perfection. I'm a goddamn siren.

That mentality shift has certainly helped me speak up and tell Rafael when I'm needy. But at the same time, I feel bad that all my thoughts are consumed by the following:

1. How sexy Rafael is and how he'd be crazy not to fuck me every second of every day.

2. Researching *everything* about birth and raising babies.

That's it. That's the whole list. I forget about my family, my job, even Cora. Thankfully, Raf sees both of us on a near-daily basis, so he reminds us to call each other. Which

I should really do again because I haven't been totally honest with her.

Raf grabs a cart as I pull my phone from my purse and press her contact. "Angie babe, how are you?" Cora says after the third ring.

"I'm good. Just at the store with Raf picking up a couple things for dinner tonight at Ana and Christina's." I answer, already forgetting what we're supposed to buy. "We're spending the night, and then seeing my dad in the morning. What are you doing?"

"We had lunch with Jay's parents earlier and now the three of us are getting a mani pedi."

"Ooh, that sounds nice. I'm due for one. What color is Marco getting?"

"Oh, he's getting a full set in highlighter pink, obviously." I can hear him in the background ask what that means and she giggles, but doesn't answer him. "How are you feeling?"

It's the most common question we ask each other since we've become pregnant. Feeling means physically and emotionally in these instances. Both are intrinsically tied to one another and change every day, but the thing that hasn't changed is the thing I've been keeping close to my chest—my sore and sensitive chest.

I meander through the produce section aimlessly while far ahead of me, Raf starts collecting what we need. I clear my throat. "My nausea is totally gone now and has been replaced with outrageous confidence. The babies love to kick me at night when I'm at my most relaxed state, and Rafael and I are fucking like rabbits," I wince, ripping the bandage off. There's such a long pause that I look at my screen to check that the call didn't cut out. "Cora?"

"Did you just say you're sleeping with Raf?" she asks in a serious tone that brokers no other meaning.

"Yeah?"

"Angie! Oh my god, I knew this would happen!" she screeches.

"You did not."

"Yes, I did. Just like how you manifested a sexy three-some for me, I did this for you! You're welcome. You can repay me by naming your children after me."

Thankful that I'm laughing and not cowering, I ask, "Both of them? What if I'm having boys?"

"Cora is a gender-neutral name. If you think about it, all names are gender-neutral, Ang. Alright, stop distract-ing me. How long has this been going on?"

My wince comes back. "Since the beginning of July?"

"What?" she hisses. "On the camping trip?"

"Yeah," I confirm, taking four pieces of sample cheese from the display tray and completely losing Rafael in the store.

She lets out a sigh that sounds like she's trying to calm herself down. "You need to tell me right now: is it good?"

I look over my shoulder to make sure no one is nearby before admitting, "It's the best. He's an animal, Cora."

This time her sigh sounds like relief. "Good for you. This is so fucking weird though."

"You said you manifested this!"

"I did, but it's still weird that my best friends are fucking—I'll tell you everything when I get off the phone, Jay," she says a little quieter before coming back at full volume. "How are you feeling about this set-up with him? Is it a romantic thing or a friends with bennies situation?"

"Well," I drawl and contemplate telling the truth. Cora's my girl though, and I'm sick of keeping the truth locked up. I need someone on my side that can keep her mouth shut. Granted, she will tell Jay and Marco, but I trust them too. Taking one more scan for Rafael, I continue. "It's friends with bennies that's only supposed to last until the babies are born, but..." I sigh as my gut drops and palms start to sweat. "I might be in too deep, Cora."

"Has that tiny crush come back?" she asks graciously.

"Yes," I admit. "And it may be a little more than a crush now."

"Oh, Angie," Cora says softly. "It's been like this for a while, hasn't it?"

I've always been upfront with her with everything except this. I've never wanted to admit my feelings for Raf aloud, never wanted to make them real. It's not a healthy thing to do and as a counselor I know this better than anyone; but it's been so easy to ignore until now. I've been able to date and have romantic attachments to other men in the past and maintain my friendship with him, allowing my unreasonable unrequited feelings to simmer. But now, simmering has turned into boiling and the steam is burning me.

"Yeah," I tell her, "It's been like this for a long time actually."

"It's about time you admitted it."

"Thanks for pretending you didn't know," I chuckle.

"I knew you'd tell me eventually. What does this mean for you guys right now? Does he seem like he's interested in commitment? I know that's important to you."

Cora's not wrong—finding a committed partner, a husband, is crucial to me. I watched my dad struggle for decades after my mom passed away—a shell of the man he once was. I felt sad for him, not because he needed help with raising kids—I was blind to that then—but because of how lonely he was. His life could have been richly colorful like it had been when my mom was alive. To this day I still look up to my parents' marriage, even if it was through the lens of childhood.

I've been committed to everyone else in my life, so yes, I'm desperate for that same kind of unwavering, unconditional support in return. I need to know that someone is always going to be there for me no matter what, and I refuse to put that responsibility on my own children.

My desire for that kind of partnership has only been laminated by the countless romance books I've fused into my soul. Is it really too much to ask for a man to be obsessed with me? Someone who takes care of me and recognizes everyone I've been supporting?

Sure, Rafael has always been around for me, and I've never felt lonely in friendship, but could he turn a new leaf? I love picturing it, but there's always a sharp stab of worry telling me, *He'll never change. He's a flight risk.*

"As far as I can tell, he still has the same attitude," I tell Cora. "But oh my god, when we're having sex, it's so hard not to picture us—you know what I mean?"

"Yeah. He's been treating you like a girlfriend forever, hun. I've never seen someone as comfortable together as you two are. You have such an intimate friendship, so it makes complete sense that your heart connects so fiercely."

When I step into a new aisle, still lost in our conversation and my feelings, a booming voice yells, "Hey, sweetheart!" My head pops up to locate where the sound is coming from, when I spot Rafael at the end, holding a huge plastic package up in the air. "Are these the right adult diapers you need? Ultra-absorbent?" he bellows, and I roll my eyes, totally unfazed. He's chuckling, but I shake my head and leave the aisle.

It's not the first time he's tried to embarrass me. You can't grow up with someone like him, like my brothers, and not be accustomed to this kind of juvenile behavior. It's better to ignore him.

"Oh my god," I whisper.

"Did someone just yell about Depends?"

"That was Raf," I hiss.

Cora snickers on the other line. "You see, this is what I'm talking about. You two are way too comfortable with each other. Now tell me, are you going to talk to him about your feelings?"

"Wasn't planning on it, no."

"Ang."

"No. There's no point. This arrangement will end when the twins are born and we'll go back to friendship as usual."

"Uh-huh," she deadpans, like she knows everything. Ugh.

"It will. We're going to be great co-parents."

"Are you planning on living together forever?"

I find myself back at the cheese station and grab four more pieces. "We decided we're gonna live together until it doesn't work."

"What does that mean?"

"It means if we start to feel like it isn't healthy for us to live together, then we'll live separately." Cora's harrumph on the other end stirs my curiosity. "What?"

"I don't know," she says. "It already feels wrong imagining you two not living together." She's not alone in that feeling.

"Well, I'm not planning on moving out, so it's unnecessary to worry."

"I know," she says. "I'm just a little extra worried about a lot of things right now."

That has my focus shifting. "Like what?"

"Like I'm worried I might not carry to full term," she says solemnly, and I get it. She's been battling depression and PTSD. She's had various forms of grief to work through and it's totally natural for her to have this worry. I haven't been through half of what she has, but my heart sinks with hers.

"I know. I've been worried about that for both of us."

"I've been trying to stay positive and talk to my therapist about it."

"That's good, Cora. It sounds like you're feeling your feelings, acknowledging them, but trying to see a positive future too. I should keep reminding myself to do the same."

"I'm so glad we're doing this together, Ang. I feel so much closer to you for it." Tears prick at my eyes as Cora's sentiment hits me hard.

No, *do not cry in Wegmans*, I think to myself.

Too late.

"I'm so grateful for you, Cora. If we can't have our moms by our sides for this, then I'm glad I have you."

"Shut up, you're making me cry."

I wipe the tear streak from my face with the back of my hand. "We were laughing like two minutes ago, what the fuck?"

"Okay, okay," my bestie inhales raggedly, trying to calm herself down. "Let's change the subject. Have you thought of any names?"

Centering myself to answer her question, I inhale along with her. "Yeah. Raf likes the name Chlamydia, and I thought it was a joke at first, but I think he might be serious."

"No, he doesn't," she chuckles in disbelief.

Knowing Cora is smiling makes me do the same. "He also suggested Olbric, but I had to veto because that's the name of my favorite sex wizard, and I refuse to let him take away the ability to read my favorite erotic fantasy series."

"Yes," she hums. "A very reasonable explanation indeed."

When I turn another corner, I find Rafael in the health and beauty aisle looking at something. As I take my first steps in his direction, the woman standing behind him with a store basket in the crook of her arm, comes up to his side and places her hand gently on his exposed bicep.

And I...see...red.

She's slim and blonde and so fucking pretty I could scream. She's exactly the type of woman Raf usually goes for.

My eyes stay glued to the pair of them. "Cora, I'll have to call you back. I love you."

"Oh. Okay. Love you too."

Before the call ends, I devise a half-baked plan, but I'm not entirely sure it's me doing it.

He's yours, the hormones hiss. *Eliminate her.*

Her hand is still on his arm as he looks down at her and she gives him a saccharine smile, pointing to an item in front of his body—at a level she could easily reach if she only waited ten more fucking seconds for him to get out of the way. Like a normal shopper!

Sweat forms under my arms as my heart mercilessly pounds, but when my eyes catch on a box of condoms next to me, my plan becomes fully baked.

I'm going to walk up to him with this box and say, *They don't have the extra small condoms you like. Will these work?* Then I'll turn the box to read them like I have no other concern. Before he can answer, I'll say, *Nah, you're right.* I look over at blondie and ask, *Do you work here? Do you carry extra small condoms?*

But for once, my logical brain pipes up before I make my move. *That's too harsh,* it tells me. *Take it down a few notches.*

Taking a deep breath, I calm my nerves and put on an unaffected front as I walk toward them. Raf has already handed her the bottle of whatever, and he's smiling back at her. It's his run-of-the-mill grin, but I know better than anyone that smile can make panties wet.

When I reach the cart, he finally sees me, but he doesn't look the least bit unfazed. The woman's head turns as well, and her hand immediately releases. The dress I'm wearing does a pretty good job at covering my pregnant belly, so I push it out as far as I can and rub it.

"Hey, sweetheart," I mock the nickname from earlier but keep a neutral tone. "Are you ready?"

Blondie's face falls and she finally backs away to an acceptable distance.

Raf nudges the cart forward, leaving the woman standing there with wide eyes, and I can tell he's holding back a fit of laughter. "Come on, *sweetheart*. I think we got everything we need."

Chapter 19

August 24th

Angie

"Where are you pulling that cheese from?" Rafael asks as he opens the back door to his moms' house with a reusable grocery bag slung over his shoulder and carrying a ten-inch glazed fruit tart, which I plan on eating half of.

I glance at my hand then back to him. "My pocket."

"Why do you have cheese in your pockets?"

"They were free samples. They want you to take them," I say with a furrowed brow and follow him into the kitchen from the back deck.

His dimples dig in. "They want you to take *one*."

"There's no sign. Are you cheese-shaming me? The woman who is creating human lives—your offspring, the fruit of your loins—and you're shaming her?"

"*¿Qué pasa?*" Ana admonishes her son instead of greeting him, lightly smacking him on the shoulder. She's wearing a casual, dark brown tank dress that's fitted nicely over her mid-size body and her long dark hair is pulled up in a styled ponytail. It's a hot day, so once again stepping inside to glorious air conditioning is a relief.

"When someone pulls cheese from their pocket," he says, switching to Spanish and setting the bag on the counter, "and they left home over an hour ago, I think I have the right to ask questions."

"She's right," Ana says, taking me in her arms before her own son and hugging me tight. "She can eat whatever she wants. My grandchildren require a happy mother. How are you, darling? You look perfect."

"Hungry all the time," I sigh, breaking the embrace.

We told our families about the twins shortly after finding out, and it was like telling them we were pregnant all over again. They went berserk, but again, his father had a similar unenthused reaction, but kept a jovial tone through the conversation at least.

"Well, you're in luck," Christina says, walking into the room in her summer home uniform of tan cargo shorts and a gray cotton T-shirt. "We made beans and rice, and the enchiladas will be ready in ten minutes."

My stomach churns at the thought of meat immediately. *Okay, just breathe,* I tell myself. *You still have salad, rice and beans, fruit tart, and a few pieces of pocket cheese jangling around.*

"What kind did you make?" Rafael asks, taking the salad contents out and finding the big wooden bowl in the cupboard.

"We made two: cheese with green sauce, and potatoes with mole. We weren't sure which one you'd prefer," Christina shrugs. "If none of that sounds good we can whip up something else," she adds with a genuine smile.

Confusion dawns on me. "Where's the meat?"

Ana puts the tart in the fridge and then turns her head to me with a pinch between her sculpted eyebrows. "Rafael said meat makes you sick, so we didn't make any."

If I was running right now, I'd stop in my tracks. "You didn't have to do that," I say. I don't think I've ever attended a meal at this house where meat was not served—it's integral to their family's food scene.

"Of course we did," Ana shrugs like I'm silly. "I also made this extra spicy," she smiles, pushing a dish of dark reddish-brown salsa across the island counter to me. "My son here said nothing is spicy enough for you right now, which is hard to believe, so I'd like to see it for myself."

A giggle bursts out of me and I stare mouth agape at my best friend. "What?" First, I can't believe he would even think to tell his moms to make a meatless meal. I expected carne asada, tacos al pastor, anything but cheese and potato enchiladas. He did this for me?

Thankfully, Ana cuts in before I start crying at the simple and sweet gesture. "I tried it myself," she says pointing to the dish, her smile disappearing. "I can't handle it." Incredibly tempted and already salivating at the thought of something finally being spicy again, I quickly take a tortilla chip and scoop a large portion of salsa.

"Whoa," Raf mumbles. Apparently, he expected me to daintily dip the chip to test it first. I didn't come here to fuck around.

Just looking at the salsa I can tell it's mostly made of peppers and seeds. What kind? I don't give a shit as long as it lights up my mouth. My first registered taste is salt and the corn of the tortilla. Next is the tomato, and then...

No.

No.

I can't taste the heat—the spice—the whole reason I eat salsa in the first place! Everyone has halted what they're doing to watch me closely. Maybe it's a delayed heat? I finish chewing and swallow then suck in a little gasp of air, hoping the heat will be triggered by air flow.

Nothing.

I take another chip, a bigger scoop, and a faster bite.

Nothing.

"What kind of peppers did you use?" I ask a wide-eyed Ana.

"Chipotle, jalapeño, but mostly ghost peppers."

"I have to try this," Raf says, reaching next to me and taking his own delicate bite and immediately coughing, tears springing from his eyes. "Jesus Christ, Ang. I need milk," he wheezes, launching for the refrigerator and chugging the two percent.

He's so theatrical sometimes.

Raf sets up some dinner music, a low instrumental playlist of pop songs throughout the decades. When we finally sit, the anger at my nonexistent spice palate flits away when the first bite of seasoned potatoes and mole hit my tongue and memories flood back. Ana's mole is powerful like that. The first time I had it I was eleven or so. I remember being confused as to why cocoa and nuts would be in a sauce and it wouldn't be sweet. It took me a few dinners to get used to it, but once I did, I begged her to make it all the time. By the time I was thirteen, I was making it myself and serving it to my family. I'm not sure if Ana knows that the Johanssen family mostly ate what she taught me. What Christina taught me about grilling too.

What these women taught me wasn't always about food though. They showed me how to be a child while taking care of a family. They provided me space to be free and stupid and creative. They watched my siblings when Dad was working on the weekends, invited us all over for fiestas, movie nights, and board games. They'd come over with bags of corn husk tamales, enough to feed everyone for a week—at least until my brothers were all teenagers, then it fed them for a day.

When my siblings got older, we'd all go over and help prepare food together—forming an assembly line to make homemade corn tortillas and trays of enchiladas to be frozen. I don't even want to think about how many thousands of dollars these two women spent on feeding and hosting us.

They didn't have to. They could have let us struggle to find attention. Could have let us eat peanut butter and jelly sandwiches most nights. Could have ignored the signs of children desperate for more love—more than a single, grieving father working hard to make ends meet could give.

Of course, I still ended up being a parentified child, despite Christina and Ana's efforts—I don't think I could have avoided it entirely, but it could have been so much worse.

College was the first time I was able to break out of that role thrust upon me. Our college was two hours away—just far enough from home that I could live on campus but be home every weekend if needed or for an emergency. Isaiah certainly stepped up to take care of the rest of our siblings, but he'd still call me every other day for advice.

The transition to college wasn't a difficult one for me. While I saw students fail out left and right that first year, I always wondered how they managed to do that. It wasn't until I was older, and it dawned on me that many of the students didn't know how to live on their own, manage their time, personal life, and classes. It came so naturally to me because I had been doing this for myself and my family for years.

Responsibility for myself and others has been ingrained into me—it's something I rarely shed except around people like Cora, Rafael and his family. College gave me the opportunity to find myself outside of my siblings—to live and experience life as a young woman.

When Raf and I tried to find ourselves in high school, to find where we fit in, I was still largely responsible for my brothers and sister. When we went to college though, I tried to take those countless interests and hone-in on what really inspired me. By the time I graduated with my master's degree, I was a different woman entirely to the innocent freshman I once was. I had grown in confidence and understanding of myself, and what I knew for certain was that I was curious.

That's what it all boiled down to.

Curiosity.

Our random playlists. Our diverse friend groups. Our questionable wardrobes.

Becoming a children's counselor made complete sense because I had been playing this role with my siblings. So it was all too fitting to learn while taking those courses what I was made into, and then learn that the only way to heal was to have emotional awareness of it.

When the instrumental music changes to *Dancing Queen*, Christina gasps a little as she slices up the fruit tart. "That reminds me. There's an ABBA cover band coming in a couple weeks, so if you want tickets let me know."

"Yes, please," I beam.

"I'll tell Jay," Rafael chuckles and pulls out his phone to text.

"He'll go ballistic."

Ana steps back into the dining room with a stack of dessert plates in one hand and a large book in the other before placing it in front of me and Raf. "I know it seems like I do this every time you two are here, but I found another photo album," she grins.

We flip through the pages together and it's mostly our junior year of high school. Rafael in a baseball team photo, Joaquín in softball. Raf and I in our black formal orchestra outfits, him standing next to his bass and me next to my violin.

"We were awful," I muse.

"They would have kicked us out if they could have," he smiles and then turns the page.

"Oh, look at little Dane!" It's a picture of thirteen-year-old Joaquín in a one-piece electric blue swimsuit standing in the water at the beach with Dane on his shoulders.

"Dane is such a good boy," Ana says. "Tell him to stop by more."

"I will," I nod, then look back to the photo album and Raf turns another thick page.

"Nooo," he chuckles. "Not the underwater robotics team."

"Gasp!" I hiss. "So this is where those photos ended up. Oh my god, who let us name our robot Nauti Nautilus?"

"There was no stopping you two when you made up your minds," Christina says, taking a bite of her fruit tart.

"Oh jeez, junior prom," I drawl, staring at myself in a yellow and faux-crystal strapless hand-me-down dress from my older cousin, standing next to my white-blonde date, and Rafael with his date Abby.

"I can't believe you went with Will Parker," Raf huffs disbelievingly.

"Why is that?"

"I don't know. We had all these friend groups we were a part of, and he was never in any of those groups."

"Well, I was getting desperate for a date and he was just sitting there in the computer lab next to me." Truth be told, I was getting desperate because Rafael had a date and I didn't. We could have gone together like we talked about, but then he blindsided me and asked Abigail Martin. "It's not like anyone was going to ask me anyway," I sigh.

"That's not true."

"You know, come to think of it, me asking Will to go to prom might have been the turning point of my confidence. I flat-out asked him if he wanted to go with me, and he said yes. I didn't put any more thought into it beforehand."

"Clearly," he mumbles.

My eyebrows furrow. "What?"

"I'm just saying... You were pretty blind to when guys liked you."

"No I wasn't," I retort.

"Ha, yeah, you were. For example, it was clear Will had a crush on you all through high school. He kept his distance because he was nervous."

I roll my eyes. "You're making that up. How would you know?"

"Because I always knew who had a crush on you. Will Parker, Troy McAlister, Jerome Warner, Corey Sabin-Clark," he lists, counting on his fingers.

"What? No. None of those guys did. They used me for homework answers or never talked to me. Like Will."

"Oh, Angie. You're so stupid," he grins affectionately. "We were teenage boys, that's the best way we could tell girls we liked them. I couldn't even look at guys then. You either keep it bottled up or study with them."

"Well, we studied together, and you never had a crush on me."

Christina pushes her chair away and stands up. "Think I'll clear the table," she says to herself.

"Me too," Ana adds, following suit and exiting the dining room.

My eyes focus back on him. "And that doesn't hold true. If it did, you would have never asked Abby Martin to be your date."

"I didn't have a crush on her," he says simply.

"Then why did you ask her?"

He fidgets with his napkin. "Because I was afraid to ask you."

Before I can let that statement sink in, I blurt, "That doesn't make any sense. We planned on going as friends until you—" It's then that his words hit their target and my mind starts processing. "You wanted to ask me to prom?"

"I was never going to until Mom said I should, then the idea of really asking you scared the living shit out of me." He swallows. "I was so nervous you'd see right through me that I asked Abby the next day after math class."

"You had a crush on me?" I ask, slowly coming to terms with this.

"Yeah," he sighs. "I don't really know what happened to that crush, but I knew keeping you as my friend was always in the stars."

So something happened to that crush, which probably means it's gone, unlike mine.

Chapter 20

August 24th

Angie

M y best friend's admission buzzes in my head like a
bee as I curl up in the guest room bed after a shower.
It's after 10:00 pm, which for me these days equates to mid-
night. When Ana and Christina came back into the dining
room to gather more dishes, our revealing conversation
came to a halt. Their presence broke the tension that we
didn't want to put back together or explore any further.
Why would I want to with him? What good would it do?

Unable to focus on the mafia romance I was reading,
I close my Kindle and set it down. Instead, I think about
Abby Martin and the wrongful pedestal I put her on all my
life. The pedestal with bright showcase lighting demanding I pay attention to everything she was that I never could
be.

He didn't even like her, I remind myself. He had a crush
on you.

Even with this new information tapping at my brain, I
still can't erase the years of what his dating habits have
shown me. The woman at the store being a prime example.

I can't believe how jealous I became. What is wrong
with me? I'm the one who said we should have an open
arrangement. He should be free to see whoever he wants.
Hasn't he been? I recount the months that have gone by
since we struck this deal. He hasn't gone out once and no
one has come over, that's for certain.

I cannot be getting this attached to him; I know better.

From inside my belly, one of the babies kicks, followed by another and another in rapid succession. I giggle, "Okay, you two are right. Mama will stop being so jealous." My appeal to them doesn't soothe their headbutting so they continue to party, uncaring that I'm tired and desperate to shut off my brain for the night. They're usually at their liveliest at night in bed, but tonight, unlike most recent nights, I'm alone. I've grown accustomed to Rafael's body pressed into mine, his big hand splayed out on my round belly, waiting for every kick and tumble these two offer.

Tears threaten to burst when I think about being alone for the rest of the night, and maybe for the rest of my life. Dating is going to be so much harder after kids, as if it wasn't already hard for me. But am I upset at being alone, or am I upset that after our arrangement, there will be no more Rafael in my bed?

I know the truth.

My phone buzzes from the nightstand and I'm grateful for the momentary distraction. It's a text message from Raf with a picture of what looks like his old physics binder. Zooming in, I take a closer look at all the notes scribbled in the margins. Notes between the two of us, because of course we sat next to each other in any class we could. Then I see a sketch I drew of Mr. Forton and Big Mean Kitty (the stuffed animal he'd use for experiments) getting married.

I'm helpless against the smile that curls on my face, but the warmth that spreads isn't enough to distract entirely from my earlier thoughts. Regardless, I stare at the picture long enough to remember the simpler times.

When a soft knock raps on the door, followed by a slow crack, I look up to see Raf's head pop in. "You awake?"

"Yeah. Just looking at the picture you sent me."

Opening the door all the way, he steps in wearing only a pair of gray cotton sleep shorts. "Come with me," he grins, throwing open my covers and taking my hand. "I have to show you something."

"Okay," I breathe, then stand with him and straighten my short floral nightgown before following him hand-in-hand to his bedroom across the hall.

Shutting the door softly behind me, he has me sit on the edge of his bed. His room has changed a little bit since he moved out—the dark blue and tan plaid comforter replaced with a warm gray duvet, yellow accent pillows and a throw blanket. Floating bookshelves grid the wall at the head of the bed along with matching modern lamps, once in the shape of different sporting equipment. The formerly mossy green walls are now a matching gray, but they're still covered with his posters, medals, and artwork.

"Look what I found," he whispers, even though his moms' room is at the other end of the hall, and he pulls out an iPod Classic from his drawer.

"No," I exaggerate.

"Yes!" He smiles then sits next to me, handing me a wired ear bud. "It still works." I still have mine I pull out for occasions I don't have wifi, but I thought he lost his.

His bare thigh presses against mine as he holds the brick of technology between us, scrolling in a circle with the pad and clicking until he finds a playlist titled RANGIE JAMZ.

"Oh my god," I say, shaking my head. "This was back when we had to burn CDs in order to share music."

"Mika!" he hisses, pressing play on *Grace Kelly* and immediately triggering my lyrical memory. It's the kind of memory that makes you remember every single word because you've sung it over a hundred times. It's the kind of memory that makes you anticipate that the next song will be *Roses* by Outkast because that's the way the CD was burned. It's the kind of shared knowledge only Rafael has with me.

"I think they like this song," I smile, leaning against his shoulder and placing his hand on my stomach when the babies start kicking again.

"Come. Lay back with me," he says, shifting us into place under the covers and wrapping his arm under my belly as he lays propped up on his other arm. His fingertips play along the thin flowy fabric as he waits for more kicks. "Oh yeah, they're fans," he chuckles, then leans in to talk directly to them. "Do you know how lucky you are to have two parents with excellent taste in music?"

"What do you think about when you hear this song now?" I ask him, rolling my head to the side to admire him.

It takes him no time at all. "I think about listening to it endlessly with you, hunched over the computer down-stairs, and which one of us could memorize all the lyrics first." My belly bounces up and down as I giggle at his memory because it's the same one I have.

When the song ends and starts playing No One by Alicia Keys, my heart sinks, but he must be unaware because he asks, "What do you remember when you hear this song?"

Afraid to put words to it, I deflect. "What do *you* think about?"

"Hmm," he considers. "That time you failed your chem-istry test and we drove to the park for lunch. Do you remember?" I nod once but keep my mouth shut. "You studied so hard and were so upset. I knew you needed to belt something at the top of your lungs to feel better."

It was a cold and damp spring day, but we blasted the song from the speakers of his little blue Impreza as I sobbed and released all my pain. I wasn't someone who did well with failure when it came to schoolwork. I didn't mind being bad at extracurriculars, but when it came to my academic success, I took it personally.

I remember that day. I remember being grateful for a friend who knew what I needed more than I did at the time.

I couldn't see past my anger and self-hatred, but he could, and he made me breakdown in tears in the middle of a desolate park on a Friday. He knew it would heal me. No one else knew how hard I pushed myself to get good grades. No one else knew the struggle I faced trying to be a role model to my siblings and keeping it all together for their sake.

But Raf did.

He could remind me to let go and scream until I could feel other emotions again. That it was okay to be mad, but to remember grades did not define me. He did it then, and he did it throughout college too.

But *No One* by Alicia Keys doesn't trigger that memory for me.

"Is that what you think about when you hear it?" My best friend asks, scooting up to lay his head next to mine, his hand still caressing my belly.

"No," I admit.

"Then what? I thought for sure it would be that."

Maybe it's because of that park memory and what Raf can pull from my emotional bank, but since our crush conversation earlier, it seems fitting.

"I think about you dancing with Abigail at prom when I hear this song."

"Did I?" he asks, his face serious.

"Yeah. I was standing with Will near the entrance and I watched you dance together."

"Why weren't you dancing with him?"

"Because I didn't want to slow dance with him," I whisper. I wanted to slow dance with you, I think to myself.

"I don't remember what happened that night much, to be honest," he says in a low tone that captures my full attention, and then he glides his warm hand to the nape of my neck. "What I do remember, was how beautiful you looked and what a fool I was for not asking you myself."

Oh fuck.

Let me just step off this cliff and—yup—fall to my death.

When his forehead presses against mine, my eyes fall shut. "You thought I was beautiful?"

His lips dust over mine before he whispers back. "You still are, Angel."

His tender kiss is like one of our songs—a touch that elicits a memory. We've only been kissing a couple months, but the memories he transfers in the brush of his lips aren't that of an act; they're that of a love that's been growing alongside us. It's bonded our trust and care and mixed feelings into something that, even if we tried to break it, could never be.

Our kiss is slow and warm. Impossibly intimate. Every nerve ending I possess comes to life with each shared breath—with every graze of his lips against mine. His hand is still cupping my jaw, and I need nothing more than for him to keep it there. To keep me at his mercy. To kiss me like I've always dreamed he would.

As our kiss deepens and our tongues dive for the other, our breathing picks up. The weight of his body shifting causes the mattress to dip slightly as he braces his arms on either side of my head and lets his lower half fall against mine, his erection growing stiffer by the second.

This is a first—Rafael initiating that is. It's always been me leading our games. That's the way it was designed; I simply tell him when I'm horny and he takes care of it. Now he's making the first move and with so many feelings wrapped up from our conversations tonight, I'm not sure it's a good idea.

It's *a fucking great idea*, my hormones shout. Wait, no. That's my heart talking, not my hormones. He said you were beautiful, my heart pumps.

"I wanted to slow dance with you," I exhale into his hungry mouth before I can stop myself.

"Me too, Angel. I wanted to kiss you then like I'm kissing you now."

"I wish you would have," I whisper, and his mouth drops to my neck, sucking gently and dragging his lips lower, across my shoulders and down to the stiff peaks forming under my nightgown. He lifts it off quickly, straddling me, running his hands over my breasts and stomach, admiring.

"I wouldn't have known what to do with you back then," he says almost to himself. "I had no game, no experience, no idea what I was doing."

"You didn't need game, Raf."

"No, I clearly did. You had no idea how bad I wanted to simply hold your hand in the hallway. I wanted to carry your backpack and all your worries." My heart stutters and my mouth goes dry listening to him admit this. "And I was being serious before, when I said I've never been with someone who looks like you." His wide muscled chest rises and falls as he pets my hip. "It was on purpose because there's no way I could have gone through with it without thinking of your incredible body."

"Oh yeah?" I tease "My small chest, lack of ass, and thick ankles... That gets you going?"

"Angel, you rev my engine." He leans down for a drugging kiss and his words wash away the whispers of my former insecurities—the insecurities I banished, but still itched in the back of my psyche from time to time.

"I have lost time to make up for, *sweetheart*. I want to touch you like this whenever I please. I want to watch you come because of what I do to you." He pinches one of my aching nipples, shooting a direct pulse of desire to my pussy, making me forget that I'm supposed to be the one calling the shots. "Those were the dark days, the foolish days," he rumbles, then pushes himself down my trembling body until his mouth hovers above my mons. "Let me prove to you just how much I crave this body."

· · • • • · • • • · ·

Rafael

She smells like the shower she just had, but tastes exactly like what I'm growing fond of. "Already so wet, Angel?" I hum, pushing my nose through her slit and dragging my tongue along for the joyride.

"Yes," she breathes.

"Can you be quiet for me?"

"Yes, Sir."

"Good girl," I whisper back, licking at her entrance in slow measured strokes. From this angle, her rounded tummy is more pronounced than ever and a boost of masculine pride fills me.

I did that to her. She's round with my babies.

But it's not just me—I'm proud she's the one carrying them. We may have stumbled into this by mistake, but it's hard to see it that way when, if given the choice, there's no one better suited to have my babies than Angie. No one is better suited to raise them with. No one is better suited to me.

Her adorably sexy whimpers encourage me to keep teasing her with my tongue, nipping at her softly with my lips. "I need more, Sir."

"I know you do, Angel," I smirk. "But I need this more. You'll take what you're given, is that understood?"

She lets out a resigned sigh. "Yes, Sir."

"Good," I growl, then use my thumbs to spread her open for better access to that perfect little pink pearl at the top. She writhes above me once my flat tongue drags over it, pulling a pillow over her head to muffle her moans.

When her fingers tighten in my hair and her muscles begin to contract, I know I have her on the precipice—and it's then that I pull back my aggressive tactics and start slowly, gently, again. Angie whines and lets out a huff of frustration that makes me smile. This time, I enter her with two fingers, carefully pumping into her without touching her clit or her G-spot. I revel in her warmth and my trapped cock begs to be let free inside her. She's more than ready to take me, but I can't stop watching the way her bare and beautiful chest lifts and falls and the way her fingers play with each stiff peak.

"Please, Sir," she whispers. "Please make me come. I don't care how, just please make me come."

"I don't know," I tease, then curl my fingers inside her to flex along her G-spot and she gasps. "I told you to be quiet and you didn't listen." She covers her mouth with her hand and her brows raise to watch me suck on her clit and fuck her with my hand. "See, good girls get rewarded." Her low moan reverberate through her body, but it's nothing compared to the spasms I create for her as she bears down, clamping my head between her soft thighs and riding my face like she owns it.

"Yes," she hisses, but it's more like a croak. She's barely hanging on to her own sanity as I pump into her, curling my fingers and devouring her without mercy.

Before she can come back to reality, I pull her up and toss her onto her hands and knees. She immediately falls to her elbows and rests her head against the sheets, panting hard. Her breathing is interrupted by a string of small gasps when I plant my face directly in her ass and flick that teasing little rosebud. We haven't done rimming until now, and I'm wondering why the hell not? Goddammit, I'm adding her ass to my diet from now on.

"Oh fuck," she grits out and I spread her wide.

"That's right, baby," I purr. "I'll fuck this one day soon. Would you like that?"

"Yes, Sir."

I lick from her dripping wet pussy to her ass and shove my taut tongue inside her, fucking and massaging her with my mouth, then adding a couple fingers back to her clit and circling, pressing, pulling on it until she comes undone once more. The pillow beneath her face absorbs most of her cries, but just enough escape to make me swell with satisfaction.

I sit back on my heels for a moment, admiring her backside and toying with her slick center, as it pulses with arousal. "You were a very, very good girl, Angel. Now it's time to take what's mine," I whisper, moving up with my cock in hand, dragging the sheathed tip through her wet folds, then coating the rest in her fluids. "Are you gonna take my big, bare cock?"

"Yes, Sir," she whines. "Please."

"That's what I like to hear, baby," I grumble and push in the first couple inches—just enough for my eyes to roll back in my head as I plant my hand on her ass for support. "Fuck, you feel so good." I slide in a few more inches, then pull them out, watching her lubricate my shaft.

When I'm all the way in and her ass kisses the base of my cock, something in me snaps and I can't stop the beast within me. I can't play the slow and steady Dom anymore. It's like her pussy is eating my control and every brain cell I hold—leaving only base animalistic urges. I want to kick out her knees and lay on top of her, pinning her down and rut into her, but the one brain cell she's left me with reminds me of our babies she's carrying, so I change tactics. Leaning over her, I give several deep thrusts, then scoop under her shoulders and pull her back up with me.

"Oh fuck," she whispers, but I throw a hand over her mouth and let her sink down even further, letting her weight settle against my lap and chest.

"Hold onto my head, baby," I whisper in her ear. "You're gonna need stability in a second."

"Hmm?" she whines beneath my hand before I thrust into her hard and her hands fly behind my head and lock in place. I pound into her from the bottom while I hold under her belly with the other hand. From this angle, I can watch her full breasts bounce with every hit.

I know she's enjoying this, but I can tell she's straining. "Lean all your weight against me, Angel. All of it," I growl in her ear, and she obeys perfectly, her head lolling against me and her shoulders sagging. It already feels better for me too.

"That's it. Give yourself to me. All your worries. Your pleasure. Your body. They all belong to me," I soothe, drawing my hand from her stomach to her mons and pressing my flat palm against it enough to feel my own dick rocking inside her. Her moans tell me that added pressure is hopefully rubbing her G-spot against my cock.

Her tongue darts out and playfully licks between my fingers, but I clamp them tighter around her face and start strumming her clit with two digits. Her pussy squeezes me tighter, causing me to curse, and the last shred of control I held snaps.

I make it my mission to make her come again as fast as possible because I can't hold back much longer. When she does, it's glorious. Her whimpers drive me mad with lust as her pussy flutters around my buried dick. I'm about three seconds from coming inside her when I quickly remove my hand from her mouth and pussy and wrap my arms around her chest from behind and pummel into her core—the tight build bursting inside her.

The hair on the side of her face flies when I exhale heavily against her head. Sitting back on my knees and taking her with me, her soft body is made even softer by her limp and sated state. I'm clutching her like a pillow as I catch my breath.

"Fuck, Ang," I exhale. "That was insanely good."

"I feel high," she whispers.

"Yeah? Nothing's sore?"

"Not right now. I only feel pleasure," she hums, and I catch her smile.

"Good. Me too. Hopefully hooked-in was a sex position you read about and wanted to try," I chuckle, crossing my fingers.

"It wasn't but based on my very recent experience with it, it should have been. Good call."

I love when she compliments me like this. It's exactly the kind of aftercare I want when I dominate. I want to know beyond a shadow of a doubt that my partner is happy—so her feedback and praise she so freely gives me is just as important as everything else we do.

I hug her a little tighter before murmuring, "Thanks. Now, let me clean you up," and then I'm pulling out, twisting her, and setting her down on the bed where I quickly latch my mouth on her wet center.

"Oh," she gasps. "You know, one of these days you're going to let me return the favor."

"That's not gonna happen tonight," I mumble through her folds, lapping at my own release spilling out of her. "Tell me, what's still on your smutty bingo card?"

She snorts but it vanishes when I start to pay closer attention to her clit again, replaced by her face relaxing, mouth hanging open. "Um," she pants. "Fuck, it's hard to think when you're—oh god."

"Tell me," I drawl, working my jaw in tandem with my tongue into her heat, "what other fantasies you want to try. How can I please you?"

"Fuck me with a gun," she blurts breathlessly.

That causes me to pull back immediately. "I'm sorry, what did you say?"

"Please, Raf. I want you to fuck me with a gun."

Angie has shocked me before with her requests but nothing at this level. "What? No!"

"Why not?" she whines, her hand flying to stroke her pussy and replace my mouth.

"Because I don't even own a gun! And you're pregnant!" I hiss. "Are you kidding?"

"No. I want it. Please," she begs.

Her hand continues to play with her clit and I roughly snatch it away. "Don't you touch what's mine," I growl, white-hot anger lancing through my blood. I have no idea how I'm going to get a gun or safely use it with her, but I know I'm going to make this happen as much as it freaks me out. "Can we table this fantasy for later, Angel? I need to work through some things."

"Of course," she smiles, then bites her lip.

Fuck, she really wants this.

I spend the next fifteen minutes eating her out again and making her come on my chin and fingers two more times. When I return to her rumpled and satiated body with a warm cloth to actually clean her up, she lets me maneuver her legs where I need to as she nearly passes out.

Good. I didn't want her to return to the guest room anyway.

Folding back the covers, I climb into bed and take my new favorite spot—spooning her with my hand covering her stomach while her neck rests against my other arm.

A small hum comes from her lips and a contented sigh. "Are you happy, Ang?" I whisper.

"I am. I'm also tired. You wore me out."

"That's high praise coming from you."

"If you wanted to sleep-creep me, that would be fine."

Her ridiculous words make me smile. "I believe that's illegal and morally wrong."

"Mmm, no. I'm giving you consent ahead of time."

Once again tonight, my brows pinch together. "You want me to fuck you while you sleep?"

"It's more like, I want you to fuck me awake."

We've come close to this since we've started sleeping in the same bed, but Angie has always been the one to give me the indication to wake up and slide into her. It goes against every fiber of my being to ignore that drilled-in teaching that verbal and enthusiastic consent is required before having sex. It was different when I was chasing her in the woods. I knew ahead of time she was going to say no, going to refuse me, but I had her safeword. It was all laid out ahead of time—between two conscious people.

"I need to think about this one too, Ang. I promise to take care of you in the morning, but I don't know about this yet. Is that okay?"

"Of course. Let's just go to sleep and pray your moms didn't hear us."

That makes me smile. "You know, I've never had a girl in my childhood bed before. This was pretty sweet."

"Yeah. Your moms were kinda strict about that back then."

A small laugh rumbles up from my chest and I pull her in tighter. "Probably because they thought I would get you pregnant if we did."

"We showed them."

Chapter 21
August 25th

Angie

"Hey, bunny," my dad grins, bringing me into a familiar hug and wrapping me in his scent. His scratchy, short salt and pepper beard tickles my face as he plants a kiss on my cheek. "So good to see you."

"Good to see you too, Dad." Once again surprising me, he's quite put together wearing nice jeans and a dark blue T-shirt that actually fits and doesn't have holes in it. Who is this man? If my dad isn't at his office job working in a sad polo, he's home or working a side job wearing clothes that most people would deem rags. Even his short hair is trimmed up and styled. "You look great."

"Not as great as you, honey. And Raf, how are you, son?" he asks affectionately, the way he always has to my friend.

"I'm good," he says as we step inside my childhood home. It's a small two-story house that would suit an average size family of four just fine. But somehow the giant Johanssen family squeezed in here all these years. My dad and brothers are all over six feet tall and so is Ivy. I'm the shrimp of the family and I'm still above average height for a woman. Dad's tall Swedish genes did not miss our family, that's for certain.

"Bunny, can I get you an iced tea? Raf, a beer?"

My eyebrows raise at that. "You have iced tea?" This man never has anything other than water and the occasional warm Mountain Dew hidden away in his workshop.

"Yeah," he nods, making his way back to the kitchen from where we're standing in the living room.

"Okay, I'll take a tea," I say.

"I'm not drinking," Raf says. "I'll have an iced tea too."

When Dad disappears into the kitchen, I turn to Rafael. "You're not drinking?"

"No. I haven't had anything to drink since you found out you're pregnant."

"You haven't? But there's been so many socials since then."

He simply shrugs. "I'm doing it for solidarity."

Well, that's freaking sweet of him. "I had no idea. Thank you, that's—really nice actually."

"Actually? Am I a douchebag normally?" he chuckles.

"You know what I mean. Thank you."

"How's the season, Raf?" Dad asks, walking into the living room with our drinks, the hardwood floor creaking with every step.

"Good," he smiles and we all take a seat on the oversized leather sectional. "We just had our first official fall match yesterday morning against Pittsburgh. Smoked 'em."

"Good for you. And how about you, Ang? How's work going?"

"It's great. I just wish I could stay awake all day. I feel bad for zoning out on the kids sometimes," I admit with a grimace.

"Can I?" Dad asks softly, hovering his hand over my baby bump and looking a little sheepish.

"Knock yourself out. They're not kicking right now, but you never know."

He quickly sets his beer bottle down on the coffee table and places both hands on me. "Can I...talk to them?"

Shut the fuck up, this man is going to make me cry.

"Yeah," I swallow thickly.

"Hey, little ones," he coos, bringing his mouth only a couple inches from my stomach. "It's your grandpa. Are you giving Mama a hard time?"

That makes me giggle. "Yes, they are. The heartburn is starting to kick in, and last week I thought it would be a good idea to make enough homemade pasta to last through the next presidential term."

"And then she fell asleep halfway through making her last batch," Rafael adds with a smirk. "Found her on the couch covered in flour with Goodbye Earl blasting through the speaker."

"This morning I got winded putting on my sandals."

Dad pulls back his head to look at me, his crooked smile small but present. "Yeah, I remember your mom going through that like it was yesterday."

Proceed with caution, I tell myself because never, and I mean never, has my father spoken about my mother outside of the occasional fact.

I swallow my nerves and try to nudge him. "Yeah?"

"She was just as beautiful as you, bun. She glowed when she was pregnant. Went through the ringer with symptoms, especially with the boys," he says fondly and my pulse picks up its pace. Maybe if I pay closer attention, I'll be able to brand this moment as a core memory. I can sense Rafael's stillness on my other side, like he, too, is afraid to make a move so as to not scare off these rare glimpses into my mom's life.

"Did she have any cravings?" I ask gingerly, desperate for any scrap of her.

"You know, now that you say it, I do remember her eating a lot of grapefruit. And nothing was spicy enough for her."

"Really?" I interject. "Me too! Well, not about the grapefruit, but the spicy food, yeah."

"I guess that makes sense; you two share so much as it is." His expression turns unreadable for a moment as his focus shifts elsewhere and then he clears his throat. "I'm not sure you know this, but twins actually run in your mom's family."

"What? Really? I thought I was an outlier."

"No. Um," he says, then grabs his beer bottle and sits on the edge of the couch with his legs spread and elbows on his knees. "Your mom's mom, Grandma Dabrowski, was a twin."

"I didn't know that," I whisper. I knew my grandma had a sister in Poland, but I didn't know she was her twin.

"And," he pauses. "Your mom was actually pregnant with twins when...she was...killed in the car accident."

"I'm sorry, what?" I would ask him how am I just hearing about this, but he's never uttered a word about my mom or her family since she's been gone.

The label on his full beer bottle is slowly and methodically being pulled away when he speaks again, not looking at me. "She was only twelve weeks along. We had just found out we were having two, and we weren't expecting any—they were a surprise, but a welcome one." I'm fascinated and in shock. His eyes slam shut and he shakes his head. "How Ivy survived that accident is a miracle."

I've always thought that too, and it's no wonder everyone else in the family babies her. I've also put myself in my dad's shoes more times than I can count, thinking what he must have gone through losing his wife in a horrible car accident and almost losing his youngest child—and I sympathize with him because it's impossible not to. But knowing he's been holding on to this extra loss the whole time brings renewed grief, understanding, and sorrow along with it.

"Why didn't you tell me until now?" I choke out, tears springing.

"I was never planning on telling you, truth be told. But I've been seeing a therapist for the last six months, and I realized there's a lot of things I need to come clean about and make right with you kids."

"Dad," I say, my voice pitchy and small.

"I know," he nods then finally looks at me, a single tear threatening to escape. "I should have gone a long time ago. I'm sorry I didn't. I wasn't the father you kids needed me to be, but I hope there's still time to be."

"There is," I cry, then throw myself into him as we wrap our arms around one another. "I'm so proud of you, Dad. I hoped someday you would get here, but I never thought it would come."

"Thank you, bunny. Thank you for waiting." When we pull away, each of us wiping at the remnants of tears, he says, "There will probably be a lot more apologizing in the future, so get ready."

"Will I also get more stories about Mom?" I ask hesitantly.

"I'd love to share them. Would you like her journals?"

"She had journals?" I exclaim.

Chapter 22

August 30th

Angie

I didn't think it was possible, but something other than my raging libido has taken up every inch of my brain this week. The journals my mom kept have been the only thing I've cared about, analyzed, and sobbed over. She kept one journal for each of her pregnancies up until each child turned one. Including the two blank journals she never had the chance to fill in.

"What did Isaiah and Dane say when you gave them theirs?" my sister Ivy says over a video call, the sunshine still vibrant in her small shared apartment in the background compared to the setting sun outside my window. Even though I know she's tired, she still looks beautiful in her sundress. Guatemala looks good on her—still doesn't ease my worry for her safety in another country without any family around.

I roll my eyes and sit back on the couch with a mixing bowl full of cut melon and a fork then look at Ivy. "Our brothers did not find these journals nearly as earth-shattering as you and I."

"Typical," she snorts. "Thank you for scanning and sending every page of mine by the way. You didn't have to do that."

"I couldn't stop myself. I did it for everyone. Stuff like this is too valuable. Which reminds me," I say, then pop a piece of sweet cantaloupe in my mouth and continue talking because what are manners between sisters? "Jonah isn't getting his journal until he can be trusted not to lose it."

"I bet he'd use it as wrapping paper if it was nearby and he ran out."

"You assume he would wrap something in the first place?" I grouse.

Ivy brings a glass of water to her lips before saying, "I bet if we told him this was the diary of Anne Frank he would believe us."

"That's *if* he knew who Anne Frank was."

"Good point," she giggles.

"I don't understand how he's made it this far in his life."

"He's charmed his way through everything," she answers.

"It might also be pure luck." Ivy gives a considering smile as a pause lingers between us. "How's your training program going? Are you a certified midwife yet?"

She smiles, "Not yet. But it's going great. It's hard, mostly because of the hours. Babies don't care about other people's sleep schedules, it's so rude." That makes me chuckle as I take another bite of melon. "I won't be certified until I come back to the States and work under another midwife, like an apprenticeship. But for now, I'm gaining a lot of experience. Just yesterday I participated in my two-hundredth birth," she says proudly.

"That's amazing, Ivy!"

"Yeah, it was pretty wild, too. This mom of five just walked into the birthing center with all of her kids, in labor, and within twenty minutes the baby was born."

"What?" I exclaim.

"Yeah, she just had a *been-here-done-this* attitude."

"I should channel that woman's energy when I give birth."

"Why? Are you freaking out?"

"A little," I sigh. "It's a lot of little things I worry about. Like the mind-blowing reality of two babies exiting my body."

"Are you still trying to have a vaginal birth?"

"Yes. The doctor thinks I should have a c-section, but I want to try giving birth vaginally."

"And we're still on for a hospital birth?" she asks calmly, jotting down notes in what I assume is her file on me. I still have an obstetrics doctor who I see for all my prenatal appointments, but Ivy's been following along the whole time and giving me advice.

"Yeah. I did confirm with the doctor that I'm allowed to have you with me as a midwife in the hospital."

"Perfect. And how does Raf want to support you on birthing day?"

"Oh, he's already read all the birthing partner books you recommended. I think he wants to catch the babies," I chuckle.

"That's great! It sounds like he wants to be involved in the whole process." He really does. And it's more than just being an active birthing partner. When we came home from my dad's house yesterday and read through the journals, he was the one who suggested we do the same thing. Each of us writes in a journal for each baby. I was floored by that.

Then I remember what he did last week and smile. "Oh my god, Ivy, I started looking into hypnobirthing and he created a playlist for me."

"Aww," she coos. "Where is he right now?"

"He has an away game tomorrow in Norfolk, so he left this afternoon."

She gives me a suggestive hum and raises one eyebrow. "You didn't go with him this time? Dane said he—"

I cut her off. "We are perfectly fine not spending every weekend together," I lie. "We're not that codependent."

She levels her stare. "That's not where I was going with that."

Before she can launch into questions about me and Raf and what we are, I steer the conversation in another direction. "So when will you be back?"

"Well, let's see," she hums, peeking at her notes, "You're due December 28th. I'll be back by late November, so even if your doctor has you induced, or you go into labor early, which is common for twins, I'll be there." The relief knowing my sister will be by my side gives more peace than I expect.

Even with three thousand miles separating us, I can see how much she's grown into herself. When she first told us she was joining this midwifery program in Central America, I was naturally fearful. This girl didn't even talk to us about it beforehand—she just signed up and committed herself out of nowhere. She would be gone one full year in a country we knew no one and nearly nothing about.

Well, not *no one* exactly. Rafael's cousin Daniel knows a guy who knows a woman in Santa Catarina Pinula who's keeping an eye on her. I guess they have breakfast together sometimes. That's the best we have.

But maybe this was the right move for her. She's been reliant on me for everything, and now here she is, living on her own—well, with a roommate from her program—making something for herself. It's incredible to witness, but heartbreaking to be separated from.

"Good," I tell her. "I know Dad misses you like crazy. Are you going to move in with him when you come back?"

"I don't know," she winces. "I'd rather live on my own, but I might have to."

"Let me talk to Raf and see if you can live with us," I offer without thinking, immediately chastising myself for not sticking to my boundaries.

"That's really nice of you, but I'll figure something out."

Holy cow. Who has this girl become? But there's a tiny scratch of uselessness etching itself in my heart at her words. *You're not her parent,* I remind myself. *This is a good thing.*

"I don't know, sis, living with Dad might turn out to be a healing experience now. You might get to hear him apologize to you too."

"I'm so freaking jealous of you, by the way," she says, her teeth peeking through her disbelieving smile as she crosses her arms and sits back in her chair. "That might be worth moving back home for. I can't believe he's in therapy."

My gaze drifts from my phone screen propped against a candle on the coffee table to the silver words emblazoned on the bound book a few inches away.

The Journal of Zofia Dabrowski.

"Okay, I gotta run," Ivy chimes back in. "I'm meeting my roommate for dinner."

"Oh, sure. Have fun. I love you."

"I love you too," she smiles, then leans down to end the call.

Setting down my empty bowl, I then pick up the well-worn white journal and flip to where I left off in my fifth read-through near the beginning.

8/1

Hello my little peanut,

Your father and I got married today! But don't you worry, we wanted to get married before we found out about you. I'm not sure what the future holds for us or what will happen to my college attendance, but what I do know is that no matter when you came to us, it would have always been the right time.

Your father looked very handsome today. I'm the luckiest bride. I love him so much it hurts. He brings me so much happiness and cares so much for me. He's going to be the best dad. I hope one day you find someone as special as he is to me.

I can't wait to meet you, my little peanut.

It would be nice if you let me go more than twenty minutes
without needing to pee though.

Love,

Mama

Chapter 23

September 17th

Rafael

T oday was a rare morning where I got to spend most of my time diving into spreadsheets and figures like I used to. Normally the small team of finance employees that works under me at Define are the ones producing the reports, but with two of them out on vacation this week, I've been able to dig my fingers in like the old days.

Financial math has always clicked for me. I like how I can find answers to real-life problems through it. Struggling to make ends meet? Look at your spending and adjust. Maybe that means cutting back on the amount of food you DoorDash to your best friend's cat, or maybe that means getting a second job.

In this case though, it looks like Define's misfortune has turned around. Ever since our company was hit with that lawsuit and we lost clientele, we've slowly but surely made our way back into the community's favor it seems. Based on the figures on my screen, I'll be able to let Cora know we can hire more staff for the increase in business we've accumulated. I'm excited to tell her.

I've been working my ass off here—partly to prove to Cora that she made the right choice in hiring me, but also because I took over during a tumultuous time for Define. I took over from a well-seasoned CFO and I needed to prove that I could do it. Taking this job was a huge step up in my career, and even now, with good news for the company on the horizon, I still manage to feel like I'm not doing enough.

Will I ever?

There's a soft knock at my open office door. "Hey, did you bring gym clothes today?" Jay asks, leaning against the frame. We've been working out in the small office gym together a few days a week during our lunch break recently. It's usually a quick thirty-minute run on side-by-side treadmills, just enough to keep up my cardio during rugby season between practices.

I quickly look at my watch. "Oh shoot, is it that time already?" I ask, standing up and collecting my phone, wallet and keys. "Sorry, I can't today. I have to make a quick trip over to Chestnut Street to talk to the contractor. Joaquín can't be here and they need approval before installing the kitchen counter tops."

Jay chuckles, "Oh yeah. What is this, the third time they've tried to install it now?"

"Yeah."

"I don't know," he muses. "I think you should have kept the pink marble they tried to give you the first time."

••••••••••

My trip to the property proves successful and worthwhile. The countertop installers had the right lightly veined stone this time and did a perfect job.

This house is starting to grow on me. I was considering selling it after a couple years, but now that the floors are in, the casework has been renovated, a new roof, the kitchen is almost complete and the bathrooms totally overhauled, there's a soft spot growing in my heart for it. Joaquín knows what the hell he's doing, that's for certain.

I have a few more minutes before I need to drive back to work, so I take the opportunity to look around at each room. Even through the heavy thumps and bangs from the crew working inside the house and scraping cadence of the masons working on the exterior, everything falls away as I walk through the top floor bedrooms, envisioning my babies in here. Angie sent me several articles saying even if the space is available, keeping twins in the same room helps with anxiety for both the parents and the babies.

But what I see even clearer is her.

Here.

I see her in my bed after we've finally put the twins down to sleep, both of us exhausted beyond belief but happily curling into one another. But then I remember she won't be in my bed and I won't be in hers, and somehow that feels utterly wrong. I know living together is the right move for us and our family for now. Between her comfortable bed and comfortable body, I've fallen into a comfortable pattern with her, just like I've always done with Angie. Everything about her is my comfort zone—even when we're trying some new kinky fantasy involving me pretending to be a duke with a penchant for tavern wenches tying me up—even then I find comfort in her attention. Comfort is not something I have ever found with sexual partners.

I think about her more as I walk down the refinished stairs. Maybe this arrangement between us will end like we agreed, but I cannot let her move out. I want her to stay. I want her to want to stay.

When I reach the main floor, the light pouring in from the sunroom on my right catches my attention. Whenever Angie comes over, she gravitates to this space. So far, there hasn't been a plan for it other than a new floor and windows, but as I stare at the blank walls, an idea comes to mind.

There's enough space for that, I think to myself, then shoot off a text to my brother with the change order. Right as I hit send, a call comes in from Angie, her picture lighting up the screen. She says it's the worst photo ever taken of her, but I think it's hilarious and perfect. It's a candid shot of her vulgar gesticulation on the sidelines of one of my games years ago. It was taken by our team photographer and it makes me smile every time I see it. She looks more like a fuming coach rather than a spectator.

"Hey, what's up?" I answer.

Her audible groan sets me on edge. "Ugh. I'm about to call a tow truck."

Even though she is talking to me and sounds safe, my heart plummets as I think of her mom. How can I not? We've been spending almost every night reading her journal entries since she got them. We read about the love she had for her family and her life. But as soon as I imagine a tow truck, it's only Zofia's death I picture, and this time, Angie's in the car.

"What happened? Where are you?"

"I'm in the parking lot at work," she says casually. "I tried to leave for lunch but my car wouldn't start, and when my coworker gave me a jump, it turned on, but before I could even get to the road, it started smoking and died again."

All I can envision is her car aflame as sweat begins to form all over my body. "Is it currently smoking? Are you inside it?"

"I'm walking back into the building right now," she sighs, unaware of my turmoil. "Yeah, it's still smoking."

I sag in relief and I'm already running out of the house and hopping into my SUV. I've had enough of that piece of shit car of hers. "I'll be there fifteen minutes, Angel. Just stay inside and rest. I'll call the tow truck," I say, but when an idea pops in my head, changing my mood, I smirk.

"What? No. You have work. I can handle this."

"Ang," I deadpan. "Last time you called a tow truck they tried to charge you fifteen hundred dollars to tow it five miles."

"It's not my fault I didn't know how much tow trucks are supposed to cost."

"I'll come get you, I'll take care of the tow truck, and we'll get some lunch. I haven't eaten yet either. I've already sent a text to Cora letting her know what's going on and that I might be gone the rest of the day."

"The whole day?"

"Don't worry," I soothe. "You had an office day today, right? No patients?"

"Yeah," she drawls, and my plan solidifies.

"Can you take the rest of the day off? We're buying you a new car."

· · • • • • • • · ·

I called the tow service and had them haul her hunk of junk Ford Fiesta to the scrap yard because no dealership would ever take that flaming pile of garbage. She tried to tell me over lunch that it was probably a simple fix. But when I reminded her she's had several major fixes in the last year, and then showed her my handwritten calculations on the back of the diner's paper place mat, she relented. In the last year she had spent three times what it would cost to have a new vehicle.

"How about this one?" she asks, walking away from the big SUV I was just pointing to, wearing a casual white and blue striped dress and sensible flats. I know her feet are starting to hurt carrying the extra weight and I can see her ankles swelling a little from the heat—further fueling my desire to get this over with and get her home and resting.

She bellies up to a ten-year-old Impala and tries to look inside, placing her face against the window and blocking the sunshine over forehead.

"You remember you're having twins, right?"

"You remember my budget, right?"

"Ang, come on. We need something bigger than a sedan."

"You have your Range Rover and I'll have a car. It's what I can afford, Raf."

"Let me help you with the cost."

She cocks her head back like she's rubber-necking next to a traffic accident. "Excuse me, no. I can pay for my own vehicle, thank you very much."

"I just mean... You're having my babies too. I want to make sure the cars they ride in every day are safe."

As she turns around to face me, her posture immediately changes into something rigid, her shapely eyebrows pulling together. "Are you thinking about what happened to my mom?"

"Kind of, yeah." I admit, coming to stand next to her and leaning my hip against the front driver's side door. I want to smooth a finger over the crease above her slender nose. Instead I sigh. "I'm not saying her death could have been avoided by having a safer car. I'm just saying I'd like to make sure that box is checked. I want you in the safest vehicle possible, not the safest for your budget."

Her eyes narrow and she considers me for a long moment before saying, "Maybe. How about I contribute what I planned on paying monthly? Like how I'm paying for living with you."

Oh. You mean the money I've been funneling into a high yield investment account for you? I think to myself. Instead I say, "That works."

"Hey there, folks," a slender white car salesman waves, walking up to us with that customer service grin you know he's required to have. "What can I help you find today?"

"My car died," Angie says and I want to cut her off and whisper in her ear to not look so desperate. He can smell the sale. "It's time to replace it."

"Oh no," he replies, putting his hands in the pockets of his khakis and rocking on the balls of his feet. "Alright, well, I can definitely help you find the right vehicle. What color are you looking for?"

Angie goes still and I watch her mouth slowly drop as she twists her head to face me. Her eyes are wide, a little crazed even, and I know exactly what she's thinking before she even says it.

Get him, Ang.

She turns to him and crosses her arms. "Why is that the first question you ask me?"

"Um," he drawls.

"Would you have asked him that question?" she asks with a nod in my direction.

"Probably?"

"I don't think you would've," she whispers. "So why don't we start over and you don't pretend I know nothing about cars and I don't pretend you asked me that sexist question?" Her cheshire grin has made its way to my face now.

"Yes, ma'am," the salesman swallows.

"Good."

When there's a pause in conversation, I offer him some help. "She's looking for a safe vehicle. The newer the better."

"Oh, yeah. We have lots of options, sir."

"You're not selling to me," I say. "You're selling to her. Talk to her."

"Of course. Sorry," he stammers. "Ma'am, if you'll follow me I can show you some options."

Angie humors me and test drives an enormous Expedition, but when she turns down a tight street, she white-knuckles the steering wheel. "No, Raf. Hard no. This is way too big, and we're not even in the old part of Philly where the streets are smaller."

"Ang, we're having big kids," I say from the passenger seat as she leans forward trying to get a better look of her surroundings and pushing past parked cars on the street.

"Between the giants in your family and mine, there's no way our kids will be small. We need the big one."

"I'm not pushing out NBA players, dude. They don't need much space until they're older, and by then we'll have different cars." She looks in the rear view mirror at our salesman, nearly sideswiping a BMW. "Are you gonna sell us our next car, Brian?"

"Sure," he winces, holding onto the oh shit handle.

"Good. I'm turning back and we're gonna try that Subaru instead."

Apparently Brian can't handle a little aggressive driving from Angie, so he lets us take the next car by ourselves. I'm surprised at how spacious this one is for the size and after reading through the safety accolades online, I give her the thumbs up. This is a good choice, a good middle ground between a small city car like she's used to and a school bus—her words—that I originally wanted.

When we pull back into the parking lot, I ask, "Do you want to negotiate or do you want me to do it?"

Angie puts the car in park and turns it off. "Knock your-self out," she says with a smile.

Brian and all his nice guy energy came to a screeching halt the moment I told him we were ready to pull the trigger. I know for a fact this car is listed two grand over market value, but he's not budging a cent. In fact he's added costs for bullshit like documentation fees. I've never been dicked around like this while buying a car. Do I have the money to pay for this car outright? Yes. But as a matter of principle, I will not pay more than this car is worth. I don't want to leave here without a car for Angie though—I mean we've been here for four hours already. Ang had a pizza delivered for Christ's sake.

"I'm sorry," Brian shrugs. "That's the best we can do."

I take a deep breath while gritting my teeth. "I'll be right back," I say, turning on my heel and crossing the showroom floor to find Angie sitting in a chair with a slice of pizza in hand. "If you wanna take my car and go home, I'll meet you there. I'm gonna be a while longer. He's not budging."

She swallows her bite. "Really?"

"Yeah," I huff. "I don't know what his deal is, but if I have to stay here after closing I will."

"Let me try," she smiles, then stands up and stretches her back. "Stand about ten feet away when I talk to him and keep looking like this," she waves her fingers in front of my face.

"Like what?" I grumble, following her.

"Like you're on the verge of hulking out."

"What are you—" I start, but she presses her index finger to her mouth to shush me.

My best friend walks over to Brian who's talking with another sales guy and interrupts them. I can barely make out what she's saying. With one hand still holding a slice and the other caressing her large baby bump, she coos, "Brian honey. Do you see how pregnant I am?"

"Yes, ma'am."

"Do you have any idea how tired I am?"

"No, ma'am."

"Very," she smiles. "I want to go home. I want to go home with a car tonight, but if you don't give it to me for the fair price he wants," she gestures to me, "then we're not buying it. And we're not gonna buy from here ever."

"I understand, but—"

"Brian, he's about two minutes away from having a breakdown. Numbers are his thing. If you can't make the numbers work, then I'll just keep driving around in my unsafe tin-bucket of a car that smoke billows out of and he'll keep barking at me to get a new car." She looks down at her belly, causing his eyes to follow hers, and then I think I hear her sniffle. "Maybe if he sees that I have my shit together," her voice cracks, "then he'll want to marry me."

I'm frozen in awe of her. She claims I'm dramatic, but this is Oscar-worthy.

"You're not married?" he asks, genuinely concerned.

She shakes her head. "No. I'm carrying his babies and he won't put a ring on my finger."

"Oh my god," he says as his lip curls in disgust when he looks over at me.

Then, as if there's a dial to increase the size of doe eyes, she peers at him from beneath her lashes and pouts. "Do you think you could cut me a break, Brian? I could use one."

"I... I think we can make something work. Dave?" he asks his manager next to him.

"Whatever she wants," he nods, and I'm floored to see tears welling up and a frown he can't seem to remove.

"Thank you," Angie beams. "Can I go eat the rest of my pizza now and Raf can settle up with you guys?"

"Oh, sure! Yes, please go ahead and eat. We'll take care of everything," Brian says.

Holy. Shit. She just swooped in and out-negotiated me in less than five minutes. I didn't even know this side of her existed. Where did she learn to buy cars and act? Did she study at the school of Glengarry Glenn Ross? How many times has she watched The Wolf of Wall Street? Based on the chub I'm tucking away, maybe I should consider financial domination after all. What's the equivalent for getting off on good negotiation?

"You guys are the best," she says and then makes her way back to me with the same smile. "Alright, close it up."

"That was fucking hot," I whisper. Seriously my cock is becoming a problem. She may have appeared to be a damsel in distress, but I knew the truth: she used his sexist mindset against him. I know she doesn't think we have to get married just because she's pregnant—but he doesn't know that.

"I think I have a lady boner," she whispers and shimmies her shoulders, giving me a smirk as she saunters past and sits back down. She takes another bite of pizza and arches an eyebrow. But my eyes land on her unadorned left hand.

It would look better with a huge fucking ring on it.

"Mr. Jimenez?" Brian says, derailing my train of thought and I turn in his direction. "We'll take the two thousand off."

· · • • • • • · ·

"Why are we here?" Angie asks, stepping out of her running car in a park outside the city. It's been an hour since we've signed all the paperwork, and she followed me in her own new car where I know traffic wouldn't be an issue.

"Don't you remember our new car tradition?" I ask, shutting my door and locking it. Her expression tells me she doesn't. "We gotta [1] ghost ride the whip, Ang," I say with a shit-eating grin.

She buckles over in a low laugh, "No."

"Yes," I reply, opening the passenger side door and sitting down. Connecting my phone to her dash, I then peer up at her standing on the other side. "Get in, Angel. We've done this for every car purchase since we were sixteen and we're not stopping now."

She climbs back in and stares at me. "I think our circumstances have changed," she says with wide eyes and a nod to her belly.

"We'll do a modified version," I say, pressing play on the touch screen. "Put it in drive and head back to the road."

"You're insane," she giggles, but quickly slams the door and makes her way to the vacant street. She stops and

---

1. *Ghost Ride IT*

checks the mirrors. "How are we supposed to do this? I can't stand on the roof of the car while it's moving."

I open my door. "Just put it in drive, let it idle, and walk on the street with the door open like this," I say, before boosting the volume to a terrifying level and jumping out onto the pavement.

Angie's giggle tells me everything I need to know. She's bursting with excitement as the lyrics hit us like a memory and the beat guides our steps. There isn't another car in sight as we belt the tune and swagger our way through the street next to the car, dancing like idiots.

"This is entirely the wrong kind of car to ghost ride," Angie hollers at me. "It's a mom car!"

"Yeah, but it's a cool mom car!"

"No, it's not. It's a Birkenstock-wearing, dog-owning, cross country skiing, farmers market-loving, mom car!"

"You love all of those things," I laugh. "This car was made for you."

"Ghost ride it!" We both shout when the chorus hits, unable to refrain.

It's then that another car comes into view, and we quickly hop back in with a fit of laughter as it drives past us. The look on her face is the one I think of when I think of Angie Johanssen.

Pure silly bliss.

Laughing so hard she can't breathe.

Unable to look directly at me in fear that she'll pee herself.

That version of her fills me with pride because she shares that side of herself with me, and there's no better feeling than when I've made her happy.

Chapter 24

September 17th

Rafael

When we get home, she pulls into the single car garage and kills the engine. But as soon as she shuts her car door, I'm on her, pushing her into the side and caging her in. "Hey," I rumble.

"Really? Right now?"

"Do you have any idea how turned on I was watching you negotiate?" I hum against her warm neck, her peachy perfume still lingering behind her ear after all that's happened today.

"That got you going?" She may be questioning me, but her hands are sliding up to my chest and she tilts her head, offering me better access.

"Mhmm. Would you like for me to be your good boy?" I need to remember she calls the shots here. Ever since our sleepover at my moms', I've been too reckless with the rules. But how can I not? I think about her constantly. I fantasize about her. I fantasize about what astonishing scenes she wants to try and somehow, she still surprises me. Now that I've seen this wild, lusty side of her, what we do together is anything but transactional. This isn't me simply taking care of her needs—this is me desiring her and needing to please her. It doesn't fucking matter if it's through domination or submission because every little touch from her is like a craving being fulfilled.

A breathy whimper escapes her, "Yes."

"You wanna christen the car?"

"Fuck yes."

"Let me make room," I huff and then quickly open the back door to fold the backseats down. Angie takes the opportunity to close the garage door so our neighbors don't get a full view of us going at it. After opening the hatchback and laying the back seats down, I guide her inside. She lays back against the floor and I take her mouth with mine before she can even rest her head back.

Fuck. Every time I get to kiss these plush lips I'm transported to a better place. A place of soft, ooey-gooey sweetness and magic. A place I didn't know existed until her.

"You were incredible today," I murmur against her full lips and her legs spread even wider for me to settle into, her dress hiking up to her waist. Her stomach is getting larger by the day, but there's still plenty of room for us like this. "The way you took charge and got exactly what you wanted," I groan and grind my dick against her. "So sexy."

"And you think I get turned on by strange stuff," she mocks.

"It made me want to get on my knees for you right there in the showroom."

Her hips begin to match my grinding. "Oh yeah? You would have looked so pretty like that. Showing everyone who fucking owns you."

"Yes, Ma'am," I moan, crumbling at her words and every shred of dignity and control evaporating from my being—desperation taking its place as I lick down the column of her neck. "Am I your baby?"

I feel her swallow thickly against the light suction I'm applying. "Yes," she sighs, her hands making their way into my hair and massaging. "Yes," she repeats, and her body relaxes more before treating my ears to her melodic praise. "Baby, that feels so good."

"Can I lick your pussy, Ma'am? Please."

"How can I say no when you ask so nicely?" I can practically hear her smirk.

"Thank you," I say eagerly, kissing and kneading my way down her heaving body, stopping to pay attention to her baby bump. With both hands, I press gently against it and close my eyes before silently adding another *thank you.*

My hands glide down her hips and I slip her sheer pink panties off and pocket them. There isn't enough room for me to sit back on my knees and watch her the way I want to, but there is enough room with the hatch open to plant one foot on the garage floor and the other knee bent up to hold myself in place before her, marveling as I push her stretchy cotton dress up and over her stomach.

This. View.

Fuck.

My cock is leaking precum as I stare at my best friend—her round middle and glistening pussy causing me to lose every logical thought I possess. "*Eres bella.*"

"So is your mouth. Use it."

My stomach drops and the pool of arousal in my groin deepens.

Damn, Angie.

Before I can get a taste, the warm, earthy smell of her cunt washes over my senses, heightening my need for her. I gently lick a stripe through her slit, collecting and following her wetness as it leads me home. I tease her clit with a hardened, fluttering tongue and once again, her fingers slice through my hair and clutch in, the sound of her heavy breathing stirring my own desire.

"That's it, baby. That's it," she gasps. "Oh my god, I'm almost there," she says like she can't believe it herself. But getting her off as fast as possible and as many times as I can manage has been my own personal goal. Sure, sometimes I like to tease her and build her up until she's reduced to nothing more than a whining, whimpering sub begging for relief. But most of the time, I want her to light up in ecstasy until she's whining and whimpering for me to stop.

I thrust two fingers inside her and curl them across that rough patch. "Please come on my face, Ma'am. *Ungh*, use me."

"Fuck," she chokes out, pulling hair until I feel the sting lance through my scalp and down my neck. Her whole body clenches, everything from her shoulders to cunt to her feet constrict, trying its best to keep me right where I am.

Far be it from me to deny her body what it wants.

My hand fucks her through her orgasm and I suck her clit harder, growling into her spasming flesh until she's crying from overstimulation several minutes later.

"I can't take any more," she exclaims, pushing my head away from her warm center as a trail of saliva forms a bowed line between us. Her hooded eyes and gaping mouth stare at me. "That... You're... You're a very good boy."

Her words comfort and reward me. "*Gracias.*"

But when she sits up abruptly and takes my belt in both hands, I think she's about to rip my pants off so that I can bury myself inside her. Instead, she whips my throbbing erection out and proceeds to push me down to where she was just laying, and quickly swallows the head of my cock.

"Oh fuck," I whisper out of shock. "You don't have to do this, Ang." In all our time fooling around with each other, I've been hesitant to let her go down on me. It feels too mutual for what we're doing. But when her velvety wet tongue slides down my shaft, her face softens, her eyes close, and she fucking purrs.

Dios Mio, que rico se siente. Mi angelita con esos labios tan pecadores / Oh my god, it feels so good. My little angel with those sinful lips.

Her slick hand slowly jerks me as she takes her mouth off just long enough to say, "I want to, baby. I want this so bad. Give me this."

The last thread of my resolve gives a valiant if not pathetic sounding reply. "Do you... Don't you want me inside you?"

Her mouth pops off my cockhead, but she nuzzles her face against my shaft like it's a jade face roller and it's going to cure all her skincare needs. "I want this more," she pants, then her seductive gaze shoots to mine. "Tell me you want this too, Raf."

Raf.

Me.

She could have said slut—my subby name I love but has a clear distinction of what roles we play. She could have said baby—the name that makes me soar with giddy pleasure but leaves me a little confused still. Maybe that's because we only say it in the heat of the moment. When she says it, the door to my vulnerability blows open, and it's precisely because of that exposure that I submit and fall into her.

But Raf. I'm always Raf to her. That's who she knows outside the bedroom, the car, the games. That is who she trusts. That is who dances with her. That is who will raise children with her.

Maybe I'm thinking too much. Maybe I'm reading into nothing and I should simply erase my intrusive thoughts and mindlessly give in to the hedonistic pleasure she's eager to give me.

"I want it," I whisper, deciding to think about this later because the idea of stopping her right now is a crime.

Angie's mouth envelopes me once again and her tight right fist strokes down to the base and back up to meet her lips. She slides her other fingers through the dripping saliva, and then presses her fingertips against my taint, slowly stroking me and causing me to moan louder than I expect.

She pops off my cock for a second—only an inch or two away—to marvel at me while still stroking my shaft and kneading behind my balls. "Look at you, taking my mouth like a good boy."

Oh shit. I've never heard someone phrase it like that and it sets me off even more. *Me voy a morir* / I'm going to die.

Once again pushing her tight mouth around my length, she slides herself down and takes as much as she can fit. This might be the sloppiest blowjob I've ever had, which is to say the best. It's so precise, but wet, nasty, and erotic at the same time. Her left hand searches up from my taint to my tightening sac and she plays with my balls, all while moaning around my cock.

"Goddammit, Ang. I mean Ma'am," I correct. She doesn't lift off but I can feel her smile. I want to praise her, but that's not what this is. "Thank you so much, Ma'am. Thank you. Thank you," I chant. I don't know how many more times I thank her because my brain is gone, replaced by my impending climax curling into a tight pressurized bundle in my stomach.

"I'm going to come," I grit. "Where do you want it?" Her stunning blue eyes fixate on mine and it's a death glare if I ever saw one. Hoping I'm reading the right message she's sending, I ask, "You want me to come in your mouth?" She nods like *of course I do and if you don't, I'll murder you.* "You got it," I breathe. "Fuck. Yes, yes..." I moan through my release as it shoots out and paints the inside of her luscious pink mouth.

Her eyes roll back and her throat works as she drinks me down. She waits a long, drawn-out moment before she slowly and torturously takes one last suck, then pulls off. Her playful tongue gives my cock one last lick as I lay here in blissful disbelief. "Jesus Christ, Ang. That was the best blowjob of my life."

"That's high praise," she smirks.

"Come here," I growl and force her to fall next to me so I can kiss the living daylights out of her, my thoughts on what we should and should not do be damned.

"Let's go inside," Angie says, melting into my touch. "I'm not done with you yet."

···•••••···

A little while later I'm laying naked as the day I was born, fresh from a quick shower and on Angie's soft pink and white duvet. "When did you get that?" I ask in surprise, as my soft cock stiffens again watching her take out and step into a beautiful purple strap-on.

She tightens the jock-like harness snugly against her hips. "A little while ago. Cora sent it to me."

That part has me raising an eyebrow. "Is there anything off limits between you two? Is there no room for mystery?"

"Why would we do that? That's no fun. Besides, she swears by this," Angie gestures at her hips and gives a test thrust, letting the lengthy dildo swish around. "And I've always been curious," she says with a roguish grin.

Throwing my hands behind my head on the pillow, I settle back and admire the view of my best friend in nothing but a sheer pink bra and a fitted strap standing before me, excitement bursting from her face. "It won't be my first time getting bent over and fucked, but it will be getting pegged."

Crawling onto the bed, Angie straddles my lap and lets the strap rest on my stomach. "When was the last time you had something inside you?" she asks carefully.

"It's been a while. Maybe six months."

Her fingertips ghost over my abdomen and chest before she asks, "You never played with yourself since then?"

"I don't know if you know this, Angie, but you've been occupying all my free time and siphoning every ounce of sexual energy I'm capable of. I haven't felt the need to do that in a long time."

"Is that something you miss? Being penetrated?" she asks with a softness in her eyes.

"Not until this very moment, watching you parade around here with this thing."

"Yeah? You wanna take my cock, Raf?" she says in a sing-song tone.

My hands fly to her hips and my fingers slide between her skin and the thick black straps; all traces of my smile are gone. "Yes, I do."

"You want this soft, pregnant woman to fuck your little hole like the slut you are?"

"Stop teasing me, Ma'am," I say as defiantly as I'm willing to get. She leans over to grab the lube she's already placed on the edge of the bed and I take the opportunity to caress her large ass as she brushes her belly against mine.

"Getting handsy I see," she admonishes, but the smile she tries to hide betrays her dominance.

"You're worth getting in trouble for," I quip.

"If you keep doing as you please, you're going to find yourself with a red backside and a cock in your ass."

Throwing her off me, I quickly flip over, press my forearms into the bed and arch my back with my ass on full glorious display. "Oh no," I whine, my butt swaying side to side. "I would hate that."

Angie dissolves into a puddle of laughter forcing me to follow suit. "Stop," she musters out. "I can't be a good Domme if you make me laugh like this."

"Are comedic brats a thing?" I chuckle.

"I'm not sure," she says, trying to catch her breath. "I've never read about them."

"Time to create some original content. Save it for your spank bank."

She finally sits up to kneel behind me, smoothing her hands over my ass, and then dragging her nails against my skin. "Oh, I'll be depositing spankings alright. What's your safeword, Raf?"

"Kenny Rogers," I answer, quirking an eyebrow. "Are you—fuck," I hiss after her hand makes abrupt contact with my right cheek, and my smile packs its bags as the sting sinks in and the heat rises.

"Wow," she says calmly. "That deposit was pretty easy. I think I'll make some more," and she smacks me again. Her slaps have me clenching my whole body in pain and anticipation. "This is by far the dumbest tattoo you have," she says affectionately while taking a break to graze her fingers over the word *butt* inked on my right cheek. "I think the funniest part is that the font is comic sans."

I got it after scoring my first try freshman year. Most teams make their rookies run a naked zulu lap after scoring their first try on a team, but not Penn Valley University Men's Rugby Team. Oh no. They make you get a tattoo of the veterans' choosing, inked right there at the social immediately following the game. I could have opted out and run a naked lap, but I thought this sounded more interesting.

It was my first tattoo and I remember Angie dying with laughter when I showed her. Soon after that, the tattoos came more frequently. The team crest on my thigh, Prison Mike from The Office on my inner bicep—that was quickly surrounded by the Japanese waves cascading down my upper arm when I studied abroad there for a semester sophomore year.

But none of my tattoos mean as much as the letter J inked over my heart. The same one Angie has slightly below her left collar bone in a more delicate font. It was our gift to each other when we graduated from undergrad—a testament to our friendship both for the past and the future.

Johanssen and Jimenez. We were always meant to stay together.

Were we always meant to become this? A couple of friends playing with Dom/sub dynamics and wild fantasies? Having children together? Being so intertwined into each other's lives that removal would be unfathomable?

Did I ever think my pretty best friend would see me as this? No. I was perfectly happy being a bachelor. But here I am, laying naked in front of her, wishing for her to spank me, praise me, degrade me, put me in a hog-tie and attach a vibrator to my balls, not because of the arrangement we struck, but because I wouldn't want to be anywhere else—with anyone else.

The thought of going back to what I was before getting Angie pregnant has lost all its appeal. Maybe that's because I can't see myself leaving for a hookup while being a new father. Maybe it's because the feeling I get from those hookups is no more exciting than dragging a lit sparkler through dusk. When I'm with Angie, it's like a grand finale of fireworks.

Out of nowhere, my father's voice rings like it always has. *Women will only ruin your life, mijo. Never get close.*

And for the first time since he told me that when I was fourteen, I question it. It's the smallest of irritations, like a tiny pebble stuck in my shoe, just bothersome enough that I could easily ignore it for another time, perhaps when Angie isn't about to push a purple dildo inside me.

"Are you ready, baby?" she asks in a sultry tone as the kiss of a slick phallus grazes against my back entrance.

Yeah, now's not the time for this mental unpacking.

· · • • · • • • · ·

Angie

"Yes," he sighs. For a moment there I was concerned he wanted to stop. He seemed like he was lost in thought.

"I'll go slow," I coo. I've already applied the lube directly to him and my strap, but I take the time to insert one then two fingers, scissoring his tight hole until it gives way for a third. Rafael doesn't need any instruction from me to relax—he definitely knows what to do. I've never experienced this side of things, but watching him breathe deep and moan as I gently massage him open is beyond my wildest fantasies. I'm in awe. "You're doing so good, Raf."

"I'm ready."

"Are you sure?"

"Yes. Please," he whines and spreads his long, toned legs even further apart to line up with me.

Grabbing my fake shaft, I can only see the end of it past my stomach, but I press the tip against his hole again, this time pushing in ever so slightly. "Oh shit," he whispers, and his right hand fists the pillow. "Yes. Don't stop." I'm not, but I'm still taking my time entering him at a glacial pace. When I'm mostly in, his entire body relaxes. I'm having a hard time playing Domme right now because I'm mesmerized by what's happening before me.

I intend to use the little remote to turn on a vibration setting, but I didn't expect to actually feel something while wearing this. It's not stimulating my clit, but there's this phantom feeling when I drag out and push in. Maybe it's all in my head; but it's the way the hip straps bite at my flesh when I'm pulling out of him and the way his hot skin kisses my thighs when they meet—it's so damn beautiful and real.

"Oh my god," I whisper. "I feel so...fucking powerful like this." I start to thrust in earnest, and Rafael's moans are his only reply. "Talk to me, baby. Where are you?"

"I'm so...so good," he says, followed by a string of mumbled expletives.

"You like taking my cock, you little slut?" I bite out.

"Yes, Ma'am."

"That's right," I say, running my hands on the side of his ass to his narrow hips and holding tight, using his body as leverage to pump harder and faster.

A round of applause to tops, though, because this is a lot harder than it looks. I get winded so easily these days. This is taking a lot of strength.

Grabbing the little black remote next to my knee, I press the button and quickly find the right vibration setting.

Why sex toy manufacturers give us more than two options is beyond me. Low and high. That's it. I don't need Morse code to get me off.

I'm pleasantly surprised at the amount of sensation against the outside of my pussy—and Raf is too. He gasps, "Sí sí sí. *Unghh.*"

"Touch yourself. Stroke that pathetic little cock you have." He obeys and shoves a hand between his legs. A tendril of perverse thrill rushes through me after degrading him like that.

"You're so good to me, Ma'am. Thank you."

I grind my hips against him to capture more pressure and rub the harness material into my clit. "Shit," I hiss. "That's so good, baby." I'm vaguely aware that I might be getting fast and loose with the baby's but I can't care when he's grinding against me too.

Out of nowhere, Raf slips away, gets to his knees and pushes me down on the bed. "That's enough," he growls and his eyes are like burning pools of desire. He looks feral as he spreads my legs open and moves the thin harness strap away from my pussy. "I need to be inside you. Now."

Apparently I'm not a very good Domme because I fold instantly, slipping into submission effortlessly. I barely squeak out a *yes, Sir* before he's thrusting inside of me in one powerful stroke and I'm gasping for air.

"*Ay dios mío. Mierda. Estás bienmojada, Ángel* / Oh my god. Shit. You're so wet, Angel."

He sounds so sexy when he speaks in Spanish. "*Sí. Siga hablando en español, por favor* / Yes. Keep speaking in Spanish, please," I whine.

His large hands glide into the crevice between my hips and thighs, squeezing me and pulling me into him. "*Este coño es perfecto. Eres tan hermosa así.* / Your cunt is perfect. You're so beautiful like this."

As Rafael pumps into me I find pleasure not only in what he's doing to me, but what he's giving. His handsome face contorts like it pains him to have this much pleasure.

This, though. This power exchange. This switching of roles and the push and pull we have with each other—it makes so much sense for us. We are a million things, him and I. We don't fit in any one category or genre. Our interests are vast and our curiosities insatiable.

He adds a thumb to my clit and I buck into his touch, chasing my orgasm like a moth to flame. "*Oh Señor, sí. Más. ¡Me voy a correr! Mierda. ¡Sí!* / Oh Sir, yes. More. I'm going to come! Fuck. Yes!" I whimper, and clench around him, arching my back and digging my hands into my tender breasts. But he doesn't stop, doesn't relent. He fucks me harder, making my orgasm span out and I'm free falling with no end in sight.

"*Eso es mi ángel, úsame para tu placer. Quiero que te sigas viniendo en mi verga. Quiero que siempre estés llena de mi esencia. Dime que tu lo quieres también.* / That's it my angel, use me to please yourself. I want you to keep coming on my cock. I want you to always be full of my essence. Tell me you want it too."

"Sí," I whimper.

Suddenly he leans over, arching over my bump and takes my mouth in a frenzied kiss. His arm braces on one side of my head and his other hand clasps behind my neck. He bites my lips like they're the only thing anchoring him to this world.

"I have something for you," he whispers. Before I can form the words to ask what it is, he's pulling something out from under his pillow. His face lifts from mine just enough for me to turn and see him holding a blue and red water gun.

"No," I bellow in laughter as my orgasm finally dips.

"Yes," he replies, eyes wide and grin wider. "You asked for it and this is what I'm comfortable with."

"Oh my god. I applaud the commitment. Let's fucking do it."

"What's the scene, Angel?"

Plucking the fantasy from my mental bookshelf, I say, "Your father is the city's crime boss and you're his heir. I'm just a girl in the wrong place at the wrong time and witnessed too much. You've been sent to kidnap and torture me to get information. But I'm tougher than I look! You're beguiled by my beauty and brains, so you try to seduce-torture me with your cock and your glock."

"Jesus fucking Christ, Ang."

"It's hot, I know."

He starts to peel off my strap. "Maybe someday I could be a kraken crime boss."

I go silent as the wheels turn in my brain. "That's not a bad idea."

Tossing my lady cock and harness to the side, he then trails the tip of the gun against my inner thigh. "The bad idea," his voice dropping, caressing my ears like velvet. "is me leaving here without any answers." The gun then taps at my wet center and my entire lower half tightens in fear. He throws my hands above my head and pins them down with one of his. Faster than I thought possible, I immerse myself into the scene. "So you can either tell me what you saw by the docks, or we can play Russian roulette with your cunt," he growls.

He. Growls.

"Oh my god," I whisper, and then dry swallow. "I told you; I didn't see anything."

"You're fucking lying, and you're lying to yourself that I don't turn you on. You think you're so innocent, but you're a thief. You have information that doesn't belong to you." The gun thrusts inside me and the foreign object is every bit as intrusive, bizarre, and hot as I dreamed it.

My whimpers are lost under his commanding voice again when he says, "I'll give you one minute after each pulled trigger to try and get off." He pulls the gun out of my pussy and replaces it with his own thick length, then presses the gun firmly against my clit, making me shiver. He smirks. "You'll have up to six minutes or no time at all." Then he pulls back the trigger and a shot of cool water scares the living spirit out of me.

My chest frantically shakes as I try to catch my breath. Shit. I did not think I'd be this frightened, but my raging lady boner is hard as a rock, and I'm not talking about the purple dildo sitting next to me.

"Do you understand me, little thief?" he bites out, then throws his hips against me with the gun rocking against my clit.

"Yes!"

He's caging me in, forcing me to submit like a captive as I let the fear amp up my arousal. The gun's ridges and unforgiving material bite against my sensitive flesh. Panic sets in with every passing second that I don't come; and when he slows his thrusts to pull the trigger again, I'm reaching for his wrists and squeezing them like they're going to save me. The shot of cool water once again shocks me, but it's the dripping water down my ass that has me focusing on the task at hand.

"You don't have to do this," I plead.

"Of course I do. They'll kill me if I don't come back with answers, and then they'll kill you—and they won't be so nice about it," he snarls. The speed and pressure of his gun against my pussy increases to a painfully pleasant experience to which I'm grateful because before the next shot, I'm wrapping my legs around his waist, locking him in place as I reach my climax and ride it out. Between his dick buried to the hilt and the hilt of the gun in his hand being shoved against my soft sensitive flesh, I rock and clench into him.

With only a few more thrusts, he releases himself inside me with labored grunts as my own orgasm finally makes its slow decrescendo.

Moments later, his mouth finds mine and our bodies relax. Our kiss becomes kisses. Small. Sweet. Tender. Rafael rolls us to our sides but our faces stay pressed together. When his hand moves near my pussy, I think he's about to fuck me with the gun again; instead, with a steady hand, he pushes all four fingers against my slit, pushing his release back inside me.

Kill me now.

It's *all part of the game*, I tell myself weakly. But the hormones clap back. *Breed me, Rafael.*

"Who's turn is it for aftercare?" he smiles against my lips and I snort.

"I think after that we're both due."

We take turns cleaning the other and soothing any sore spots. We check in on our experiences and where our emotional loads lie. Like always, I tell him the truth, but only enough to not disrupt the delicate ecosystem of our friendship.

When we've both washed up and used the bathroom, then brushed our teeth next to one another, we make our way into bed with fresh pajamas and satisfied bodies. He places an antacid chew in my hands because he knows I get raging heartburn at night and I chew it with a smile. Then he wraps me up in his arms and Razz—all twenty pounds of him—jumps up to join us.

Has he been in here the whole time? Yeesh, how much did he hear?

My boy nuzzles and purrs his way into the space between my chest and pillow as Rafael spoons us and pets Razzle's one-eyed face.

It's so painfully right.

"I was thinking," he murmurs into my hair. "Since we're moving into the house on Chestnut before the babies come, would you like to help decorate?"

"Really?"

"Yeah. It's going to be as much your home as it is mine."

"Well, that's not true at all. You own it. And aren't you going to sell it when the market is right?"

"I don't know," he hums. "It's growing on me. I feel like we could really lay down some roots there." My heart pitter-patters at his future plans—the future plans he has for us.

"Um...okay," I smile because what else does one do when the person they love most wants you to make his home yours? "So like, furniture and stuff?"

"Furniture, paint colors, light fixtures, you name it. Whatever you want, I want that too."

If only that were true outside the context of our house, I think to myself.

"I'd love that," I say with heartbreaking honesty and guilt swirling together in my gut.

"Good. It'll probably help with your nesting habits too."

"What are you talking about?"

He stiffens slightly. "The...weekly deep cleans of the entire townhouse? You cleaned the tops of the cabinets and the legs of the dining chairs. You steam-cleaned every piece of upholstery last weekend."

"That's not nesting," I drawl. "I'm just a clean person."

He chuckles. "We have a housekeeper, Ang." He might have a point. "We can go over there soon and let Joaquín know our choices."

"Oh really? I can paint. I love painting actually."

"Ang, you get winded taking the laundry out of the dryer these days."

"Hey," I playfully scold. "I can handle a little paint."

Chapter 25

September 22nd

Angie

T urns out I cannot handle a little paint.

I stare at the blood red wall in front of me as I splay out on the tarp-covered floor of the living room. It's only half painted, but I'm so out of breath I need this break. Yesterday, Raf and his moms helped me paint the nursery a sweet pastel yellow, and it turned out perfect. But today I'm here by myself, and after switching paint colors last minute at the hardware store, I made a slightly bolder choice to axe the eggshell-finish cream and go for blood. I mean red.

I like it. I just wish I had enough energy to finish it.

Finally catching my breath but still sweating, I dial Joaquín.

"Hey pretty lady," he says cheerfully. "What are you doing?"

"Painting the living room."

"Raf there?"

"No. He's doing some charity fundraiser five-k with the team today."

"Oh that's right. So what's going on?"

"Well, turns out I'm not as physically capable as I once was," I admit. "Raf told me to tell you what colors and lights to order?" I trail off, hoping he knows about that.

"Yeah, of course! You need me to get the crew on it?"

"Yes please," I sigh. "I got all the paint and wallpaper, I just need everything else taken care of," I laugh.

"You got it. Do you have any inspiration pics you can send me?"

"Oh yeah." I perk up at that and start scrolling through my phone. "There. You should have them now."

"Oh," he says ominously. "Are...are you sure about this? These are all so...unique."

"I thought so too," I cheer.

"So this kind of gothic red and black one... This would be for...?"

"The living room," I say flatly.

"Okay," he drawls. "And this Barbie Dream House?"

"All the bathrooms."

"And this hobbit-like dwelling with all the mushrooms and crystals and plants?"

"The sunroom. Oh, and the stairs and the halls. You know, for cohesion."

"Gotcha. Welp, I don't see any need to run this past my brother, do you?"

"He's gonna love it," I beam.

"Okay, I'll tell the crew and make sure they know the library will be giving cottage-core vibes."

"The what?"

"The library," he repeats.

"There's no library in this house."

"Yeah. Raf said the sunroom is supposed to be a library for you. I have custom shelving being installed in a few weeks."

"What?" God, I sound like a broken record, but—what?

"Yeah. They're beautiful. You're going to love them."

I'm stunned. He's giving me a library? Once again guilt gnaws its way into my gut, but it's surrounded by tiny fluttering pink butterflies.

"I've always wanted a library," I whisper to myself.

"I know," Joaquín says with a lilt. "Your romance books will be so happy in their new home. By the way, that queer

orc romance with the drag queen was a great recommen-
dation. Five stars. Alright I gotta go but send me anymore
inspo pics you have, and I'll get it all squared away with the
crew."

"Okay," I say, still taken aback by this new information and
what it means, if anything.

"*Te quiero.*"

"*Te quiero*, Joaquín..."

Chapter 26

September 28th

Angie

"Did your brothers say why they wanted us to come early today?" Rafael asks, turning into the home field park.

"Not really," I say. "But apparently Jonah is bringing Yogi and Rugger."

"God, they're cute. I still can't believe he got two dogs."

"I can't believe he found two Great Pyrenees pups at a shelter. Not exactly a breed you'd see there often."

When we step out of the car into the dewy morning air, the two white fluff balls are rolling around and play-fighting with each other. They're much bigger than the last time I saw them when Jonah tried to bring them to the beach.

There are a few other players getting here at the same time, but we make our way to my three brothers all standing in a little huddle with their kits on the ground nearby. They're still in their warmup sweats and sandals, and Jonah's mop of blonde hair doesn't look like it was combed this morning and his whole body is covered in white dog hair.

Looking at the three of them, I'm reminded how the hair color of the Johanssen kids looks like the printer ran out of ink. Me and Isaiah have the darkest, followed by Dane with a sandy brown, and Jonah and Ivy with blonde.

Their demeanors sort of match that now that I think about it. Isaiah is gruff and grumpy. Dane is naturally a social person, but he also gets a little grumpy when things aren't going his way. And Jonah... Oh, Jonah. Brother Sunshine. He's never met a person he can't charm.

"I'll let you catch up with them," Raf says. "I'm gonna help Snarf line the field."

"Sure. I'll see you in a bit."

He walks away carrying my bag chair, blanket, and his kit before turning to my younger brothers.

The three of them spot us just before Jonah throws his arms open to hug me. "Angie-Pangie! Did you bring orange slices today?"

"Of course I did."

"Dude, come on," Isaiah grumbles. "We talked about this."

Jonah pulls back and crosses his arms and his expression changes from his natural smile to a frown.

My head rears back as I take them all in. "What's going on?"

Isaiah clears his throat. "We know you two shared a room when we were in Saranac."

"What's your point?" I say calmly, but a burst of panic sets in. This shouldn't be worthy of discussion with them. It was never uncommon for us to share a room or a bed from time to time if the situation called for it.

Dane goes next. "Wheels' wife said she saw you two out at dinner the other night."

"So? People eat together."

I think I know what night he's talking about. We were at a trendy restaurant for a mocktail happy hour that turned into apps and dinner, and when the Cuban music started playing, we had to dance.

You know, normal friend stuff.

Well...normal for us.

Dane then pulls his phone from his pocket and shows me a picture from Jay's social media account. "What about this?" he accuses.

It's a series of photos from the ABBA cover band concert we all attended last week. But the specific picture Jonah shows me is of Cora in Marco's arms smiling at the camera, pink and purple lights cast over their bodies and illuminate their surroundings. Jay's focus was to take a picture of his husband and wife, but in the background is a picture of me and Rafael in the same exact pose. His big arms are wrapped around my shoulders and his chin rests on top of my head. We were swaying to the music, entranced by the performers.

I don't blame Jay for posting that picture. In fact, he asked for permission to post them before doing so. We approved the pictures because, well, we didn't see anything wrong with it. That's us. That's the normal level of affection we've always shown each other.

But as I study it under the lens that I think my brothers are, my knees go a little weak and my gut drops. Can they see it? Can they see the unrequited feelings? Can they see how I've let Rafael use me like an unacknowledged girlfriend all these years?

I've let him play pretend with our relationship for as long as I can remember because I'm weak for him and if I ever called him on it, I'd expose us. I'd expose the part of Rafael he's worked to keep locked away from fleeting partners. I'd expose that I've known all along what he's been doing, and that I've encouraged it. I've leaned hard into it with sex, decorating the house, and the intimate conversations about our teenage crushes—it's all led here.

I've allowed this to happen and blatantly ignored the inevitable destruction of my heart. I did this before he got me pregnant, and now I've amplified it.

Goddammit.

I try to hide my fear and shame from them before shrugging, "It was just a concert."

"You look like you're in love," Isaiah says bluntly.

"It's the lighting," I smile weakly.

"Shut up, it is not," Jonah finally interjects with an eye roll.

It's my turn to cross my arms. "Are you guys going to get to the point?"

"Yeah!" Jonah says, then turns to Dane. "You tell her."

"Jesus, dude," he mutters with a shake of his head and then asks me, "Why aren't you getting married?"

Okay, that's not exactly where I thought he was going with this interrogation, but my cheeks heat regardless. My gaze darts away. "Because people who are just friends don't get married," I say quietly.

"Cut the shit, Ang," Isaiah groans. "Listen, I don't like the idea of you and Raf as a couple any more than them," he snarls with a hooked thumb pointing to Dane and Jonah. "But that's only because we see him and Joaquín as our bonus brothers."

Dane winces. "Well..."

Isaiah ignores him and continues. "But are you really going to stand here and lie to us that something isn't happening between you two?"

I am far from admitting the truth to these three. I don't owe them anything. The only people who know about the true arrangement Raf and I have are Cora, Marco, and Jay, and it's going to stay that way.

"Nothing is happening, guys," I smile in an attempt to deflect.

"Oh okay," Jonah says in a mocking tone. "Let's pretend nothing's happening. Sure. Irregardless—"

"That's not a word," I mutter.

"—you guys should get married anyway. For the kids."

I stare at him, dumbfounded.

I stare at Dane.

I stare at Isaiah.

"All three of you think that?" They all nod in various degrees. "That's fucking ludicrous, you trad-family-at-any-cost morons!"

Jonah's brow furrows. "Huh?"

Shaking my head, I level a glare at them. "I'm not going to marry him just because I'm pregnant. That's some patriarchal bullshit fueled by religion."

"Why not? Mom did and they were happy," Dane argues.

"No, she didn't! She wrote in my baby journal that they planned on getting married anyway. And that they were very much in love."

"Oh," Isaiah says in flat understanding.

"I'm not going to enter into a marriage with someone who doesn't love me." Dane tries to add something, but I cut him off. "In that way. I deserve someone who wants to be married to me simply because they love me—not out of obligation."

"Ang," Isaiah sighs.

"No," I say, lowering my voice to a level and a tone I haven't used with them in a long time. "I've said all that you need to hear. You're not going to pester me or Parent Trap me into marrying him. End of discussion."

When their silence drags on too long and their heads lower, I know I've won, but the victory feels hollow.

"I just don't want to see you alone," Isaiah mutters, his words pinching at my heart in a surprising way.

"You don't have to worry about that," I say gently. "And Raf's always going to be around, you guys."

"He better be," Dane says under his breath.

My gaze travels to a handful of other players who have arrived and are starting to gear up. "Thank you for your misplaced brotherly love, but it looks like you should get ready with your team. Oh hey, Isaiah—is that Robyn and her dad walking over here."

His head whips around to see where I'm indicating. "What?" he asks, suddenly on high alert. "Crap. Why is she—I gotta go warm up," he stammers then wraps me in a quick bear hug. "Love you, Ang."

Isaiah books it for his teammates, and then Jonah and Dane each give me a hug and when they've sat down to start booting up, Raf comes toward me in a jog from lining the field. "What did they want?"

I shake my head. "You're not going to believe this. They asked me why we weren't getting married."

"What?" he asks with his eyebrows sky-high.

"Yeah," I sigh.

"Wait... Do you want to?"

It's my turn to be surprised. "What? No," I say immediately, but not before my heart leaps at the saddest excuse for a proposal I've ever heard.

Is that really his response? Is the thought just now popping into his thick skull? I try to shake off the idiotic response my brain is firing at me. Didn't I just ream my brothers out for thinking the same thing?

"Yeah, I was going to say..." He smiles and for the first time those dimples of his piss me off. "I didn't realize they felt that way. Alright, well I'm gonna get ready with the team. I'll see you after," he smiles again and jogs away.

He smiled.

He smiled because it's so fucking ridiculous for him to imagine being married to me, to commit to me. I feel the babies kick and I take that as solidarity.

This is my own fault. I opened this door. I repeatedly ignored my feelings, ignored my heart and its stupid attachment to him—the attachment that has only grown stronger since we've started fucking.

Even that word doesn't feel right.

We haven't been fucking. Not even from the beginning. Yes, they've mostly been fantasies we've enacted but... I haven't been fucking him. I've been... Shit. I let the person I trust more than anyone else make love to me. He might not know it, but I do.

I've been purposefully ignoring my true feelings just like I have my whole life with Raf. How can I be so honest everywhere else when it comes to what I feel and how I communicate, but I can't get it right with him?

Because if he knew, everything would end.

I would ruin everything. The closeness. Our laughter. His family. I'd lose my living mothers, Ana and Christina.

By keeping my mouth shut, I've been protecting my heart and almost everything it values. I've grown accustomed to hiding, but can I keep doing this after everything we've been through in the last six months?

But I know Rafael better than anyone, maybe better than himself sometimes. He's a loyal friend and brother. I know beyond a shadow of a doubt that he's going to stick around for these babies. I'm not even remotely concerned about that. So if that's the case, maybe it is a safe time to step back.

From this arrangement.

From him.

From us.

I need to put up the divider that I needed a long time ago. Just like the first day we met, I need to draw a line down the middle of our desks and create some semblance of separation.

My heart needs the boundary if it's ever going to survive.

It's time to end our arrangement. It's time to dissolve our too-close friendship. The platonic intimacy he seeks is too fucking real to me—it gives me unwarranted hope, which only fuels the desire to keep it burning.

I feel like his shameful secret—the one he parades around in plain view of everyone. I can't be the girlfriend or wife he says he doesn't want.

Chapter 27

September 28th

Rafael

A fter the game and social, adrenaline from the win is coursing through my body. We've been undefeated this season and it only rockets my enthusiasm as well as the team's. Though the Johanssen brothers don't seem too keen to share a non-alcoholic beer with me at the social, I shrug it off. They'll get over it. Once the babies come, they'll be too wrapped up in being uncles that they won't bring this up again.

Maybe.

"Woof," I sigh, stepping into our place behind Angie and immediately slumping into the couch and kicking off my slides. We've been gone all day and the sun is already making its way down. "I'm whooped. I need a shower, food, and—oh, *muchacho time!*" I croon, picking up Razzle Dazzle and placing him on my chest. "Hi, buddy."

"I'm gonna change out of these jeans," Angie says, unbraiding her hair as she walks toward the stairs.

"Hey wait, why don't you join me in the shower?" I smirk, hoping she turns around and throws one back.

But she doesn't. She doesn't even turn around or stop.

"No, that's okay."

What? Is she okay? She never declines a sexy shower. They're usually her idea after a game.

"Are you sure?" I blurt and quickly get to my feet to follow her with Razz still against my chest. She's halfway up the stairs when I say, "I could be your good boy." I realize how desperate that sounds once it leaves my lips, but I don't give a fuck.

When we reach the top, she finally looks at me with a smile that doesn't reach her eyes. With a tiny nod to the bathroom door, she says, "Why don't you take a shower and I'll make us some dinner."

"Are you okay?" I ask, placing my free hand on her hip, but she backs away.

"I'm just tired. Go. I'll meet you downstairs." Before I can respond, she's heading for her bedroom, leaving me perplexed and a little defeated.

I soap up and let the hot water rinse away the dirt and uncomfortable niggle in my gut the best I can. When I step out, I pop a low dose pain killer to stave off the future aches and pains I'll have in the morning and head down to the kitchen wearing only the thin, gray joggers I know drive Angie crazy.

I'm not over this.

It's fine if she doesn't want to have sex—that's not what's eating at me. She seems distant and cagey and I want to figure out why. Maybe I'm using the gray pants as bait, but I'm going to get answers one way or the other.

When I get to the kitchen, she's at the stove mixing pasta and a light green sauce and plating it up. "Smells good," I lie and cozy up to her back, placing my hands on her hips and kissing her neck.

"Oh," she says shakily, almost like she's nervous. "Yeah, this sounded good. I'm just," she huffs and squirms from my touch again. "Sorry, I'm just not in the mood. I'm starving. Let's just eat," she smiles and takes both plates to the dining table with silverware.

She walks away, and I slowly follow and pull out her chair. "I thought you said watching me play rugby turned you on?"

Setting the plates at our spots but not looking at me, she says, "Did I? Oh. So how's work going? You never talk about it. Is Cora a good boss?" She's obviously trying to change the subject, so I let her. If something is really going on, she'll tell me when she's ready.

After she takes her first bite, I take mine and nearly choke, but I try to hide it. She's already having a third bite when I ask, "This is great. What's in this?"

"It's linguine with alfredo and pesto mixed together. I added some vinegar. I think it really adds that umami flavor, you know?"

It adds something alright, I think to myself. Her tastes have been out of control lately, but I'm not going to say a word. She's carrying my children and I won't make her feel weird for liking what she likes. She's still mad about the ghost pepper salsa.

So I eat it—every bite—and tell her about how much I love my job and working for Cora. How the company has turned a new leaf and how much I'm trying to prove myself.

When she goes back for seconds, I take the opportunity to clean everything up and make some Old Bay-dusted popcorn. Because tonight is trash TV night and it's our tradition. She seems on board with our routine, and when I hand her the bowl, she takes it with a real smile and makes her way to the living room to turn on Million Dollar Listing.

Finishing up, I press start on the dishwasher and head for the couch where she's already sitting with her feet up on the cushioned ottoman and Razz perched behind her. She's changed into one of her loose-fitting maternity nightgowns. It's pretty on her. It's short sleeve and me-dieval-looking. Reminds me of that time we played the duke and tavern wench, and I chuckle to myself at the fond memory.

Taking my place next to her, we comfortably watch and banter back and forth about the stars of the show and their methods of selling high-end real estate in Los Angeles. When the popcorn runs out, I set the bowl on the side table and lean over to place my head in her lap like I've done for years. Except the softness and warmth I expect is stiff and jerky.

She nudges my shoulder. "Can you get off me please? You're just...really warm and it's too much."

"Oh, sure." I sit up right away because I know how over-stimulated she can get lately. Just the way a fabric will rub can send her senses on high alert and her heart rate skyrocketing.

So we just sit there. We're a couple feet away from each other, and even though we're on a plush, oversized couch, I'm uncomfortable.

What is going on with me?

When the commercials run, a steamy movie trailer plays for some action-romance that I think she might be interested in. Hell, I'm interested in it based on the way my groin perks up. But when I side glance at Angie, she's looking anywhere but the TV. Her throat swallows on nothing and she's fidgeting with a seam on her nightgown.

I'm about to ask her if she'd like to see the movie, but she bolts up. "I'm tired," she says, then makes her way to the stairs. "I'm going to bed."

Shutting the TV off, I follow her. "Okay. We can go to bed now if you want."

She spins on her heel and puts up a hand to stop me from coming closer. "No," she spits out with eyes round. "I want to sleep in my own bed tonight." I study her. "Alone please," she adds.

Now I'm really worried. I thought what we've been doing has been working out great. I've grown accustomed to her bed and our bodies tangled in it. I thought she liked it, too. I thought she wanted it.

She has the right to sleep alone if she wants to, my conscience reminds me. But this distance between us today has me on-edge.

I force myself to stay planted where I am as I watch her ascend the stairs again without a look back. She gives me a perfunctory "Good night," and then the latch to her door clicks.

I stand there dazed and replaying everything that has happened since we got home. Because that's when it all changed. But what exactly is *it*? What changed? I can't pinpoint any one thing. Something is off between us and it's making my skin crawl.

In a swirl of distress, I shoot upstairs with feather-light steps and lean against the door frame. When I make out the sound of her crying, every nerve in my body electrifies, and I can't stop myself from knocking. "Angel, what's going on? Can you talk to me?"

Immediately her crying stops and her throat clears. "I'm fine, Raf. I just need some space."

"You're not fine—"

"Raf," she bellows. "I swear to god, if you don't leave me alone, I'm going to castrate you!"

Taking the not-so-subtle hint, I back off. "Okay. Fair enough. Goodnight, Ang." Maybe this is a mood swing. I've read numerous pregnancy articles and blogs about this very thing. She's probably just been out in the sun all day and she's tired. If she wants space, I can give that to her. *I'm here for her no matter what she needs*, I remind myself.

As I step away from her door, I hear music play. Lingering a moment longer, I recognize it as *Fancy* by Iggy Azalea and I try to put together the most impossible puzzle in my mind.

I say nothing when the song plays on repeat all night.

·· • • • • • • ··

Angie

Turns out my patient was a liar. Listening to *Fancy* did not make me happy.

Chapter 28

October 4th

Rafael

Angie's been keeping busy between work and the Chestnut street [1] house. Every day this week, she either gets out of work and goes straight there, or she's video chatting with Ivy in her room all evening. She only goes to the fixer-upper when she knows I can't. Like when I have practice after work.

When I went there a few days ago and saw the red and black walls in the living room and hot pink in the bathroom, I knew without even asking that this was her doing. I'm not going to question it. If this is what makes her happy and makes her want to live there with me, then I'll let her paint the outside in glitter for all I care.

I'd love to talk to her about it, but my gut is telling me she's intentionally avoiding me. Of course I scoured the internet looking for evidence, hoping that this behavior is normal for pregnant people. I easily found a reassuring answer, but I'm no less convinced this isn't my fault.

Tonight, I'm going to sit her down and talk to her. We've always had great communication, so what's going on now?

"Hey, I'm heading home early today," I tell my staff as we wrap up the next year's budget meeting. "Feel free to do the same."

---

1. *Shaky Hands* by VACAY

"Cool," my controller, Michelle, nods. "How's Angie doing?"

It's not uncommon for me to field questions like this. I actually love it. Before she was pregnant, I only got them from family who know how close we are. But now that she's carrying our babies, anyone who knows me even a little bit asks about her.

"She's doing great," I say, the half-truth eating away at me. "Babies are measuring on track. They're kicking relentlessly now," I smile, packing my laptop up. At least Angie has let me touch her belly this last week in a few fleeting moments. Nothing else though, and no sleepovers either.

I fucking hate my bed now. My room might be the same temperature as hers, but it's cold and lonely.

But I don't let that image stop me from my mission tonight. I'm going to head home early, make all her favorite foods, and talk to her. I've already canceled my plans with a couple of my teammates that we made a while ago. They're both dads, so I didn't have to explain myself to them. They get it.

I didn't tell Angie I canceled my plans though, and when I glance at my messages as I walk out of the office, I read the last text from her sent yesterday.

> **Angie:** Are you still planning on hanging out with Small Fry and Wheels tomorrow?

> **Raf:** Yeah. Why? Do you need me to cancel?

> **Angie:** No. Just wanted to confirm.

> **Angie:** Thanks.

Thanks, period. Like it was an after-thought.

I take my time grabbing every grocery needed and extras just in case. As I check out from the bougie store, I see a phenomenal display of fresh flowers and grab a large bouquet. I've only bought her flowers on her birthday before. The weather is always so cruddy on February 20th, so I always get the brightest, summer-like flowers I can find. But based on the outfits she's been wearing lately, I know she's loving the fall season, so I make sure to pluck an autumn arrangement.

As soon as I get home and give Razz some quick loving, I put the flowers in a vase and get to work. I don't even change out of my work clothes—I just get to work on the random assortment of dishes. Veggie tostadas, enchiladas, rice, beans, fresh fruit, a meatless meatloaf, garlic-mashed potatoes, broccoli with butter and a heavy dusting of Tajin. I even have several chocolate mousse tarts she's been inhaling lately from the bakery. I have no idea what she's in the mood for, but something here must be it.

As I take out the enchiladas from the oven and place them on the table with everything else, I hear the door open and my heart pounds in my ears. Suddenly I'm incredibly aware of our playlist filling the room. It's a sexy little salsa number we love dancing to, and even though it's one of our favorites for years, at this very moment it's wholly wrong for what I want to convey. I don't want her thinking I'm doing this as some grand gesture to get back into her panties or her bed. I simply want us to go back to what we've always been, but I need her to talk to me.

Angie's rightfully shocked to see me here as she hovers in the threshold, hand still on the doorknob and wearing that cute olive-green dress I like. "What's going on?" She looks at the flowers in the center of the table and back at me. "What is all this?"

Eagerly, I take a few steps toward her and smile before taking her into a hug. "I thought we could eat together and talk about what's going on. How you're feeling."

She pushes me out of the hug gently and looks up at me with soft eyes and a confused look. "Raf, I'm sorry, but I made plans tonight," she says and my heart sinks. "I wish you would have—" she cuts herself off from saying anymore.

I tug at the back of my neck. "I thought this was a nice surprise. Look," I say and gesture to the table. "I made all the things you've been craving lately."

Angie's pained expression cuts my chest open. "I... I'm sorry but I made plans with someone tonight and I don't want to cancel on them, Raf."

"With who?"

"Don't worry about it."

Did she really just say don't worry about it to me? That might be the most bothersome thing she's said to me yet. Reaching over to the console behind the couch, I turn the music way down so it's not distracting.

She closes the door, and tries to take a few steps away, but I juke to make up the distance. "What's going on with you, Angel?"

"Don't call me that anymore," she mutters.

"Why not? Hey, wait." I urge and place my hands gently but firmly on her shoulders to stare her in the eyes. "Talk to me. You've always been my An—"

"Don't," she cuts me off from saying her nickname. "Don't do this to me, Raf."

"Don't do what?"

"You know exactly what I'm talking about."

"No, I don't. Enlighten me."

She sighs and looks at the table before turning to meet my eyes. "You know by calling me Angel, I'll crumble for you. I'll do whatever you want me to. It's the button you push when you want me to be soft for you. And I... I can't do that anymore. I can't keep pretending all the innocent touches and smiles and nicknames don't affect me. I can't keep letting you use me!"

"Angie, when have I ever—"

"Emotionally, Rafael! You use me emotionally. I've always been here for you to let your guard down and be your true self; and I love your true self—"

"I love you too, Ang," I say softly.

Her huff of frustration forms into a single tear falling from her beautiful blue eyes. "You love me like a friend, Raf. I don't have any qualifiers. I love you."

All at once, the air is sucked out of the room and everything in me stills except the thunderstorm in my heart. A tightness pulls across every inch of my skin and the hairs raise on the back of my neck.

She loves me?

"Since when?" I manage to ask. But before she can answer, there's a knock at the door. I'm too stunned to move or care who's there.

"Does it matter?" she says defeatedly, then opens the door like she already knows who's waiting.

There stands Jared Holloway, just as shocked to see me as I am to see him. My mind reels back to that night freshman year when she left me at that party to lose her virginity to Jared—and all the nights following when she'd leave me to hook up with him.

"What's Rafael doing here?" he asks her.

"I live here, asshole," I seethe.

"You live with Angie?"

"Were you going on a date with him?" I accuse her and she rubs her forehead with a sigh.

"Ang, are you okay?" Jared asks, reaching for her arm and stroking it gently. "You look like you've been crying."

"Don't touch her," I snarl.

"That's enough!" Angie barks. "Jared, could you please give us a moment. I'll be right there."

He looks at me warily but nods to her. "Sure. I'll just...be out here."

When the door closes, so does my resolve. "Were you going to fuck him?" She crosses her arms and stares at me in response. "Were you?"

"I don't know."

To my surprise, my throat locks up and tears start to form. "I thought we had an agreement. Why would you fuck him when I'm right here?"

"BECAUSE HE DOESN'T MEAN EVERYTHING TO ME!" she shouts, but I'm too pissed and stunned and miserable to say anything back. "I can't be casual with you, Raf," she cries. "My heart demands more. I want, I need commitment. I want to be so thoroughly loved and committed to and labeled as yo—someone's partner. Not a fuck buddy. Not a baby mama. I am wife material, Rafael. You can't keep pretending I'm your wife just because you can't let anyone else in. I'm sorry, but I need to stop."

"Stop what?"

"Stop with all the affection. As platonic as it may seem to you... I can't do it anymore. My brain—my heart—can't separate platonic from romantic with you. We're going to be seeing a lot of each other for the rest of our lives," she says through more broken sobs, touching her belly. "And I can't keep doing this to myself, Raf. I think this is the only way I can keep you in my life."

Has she been considering cutting me out of it? The thought cuts me deep—deep in a place I didn't know existed. How can she possibly consider that?

When she opens the door again, Jared is standing on the sidewalk with his hands in his pockets. He looks up at us, swiftly climbs the stoop and reaches for her hand.

With every ounce of desperate pleading, I choke out, "Please don't leave, Angel."

She's already one foot out the door when she turns back with a serious set to her brow as she tries to push through the tears. "Why, Raf?"

She crosses her arms and gives me a moment to speak, but nothing comes out.

"I don't see how this can keep going the way it is," she continues. "Tell me you love me like I love you. Tell me this isn't hopeless. Because I either need all of you, or I need to find someone else who can."

Everything inside me begs for me to respond, to say something—anything—to get her to stay, but I'm frozen. Why can't I say anything? I love her so much. I care for her deeply, but there's an internal force blocking me from telling her more. I do love her as a friend, but it's not enough. Somehow, it's both not enough and too much.

You're never enough, I think to myself.

Angie wipes at the tear streaking down her face and sighs. "That's what I thought."

And just like that, she leaves me silent and crying as she climbs into the car of Jared fucking Holloway.

Chapter 29

October 4th

Angie

"**A**re you sure you wanna be dropped off here and not at home?" Jared asks, putting his sleek BMW into park in front of Cora's house.

"I'm sure," I reply with a sigh. I'm drained from the events of tonight. I admitted to my best friend of over twenty years that I was in love with him. I can't go back there right now. I don't know when I can. I don't know when I'll be able to face him again.

I already texted Cora the situation, and she told me I was more than welcome to stay with her.

Jared has been nothing but a gentleman tonight. He's sent me several text messages and calls since I last saw him, before he had knee surgery and retired from playing rugby altogether. Our conversations were always brief, and like always, he was flirtatious. But I had no interest in going out with him until this week. Until I pulled the plug on the arrangement with Rafael—pulled the plug on affection and sleeping in the same bed.

When he asked me out, he knew full-well I was pregnant, and I knew full-well I had to replace Rafael in my heart. I was grasping at straws. I was hoping to find a deeper connection with Jared—someone I used to trust with my body, but not to the same level I trusted Raf. I wanted to see if there could be more with him.

And in my desperation, I hurt my best friend. My plan was to quickly change from work before he picked me up—not to find Rafael at home waiting for me and cooking enough food for a family holiday. He was never supposed to know about my evening with Jared. I know it blindsided him and I feel like shit for the way he found out.

I had no intention of sleeping with him tonight though—I knew I couldn't do it. Not out of consideration for Raf, but because the idea of sleeping with someone else feels completely wrong, even with someone I trust like Jared.

"Thanks for dinner and letting me talk about it with you, Jared. It means a lot."

The corner of his mouth curls up, then he puts his hand on my knee and strokes his thumb against the fabric of my maxi dress. The placement is low enough that it reads as friendly and not suggestive—a perfect picture of how tonight's date has been with him. Jared might be a little dumb, but he knows how to read a room and be a friend. Maybe I was too shaken with emotion to properly evaluate him, but that outside-the-bedroom spark doesn't exist between us. The spark I know all too well, as misguided as it is.

"Anytime, Angie. We go way back. Call me whenever you need to."

"Thank you," I say softly and reach for the handle.

"Let me get that for you," he says, jumping out of the car and coming to my side. And even though it's Jared opening my door, all I can picture is Rafael doing it for me.

When the door opens and I swing my legs out, the car is too low to the ground and I'm too round to get up without looking like I'm crawling out of a mud-wrestling pit. He smiles and extends his hands to lift me out. "Let me help." Finally standing up with a lady-like grunt, I take a deep breath and thank him again.

Jared holds my hand for a few steps before the memory of Rafael's confession strikes. *You had no idea how bad*

I wanted to simply hold your hand in the hallway. Like a reflex, I retract my hand.

What happened tonight hurt Rafael, I know that. I should have handled it in a calm manner, but my emotions are all over the place lately. I hate this unhinged version of myself. I'm supposed to be a reasonable person. I'm well-educated and guide my patients into having meaningful conversations, but I still snapped. I don't want to use my hormones as an excuse, but I was a completely different person back there. What I said needed to be said though. I know that.

Cora's already standing in the doorway to her beautiful townhome when we climb the stairs.

"Thanks for bringing her," Cora says before giving him a friendly hug. "It's good to see you again, Jared."

"It's good to see you too, Cora." He pulls back and looks between both of our prominent bellies. "Looks like a couple of best friends are making some best friends."

A needed smile finally crosses my face as I lean in for a hug as well. "That's the goal. Thanks again." Before he backs away from the embrace though, he places a soft kiss on my cheek and all at once a flood of guilt hits me.

Dammit, I think to myself. Raf doesn't have any claim on me. I'm not his. I'm free to let other men kiss me, as chaste as this is.

"Have a good night. And call me if you need me."

I give him a short nod and step inside because if I open my mouth, I'm going to cry.

As soon as Cora shuts the door, I fall apart anyway.

"Oh honey, I know." Cora holds me as fiercely as she can, our bumps bumping and our hands gripping the other for dear life.

It's the kiss. It's the guilt. It's the heartbreak and fear of the unknown raining down on me. I want it to wash away everything in its wake and leave me new again. Leave me the girl I always wished I could be—the one who isn't in love with her best friend.

But I know that's not how this works. I'm going to let it all out and feel a sense of relief once the tears stop, but my mind will keep going until something new hits me and it'll start all over again.

I'm vaguely aware of moving to the couch as I continue crying and a box of tissues appears. I'm overwhelmed with a menagerie of emotions including immense gratitude for Cora. I might be in total distress right now, but I haven't felt this level of comfort all week.

Finally catching my breath and dabbing my face dry, I give Cora a weak smile. "Thank you."

"Tell me what you couldn't over text," she says calmly and hands me a glass of water from the coffee table. I didn't notice until now, but it's covered in glasses of water, wine, chocolates, nuts and cheese.

"Wine?" I ask, a little confused.

"We're allowed a little. Tonight seemed like that kind of night."

"Bless you," I whisper, grabbing the stem of the glass and taking a sip. Cora does the same. It's only about four ounces, but I relish in it as the wine seeps into my tongue and stare blankly at the wall of books in front of me.

Right as I'm about to speak, my phone buzzes incessantly from my purse next to me. Pulling it out, I see it's yet another call from Rafael which I send to voicemail.

"Is that him?" Cora asks.

"Yeah," I sigh. "It's the seventh call since I left. I should text him what's going on."

> Angie: I'm at Cora's. I don't want to talk right now.

Instantly I get a reply back.

Raf: Do you need me to pick you up?

Angie: No. I'm staying here tonight. Maybe all weekend.

Raf: Please come home. Let's talk about this.

Angie: Not now. I need space and I need you to respect that.

Raf: <sad face emoji> Ok. I'll be here.

I set my phone back down. "Raf got me bookshelves," I say flatly and let that statement marinate. When Cora doesn't say anything, I continue. "He's having them custom-made for his house on Chestnut. For me."

I turn my head to see her confused expression. "He really wants you to stay with him, doesn't he?"

"What's wrong with me? Why do I fold for bookshelves?"

"Because it's not about the bookshelves. It's about him. It's about what he means to you. He could give you a cup of dirt and say this reminded me of you, and you would swoon."

She's not wrong.

Swirling the wine, I stare down at it. "You were right, before. When you said he treats me like a wife. I think I've—no—I know I've been letting him do that. For a long time." I swallow. "I know I was torturing myself, but with all my inconsequential, painful, terrible dates over the years, having him treat me like that was nice. Comforting. The most reassurance I've ever felt. It's my own fault."

"Don't do that," Cora says, placing a hand on my shoulder. "Whether he knows it or not, he's been using you too. You're allowed to feel at fault and guilt, but you're allowed to be angry at him." She takes her hand away and seems to refocus. "Tell me everything you're feeling, regardless of it making sense."

God, she gets it. She gets that even though I'm a therapist, it doesn't mean I'm perfect at regulating my emotions. Logic and emotion do not always march hand in hand, especially since I've been pregnant.

Closing my eyes, I take a deep breath and take inventory. "Shame. Fear. Guilt. Heartbroken. Anger... Anger," I repeat.

"Why are you angry?" she says, like she's opening a door for me.

"I'm angry...because he can't love me the way I love him. Because he got jealous of Jared and still couldn't do anything about it. Because I may have just broken whatever relationship we had and it's going to hurt our kids. Because he would make the best fucking partner in the world if he just got over his stupid fucking commitment issues! Fuck!"

"Yes, Angie. Let it out."

"How can he be the most committed friend, but he can't romantically commit? Like, what the fuck? How is it different?" I ask rhetorically.

"He only lets me see the real him," I say, then take a sip. "And he uses my affection for his own comfort so he doesn't have to seek it out from anyone else."

"He told me he had a crush on me in high school. He told me how beautiful and perfect my body was while he worshiped it. He made me feel like our arrangement was more," I cry out. "I'm fucking mad!"

"That's it," she snarls in agreement and gets up to power on her Bluetooth speaker on the shelf and tap away on her phone for a second. "We're going to let our feminine rage out."

When the melody to Miley Cyrus' *Wrecking Ball* takes over, there is absolutely no stopping me from standing up, taking one more swallow of my pinot, and joining my best friend on the rug. Letting myself succumb to the almost unfairly-accurate ballad, I lean into the dramatics of all—raising my fists to the sky, belting out lyric after lyric next to the woman who's stayed by my side through everything and let me be there for her too. Through every heartbreak and all-nighter in college, through every death and moment of pure bliss, we have always been there.

As I sing and sob, I think of how Rafael has been that person for me too.

I think about how the relationship between Cora and me is going to change once we have kids. We won't have the time to see each other like we used to. We're going to be wrapped up in our own bubble. Will we be able to make the effort to see each other like this?

I think about how I've ruined what Raf and I have. I want us to stay friends, not just for the sake of our children, but for ours. I just don't know how our puzzle will fit together anymore.

I think about my mom and how much I wish she was here now. I wish I had more than her journals. I wish I had that close mother-daughter bond. I wish she was still alive, and I could giggle and agree with other girls when they talk about how annoying their moms are, how they all hate their moms just a little.

I'd rather hate her a little but love her a ton than miss her so much it hurts.

Between verses, I spot Jay barreling down the stairs with Marco stepping behind him. Jay joins the rage-a-thon in solidarity or because it's just too good of a song not to belt from your lungs. But I think it's the former.

Marco joins us and he takes my hands in his, stares directly at me and hammers the chorus along with me for a couple of lines—it's intense and it fuels my emotional fire. I'm caught off guard when he turns behind me, inserting his forearms under my arms and hoisting me like he's a forklift. Squealing, I let a smile cross my face and he twirls me around slowly.

The last of the lyrics are spent with me feeling like Rose on the deck of the Titanic, except it's not romantic love coursing through my body for the man behind me. It's a love for all three of them—a love for the kind of people who let you free yourself with ballad rage and join in.

Chapter 30
October 5th

Angie

T iny kicks from inside wake me up the next morning and I'm greeted by a cat that's not mine. "Good morning, George," I mutter, staring at Cora's gray cat as she sits on the floor watching me like a psycho. "What? Didn't feel like joining us last night? You seem like someone who'd enjoy a good fem-rage."

We stayed up until our pregnant hips got too sore to sway and our breath ran out. Last night was exactly what I needed. It doesn't mean I'm ready to face him though. This time away needs to be spent reevaluating our dynamics and how I'm supposed to move on from him.

A soft knock has me looking to the door where Cora slips in wearing a matching white pajama set and carrying a tray. "Morning," she sings sweetly. "Want some breakfast?"

"Of course," I smile, but when I shift my round body to sit up, I feel the urge to pee like a racehorse. "I'll be right back." Cora chuckles knowingly, and when I return, she has the tray sitting on my bed.

Sitting cross-legged on the bed in my borrowed mumu, I look at the tray. Fresh fruit and tea, but then I see the two things I've been having every morning for weeks now. "You have a craving for cottage cheese and mustard too?" I ask her. Before she answers, I add with a pinched brow, "Wait, is this carrot and turmeric juice? I love this."

"Um," she hesitates. "Actually, Rafael dropped them off on our porch this morning. Along with a ton of homemade food, your Tums, pregnancy pillow, and a small weekender bag."

My head falls into my hands and I groan. "How am I supposed to fall out of love with him when he does shit like this?"

"I don't know," she says solemnly.

"I think I need to move out, Cora." She sighs and waits for me to continue. "As much as it pains me, as much as I know it's going to be harder as a mother of newborn twins, I don't see how else I'm supposed to get over him."

"Have you considered, oh, I don't know, talking to him about the possibility of being together?"

"You and I both know where he stands."

"No, babe. That was with other people. They're not you."

Her statement hits me harder than I expect it to. Maybe she's right. I know I have to talk to him, and I will. I want to. But this is something I can't bring myself to fathom. Can Rafael change? Does he want to? Based on the way he looked when I finally confessed my love to him, he's never even considered me as more than a friend. As more than a teenage crush.

"Good morning, ladies," Marco says, peeking into the room and holding my bag Rafael apparently dropped off. He sets it down and leans against the door frame. "Sweetheart," he says to Cora. "Are you ready for your prenatal massage?"

Her shoulders bunch up in excitement. "Yes, please."

This lucky woman gets to be married to a massage therapist. I envy her.

"Angie, would you like one after Cora's done?"

"Yes please!"

"Okay. You're up first, my love," he smiles, then heads down the hall to his home massage room.

"We'll talk after?" Cora asks, squeezing my hand.

"Yeah. I'll enjoy my breakfast. Go ahead."

After she leaves, I open my weekender bag and immediately am surprised to find my mom's journal on top as well as my Kindle.

Of course he would do something nice like this. Ugh.

Taking both, I sit on the bed again and crack open mom's words, hoping to find solace in them.

4/18

Today my sweet girl, you had a poop so big you scared yourself. So while I finished folding laundry, Dada changed your diaper. You were so upset, screaming and crying. But I listened from the other room as he sang the silliest little song to you. And that was it. You stopped crying and listened to his awful singing voice while I fell deeper in love with him.

He's wonderful with you, Angela. Serendipity brought you to our lives, but I know it was for a reason. He was made to be your father, I just know it. I know it like I know everything about you.

You're almost two months old and I can't believe it. It's been both the hardest and most joyful time. Time has slowed. Our days and nights are the same. But you remain our bright light.

Never dull your shine, baby girl.

Love,

Mama

4/19

You smiled today, my sweet girl! Your first real smile, and of course it was because of your father. Apparently him blowing tiny raspberry kisses on your belly is the funniest thing.

We were obsessed with watching you. I don't think I understood or experienced true joy until that moment. Sure,

I've been happy, in love, and excited before... But until that first smile of yours, I can't remember a time I felt that level of profound emotion.

You're incredible.

Also, please stop scratching my breasts when you nurse. I love you, but that hurts.

Love,

Mama

4/20

Two months old and the doctor confirmed our suspicions today: you are perfect. You're extra perfect because you slept for seven hours straight at night, and then took a three hour nap in the afternoon. Well, <u>we</u> took a three hour nap in the afternoon, so thanks for that. Mama needed it.

You've been eating so well lately, and it looks like your father and I have a routine down. At night, if you wake up, he changes your diaper and brings you to me and I feed you, then he takes you back and rocks you to sleep.

I don't know what I would do without him, Angela.

Love,

Mama

4/30

You rolled over today my strong girl! It took us by surprise but we stopped everything we were doing to watch you. I was so happy your father was home from work to catch it. He was the one who alerted me. "She's going to do it, Zo!" he hollered. It was like watching the finale of a TV show or a tied game being battled to a nail-biting finish.

And we saw it. We watched you take your first roll from tummy to back like the champion you are.

I'm so proud of you, my sweet girl.

Love,
Your cheerleader, Mama.

I read dozens more journal entries over the next hour as Cora got her massage. All of them are similar and yet unique. My first this, my first that. More gushing about my dad and how tired but happy she is.

Her words ruminate as I lay on the massage table and wait for Marco to enter the room. I've had several with him over the last six months or so and that man is talented. What's even better is this table having a cutout for my belly so I can lay face down. What a luxury that is these days.

At my request, Cora sits in the chair in the corner of the tranquil room as Marco starts to dig his fingers into my stressed back.

"Maybe moving out isn't the right thing," I tell her while staring at the floor with my head in the padded cradle.

"Why's that?" she asks.

"I was just reading my mom's journal, and I'm afraid if we live apart, both of us are going to miss out on those special first moments, you know?" What I don't voice is how painful it would be to miss out on those firsts. How painful it would be to witness those firsts and know Raf isn't there to see them, too.

If we can just get back to the way things were before I got pregnant. Before the arrangement. Before the confessions.

How can I erase mine? How can I forget his?

"So, what does that mean for you and Raf?" Marco asks, pushing his thumbs into my neck.

"It means I need to set clear boundaries. Maybe in a more rational and less emotional way than what happened last night," I mutter. At that, the twins start kickboxing, making me giggle. "Or maybe not. These two seem to like the theatrics."

"Speaking of theatrics," Cora says. "Jay's mom, Kathleen, showed me the invite list to our combined baby shower, and it's huge, Ang. She rented out a country club for this."

"Does she know what kind of buffoons rugby players are? That seems far too nice for the likes of us."

"She's going hog-wild," Marco adds. "No expense is too high."

"I think she's making up for the fact that we got secretly married," Cora says.

"Well, I'm not stopping her," I say.

Marco chuckles, gliding his broad hands down to my lower back. "I can't wait to see what kind of event *our* mother-in-law and *your* brothers put together."

Chapter 31

October 6th

Rafael

I played like shit [1] yesterday. I was either yelling at my teammates for miniscule mistakes or my head was in the clouds and I should have been yelled at. I missed tackles, my passes were sluggish, so coach pulled me before the first half even ended. I don't blame him. My head wasn't in the game because all I could think about was how my best friend loved me, then walked away and cut me off. Anxiety has been crawling its way through every inch of my body and soul since then.

As soon as she left Friday night with Jared, I stood there dumbfounded in my living room for a long time. How long has she loved me? Part of me wanted to say it back. A part that's been growing more and more comfortable with the deeper level of intimacy between us since our arrangement started.

All I wanted was for her to talk to me, but I wasn't expecting that. I wasn't expecting the reason she was making herself scarce was because she wanted to end what we have. Logically, I knew we were going to end, but I thought I still had a few months, and I was going to do my best to prolong that as much as possible.

---

1. *Mr. Brightside* by The Killers

Now here I am, wallowing in my bedroom with Razz like I just got broken up with even though we were never... We were never...

I can't even say it.

My body is sore from my rugby game yesterday, but it's nothing compared to the ache in my heart.

Her confession threw me off kilter and now parts of my conscience are fighting for the spotlight.

She loves you too, my younger self squeals. Is it just my younger self? I mean, I do love her. I love her more than the average friend without a doubt. When I lived in DC, being away from her for weeks at a time became a normal ache—one that was soothed when we visited each other. But living together again has been everything I wanted. So what the fuck is wrong with me? Why am I in so much turmoil over this?

She chose Jared over you, I sneer at myself. *Again.* I know we said this was open, but it doesn't hurt any less reminding myself. She probably blew his fucking mind in bed. I wonder if she asked him to role play? I wonder if she was comfortable enough to ask for something kinky and depraved. The thought crushes me like an avalanche. I'm that for her. She told me she's never been able to trust a partner enough to ask for this stuff, and I took that as an ego boost. I nestled that little fact into my chest for safe-keeping.

God forbid, but if they did sleep together, I hope it was vanilla. What am I saying? I hope it was terrible or better yet, I hope it didn't happen at all. I hope he repulsed her.

You're going to lose her, I chide myself. She said she couldn't be affectionate with me anymore. What would we even look like without that? To what level does she want to back off? She's my solace, my comfort. I can't imagine our relationship without affection. Who else would I have this with?

There's Cora, and while she and I are close, we're not nearly as affectionate. I think about what our friendship would look like if we were as intimate, but I immediately think of her husbands and I don't think they'd be happy with me if she and I had that same level of familiarity.

Angie's words ring in my head again. *You can't keep pretending I'm your wife just because you can't let anyone else in.* Is she right? Have I been treating her like a wife? An image of my moms plays in my mind like an old-timey film. The way they support each other, the way they touch even when one of them is passing behind the other in the kitchen. The way they laugh with each other and the way they would do anything for the other.

Maybe Angie is right.

But *I don't want a spouse,* I remind myself. Why would I treat her like a wife if being a bachelor is all I've ever wanted? Relationships are work, and while I work hard, they're not a stress I should be adding to my life. I have enough on my plate. Adding more might mean I'll lose focus on everything else, and I can't afford to slip.

I'm not enough for her. I'm not enough for anyone.

The battle in my brain comes to a halt when I see my father's incoming call. Since Friday night, I've been ignoring every phone call and text if it wasn't from Angie. But a phone call from Papá is rare so I take the opportunity and clear my throat before answering.

"Hey," I smile.

"Mijo," Papá bellows in that raspy Texas baritone I miss. "How are you?"

"I'm doing great," I lie. "How are you?"

"Pretty good for an old man," he chuckles. "Those babies come yet?"

"No. We'll be sure to tell you as soon as they do." God, just saying we has me missing her again. "Why? Have you booked your flight for when the babies come?" I think about him holding the twins and my heart soars. What a sight that will be.

"What? Oh," he chuffs. "No, uh, not yet. But hey listen. I got a couple of tickets to the Texas Rangers verses Phillies for next week."

"You got tickets to the World Series?" I ask in disbelief.

"Yeah. Pretty sweet. So anyway, my old pal Carlos moved to Philly a few years back, and he was supposed to come with me, but now he can't."

Oh my god, is he going to ask me to go with him? He's the one who got me into baseball as a kid. My inner child tenses waiting for him to continue.

"Oh yeah?" I ask.

"Sold his ticket online and got a pretty penny back."

I deflate. "Oh."

"Anyway, thought since I was going to be in your neighborhood, we could see each other. Maybe grab lunch," he says casually, which throws me off.

"You don't wanna stay with me? I have a guest room." Can he hear the desperation in my voice?

"Nah, nah. That's okay. I don't wanna bug you. I got a hotel anyway."

"Papá, you won't be bugging me. I haven't seen you in...years," I admit, feeling like an ass for even bringing up the fact that I haven't made a better effort to visit him.

"That's why we're going to have lunch, *mijo*. I'll send you my flight details tomorrow, yes?"

Unsettled, I sigh. "Yes."

"Good. I'm excited to see you. I gotta go now. I'll see you next week," he says in that persuasive tone he's always had.

"Okay. *Adios*, Papá."

The call ends and for the first time ever, the weight of the missing *te amo* feels fitting. I don't expect him to tell me he loves me. I didn't realize until college that his love was conditional. I've heard him say it to his friends and relatives in a jovial way, and that's how he's always said it to me. It's always been after I've done something he's proud of.

A big part of me is thrilled he's coming though. So what if I can't go to the World Series with him? That's fine. It's not like I can just get a ticket for one of the most anticipated games of the year. Maybe with his visit we can weave our relationship back together and we'll start seeing each other more often because of it. Yeah.

I can turn this around; and if I can make this work with him, maybe there's a chance I can make this work with Angie.

If only I could figure out what this is.

Chapter 32

October 7th

Rafael

When I get to the office Monday morning, I'm no less at ease than I have been all weekend. Angie didn't come home last night like I was hoping. She sent me a text a couple hours after I hung up with my father saying she was going to stay a few more nights at Cora's.

After typing out and deleting several drafts, I reluctantly settled on:

> Ok. I'm ready to talk when you are.

And yeah, I wanted to hug her after sending it, and in turn, made me upset realizing hugs might be coming to an end. If I'm honest with myself, I know I'd want to add a kiss to the top of her crown and maybe get a little whiff of her shampoo while I'm at it.

God, I miss her.

I'm trying to play it cool at work, but I'm dying to talk to Cora and Jay. I'm sure they know everything, and I would do anything to hear the smallest scrap of intel.

I only make it to 11:00 am before I'm knocking on her open office door.

"Hey, Raf," Cora says casually, like she doesn't hold all the secrets. Wordlessly, I close the door behind me and let the meaning sink in. "Okay," she says with a wan smile making me feel infinitely worse.

We both take a seat on her mauve designer sofa, and I ask, "How is she?"

"She's not great," she sighs.

"Is she eating? Sleeping? How's her heartburn? Did she take the Tums I sent?"

"She's been eating, but not much. She's been using the pregnancy pillow and taking the Tums you brought over."

"She's not eating much? Does she want something different to eat? I can bring it to her—"

"Raf."

"Or I can have it delivered."

"Raf," Cora says again. "You know she's not eating much because she's sad."

"How sad?" I ask, and like a sickness, the tension grows at her lack of answer.

"She went to The Shore by herself yesterday," she exhales with a knowing look, and I nod as the weight of Cora's words fall upon me.

If Angie is going to the water, she's seeking comfort and answers. She's seeking peace. I hate myself for being the reason she's in this head space and I'm worried for her—the stress she's carrying isn't good for her or the babies.

"What can I do, Cora? I feel helpless. All I want to do is take her hurt away."

"You want to protect her?" Cora asks.

"Of course."

"You want to hold her right now, don't you?"

"Yes," I reply without reservation.

"And would that make you feel better or her?"

I look down at my hands before answering. "Me. But what can I do? I have to fix this, Cora."

"You have no idea what fixing this means, do you?" she asks, but it's more like she's saying it to herself. I shake my head. "Ugh, I love you both, but you're idiots."

Just then a buzz comes through and it's a text from my brother reminding me to sign some documents for our realtor. It only takes a second to read, but I don't reply.

"Why do you work so hard, Rafael?" my boss asks.

"Because I always have," I reply honestly. "Everyone in my family does. I don't know. We were born to."

"What would happen if you didn't work tirelessly?"

The words don't come, but emotion does. Pain lances through me at the thought of disappointing my father. I think about not working as hard and all the resulting mistakes—about the effort it would take to make up for them—and I'm exhausted at the thought alone.

Cora raises her eyebrows waiting for my response. She's not my boss right now. She's my friend.

What would happen if I didn't work tirelessly?

And for the first time I say the frightening words aloud. "My dad might think less of me."

Cora sighs. "You look up to him," she states, quietly understanding. All I can do is nod. "Do you think he would love you less?"

"Without a doubt," I tell her. I work hard, but I work harder for his love. God, what would it even be like to have it all the time—without the effort? Freeing. My body sighs in relief at the thought. But it's never been a possibility. The moments he shows his love are fleeting.

"I'm sorry," Cora says. "I know there's more inside you. You want to know what you can do? You wanna know what would show Angie a little bit of faith?"

"Yes. Please," I beg.

"Go to therapy," she says slowly. "Whether you guys stay friends or—I don't know—going to therapy will show her you're serious about the health of yourself and your relationship, whatever form it takes. That will make her feel better."

"Really?"

"She's scared about what this means for the stability of your future family. If she knows you're serious about making this work, that will put her at ease," Cora says with a soft smile. "And maybe there's some other things you need to unpack."

"What?"

"Just...talk to someone, okay?"

My need to please and goal-setting brain shake hands without another thought. "I'll start researching today and book something right away."

"Seriously?" Cora asks with a skeptical look, then adds under her breath, "That was easy."

So what if I'm desperate—I don't care. All I want is for the people I care about and my babies to be happy, and once they are, I will be too.

Chapter 33

October 12th

Angie

After living with Cora for a week, I'm ready to talk to Rafael. I've been taking my time going over my plan, weighing my emotions and trying my best to be logical. I'm grateful for Marco and Jay as sounding boards because bouncing my plans off another pregnant woman didn't always yield the best results.

When I suggested we all start a commune, kill Rafael, and bury him there, Cora was the one who suggested we get pigs and feed him to them so there's no evidence. She's very smart, my best friend.

Marco put a stop to it when we started looking up property for sale. *Killjoy.*

Cora hasn't said anything about what he's been like to work with this last week, and I haven't asked. I don't want to know if he's content, looks tired, or comes to work crying because I needed this time to figure myself out without his influence.

It's futile though. Every time the babies kick, I think about him and how much he'd love to feel what I'm feeling. Then guilt gnaws at me for taking these moments away from him and I cry some more because that's all I'm capable of as a human incubator.

As I walk through historic Rittenhouse Square Park, rays of sun shine through the old tree-lined sidewalks and scatter over everyone in its wake, just like the autumn leaves. I wanted to go for a walk to give Cora and her husbands some alone time, but I also wanted to be in the right mood when I send Raf the text I know he's been waiting on.

Taking a seat on the edge of a fountain, I type.

> Angie: Thank you for giving me space. I'm ready to come home tomorrow and talk if you are.

His reply comes only a few moments later.

> Raf: You needed it and I understand. I'm ready when you are. I have so much to tell you too.

What does he mean by that?

No, I stop my train of thought. *I need to stick to my guns.*

I need to tell him moving out is the best option. He's not going to like it, but I have a plan for that too. Since he and Joaquín sold that apartment building in DC a while back and purchased three more homes in the same block as the Chestnut Street house, I'm going to ask to move into one of those.

Rafael showed them to me last month, and the one looks to be in decent-enough shape to live in. This way, he'll live close but we'll live separately. It's the right choice for all of us.

·· • • • • • • ··

Rafael

It's a bye week for our team so my father coming to town works out perfectly. Since the city is packed because of

The World Series, we agreed he would come to my place, which I'm both nervous and excited for him to see. It's been a while since he's seen how I'm living. Sure, this townhouse was only ever temporary, but I hope he's proud of what I've made for myself.

I've stocked the place with his favorite beer and organized everything. Not that it was a mess before, but just in case he looked in my kitchen utensil drawer, I wanted to make sure that was presentable.

Smiling to myself as I shut the drawer, I think of Angie and her nesting habits. I guess I'm no better.

When my phone lights up, another text comes from her, and I snatch it from the counter to read.

> Angie: Ok <smiley face emoji> I'll see you tomorrow.

I might not know what she's thinking, but that emoji lifts my spirits. It's the first real sign of our connection again.

"Razzle, buddy," I sing, looking over to him lying in a sunbeam on the rug, totally unfazed except for a flick of his tale. "Mama's coming home tomorrow. Are you excited? You're right. We *should* celebrate with tuna tartar tonight."

Before I can unpack this news and what it means, there's a knock at my door and I spring into action as Razzle does the same to hide.

"¡Hijo mío!" my dad bellows with a smile as large as his personality and dimples that match mine. José Juan Jimenez is a loud, jovial man with endless stories and giver of unsolicited advice. But I couldn't care less if he does or doesn't give it right now, because it's been five damn years since I've seen him and I'm not wasting a moment. I mean shit, the last time I saw him was at my abuela's ninetieth birthday in Mexico.

I laugh to myself when I notice we're wearing damn near the same outfit—jeans and white T-shirt.

"*Papá*," I grin and lean in for a long and tight hug. "I missed you. How was your trip?" I ask, then break away and pat him on the back. "Come in, tell me everything."

"Well, airplane seats are getting smaller," he says as I lead him to the kitchen island to have a seat on the stool. "And my knees are getting stiffer, but it's all worth it for the game, right?"

Cracking open the longneck, I hand him his beer and start on opening my own. "I think those seats at the stadium are going to be even smaller," I chuckle. "So what's going on with you?"

"Ah, same old stuff. Working hard, playing hard," he winks.

"Oh yeah? What's *playing* these days?"

"Oh, you know, got a few different ladies in the mix," he smirks, and my stomach goes a little sour.

My eyebrows flick up briefly. "I see. And do they know about each other?"

"Hell no," he huffs. "Not my style. You know me."

Do I? I think to myself. He looks the same, talks the same, carries himself the same, but after all these years I'm starting to wonder if I ever really knew my papá. I know what he presents to me.

"Are they long-term type or..." I trail off.

"Nah. I'm just having some fun, you know?"

I guess I do know. I've always known he's a perpetual bachelor and he's always made it seem cool. It made him seem suave to me. But for some reason I see him differently today. He's still cheerful and outgoing; he looks to be living his best life, but suddenly, I think about how sad it is. Doesn't he want someone special to go through life with? He has a group of guys he's friends with down in Dallas, and I know he sees them regularly, so he's not hurting for friendship—but doesn't he want something more meaningful?

"You ever think about settling down again?" I ask, then take a swig of the hoppy carbonation and immediately realize I'm drinking alcohol and freeze.

"Now why would I want to do something stupid like that?" he laughs. Deciding to swallow my one sip, I then lean over the sink and empty the bottle. "Something wrong with your beer?"

"No," I say. "I just forgot I'm not drinking out of solidarity with Ang."

"Come on," he scoffs. "One beer isn't going to kill you."

"I know," I reply, then lean my forearms on the counter facing him. "So no marriage on your setting sun horizon?" I quip.

"Was that an old man joke?" he chuckles.

"It was," I smile. "I think there's a nursing home here called Setting Sun. Maybe I could get you a good deal by signing you up early."

"You know, now that you say that," he drawls, giving me an even stare and a smirk. "Maybe I should talk to my lawyer and make some adjustments to my will."

As we catch-up for the next hour or so, everything he's talking about is surface-level bullshit. I mean, I didn't expect us to dig deep, but every time I try to ask something a little more meaningful, he sort of floats back to small talk or a funny anecdote about one of his buds or work. I'm his son... Shouldn't we be able to talk about what's going on in our lives and how we feel? When I tried to bring up Joaquín, he excused himself to the bathroom and when he came back, he had another meaningless story to tell me.

I know our time is coming to end and he needs to leave for the game soon, so when he ends another story about his friend, we both know it's time for him to go.

"Whatever happened to Carlos, by the way?" I ask as we make our way to the front door. "Why did he have to sell his ticket?"

For the first time this whole visit, he looks disgruntled. He groans, "It's his granddaughter's quinceañera today and his bitch wife is making him go."

All at once irritation bites at my stomach and I'm a little stunned. I don't know Carlos and I don't know his wife, but if I ever heard my father say that about my Angel, I would lay him out in a split second.

And Carlos' wife is right. A quinceañera is a huge deal and should take precedence over fucking baseball, even the World Series. Hearing him say that tears me apart. Has he always been so crude?

I want to lay into him, but that generational respect barrier is struggling to hold me back.

"Alright, son," he sighs and brings me into a hug that feels uneven in its exchange. "It was great seeing you. Come see me soon, yeah?"

"Yeah," I say despondently, but force a smile.

When he turns to leave for his parked rental car, it all hits me.

He didn't even ask about Angie.

Or the babies.

Or how I'm doing. He didn't ask how I'm feeling about becoming a dad, about my job, about my business, about the family—none of it.

He didn't even ask about Angie.

"Hold up, Papá," I holler, making my way down the front steps where he stands waiting for me. My body thrums with nervous energy. I can't believe I'm about to do this. "Angie's doing great by the way."

He turns his head to see if anyone is coming down the sidewalk and then back to me with a pinched brow. "Yeah? Okay."

"Yeah," I huff indignantly. "The babies are too. Why didn't you ask about them?"

He cocks his head back. "Uh, it was a short visit, son. I don't know. There was so much to talk about."

"You couldn't be bothered to ask about my best friend and our babies?"

"Watch your tone," he warns, but the barrier is dissolving slowly—just enough for me to speak my mind, but not enough for me to yell.

"I'm going through the biggest changes of my life and you haven't asked about them." He crosses his arms and looks away, but I continue. "I started a new job this year, my business has grown, but most importantly, I'm going to be a father. You're the fucking king of unsolicited advice and you haven't given me a word?"

"It's your own damn fault for knocking her up," he bites out as chills run through my body. "You had a good life before this, son. She's going to take everything from you, and I'm not talking about your money, which she will. I'm talking about your freedom."

"What are you talking about? Papá, she is my freedom." And it's the truth. I'm never freer than when I'm with her. I'm exactly the person I want to be—never having to hide a single part of myself. Free to explore. Free to dance. Free to feel.

He sighs. "Then you're making your own bed." He turns on his heel and walks away but says one more thing before opening his car door. "Don't say I didn't warn you."

Everything in my body screams at me to mend the strife I just created between us, but I don't want to take back what I said. What if I carved my own path without him? Would my life be that much different?

I imagine what my life would look like if I didn't listen to him. If I didn't care about pleasing him or earning his love. Oh my god. Have I been avoiding deeper relationships because I think they're exhausting in the same way mine is with my dad?

I think about Angie. If she's right—that I've been treating her like a wife all these years—then why would I think having a deeper romantic relationship would be work? Our friendship, our relationship, is anything but.

And then it clicks: she loves me and I've never had to earn it.

Chapter 34

October 12th

Rafael

T he traffic getting to my moms' house that evening is horrendous and gives me more time to stew in the pot my papá put me in, my thoughts alternating between him and Angie. I'm still vibrating with fear from the way I stood up to him. I know it was nothing compared to the way some people can stand up to their parents, but it was monumental for me.

How could he ignore the most important person in my life? I literally brought her up when he first got there, and instead of asking about her, he complained because I wasn't going to drink a beer with him. And then when I did bring her up, he wounded me.

I feel slimy after our visit.

All I want to do is talk to Angie about it. But I guess that's what my new therapist is for. Maybe Angie was right—I do lean on her too much for emotional support.

I arrive in Radnor an hour later than normal thanks to the World Series traffic, but everything is forgotten when I walk in the door and Joaquín runs at me, jumping in my arms.

"What are you doing here, baby brother?" I laugh.

"I wanted to surprise everyone," he exclaims, then hops off me and adjusts his shirt. "Where's—" he says, cutting himself off. I only told him and our moms about what happened last week. "Sorry. I forgot," he says sheepishly.

"It's okay. She said she's coming home tomorrow so we'll figure it out."

"That's good! I think," he mutters, but gives me a raised eyebrow. "Just figuring it out?"

"I mean—"

"There you are," Mamá beams as she walks into the foyer and gives me a quick hug. "My God, you're skinny. Come, come. Food's getting cold."

When I reach the dining room with them, Mom walks into the room holding some napkins and I go in for another squeeze. "Hi, Mom."

"Hi, sweetie," she says. "Have a seat and tell us everything."

Taking a napkin from her, I have a seat next to my brother and across from them and say grace. But instead of telling them about Angie right away, I say, "Papá visited me today."

The room goes silent as everyone stops what they're doing to stare at me.

"Are you serious?" Joaquín asks. "Why was he here?"

"The game," I say with a flat tone and a shake to my head, then serve myself some carne asada.

"The game," Mamá repeats slowly.

"He's been to the East Coast *once* in the last twenty years," Joaquín says with narrowed eyes. "And decides the reason for his next trip will be for *baseball*?"

"Unbelievable," Mom adds under her breath.

"What did you talk about?" my brother asks as he serves himself.

"Nothing really," I shrug. "His friends, job. His many girlfriends." Mamá scoffs as she takes a bite. But something has me itching for answers to questions I've never had before. "Has he always been," I start, and then debate if I even want to ask this. "Has he always been so crude?"

"Yes," all three say at once.

"I didn't see it for the first few years we were together," Mamá says. "But, yes. I thought they were jokes at first, but the more he said them, the more I realized he meant them."

All evening I've been trying to replay every interaction I've had with him over the years, trying to piece together the man I talked with today to the man I've always known.

"How have I never seen that side of him?" I ask.

"Because you've been putting him on a pedestal your whole life," Joaquín mutters. "I'm younger than you, how can I see this and you can't?"

"Have I?" I ask Mamá.

She nods knowingly. "I prayed every day for a long time that you would not end up like him, *mijo*. He did nothing wrong in your eyes. He was your idol. Do you have any idea how many times you came home from school with art or an essay about him? I was never going to let you see the ugly side on purpose. I never wanted to speak ill of him in front of you boys, but I hoped you would see the truth for yourself a long time ago."

"I think the infrequency of your visits made you idolize him more," Mom adds. "You held onto those precious moments with him like they were gold."

All of a sudden I'm painfully aware of how alike my father and I are, and it's like the rose-colored glasses are coming off. "Am I just like him?"

"No, Rafael. No," Mamá soothes. "You are kind and thoughtful. You think about the comfort of others. You were raised in a better environment than he was." When I don't say anything, she continues. "Part of that was us. Part of that was Angie."

At the mention of my best friend, my heart swells. She never would have put up with me if I was actually like my father. She would have kicked me to the curb long ago if she even got a whiff of me mistreating partners.

Partners.

The term feels weird now. The idea of sleeping with other people feels weird. Unappealing.

All I want is my Angel. I want her laughing and dancing with me. I want her to be proud of me—proud that I'm the father of her children.

But she wants me to back off. How am I supposed to let that happen now? I'll do it because she needs it, but it means she'll be at a distance we've never experienced before—and something about that irritates me. Maybe it's the need to protect my pregnant...friend. *Friend?*

We're not *just* friends, and I know it deep in my bones.

···•··•···

The rest of dinner passes with no more mention of my dad. While helping clean up in the kitchen, Mom gently pulls on my elbow. "Come with me. I have something to show you," she says with a slight curve to her lips.

Setting the plate down on the drying rack, I dry off my hands and follow her into her den just off the living room. The space is filled with organized clutter—everything from tax filings from ten years ago to faded childhood art projects.

"Have a seat," she says, indicating for me to take the old leather chair as she fiddles with the ancient TV in the corner—the kind with a DVD player built right in. When she turns it on, she then takes a seat right next to me on a folding chair and looks at me. "I found this the other day cleaning out the basement."

She pushes play on the remote and a teenage Angie pops up wearing a red swimsuit, pushing a hunk of PVC pipe and cords into an indoor swimming pool.

"Oh my god," I whisper. "Is this us practicing with our underwater robot?"

"It is," Mom says, but I can't tell what her expression is because I can't tear my eyes off the grainy digital image. "And look, there's you."

I'm standing at the edge of the pool wearing plaid swim trunks with a controller in my hands. "Am I picking it up?" I ask teenage Angie, my voice echoing off the walls of the pool room.

"No, come in closer," she replies, showing me with her hands how close I am. "That's it... You got the ring!" she beams.

"I forgot all about this day."

"You two were so invested in this team."

I chuckle. "The whole team consisted of her and me."

Then the video cuts to a new location—a larger indoor pool with people filling bleachers and a judges table. Our tournament. Mamá's voice comes in and her hand is pointing to Angie and myself, both wearing a white T-shirt with the words *Nauti Nautilus* in big blue letters. We're near the pool's edge watching a TV monitor. Angie's driving the controller and I'm pointing to the screen, directing her.

I have no idea what I'm saying to her, but I watch the two of us work side by side. We're completely engrossed in our mission. Teenage me shouts and cheers as Angie drives. Then I'm lowering myself to the pool's edge to meet our robot and grab the object from it before it sinks back down.

I can't help but marvel at the team we make. How, given the opportunity, we'll always choose each other as teammates. We'll always work like a well-oiled machine.

"Do you remember how you placed?"

I have to smile at that. "Pretty close to last I think."

"Yeah," she smiles back. "That's true. But did it feel like it?"

There were dozens of competing teams from all over the state at this competition, but somehow, we didn't care that we took last place. We didn't care that our robot was clunky and made mostly out of PVC and zip-ties. We didn't care that we only completed half of the mission before the buzzer went off. We didn't care about winning. But did it feel like we lost?

"No," I sigh with a smile. We may have worked our tails off getting ready for the tournament, but we didn't lose. I walked away with pride in my heart because every moment spent with her feels like winning.

I'm going to win her back, I think to myself.

I don't want to be just friends. I don't want to be a co-parent. I want all of her. I want to take care of her, wake up next to her, and love her. *I want to love her.* Love her beyond a friendship. Love her like she deserves to be loved. Love her like I was always meant to.

I'm in love with Angela Zofia Johanssen and I'm going to make her mine.

Chapter 35

October 12th

Rafael

I kissed my family goodbye and hopped in my SUV with determination. My effervescent mood is heightened with a [1] perfect song choice—one I know Angie introduced me to, and I revel in this new and exciting sensation. Though, it isn't all that new, is it? I've always harbored these feelings for her, but I've pushed them so far down, ignoring them until I truly believed I didn't have them.

My heart pounds in my chest like I've played a full eighty. "I love Angie!" I shout to only myself and squeeze the steering wheel tight. The declaration feels like I'm carving my words into stone. I want to look up in the night sky and see our names written in the stars because I'm certain they're there. I want to scream my love from a mountain top as if I'm the first person to discover this feeling. I want to parade her around with my hand in hers and show everybody that she's mine.

That I'm hers.

As if the heavens themselves were listening, a phone call from Angie pops up on the dash of my car. The music stops playing, but the butterflies continue to erupt from my belly. Before the second ring trills, I've already opened the call.

---

1. *Run Away With Me* by Carly Rae Jepsen

"Hey," my voice waivers, and suddenly I'm confused about what to call her. "I was just thinking about you," I say like a love-sick idiot.

"Raf," she says, her voice breaking.

I furrow my brow. "What's going on?"

"I haven't felt the babies kick in a long time," she cries. "Like, at least five hours."

My gut sinks. The bubbly feeling inside my body has been replaced with a surge of panic and every hair on my body stands up.

"You're supposed to feel them kick at least every two hours, right?"

"I... I didn't realize it had been so long until a few minutes ago," she sniffles. "I keep pushing on my stomach to wake them up, but nothing is happening," she sobs.

Every fiber of my being is telling me to fix this. Protect her. Keep her and the babies safe. "Hang on, Angel. I'm going to call Ivy first. I'm driving right now, but I'll be at Cora's house in fifteen minutes. Just keep pushing on your stomach."

"Okay," she cries.

When I add in Ivy's line, I pray harder than I ever have that she picks up. She's on-call twenty-four seven as a midwife, so there's a very real chance she could not answer. But when she does, I waste no time.

"Hey, Raf," she says lightly.

"Ivy. Angie is on the call with us. She hasn't felt the babies move in about five hours. We're both freaking out. What should she do?"

"Okay, there's no need to panic just yet," she says evenly. "Angie, do you have any chocolate or coffee around?"

"Um," Ang hesitates and I can hear movement shuffling around her. "Yes. Oreos, M&Ms, and cold brew."

"Perfect. Drink some right away and eat. The caffeine will wake them up, but keep moving them around, too."

"What if I don't feel them moving?"

"If they don't start moving in the next twenty minutes," Ivy says, "then you should go to hospital."

No. No, no, no, this can't be happening. These are my angels. These are the most important people in my life and I'll be damned before I let anything like this happen to them.

"I'm almost there, Ang. Just stay on the phone with me. I'm right here. Everything is going to be okay," I try to soothe, praying that my words manifest reality.

I've never driven so aggressively in my whole life. I'm driving as fast as traffic will allow, all while waiting on bated breath for any sign of movement from Angie. I can hear Cora and the guys in the room with her from time to time, getting her whatever she needs and helping her push on her belly.

Curb-checking the sidewalk in front of Cora's place and screeching my tires, I turn off my car and bolt out like I'm on fire. Leaping through the front doors, I don't even bother closing them when I spot both Cora and Angie on the couch in tears. Marco and Jay are each sitting in an armchair, wringing their hands with pained expressions.

"Baby," I sob, launching myself for her and falling at her knees. My hands fly to her stomach and I bellow at my babies. "Wake up! Please, please wake up!" I push like I'm kneading bread and I feel Angie's hands on mine. "Please," I beg again, pressing my mouth to her skin. "Please do it for Papá. Please, I'm here. Papá is right here. Come on," I plead.

I can't lose them. They're my entire world. If I had no one else in my life, these three would bring me more happiness and love than I could ever need or deserve. Everything I love sits before me. I push against her belly again and again and again. I can feel their tiny bodies behind her protective barrier with each jerking nudge.

"*Por favor*," I beg, like my own life depends on it. They are my life. "*Te amo. Te amo. ¡Te amo!* Wake up," I cry and kiss her skin between pushes. "Come on."

Every single second that passes feels like an eternity. Like impending doom. Like if something horrible does happen, I'm not going to survive it either.

"Still nothing?" I hear Ivy's voice ask from the speaker phone.

"No," Angie whispers, her tears spilling over as I lock my eyes with hers.

"Okay. It's time to go then," Ivy says, and I know she's worried too, but she's trying her best to stay calm and reassuring.

I pull Angie off the couch, reluctance and urgency fighting for dominance in my body. "Let's go," I say, trying to keep my own voice even, but failing.

"We'll be right behind you," Cora says. "We'll bring an overnight bag just in case."

Angie is holding my hand so fiercely, I don't even bother putting her shoes on because I don't want to break contact. I simply lower myself to grab a pair of her shoes and head to the door. I'm already thinking about the best route to the hospital to avoid World Series traffic, when Angie screams.

"Wait!" We stop midway on the outdoor steps. "I think I felt a kick," she says with wide eyes and her hand glued to her bump, the other holding mine tight.

My other hand attaches to her belly and we both wait another few seconds before we feel it.

A single kick.

Another.

Another.

"Is that both of them?" I huff, my heartbeat entirely too loud for me to hear over.

"I think so," she laughs in relief. "Yes. It's both of them!"

Without another thought, without hesitation, I take her in my arms and hold her tighter than ever. My tears seep into her hair as I absorb every molecule of her—of them—and I vow right then and there that I will do everything in my power to love and protect them for the rest of my life.

"I love you, Angel," I confess. "I love you more than anyone. I want to be with you."

"What?" she asks, pulling her head away just enough to look up at me, the gaslight glow flickering against her tear-stained face.

My whole body trembles as I stare at her. "I'm such an idiot and I'm so sorry. You were right, I was treating you like a partner, but I was too stupid to realize that I love you the same way. I thought loving someone was supposed to be hard work, but it's never been that way with you."

I can feel Angie's heartbeat racing against my chest as I stand there holding her. Her chin trembles as she says nothing. Fuck. She wasn't expecting this, I know. Have I missed my chance? Did I throw it all away when I couldn't put words to my feelings last week? When I didn't understand what was really holding me back? Did I really lose to Holloway again?

"Please don't tell me I'm too late," I beg. "I—I don't care if something happened between you and Jared. Please," I pause, barely able to think through my thrumming heartbeat. "It's me and you. I love you," I repeat. "Te amo. You're everything to me. I don't want to be casual. I don't want an arrangement. I want to be yours and only yours. I want us. It was always meant to be us, baby."

"Raf," she cries, but it's a tender, sweet cry as her hands snake up my back. "You're not too late. I love you, too."

Relief washes over me and I'm soaring. Her words lift me to a plane of existence I've never been before.

I fucking won.

I gently cup the back of her head as I place my other hand firmly on my future, and I lower my face to capture her lips with mine.

And it's different.

And it's the same.

And it's new.

And it all makes sense. It all fits perfectly.

Her salt-kissed lips mingle with mine and her little whimper makes me melt as I hold her. When she opens her mouth for me, I let my tongue dance with hers—slow, steady, and promising.

"I'm yours," I murmur against her soft lips.

"You're mine."

"Um, hey guys," a timid little voice says from somewhere sounding a lot like Ivy. "I'm still on the phone. Do you still need me?"

The rumble from my chest and the giggle coming from Angie indicated we both forgot about her. Angie pulls the phone from the pocket of her maternity pants and brings it closer to our heads. "Sorry," she smiles. "No, I don't think so. Do I still need to go to the hospital?"

"No, you're fine. As long as you feel those kicks, you're in good shape."

"Thank you, Ivy. I love you so much."

"Yeah, thanks, Ivy. You're the best," I add.

"I'll leave you two alone. Sounds like there's a lot you need to tell me later, Ang."

We both grin at that. "Bye, Ivy," she says, then hangs up.

"Let's get you inside," I say. "You're getting cold."

When we step in, our friends are standing there watching us like perverts. Cora and Jay both have their hands covering their mouths and Marco has his arms crossed, a smug look painted across his face.

"I knew it," Marco says.

"I knew it first," Cora cuts in.

"It was so obvious," Jay adds.

"Shut up," Angie chuckles, tucking herself under my arm and I love the way she fits there.

Holding her close and smoothing my hand down her back, I ask, "Do you wanna stay here tonight or come back with me?"

Cora perks up, "Oh, both of you should stay here. It's late and your emotions are high; let's not add any more risk tonight."

She makes a good point. "Do you want to stay here one more night?" I ask.

Angie looks up at me, her ocean blue eyes still stained a little red in the corners. "Are you going to stay with me?"

"Of course I will."

"Yes!" Cora squeals. "We're one step closer to our commune."

"We're starting a commune?" I ask with a furrowed brow.

"Yes," Angie says. "But we'll need to make some adjustments to our plans."

"I say we keep the pigs," Cora says. "They're cute."

"Someone will need to fill me in on this," I say as Angie hauls me to the stairs.

"Goodnight, lovebirds!" Jay beams and waves us away.

After stripping naked, we both slipped under the fluffy covers of Angie's bed for the last week. It smells like her, and I remind myself that I'm a fool for ever letting her go.

"Can you just hold me tonight?" she asks, scooting her body closer to mine and planting her hands against my chest.

"Of course, Angel," I hum. "I'll spend forever holding you."

"Say it again," she whispers, tracing the letter J tattooed across my heart.

I mirror her and run a fingertip over her J, placed just under her collarbone. "I love you. I want you in my life as my friend and partner. As my lover. I want the real deal with you, Angel."

"Really?"

"Really. And it's not because we're having children together, I want you to know that. I want a life with you, baby. When the kids are grown and out of the house, I want you there with me. I want to love you forever." I lean in and kiss the tear away from her cheek. "Angel."

"I want that too," she says with a hitch to her breath. "I've loved you for so long, Rafael. You were my first crush, and I let you crush me over and over again."

"I promise I'll never let that happen again." Angie presses a soft kiss to the tattoo on my chest. "That J has always been yours, baby."

"And mine has been yours."

Chapter 36

October 13th

Angie

T he dream I'm having is too good to wake up from. A thick, long shaft prods at my pussy and on instinct, I push back against it. It pumps inside me as strong fingers play with between my thighs. Hot breath ghosts over my ear as soft rumbling grunts send shivers down my spine.

"That's a good girl," the deep voice murmurs. "So wet for me."

I know that voice. I love that voice.

Raf.

Suddenly I realize I'm not dreaming anymore. He's really here—fucking me from a spooning position. He has one arm under my head and his fingers plays with my sensitive nipple, shooting pleasure directly to my pussy. The other hand rubs my clit as he continues to thrust inside me.

"Good morning, Angel."

"Finally," I sigh, surrendering to his touch.

"This is so much sexier than I thought it would be. I'm fucking into this."

"Yeah? Oh god, yes," I moan. "Wait. No, we can't do this. Cora and the guys will hear us."

"No, they won't. She texted us that they're out running some errands all morning and we can have some alone time."

"She's the best," I huff, unable to catch my breath because he isn't stopping.

He nuzzles against my neck as he rocks into my needy pussy. "You were grinding into me all night. I knew you needed me."

"Yes, baby," I whisper. "Please don't stop."

"But you're so wet and warm," he says, adding more pressure to my clit. "How am I supposed to last with you like this? So perfect."

"I'm so close," I whimper. "Yes, yes, yes. *Ungh!*" My pussy convulses and tightens around his cock as I soar into bliss.

"More, baby," he growls, thrusting into me faster and pulling my sensitive bud between his fingers. "Keep going."

I thrash against him, unable to keep my composure and throwing out curses and moans like my body has been possessed, and he locks in tighter. My climax continues as he does his best to hold off, but it's a battle I'm all too eager to see him lose the longer I go on.

"Oh god, Angel. You're gonna make me come."

"Yes. Please come inside me," I beg.

"Say it. Tell me again," he says, and I know exactly what he means.

"I love you, Raf."

It's then with my declaration that he lets it all go. His fingers dig into my soft flesh as he musters through a string of groans. His breath is ragged as his legs shake, but he finally relaxes behind me, holding me like I'm his. I am.

"I love you too, Angel," he sighs. "God, it feels good to say that to you."

Gently slipping out of me, I moan at the loss only for a moment before he has me spun around and facing him so he can kiss me thoroughly. Hands roam over every inch of exposed skin, caressing every curve and angle, sifting through every strand of hair. Our languid sticky morning kiss makes me hungry for all the years ahead of us—of waking up in each other's arms, disheveled, vulnerable, and completely in love. And there's a new and different ache than before. Gone is the pain of unrequited love and in its place is longing for our future.

When Rafael's hand cups my swollen sex and his fingers stroke through my seam, I'm urgently reminded that a trip to the bathroom is required. "Hold on," I smile against his full lips. "I need to empty my bladder," I giggle, knowing it's the least sexy thing to say.

"Mmm," he rumbles, pulling back the covers for me. "Hurry back." He taps my butt as I get out of bed, and when I return, he's looking effortlessly erotic propped against the headboard, one leg snaking out from the bedding, showing off his long muscular legs all the way up to his bare shoulders. The sunshine illuminates him and I marvel at his beauty.

All mine.

He's scrolling his phone, and when he spots me just before I get back into bed, he gives me that devilish dimpled smile that has me rearing to go again. He taps his phone once without taking his eyes off me and the song I *Think I Like You* by The Band CAMINO plays.

"Oh, you just like me, huh?" I smirk, crawling back into bed and giving him a kiss on all fours.

"All of sudden these songs mean a lot more when they're about us."

I melt into his kiss as he brings me in to snuggle against him. But there's a lingering question that still hasn't been answered and I can't keep it down anymore.

"What changed your mind about me?" I ask. "What was holding you back before?"

Rafael takes a deep breath and pulls my head back just enough to look me in the eyes and stroke my hair. "There had always been a part of me that wanted to be just like my father." I nod because I knew that. I didn't understand it, but I knew it. "He used to say something that stuck with me. He told me women will only ruin my life and to never get close. Of course, I applied that to anyone I...dated. I saw him yesterday actually," he admits, and I jerk my head back.

"You did?"

"Yeah. He came to town for the World Series and we had a short visit. And as I listened to him, there was this repulsive feeling I got. Like I couldn't understand why I had been trying so hard to be like him all these years. I didn't want to end up like him. I wanted what we already had, Angel. I wanted it stronger. I wanted it forever."

"That's why you've never committed to someone? Because of what your dad said?"

"Mom thinks it's because I didn't see him enough. So I idolized the version I remembered as a child long into my adult years. And she's probably right. Pleasing him was always something I strived for, but after his visit, I couldn't understand why anymore. That," he sighs, "and I just realized the relationship I have with him is exhausting. I've always seen marriage, relationships, as transactional."

"That's so bizarre to me," I say, tracing my fingertips against his skin. "You have such an excellent relationship with your moms, and they've led an enviable marriage to look up to."

He sighs. "Yeah. I know I've always had their true love and acceptance—and yours—but it's always been there. I never had to work for it. But with my dad, there's a constant pressure to please him.

"I think there's a strong inadequacy component to this, too. I've done nothing but work at earning his love and I've fallen short more than I've succeeded. I also think I saw him fail at his own marriage and thought to myself, *Why would I even try if he can't make it work?* It's something I plan on digging into deeper...in therapy," he says, and I back up even further but keep my eyes glued to his.

"Therapy?"

"I started going this week."

"You did?"

"Cora suggested going would show you that I'm serious about my mental health and whatever form our
relationship took. And I agree."

Goddammit, I love my bestie with breasties. She was
right. Knowing he's trying to work on himself fills me
with a sense of pride and comfort. Yes, he's always been
a loyal friend, but before now, I never thought he was
capable of romantic commitment. He chose us last night,
and here he is now, making sure that commitment is
protected. And oh my god, he's going to uncover more
about his relationship with his father. I can't believe all
this lingered under his surface. I knew he had issues with
his dad, but I didn't know they went that deep. It sounds
like he didn't know until recently either.

"How did you get an appointment so fast?"

"Two, actually. I've had two online appointments," he
says. "I know I've only broken the surface with therapy,
and we haven't covered much yet, but I'm gonna stick
with it. Honestly, most of my revelations about myself
and you and my father have been my own digging. Cora
helped. So did my mom. You know, now that I think about
it, I should really listen to the women in my life more,"
he smirks.

"Yeah, you should," I chuckle. "You know those
tele-therapy sites sell your information, right?"

"Yeah," he says. "I kind of don't care if the whole
world knows. What I care about is being the best father,
boyfriend, and eventually husband to you."

Suddenly, my heart skips a beat and I struggle to reply.
"Husband?"

He leans in to slowly press a kiss to my forehead and
my eyes close on impact. "You heard me."

"I must be dreaming," I say breathlessly. But when the
lyrics to *Angel* by Shaggy and Rayvon start to fill the room,

we both dissolve into a laughter and I know for a fact I'm not dreaming.

Rafael lowers me fully into the bed, hovering the best he can over the enormous bump between us. He's singing each word to me like it's the performance of his lifetime and I can't stop giggling. It's sweet and stupid and perfect.

"You know," I interrupt. "This playlist is literal evidence that neither of us ever fit in. We were all over the place with what cliques and clubs we tried to infiltrate, what kinds of music we tried to get into. Don't you ever feel like it took forever for us to find our place?"

He looks at me with a pinch to his eyebrows. "My place has always been with you. You've always fit in with me because I've loved every version of you."

Chapter 37

October 27th

Angie

"You look gorgeous today," Rafael says, taking my hand as I step out of his Range wearing a form-fitting yellow sweater dress with a matching cropped sweater. The country club valet is already making his way around to the driver's side when I grab my boyfriend's arm.

"Thank you," I smile. "You're looking rather handsome yourself." His dark teal, long sleeve polo compliments my outfit just right. And paired with his slacks, expensive watch, and even a couple rings, he's every bit the sophisticated gentleman. His rich bergamot, lemon, and cedar wood scent fill my senses and wrap me in a comforting embrace as we stroll into the haughty club.

"Ms. Johanssen? Mr. Jimenez?" A staff member dressed in black pants and a white dress shirt asks, standing just inside.

"Yes," Rafael answers.

She indicates for us to follow her. "Right this way, please."

I can already hear the [1] salsa music playing. Dark wood paneling and bright chandeliers line the enormous hallway with carpet that looks like it was designed specifically for this place.

"I can't believe Jay's parents are members here," I murmur, leaning into Raf.

---

1. *Micaela* by Sonora Carruseles, Luis Florez

"Shh, blend in," he stage-whispers. "They can smell your fear."

"Shut up," I mutter, nudging him in the ribs.

"Here we are," the staff member says with a smile as she stands outside two propped open doors into a freaking ballroom. "If you need anything, please don't hesitate to ask any member of our staff."

"Thank you," we both say and step into the strangest baby shower I've ever seen.

People are mingling everywhere, and I spot Raf's moms already dancing alongside several others including Joaquín and Cora's Aunt Rose, who's throwing her head back in cheer as Joaquín spins her.

But my eyes catch on the decorations. Clearly Kathleen had one idea for décor, and... I'm guessing my brothers had another. Mixed between giant vases of autumnal floral arrangements, elegant displays of macrons, and trendy balloon arches, are Halloween decorations. Jack-o-lanterns, a giant inflatable spider, cauldrons, and fun-size candy scattered on all the tables.

Then I noticed the Día de los Muertos décor. Colorful papel picados strung between chandeliers and ceiling beams, candy skulls on the bar, and marigolds everywhere.

"They're here!" someone shouts, taking me out of my bewilderment. Jonah is the first to run up to us, taking us both in his arms. "Do you like it?" he asks cheerily.

"It's a little macabre for a baby shower," I chuckle.

"You think so?" he asks genuinely. "Jay's mom said we could help with the decorations," he says, scratching the back of his actually-styled hair.

Isaiah and Dane are the next to come up, also wearing suits. "Look," Dane says, pointing to the closest string of cut paper banners. "All the guys on the team helped make it."

"Oh my god," Rafael says in disbelief. "They managed to cut rugby balls in them," he chuckles.

"I tried to tell them," Kathleen Bishops says, coming up to give both me and Raf a hug looking every bit like a member of this country club.

"Oh my gosh, Kathleen," I beam. "Thank you so much for all of this. Everything is beautiful."

"It was my pleasure. Are you sure you're okay with the...spiders and skulls?" she asks, looking around the room with apprehension. "Your brothers kind of...showed up and took over."

"Honestly, I love it," I tell her, and I do. It's all over the place and unexpected—it feels pretty on-brand for Rafael and myself if I'm being honest. It reminds me of all the Día de los Muertos celebrations we had at his house growing up. We'd eat enough sugar to make everyone sick, sing, and celebrate our loved ones who have passed on. We didn't often talk about my mom in our house, but there was something special about this day that we allowed ourselves to open up to each other.

So yeah, maybe it is macabre for a baby shower theme, but it reminds me of happier times with our families, and it makes me hopeful for our future.

The next hour passes faster than I can process. Cora and I each mingle more with our respective crowds, but we still manage to find each other and giggle at the elegant chaos. Rafael stays close to me, one hand placed on me at all times.

We told everyone the good news of our relationship a few days after we made it official. I'm glad we did because telling them at an event like this would have been pandemonium.

I'm truly touched at the turnout for this. My family is here, the entire Philadelphia Men's Rugby Team, Cora's Aunt Shelly was able to bring her mom from the nursing home for a few hours with assistance from the facility. Even friends I haven't seen in a while like Robyn are here. She had a playoff rugby game yesterday in Maryland, and she still made it. I wish I had more time to talk to her, but she's keeping busy talking with the other ruggers. Everyone except Isaiah who seems to catch a frown every time she goes near them.

Whatever, his problem.

Rafael and I have a mountain of presents to open, and by the time we're done, my cheeks hurt from smiling for so long and Raf's pockets are full of my used tissues.

I'm sorry, but how am I expected *not* to cry when we're given tiny socks and matching outfits?

[2] When everything is cleared away and the room's chatter finds a natural lull, I stand up from my chair on the small stage and Raf grabs a microphone from one of the staff members. When he hands it to me with a smile, he then pulls out a folded piece of paper from his pocket and hands it to me as well.

Looking at Cora, Jay, and Marco sitting next to me, they all give me a nod of encouragement, so I swallow and address the room. "Thank you all for coming. This day has been so incredibly beautiful thanks to you, our family and friends. I'd like to take this opportunity to read a passage from the baby journal my mother kept when she was pregnant with me until I was one. It struck something in me and I, well, I just wanted to share it with you all."

Unfolding the print-out of her journal entry, I clear my shaky throat and try to calm my nerves by taking a deep breath. "My sweet Angela," I start, already choking at the words. "Today you are two days old," I cry. Raf's hand rubs at my back as he stands next to me, but when I look up at him, he's unable to fight back the tears, too.

"I don't know if I can do this," I whisper to him, dropping the microphone lower.

---

2. *Rainbow* by Kacey Musgraves

"I don't know if I can either," he says, sucking in a shaky breath.

"Let me, bunny." I turn my head and in front of me, my dad stands tall, wearing a dress shirt under a sweater and a look of quiet confidence.

Silently, I hand him the microphone as my smile trembles.

"Hello, everyone," he says. "My name is Neal, and...my wife wrote this." Rafael hands me another clean tissue as I let go and listen.

"My sweet Angela. Today you are two days old," he repeats in a strong and slow cadence. "You were surrounded all day by those who want nothing more than your health and happiness. You were surrounded by love. We held you close as family and friends fawned over you, my perfect girl with nothing but peach fuzz for hair and arresting blue eyes.

"I hope you know how much you're loved beyond today, beyond tomorrow. I hope love engulfs your life. I hope it drives your decisions, amplifies your successes, and heals your mistakes," Dad says, his own breathing now uneven. "I hope someday you feel what I feel for you. Love, Mama."

When he turns to face me fully, his body language remains composed, but his eyes spill the truth.

I'm not sure how the sequence of the following moments play out, but the next thing I know, I'm wrapped between my father and Rafael, crying into my dad's chest. I'm vaguely aware of Marco speaking to the crowd, but I can't hear him over the sound of my heart thumping.

"I love you, Dad," I whisper.

"I love you too, Angela."

When we finally break apart, Rafael nods to him with a sad smile. "Thank you so much, Neal."

"Just promise you'll love my grandchildren the same way," he smiles, making Raf nod.

"Done."

Chapter 38

December 7th

Rafael

I stand in the doorway to the bubblegum-pink bathroom and lean against the frame, watching my thirty-seven week pregnant Angel slip an earring in and smile back at me through the [1] mirror.

"See something you like?" she smirks.

I take the opportunity to rake my eyes over every inch of her. She's wearing a tailored-to-perfection emerald evening gown with a long flowing skirt and a slit to her mid-thigh. The wide V neckline gives me the most spectacular view of her full breasts. Just modest enough for public, but just scandalous enough to make everyone envious of me.

Stepping behind her, I lean down to run my nose along the column of her neck and inhale her peachy scent behind her ear. "I see something I love."

"I love you too," she hums, placing her hand behind my neck to keep me in place as I kiss a trail across her warm skin. "Are you sure we're not overdressed?"

"What?" I tease, now kissing along her shoulder. "Are my matching pants and black velvet tuxedo jacket too much?"

"For a company holiday party? Yeah, I'd say so," she giggles.

---

1. *Teenage Dream* by Katy Perry

Months ago, I requested our company holiday party be moved up a couple weeks to accommodate Angie's due date. Even though she's not due until after Christmas, there's a strong chance she could deliver earlier, so I wanted to make sure this night happened for us.

"It's black tie tonight," I remind her. "Plus, Jay's going to be there, so you know he's dressing to the nines and making Marco and Cora do the same."

"That's true. I do feel pretty. This might be the last time we do something like this for a long time."

Taking my lips away, I watch her in the mirror again and I hum, "Mmm, maybe. Are you ready?"

"I think so," she says, then turns to face me. "Let's go."

I take her hand and lead her down the cottage-core hallway and wrap-around wooden staircase down to our Gothic front foyer and living room. One day last week, I woke up to find Angie reading in her mushroom and crystal-adorned library, looking so peaceful it melted my heart. When I sat down next to her and placed my head in her lap, she stroked my hair with one hand then abruptly asked if she made a huge mistake with the clashing design choices.

"No," I said. "Weird and eclectic is kind of our thing."

"Aren't you worried about the resale value?"

"No," I said. "All its value comes from our happiness."

When we get to the bottom floor, Angie tries to steer us to the side door off the kitchen to head to the garage, but I stop her. "Hold on" I say, letting go of her arm and stepping toward the front door. "Wait right here and close your eyes."

"What are you doing?"

"Just do it."

Closing her eyes, she sighs, "Alright."

I open the door and step out on the covered porch, then shut the door behind me. I grab the corsage and matching boutonniere I have sitting out here, then ring the door-bell with a shit-eating grin.

When she answers the door, the exact reaction I hope she will have washes over her. "Gasp," she whispers.

"Angie Johanssen, will you go to prom with me?"

"Shut. Up," she bellows, but her stunned features morph quickly into tears. Stepping into action, I take a clean handkerchief from my pocket I got specifically for this reason and dab under her eyes.

"Is that a yes?"

"Yes," she sniffles.

I slip the corsage on her wrist and she pins the bouton-niere to my lapel. This simple moment alone is already more meaningful than every single second I spent at prom last time.

Covering her shoulders with her dress coat that doesn't fit around her waist anymore, we then step onto the porch to find a sleek black town car idling and a chauffeur standing outside, waiting for us.

"You hired a driver?" she beams.

"I had to make it authentic," I shrug.

"Good evening, folks," our driver smiles, holding the door open for us. "Welcome. My name is Leonard. Please help yourself to the sparkling juice and charcuterie. We'll be at your destination right on time."

"Thank you," we both say, sliding into the back seat. It's only the beginning of tonight, but already I have butterflies and a smug satisfaction at how well this is turning out.

Thirty minutes later when we arrive at the historic Franklin Hotel downtown, it's Angie's turn to use the handkerchief to wipe my mouth clean of her lipstick before we walk inside arm in arm.

I glance down at the foam sandals she's sporting as they peak through the hem of her dress and I smile. I'm glad she's comfortable because there's no part of tonight I want disrupting her joy.

I keep her by my side throughout cocktail hour as I introduce her to all my colleagues and keep her sparkling juice flute filled. We take pictures with the photographer I purposefully hired, standing in those classic and awkward prom poses; and I already plan on giving a copy to our parents for their refrigerators. I'm framing this shit and hanging it up.

When dinner is served, while Angie is talking to Dayo, our Director of Interior Design, I lean over to Jay who's sitting right next to me and whisper in his ear, "Everything ready?"

"It's perfect," he says. "I may have...added a little more."

"More what?"

"You'll see. Don't worry," he grins.

After dinner and dessert are cleared, the volume of the music picks up and the song switches from the festive holiday mix to No One by Alicia Keys—and the real reason we're here tonight begins.

Sort of.

Standing from my chair, I reach for her hand. "May I have this dance?"

Her gaze shifts from mine to glance around the room and then back. "But no one is dancing yet."

"We are."

"Jesus," she mumbles, but takes my hand. "Just whip your cock out and show everyone already."

I lead her to the empty dance floor, giving her a spin right off the bat, and then tucking her into my body. To make room for the babies, her own body isn't centered against mine—instead, her belly extends next to my hip. I brace one hand under her stomach and my other holds her close. We sway together and her glossy fingernails shine against the dark velvet of my tux.

I don't care if no one else joins us. I don't care if we overstay our welcome and I have to pay to extend tonight's event, because nothing could tear me away from this long-overdue dance.

"Can this be our song now?" I ask, and her sad smile fills me with warmth.

"Only if you promise to keep slow dancing with me."

"Forever, baby."

Eventually more people come to join us and even though we're surrounded by them, it somehow feels more intimate—like we've created a little cocoon within each other's arms.

"This is the best prom I've ever been to," I say to her, watching the light twinkle in her eyes.

"I feel like a princess," she smiles. "Like a huge, pregnant princess."

My chest shakes with laughter as I kiss the top of her head. "The most beautiful I've ever seen."

"Do you mind if we take a break for a little while?" she asks. "My hips are starting to hurt, and I need to catch my breath."

"Of course. Here, why don't we step into the hallway," I offer, and she holds my arm as I lead us through the double doors. There are professionally decorated Christmas trees and garland strewn throughout the hallway as well as ornate couches along the walls. But instead of guiding her to one, I pull her towards the double doors on the other side of the hallway.

"Where are we going?" she asks.

"Let's see what's in here."

[2] Her eyes go wide as she looks behind us like we're going to get caught. "Um..."

---

2. *Say You Won't Let Go* by James Arthur

"Come on, live a little." I pull open the large door and usher her inside quickly, and it swings shut behind us.

"Oh my god, no. We can't be here," Angie whispers, trying to push me back. "This is somebody else's event!"

Holding her shoulders, I spin her back around to face the room. "No, it's not. It's our event."

She turns her head to look at the room again. It's half the size of the ballroom we were just in, but the entire floor is covered in electric candles. The overhead lights are turned off, but everything glows and sparkles thanks to the large windows overlooking the city and the mirrored ceiling.

There's a string quartet playing near the corner, and I give them a wave.

Angie, however, is stuck in one spot as her jaw hangs open, taking everything in. Gripping her hands in mine, I walk backwards, pulling her through the straight path between the candles to the center of the room.

"What is happening?" she trembles as we reach the small circle in the middle.

"I'm proposing to you," I smile, trying my best to appear confident, but my heart is pounding.

"No, you're not," she says, her eyes wild and laser focused on me. "No, you're not. Oh my god, you are." I pull the ring box from my pocket and kneel. "Rafael!" she screams, then covers her mouth with both hands, like she didn't mean to blurt that last part.

"Do you want me to keep going?" I smile, and she nods frantically. "Good."

I take both of her hands in mine. "I want to start by saying I'm sorry it's taken me so long to get here. I should have been kneeling before you ten years ago."

"It's okay," she whispers.

"Angel, I've wanted to spend every single day with you since the day we met. I've been following you like a puppy and I never realized how good I had it—how *great* I had it.

Realizing I loved you was like listening to a favorite song; I already knew the lyrics, the melody, the beat... I just had to remember who was singing beside me the whole time."

Angie wipes her tears with the back of her hand as she chokes back more. With a shaky but sure hand, I open the box and show her the ring her father gave me—her mother's ring. "I love you with all of my heart, Angel—you and your wild imagination. Nothing would make me happier than being your husband. Will you marry me?"

"Yes," she sobs, and relief washes over me like a tidal wave. I was ninety-nine percent sure she'd say yes, but based on the way I'm shaking like a leaf, you'd think I wasn't sure at all.

The quartet must have been listening because they crescendo rapidly, filling the room with the notes that will become the soundtrack to our story.

Slipping the ring on her left hand, she gawks at it as her chest heaves, and I quickly stand to kiss another yes from her lips.

And another.

And another.

Epilogue

Angie

15 months later

"They're sleeping, Rafael!" I hiss, trying to shove him away from his moms' hotel room door.

"Come on," he pouts. "We'll be quiet. And if they wake up, that's their problem."

It only takes me a second to mull it over before I'm smiling. He knocks softly and a few moments later, Christina answers the door, her eyes adjusting to the bright lights of the hallway.

"Can we see them?" he whispers.

"Of course," she whispers back, opening the door just enough to let us slip inside. The skirts of my wedding dress wrestle against each other and add to the white noise machine already playing.

We're staying in a beautiful hotel in Guanajuato, Mexico, and it's late—or early. When we left, most of our family and friends were still there, dancing to the mariachi band that showed up after the DJ packed his things.

The door shuts quietly behind us and we find our babies sleeping soundly in their travel cribs. Well, they're not exactly babies anymore because no matter how much I refuse to believe it, Zofia and Dominico Jimenez are toddlers now.

Toddlers who stole the show at our wedding ceremony only eight hours ago when they ditched the pillow and flower basket they were carrying halfway down the aisle and hugged each other.

My husband pulls me into his warm chest as we stare at our little cherubs, both sucking their thumbs, faces pressed close to the mesh barrier so they can be as close as possible.

"They passed out so fast," Ana says, as both her and Christina come up to us.

"They had a big day," I smile.

I ended up being induced a week after we got engaged, and with Ivy by my side and Rafael literally catching the babies, they were born six minutes apart, screaming and perfect.

A week later, his dad flew in to meet his grandchildren. Their relationship is changing slowly. Raf has learned a lot about himself through therapy since then, but altering his relationship with his father isn't a switch that can be flipped. It's been a slow process with lots of pain points, but I can see the difference it's made with him. I still catch him trying to be the best, the most, the hardest worker, but most of the time he can catch it himself before I have to say anything. And if I do, I'm all too happy to remind him that he is already enough and worthy of love no matter what.

I'm really fucking proud of him.

"Okay, off with you two," Ana whispers, gently pushing us to the door. "Go make me more grand babies."

We both step out of the room quietly chuckling. "I don't know, I think I'm confused about the mechanics," Raf says.

"Yeah, me too," I say. "Do you have a pamphlet or something?"

She rolls her eyes and starts to shut the door. "You're both smart. You'll figure it out."

Rafael picks me up like the bride I am, and we make our way to the suite at the end of the hall. "This is giving me ideas," I smirk, waggling my eyebrows as we enter our room.

"Oh yeah? Like what Mrs. Jimenez?"

"Like I'm your virgin bride and this is an arranged marriage."

"Go on," he says, setting me on my bare feet and combing his hand through my hair.

I bite my lip before continuing. "But I've been falling for you and your charming playboy ways."

Goosebumps pebble everywhere as he slowly trails his fingertips down my neck, across my chest, and loops them under the thin strap of my dress. "And I've been fighting with myself. I don't want to corrupt you," he says, sliding both hands down to my hips and pushing his erection into me, "but I have to have you."

My gaze drops from his lusty eyes, down to his exposed chest where the top three buttons of his crisp white dress shirt are undone.

He looks like pure delectable sin.

And he's all mine.

"Turn around, Mrs. Jimenez," he commands. When I do, he moves my hair away from my neck and kisses it, sending a bolt of lightning to my core. Then he gently pulls down my zipper and murmurs, "My beautiful virgin bride. I want to show you how much pleasure a body can have." He lets my dress fall away to the floor, leaving me in only my white lace panties.

Then I feel him kneel behind me, his large hands skimming my backside as the tip of his nose runs across the thin fabric. "Tell me, baby. Tell me you want me too."

"Yes," I sigh, reaching to touch any part of him I can find. "I want you to make love to me."

"I'm going to do a lot more than make love to you, Angel."

My panties slip away quickly, and I'm left naked before him with my heart beating wildly.

These games we play have become a part of us. It's not every time we have sex, but role playing, switching, and BDSM are interwoven in our intimacy. We're both free to explore any curiosity without judgment.

He's my slut and I'm proudly his.

Except right now I'm his inexperienced bride who needs to be taught how to take a dick.

It's so *romantic.*

His lips press against the curve of my ass and his fingers dig in a little deeper, the gentle restraint starting to dissolve. "Sit on the bed, wife," he commands. But the way he says wife—like it's the most erotic thing he can imagine. Like if he said it one more time, he might get off from only that.

I turn and sit—pressing my thighs together in some futile way to relieve the building ache—only to watch him undress in front of me. His sleeves are already rolled up from a long night of dancing, and I fixate on the corded muscles in his forearms flex as he unbuckles himself. Before he drops his pants, he unbuttons the rest of his shirt, and I know he's watching me like a hawk, but I can't tear my eyes away from his deft hands.

The shirt is thrown to the floor and he finally removes his slacks and black boxer briefs. My mouth waters when he gives his massive length a few long pulls.

"Look at me, my bride. You're going to be a good girl and put your husband's cock in your mouth. You're going to feel how big and hard it is so that you know exactly how much that tight little virgin pussy needs to stretch for me. Is that understood?"

"Yes," I breathe.

"Are you scared?"

"Yes."

"There's no need," he says, lifting my chin with his fingers. "I'm going to take good care of you and talk you through everything. You're mine now, and I take care of what's mine." His thumb grazes my mouth. "Now paint my cock with those pretty lips."

Jesus Christ, I could explode with lust at this very moment.

The mouth on my husband is next level.

I waste no more time and right as I grab his thick shaft, my tongue finds his crown and I lick the bead of precum from the tip. I have to remember I'm virginal and unsure of myself, so I take a tentative lick instead of trying to deep throat this virile man like my inner horn dog tells me to.

"Like this?" I ask innocently, kissing along the snaking vein.

"Almost, baby. Open your mouth and show me that sweet tongue. That's it," he praises, then pushes the uncut head into my mouth and groans. "Now, suck me. Ungh, yes. Good girl. Make it wet. Let it drip everywhere."

When I start to stroke through the wetness, he braces his hands in my hair, holding it back for a better view. "So pretty, my bride. Doing such a good job for me," he hums, clearly enjoying my suck and twist combination.

"Okay, okay," he huffs, pulling himself out of my mouth and leaning low to kiss and taste me. "Very good. But I need you to lay back," he says, hovering over me as I scoot to the center of the bed.

"I'm going to make you ready for my cock. Have you ever had a man kiss you down here?" he asks, sliding his fingers through my wet, bare slit.

"No," I whimper. "You're the first."

"I'm the only. Got it?"

"Yes," I repeat.

While he plays gently with my pussy, he laps and bites at my hardened nipples, then takes large mouthfuls and hollows his cheeks as he rolls each peak against his tongue.

"Oh god," I breathe. "That feels amazing."

"I'm just getting started, my love," he smirks, trailing more kisses down my body until he reaches my center. "Now spread your legs and let your husband do all the work."

"Yes," I sigh when his tongue runs across my clit and he opens me with his thumbs. He dives in softly at first, building me up with every long swipe and flick. My back arches off the bed as my hands find purchase in the covers. He has me writhing and moaning his name like it's the only word I know.

Then all at once, while never taking his mouth away, he shoves one finger inside me, and I gasp like the virgin I am. "Oh god! It's too much," I feign, throwing an arm over my eyes.

"It's not," he growls. "You can take more; I know you can. Open for me, beautiful. I'm going to add a second finger, and it's going to feel good. You need to be wet and relaxed before I give you my cock. Do you trust me?"

"Yes, of course."

"Good," he rumbles, then starts suckling at my clit again and slowly adding a second finger. "That's my girl—that's my wife—riding my hand like she was made to." His fingers curl inside my body, rubbing my rough patch and sending me to new heights. "There she is. Come for me, Angel. Come on my face," he mumbles through my pussy. "And then I'll really make you my wife."

He fucks me with his hand and eats me out for only a few more moments before I'm clenching around his fingers and chasing the sweet friction of his late-night stubble. I don't realize I'm holding my breasts like stress balls until he finally releases me and slides his fingers out and licks them clean.

"Are you ready?" he asks tenderly, climbing over me and bracing his arms on either side of my head. His erection lays against my lower stomach and his heavy sac presses against my still-quivering pussy.

"I think so," I pant.

"Now's the best time."

"Will it hurt?" I ask, touching his neck and sliding my hand over his jaw.

"It might for a moment," he whispers, then leans down for a languid kiss. "But I promise to go slow, and the pain is worth it."

"Thank you," I murmur into his warm lips. "I love you, Mr. Jimenez."

Rafael pulls his right hand down to guide his massive cock to my entrance. "And I love you," his voice rumbles back through our kiss, then he nudges the tip inside me. "Mrs. Jimenez."

And true to his word, he goes slow—tortuously slow. Like he's really fucking a virgin. Pretending he can't make it all the way in when he hits my imaginary hymen. And I pretend there's real pain when he thrusts through it and I hold tight to his strong back, clinging to him like he'll heal me.

"There we are," he says in awe, finally letting himself have free reign inside me. He adds his finger to my sensitive bundle of nerves, and commands me again. "Wrap your beautiful legs around me. Hold on tight."

There's not another thought in my brain as I listen obediently, and he pounds into me while rubbing my clit between our seeking bodies.

"Yes," I cry out, digging my nails into his muscles as my entire lower body contracts around him like a boa constrictor. "Rafael!"

He loses his composure entirely and drops his head into my neck. "Angel," he grunts. "You're my...Angel." With his last thrust, he finally removes his hand from between my thighs, and slowly adds all his weight on top of me as I relax my legs, but keep my ankles locked behind him.

Both of my hands slide down the sweat beading on his back and I gently massage whatever muscles I can touch. "I love you, husband."

"I love you, wife."

We lay there, inhaling our pheromones and letting our bodies come down leisurely.

When Rafael finally sits up, he looks down at me with a smile tugs his lower lip between his teeth. "You're the best thing that's ever happened to me."

"I know," I say with a cocksure voice, making him lose it and curl over in a laugh.

"And it's because of that attitude," he says while reaching over to the nightstand and opening the drawer to pull out a small black box. "That made me think you needed something a little more substantial." When he's centered back in front of me, he opens the box and pulls out a huge fucking ring.

My eyes bug out and I sit up fast. "What the fuck?"

"I know we both love your mother's ring, and it means more than this one, but I wanted you to have something that is just ours too. Something as bold as you."

"Is that a canary diamond?" I ask, snatching the cushion-cut from him.

"Yup."

"It's gorgeous," I huff, slipping it on my other ring finger and then pulling him into a long kiss. "I love it. Thank you, baby."

"You're welcome."

"I, uhh," I stammer, suddenly feeling nervous and for my gift to him. "I got you something too."

"You did?"

"Here, sit down." I climb off the bed and pull out a larger box than what he gave me from one of my bags. I hand him the small package I wrapped myself and he opens it quickly.

Right away, he finds his name engraved in the leather cover and touches it softly. "You got me a journal?"

"Well," I say nervously. "You know how we started making our own journals for the twins once we found out about my mom's?"

"Yeah?"

"Well, read the first page."

He flips it open to find my handwriting and today's date. "Hello, sweet baby," he reads aloud with a pinch between his eyebrows. "I married your mother today and she just handed me this journal to tell me she's..." He pauses to let his mouth tremble and his eyes well up with tears. "To tell me she's pregnant with you."

He immediately closes the journal and lets it fall away so we can hold each other tight. "Are you serious?" he cries into my hair and now I'm tearing, too. "You're really pregnant again?"

"Yes," I cry happily. "I'm five weeks along."

"Oh my god, that's so much more time to prepare," he chuckles through the tears and then releases me just enough to stare at me with wide eyes. "We're having another baby."

"Who knows," I shrug. "Maybe more than one." When that thought lands, he sobers up. "Starting a commune isn't looking too bad now, is it?"

[1] **THE END**

---

1. A *Pedir Su Mano* by Juan Luis Guerra 4.40

Want to read about Angie giving birth (and maybe some extra spicy content)? Sign up for my newsletter and you'll receive a free download.

Didn't get enough of these characters? Then get ready for Isaiah's book. Do you think it's going to be about him and Robyn? Hmm. Interesting. Preorder *Every Move You Make* and find out.

Want to know all about Cora, Jay, and Marco? Read their story in The Structural Duet.
Structural Damage
Structural Support

Acknowledgements

My goodness, where to start? So many people helped me with this book.

First and foremost, thank you to my husband for giving me space and dedicated time to write. Your love and support do not go unnoticed. Oh, and thanks for getting me pregnant so I had all this first-hand knowledge lol.

To my alpha readers, Rachel and Brittni—thanks for keeping me in check as I drafted and for fielding endless texts when I second-guessed myself.

To my betas, Alex, Zsófia, Courtney, Brittni, Priscilla, Kay, and Khaos—thank you for your honest feedback; I truly appreciate it.

To my sensitivity readers, Maria and Marta—thank you for helping Rafael and his family feel real and helping me with my Spanish. And to Lizzie and Luis—thank you for answering my DMs about even the smallest cultural things. To Ruben—thank you for translating and letting me pick your brain about Mexican culture. Thank you for letting Rachel and me crash your friend's wedding in Guanajuato. It's given me lots of material for future books and memories to last a lifetime.

To my bestie Sam—thank you for all your first-hand midwifery knowledge.

To authors Gwendolyn Harper and Alethea Faust—thank you for letting me reference your delicious characters. For those that want to read about a leprechaun king who's into financial domination, read Green & Gold. If you want to read about polyamorous wizards doing it in the name of magic, read Sex Wizards.

To author Adora Crooks—thank you for your incredible support and all your strap-on knowledge! The Pink Lantern was the sexiest educational material.

I blame author Ashley Bennett for my kraken fantasies. .

To Alex and Angie—thank you for sharing your experiences as a children's therapist/counselor.

To Rhu—thank you for helping me with Joaquín and making sure he was represented with care and respect.

To my friends and few family members that know I write smut and love me for it—let me just sob in gratefulness.

To my editors Dani and Crab—thank you for making me look good.

To my illustrator Vera—I thank my lucky stars I found you. I'm obsessed with your work.

And finally, to my fans—holy shit, you're the BEST. Thank you for sharing the love on social media, interacting with my content, and recommending my books. Thank you for DMs and checking in on me. I know some of you may have found your names in this book, and that was not a coincidence. It's my way of thanking you for all your love.

About the author

Sloan Spencer lives in metro Detroit with her husband, two kiddos, and dogs. She loves nature, scandalous stories, and thick thighs. You can follow her on her social media accounts or visit her website (and sign up for her newsletter!):

Instagram: @sloan_spencer_author
TikTok: @sloanspencerauthor
Facebook: Sloan Spencer's Reader Group
Author website: sloanspencerbooks.com
Be sure to follow her on Goodreads and Amazon!

Made in the USA
Monee, IL
14 December 2024

73812357R00204